A NOTE ON THE AUTHOR

HASAN ALİ TOPTAŞ is one of Turkey's top writers. His short story collections include *The Identity of a Laugh, The Whispers of the Nobodies* and *Solitudes*. His novels have won the Çankaya Literature Prize, the Culture Ministry Prize, the Yunus Nadi Novel Prize, the Cevdet Kudret Literature Prize, the Orhan Kemal Novel Prize and the Turkish Writers' Union Great Novel Prize. His early masterpiece *Shadowless* (1995), also translated by Maureen Freely and John Angliss, will be published by Bloomsbury in 2017. He now lives in Ankara. His work has been translated into German, French and Finnish. *Solitudes* has been made into a play and *Shadowless* was made into a film in 1998.

A NOTE ON THE TRANSLATORS

MAUREEN FREELY has translated or co-translated a number of Turkish memoirs and classics as well as five books by the Turkish novelist and Nobel Laureate, Orhan Pamuk. Her seventh novel, *Sailing Through Byzantium*, was published in 2013.

JOHN ANGLISS won the inaugural British Council's Young Translators' Prize for prose in 2012. He lives in Ankara and has translated Ahmet Altan and Hakan Günday, among others.

RECKLESS

Hasan Ali Toptaş

*Translated from the Turkish by Maureen Freely
and John Angliss*

B L O O M S B U R Y
LONDON · OXFORD · NEW YORK · NEW DELHI · SYDNEY

Bloomsbury Paperbacks
An imprint of Bloomsbury Publishing Plc

50 Bedford Square
London
WC1B 3DP
UK

1385 Broadway
New York
NY 10018
USA

www.bloomsbury.com

Originally published in 2013 in Turkey as *Heba* by İletişim Yayınları, Istanbul
First published in Great Britain 2015
This paperback edition first published in 2016

This book has been selected to receive financial assistance from English
PEN's PEN Translates! programme. English PEN exists to promote literature
and our understanding of it, to uphold writers' freedoms around the world, to campaign
against the persecution and imprisonment of writers for stating their views, and to promote the
friendly co-operation of writers and the free exchange of ideas. www.englishpen.org

This book has been published with the support of the Ministry of
Culture and Tourism of Turkey in the framework of TEDA Project

British Library Cataloguing-in-Publication Data
A catalogue record for this book is available from the British Library.

ISBN: HB: 978-1-4088-5085-5
TPB: 978-1-4088-5086-2
PB: 978-1-4088-5090-9
ePub: 978-1-4088-5087-9

2 4 6 8 10 9 7 5 3 1

Typeset by Integra Software Services Pvt. Ltd.
Printed and bound in Great Britain by CPI Group (UK) Ltd, Croydon CR0 4YY

To find out more about our authors and books visit www.bloomsbury.com.
Here you will find extracts, author interviews, details of forthcoming events and the option to sign up
for our newsletters.

Why must we suffer? We search in vain for
the key to this mystery, even as it consumes us.
Avni of Yenişehir

He who kills the monster inside him turns to dust.
Hulki Dede

Contents

1

The Key

Ziya locked the door. Without pausing to pocket the key, he hurried towards the lift. Something strange had happened to the corridor. Something with the lights. The yellow globes that should have lit his way illuminated only themselves, leaving the rest of the corridor in darkness.

And the silence, it could turn a man to stone. But it did not last. Someone shattered it by slamming one of those brown steel doors on the ground floor. All Ziya could see was a shadow flying from one end of the corridor to the other, as fast as a peal of laughter, until this, too, was lost. And now, in the ill-lit stairwell, a child was howling. Then a woman, screaming blacker than the night. Then the maddening whine of a vacuum cleaner, moving this way and that, and the juddering of a distant drill. Behind the walls were other walls, and behind these were murmurings that now grew louder. With them came the sounds of the city, deeper and denser than the memories they conjured up, until the building was swaying not just to its own beat but absorbing, with every twist and turn, the pandemonium of the streets. He had never heard a noise like this, ever.

By now Ziya had reached the lift. As the door opened, he stopped for some reason and, with a sudden turn of the head, took stock of the corridor and the stairwell. Staring straight into the sounds tumbling towards him from both these places, he caught glimpses of the plastic flowers hanging from each door. Seeing all this had the unexpected effect of darkening his gaze somewhat. It also turned his stomach. It was as if he could see right through to the heart of things, to the heavy swell of dirt and darkness that now threatened to engulf him. Best to move on. He jumped into the lift and went straight up to the nineteenth floor, and in no time he was ringing the bell at number 91. Here was another brown steel door, with an enormous spyhole and two locks, and the same plastic flowers hanging over it. From the delicate ribbon attached to one of their stems was an evil eye the size of a camel's tongue. As he stood waiting for the door to open, he stared unblinking into that evil eye. He might have stayed there, transfixed, had the door not cracked open, to reveal Binnaz Hanım's honey-eyed maid.

'Good day,' she said haughtily. 'May I ask what you're here for?'

'I was hoping to return the key,' Ziya replied.

And he offered the girl the key.

'Stop!' cried the girl. She jumped back as if something had been thrown at her. 'Stop! You can't return that key to me. That's just not done. You must return it to Binnaz Hanım personally.'

'Fine,' said Ziya. 'Let me do that now.'

He followed her down a corridor whose walls were covered in green tapestries and into a narrow chamber so airless he nearly choked. Beyond this was the living room.

It was vast, and drenched with light. But what assaulted his eyes and his mind were the teetering mountains of furniture. Piles and piles of upholstered chairs, wherever you looked. Acquired from an antiques dealer, no doubt. The patterns varied, but they all had fat legs. Beside them stood ungainly coffee tables. They were adorned with embroidered table-cloths, on which stood forests of long-necked vases and glass bowls filled with baubles. The recesses of the walls were lined with shelves. In the left-hand corner, cardboard boxes. Amidst all this, and flanked by fluttering gilded curtains, was a gigantic wardrobe covered in lace. Running the full length of another wall was a second wardrobe, lurching over this sea of furniture like an overladen ship. The more Ziya looked at it, the more it seemed to recoil, and soon he could look at nothing else, while inside his ribcage he felt a stirring – something akin to a small, warm bird.

The maid pointed at a chair near the window. 'Wait here, please. I'll go and get Binnaz Hanım.'

Ziya walked over to the chair but instead of sitting down, he turned to the window. Hands on hips, he gazed sourly at the city below.

It was cloaked in a mist that didn't look like mist. Red smoke rose in veins from shadows clouded by the soiled music of despair. Glittering skyscrapers, forgotten courtyards and ramshackle marketplaces; shopping malls, ruins and factories; the enclaves of the rich and the slum dwellers' muddy hills rolling off into the distance – there was more than despair here. Despair was merely the outer shell, beneath which lurked the deepest disarray: a bleak and fearsome stagnation, an absence. A rustling, muttering fog of noxious fumes. As they climbed from wall to window, window to wall, these fumes fell silent.

As they flowed down avenues and side streets – snaking through crowded bus stops where the crowds were even thicker, filling up the city's squares and intersections and great parks – they looked, from time to time, like ribbons of unfurling smoke. Amongst them flew pigeons, mouldy and tired, their wings dyed black by exhaust fumes. They would rise out of nowhere in a single mass, leaving a smudge of grey on the pale firmament as they dived back down into the crowds, skirting car horns here and there and spreading their wings only to tire of the sky's infinities and return to the smoke. You might almost say they landed on it. Perched on them. Nudging their wings forward, they narrowed their unblinking eyes to stare blankly up at Ziya's window. And just then it seemed to him as if their countless, aimless flights had left these birds with a gaze that carried the city's stink. For a fleeting moment, he wondered if he might be imagining things. A wave of disquiet passed through him as he stared into the shadows he might have created for them. He leaned closer to the window, to put his illusions to the test. As fast as it had read his thoughts, a pigeon separated from the flock, tracing out a vast and blurry parabola to arrive level with the nineteenth floor. With wings beating feverishly against the glass, it perched on the sill. It cooed a few times, as if to assure Ziya it was real. Then it lifted its beak in the air, swelling up with such surprising speed that – even though he had seen it fly, heard its wings and was close enough to touch its feathers – Ziya again wondered if this pigeon could be real. Abandoning the window, he turned around to find himself face to face with Binnaz Hanım.

She, too, could stare without blinking. Her face was flushed, very flushed. She was standing amongst the armchairs, and although

4

he was in no doubt that she was there, in the flesh, she also gave the impression of being somewhere else. She had been watching him for a very long time, he decided. Watching him from some point in the distant past. Echoing forwards as well as backwards. Like a ghost. A huge old ghost. With huge red cheeks, no less. How to address such a creature? This Ziya could not begin to imagine. So he stood before her, shifting from foot to foot like a small child who was trying not to wet himself.

He drew himself up to his full height. 'I've come to return the key,' he said crisply.

'I know,' his landlady purred.

Already she was waddling over to the corner. Having lowered her great bulk into an armchair, she directed Ziya to another with an imperious wave.

After dithering for a few moments, he obeyed her. It vexed him that he still hadn't managed to hand over the key; he didn't know what to do, so he just sat there, rubbing the arms of his chair.

'There's no rush,' said Binnaz Hanım. She glared at him, but from the corner of her eye. 'The piece of metal you call a key,' she said finally, 'is neither as small nor as simple as it first appears. You aren't just giving me a key, after all. You're handing over an entire apartment.'

'You're right, but I fail to understand why it has taken me all day,' said Ziya. 'I've lost count of the files and documents I had to give your accountant, but for some reason he wouldn't take the key.'

With the calmest of smiles, Binnaz Hanım leaned back in her chair.

'He wouldn't because he couldn't,' she said. 'It's not his job to take the key. It's mine.'

Ziya said nothing. Or rather, he turned wearily to look out the window. He could not understand why a simple matter of returning a key had turned into this endless ceremony. The pigeon he'd been watching earlier was still there, still staring. There was a darkening warning in its beady eyes – and even in the colouring of its feathers, which seemed on the verge of changing into something else. Unnerved, Ziya turned back to Binnaz Hanım.

She was calling for the maid. 'What's become of your manners, girl? Aren't you going to offer anything to our guest?'

At that same moment, the maid ran in carrying a coffee tray. Stopping in front of Ziya, she curtsied.

He picked up a tiny cup embellished with blue flowers. 'Thank you.'

The maid responded with a solemn nod so perfectly measured that it seemed to take even its owner by surprise. For now she broke the mood with a smile. Though it would be more accurate to say that she stood in front of Ziya and stretched her lips. Those rose-petal lips – they opened and closed, wet and slippery with desire. And then she was off, this maid, leaving a lovely perfume in her wake as she darted between the armchairs, as dainty as a little bird, to take Binnaz Hanım her coffee. Standing before her mistress, she went back to playing the coquette, swaying her hips as she gazed impishly into Binnaz Hanım's eyes. Her gaze had so much life in it that you could almost see it, flowing from one woman to the other. And even, somehow, holding up Binnaz Hanım's cup. But now, all of a sudden, the tray was on the table, and this maid was fiddling with her hair in the armchair next to Binnaz Hanım. She seemed almost to be sighing. Almost, but not quite.

Sulkily eyeing the maid, Binnaz Hanım slotted a cigarette between her lips. A moment later, she took it out again. 'A light, my girl,' she said curtly. 'A light.' The maid, unfazed, produced a garish lighter. As the flame shot up, she let out a little gasp so unsettling that Ziya fell back in his chair. Only by fixing his eyes on the ceiling was he able to regain his composure. Time seemed to stop. Or rather, it turned into cigarette smoke; it was nothing more than the smoke leaking from Binnaz Hanım's mouth. Slowly Ziya lowered his head, as the girl leaned back to play with her hair again.

Ziya, who had finished his coffee by now, gave her a pained look. What was he doing here? 'I should just hand over the key and go,' he thought. But he seemed incapable of movement. Every time he tried to stand up, something pushed him down again. A crushing weight, but not the sort you could measure. This was more like a spell, a trance, a gentle wave of fatigue casting the sort of net that never lets you go. Or rather, this was what Ziya was thinking while he sat there. But even as he surrendered to this force he could not see, he of course kept his eyes on Binnaz Hanım, and on her maid.

And now, before his very eyes, a mist blew in from goodness knows where. It swirled around the room, sketching strange shapes as it rose to the ceiling, leaving tiny wisps of quivering smoke in its wake. It vanished into the shadows, rambled across walls, rose over the cabinet behind him, bounded from chair to chair, only to return as a shadow, settling on the tables and the carpets and Binnaz Hanım's chair. She was still puffing on her cigarette, and now, when she exhaled, the fog grew thicker. Another puff, and it grew thicker still. She puffed again, and she vanished into the smoke, taking with her the maid and both their chairs. Now Ziya could see nothing but Binnaz Hanım's fat fingers, glowing in her ring's reflection. And, flitting here and there through the billowing smoke, the silhouette of a handsome young man. But it did not stay long, this silhouette. It had, perhaps, been sent from far away, in error. Ziya seized this moment to place the key on the table.

As he rose to his feet, he said, 'Please excuse me, but I have to go.' His voice sounded odd, and unnecessarily loud.

No sooner had he spoken than Binnaz Hanım parted the smoke like a curtain and stuck out her head. Slowly she opened her mouth, as if to speak, but she said nothing. She just fixed her tiny raisin eyes on him. His own eyes rested on her cheekbones, which were glistening with sweat, until suddenly, impatiently, she withdrew back into the smoke.

In a distant voice, she said, 'Where are you going?'

'I've left the key on the table,' said Ziya, turning back towards the wall of smoke. 'Please take it, because I need to go.'

This time, it was the maid who poked out her head; a plaintive look and she was gone again.

For Ziya, this was the last straw. How could they have parted company, if no one had left? With a mounting sense of dread, he surveyed the room. He turned back to the wall of smoke, hoping for one last glimpse of Binnaz Hanım before he left, but he could see nothing, and all he could hear was an indistinct echo of voices rising and falling, until, without willing it, he leaned forward to listen.

It was the maid. 'Let's drop it. Let him go if he wants,' she said.

'Absolutely not.' This was Binnaz Hanım.

'Why not, though?' said the maid. 'Tell me that, why don't you? Why can't we let him go?'

Binnaz Hanım said nothing.

Or, if she spoke, her words were lost in the smoke.

Silence. First it was just inside the cloud, but then it radiated outwards. Ziya craned his neck, as if to watch it spread. Did he know what he was doing? When his eyes lit on the window, he saw the pigeon still perched there, staring at him urgently with its beady eyes. Its outline wasn't as clear as before, though. Its colour was indistinct, too. Its long wait seemed to have worn it out. You could almost see time pressing down on it, for now it had begun to quake and blur, and even to shrink slightly. And that was why, if you just glanced at it, the bird looked more like a puff of smoke resting on the windowsill, or a pale patch of sky that had somehow drifted their way. And now, seeing Ziya's eyes, it pecked at the glass a few times, this pigeon, and ruffled its wings. Was this its way of trying to tell him something? Ziya had hardly formed the question when the bird came hurtling inside, shattering the windowpane, and sending shards of glass flying in all directions. The bird flew right through the wreckage, screeching madly as it flapped across the room. After flying like this for some time, making ever-tighter circles around the chandeliers, it wheeled around to launch a vicious attack on the wall of smoke in the corner. And soon the bird had ripped the wall to shreds, and there before him were Binnaz Hanım and her maid. Who could say how long they had been gone?

Binnaz Hanım, at least, stayed calm. Every now and then she cast a sidelong glance at the new arrival, smiling as wearily as if this bird was known to her and paid her daily visits. The maid, meanwhile, was racing around the room trying to catch it. In fact, she was going so fast that her slippers began to squeak and her flyaway hair to blur. She turned into a shadow with eyes that grew wider at the sight of scattered feathers and shattered glass. Blurring even more, she began to screech, too. 'Hiiii. Hiiii!' She was faster than a fever now. Faster still. And now she seemed to be in several different places at once. One shadow was darting around the glistening shards of glass; another was in the corner, leaping up to catch the pigeon in mid-flight. One shadow was lost in smoke, while another, anxiously panting for breath, was trying to push past his chair. You might almost think they were in the grip of some larger force here. As if there was some sort of monstrous puppeteer lurking unseen above them, making one maid and multiplying her, and binding each one to invisible threads. But no matter how they ran and lunged, or how ingenious their surprise attacks, none of these puppets could catch the pigeon. For the moment they touched it, the pigeon turned into a shadow. And all that while, the pigeon kept returning to the walls, of course, fluttering so wildly you might have thought it was trying to leave this world and enter another. For now, each time it hit against that wall of smoky shadows, the bird attacked it more viciously.

And then it suddenly disappeared. Had it exhausted its reserves, perhaps? Run out of tricks? Whatever the reason, it had escaped its shadow. Or somehow, without anyone seeing, gone back out through the window. By some strange stroke of luck, the room was cleared of smoke. The maid took a few steps forward, her arms still upraised. Then she stopped, to mutter furiously. The pigeon's departure had left a pigeon-shaped gap, which seemed in turn to upset the balance of the room and sap the maid's strength. She staggered on for a while in the silence, and then she began to apply herself, most diligently, to sweeping up the glass.

Binnaz Hanım turned back to Ziya. 'Why are you leaving so soon?'

'I just have to,' said Ziya. 'I have to go.'

'Oh, but you cannot,' replied Binnaz Hanım. She lifted her hand until it was level with his shoulder. 'You cannot, absolutely cannot, leave. Because you still haven't given me the key. On top of that there is a year's worth of obligations to see to. Were you honestly planning to leave without saying two words? Saunter off, leaving everything hanging? You could never do such a thing to me. Of that I am sure. Please, sit down.'

And so Ziya sat back down. He waited in hopeless silence, his eyes fixed on the coffee table, his hands clasped. It seemed to him just then that this was the first time he'd sat in this chair. Or, at least, he wondered if what he had just witnessed was real, or if his mind was playing tricks on him again. In search of an answer, he turned his head very slowly until he could see the maid. The girl was still on her knees clearing up the glass. She made a warm and delicate silhouette, as she crept steadily towards the foot of the window.

'First let me explain this business of the key,' Binnaz Hanım said. She paused to slip her tongue across her lower lip. 'The last thing we want is for you to go off thinking we're round the bend. In all honesty, I'm not entirely sure if something this personal can even be put into words. Can mere words have the power to bare a soul? That's something else I can't tell you. Enough hemming and hawing. Let's start with the apartment block. You wouldn't know this, Ziya Bey. But this apartment block did not come to me as a family bequest, and neither did it fall from the sky in a basket. It came to me by dint of my own hard work. Year after year of fighting tooth and nail. Imagine every dream I have ever held dear. Stack them all up like a pile of red handkerchiefs. From the earliest buddings of adolescence, I harnessed my every day, my every dream, to this project. I would gaze out at the city, at these streets alive with the music of playing children, and let myself dream. And each dream was bigger and better than the one before. Whichever way you look at it, this pile of metal and concrete we call an apartment block is nothing less than my youth. It's all here, from start to finish. The time I wasted at drunken meals when I was still a pimply teenager; my voluptuous body, ripening and ripening, showing no shame, until, many years later, it was forced to retire to the corner of a draughty ruin of a home, wheezing and growing the first hints of a moustache – this is my dignity. I can't explain any of this to tenants who come here to return the key. It's not my way. But for some reason, when I saw you, I knew I had to tell you. After all, you're my longest ever tenant, Ziya Bey. Did you know that?'

'No, I didn't,' Ziya said.

'Well, you are,' said Binnaz Hanım. 'And maybe that is why I felt like telling you these things. The truth is, I've always known you were a class apart. I have such a clear memory of leaning out of this very window and seeing you next to that removal van, and thinking, this tenant is something special. I'm not saying this to flatter you – it's actually what I said. The moment I set eyes on you, I had what I can only call a strange foreboding, the likes of which I'd never felt. Please believe me when I say that, even now, I couldn't tell you where it came from. Of course, I could see at once that you were not a humble soul, which, sadly, many of my tenants are. And tall you may be, but on that day you gave the impression of being level with the earth. I could also see you had a diplomatic side to you, and a merciful side, too, but none of this particularly affected me. It was something else. Something altogether different. How can I put it? The sun was shining, not a cloud in the sky, but it seemed to me that you were standing in a shadow, and this shadow kept fluttering, the way a threadbare vest on a clothes line might flutter in a breeze, and the longer I watched you, the more I felt this same shadow weighing down on me. I feel it even now, you know. Sitting here across from you right now, I can see that same shadow. Of course – this goes without saying – I do not have the faintest idea what might be casting it. I could not even say if that shadow has a meaning in this mortal world of ours. What I do know is this: as I've already said, you are a class apart. And please believe me when I say that not once over these past seventeen years – not even once – have I wavered in this belief. Though I'll confess that, from time to time, I've wondered if the other tenants were sent here for no other reason than to make you look like you hadn't sprung from nowhere. Or at least to make sure you didn't attract too much attention. I know that sounds ridiculous, but what can I do, Ziya Bey? All I can say is I've given all this a great deal of thought. I certainly have. When I put it into words, it sounds utterly absurd. But, I mean, where exactly were the other tenants sent from? What I mean to ask, dear sir, is: who sent them? Am I to believe that there's a depot out there somewhere, filled to the rafters with tenants, waiting for the clerk to dispatch them? Don't even say it. I know. Absurd! But now listen to this: maybe what's bothering me is that this could be the last time we see each other. Maybe that's why I opened my big mouth. When the end is nigh, we let our nerves get the better of us. I've seen people yawn wide enough for someone to shove a fist down their throats. Or they swallow their lips, like a nightingale that has swallowed a mulberry. Or their jaws get going. Which is what happens to me. Once your jaws get going, of course, it's like a volcano exploding. It all comes out. You try to explain the whole world in one sentence. But when have you known anyone to talk in a straight line? The idea that anyone could broach a subject and stick to it is as crazy an idea as I have ever heard. God created a world that was boundless and endless and that's how I still see it. There are things I can never know and never *will* know. Things I've never seen and am destined never to see. If we insist on saying everything there is to say about every individual subject before moving on, we're simply overlooking the endless, boundless chaos inside our heads. That said, I have no idea how we got here. Such things are best left unsaid. I'm out of my depth. It's none of my business, anyway. At the end of the day, I'm just the landlady. You may well ask why I even brought this up. As if I had a clue, Ziya Bey! Honestly, I don't have the faintest. You say one word and before you know it, you've fallen in love with your own voice. You become a child again. A spoiled little child. On the subject of which, shall we get her to bring in another two coffees?'

'No,' said Ziya, as a new wave of anxiety passed across his face. 'Thanks, but I really need to go.'

'I'm guessing you're late for something.' As Binnaz Hanım spoke, she gestured at the maid, who was fast approaching him.

The moment her mistress had opened her mouth, she'd come rushing. And now she was standing before him with the coffee tray, making a polite curtsy.

'Yes,' Binnaz Hanım continued. 'Sometimes people spoil themselves. But did you know, Ziya Bey, that up until this moment, no one in the world has ever spoiled *me*? Every now and again, I try and convince myself that someone somewhere must have spoiled me when I was a child. And believe you me, I've pecked so hard at my memories, you'd think I was a starving chicken, hunting for one last morsel of food. Nothing. Not even a hint. It's never long, though, before I remember my mother's silence. I can see her even now, you know – floating around in the backwaters of my mind with her plastic washtub. She only ever opened her mouth to scold me. If I hadn't done something to merit a scolding, she kept her mouth shut. She used looks in place of words. She had green eyes that reminded me of unripe grapes. She would move them like this – very, very slowly – or else bounce them about, like a pair of marbles. If she did that, they would lose their sparkle almost instantly and begin to steam up, of course. And that's how she would be for the rest of the day, solemn, steamy-eyed, and silent. Was she silent to protect us from her anger, or to shield herself from the possibility of attack? I couldn't tell you. What I do know is that every time I came close to Mother, I felt like I was teetering over a deep, dark cliff. That's how I felt, Ziya Bey. In real life such things never happened, but whenever I drew close to that poor mother of mine, I genuinely felt like I was

15

teetering over a deep, dark cliff. Such a look she would give me. But then turn back to her chores. This weary shadow that was my mother would dive back into her mountains of dishes and dirty laundry. Only the dewy, shaking clothes pegs would remain in her wake. A glimmer of that red plastic washtub. A rattle of pots and pans. May she rest in peace, that's all I can say. Except that never in a million years would it have occurred to this woman to spoil her children. Neither did my father have much time for these things, Ziya Bey. As much as I longed for it to be otherwise, I only saw him a few times a month. Every morning, that bastard would be out of bed, and out the door, crack of dawn, even before the crows ate their shit. "Time is money!" he would say. He wouldn't be back until late at night, long after our fleas had started jumping. Coming or going, he carried with him the alcoholic stink of the *meyhane*. Every night he came home, I'd wake up in the morning with the same wall of fumes in my room. Sometimes he'd just stand at the foot of my bed, leaning over as if to kiss me, his shoulders trembling, his outstretched arms, too. He would sit at the edge of the bed, and while I held my breath, I would also hold his stare. I would stare into this cloud that stank of onions, and meat, and cigarettes, and beans, and vinegar and *rakı*, until it turned back into something more like my father again. Until it was a solid mass again, and put its feet back on the floor. Then I'd go to the bathroom to wash my face, race into the kitchen to make breakfast, race back into my room to prepare my schoolbag, and all the while, he stayed by my side. Except when I went to the toilet, of course. Then he would wait outside the door, as kind and patient as any father could be. Sometimes, when we were traipsing around like this, he would stagger,

16

just a little, but I didn't care: that's how happy I was to have him there with me. Because even through that quivering wall of *meyhane* stink I could feel my father's warmth, and when I felt that warmth, believe me, I would come alive again, then and there. When I felt my father's warmth flowing through me, I just couldn't bear to leave him. I'd forget about school and all that. I'd do just about anything to put off leaving. And – let me tell you – I could be extraordinarily inventive when it came to that. When no one was looking, I'd pull a button off my uniform, and then I'd take my time looking for a needle and thread, and even more time to sew it back on. Or I'd run around pretending to be all upset, and saying, "Oh no! I've forgotten to do my homework!" And then I would open up my notebook, and I'd huff and I'd puff, scribbling down page after page of whatever came into my head. Of course, my poor mother had no idea why I did all this, and because she had no idea, she'd just stand there behind the kitchen stove. Or she'd poke her head round the door or the washing basket and stun me with that peculiar, wide-eyed stare and say, "Come on now, you'll be late for school!" That's the long and the short of it – wherever we come from, it's our father who creates us, Ziya Bey, and there aren't any others that can replace him. A whiff of his scent, a glimpse of his pale shadow, a hint of his trembling form, or even just a sign of his absence and someone like me can make him into a father again. There are other ways to come alive, to be sure. Others have been known to do so by succumbing to a warm embrace, or burning in the passion of a stolen glance. They can be born again in the spirit of a book, or brought to life by a single touch. Or by any number of brilliant or moronic acts that might have slipped my mind.

Those with little souls that are easily sated can come to life just by sitting in the corner munching on sunflower seeds. Wild souls can come to life by venturing beyond the shadows to break and spill everything they touch. Or they may come to life without doing much at all. At the end of the day, a father cannot be measured by the same stick we could use on all those others. A father is a different prospect altogether. We are talking about something very old here. Something as old as the birds. As old as the clouds above us. As old as the stones at our feet. I came to understand all this much better, you know, after my father died. Though he didn't just die. What I should have said – and let me say it now, even if it grinds my teeth to dust – what I should have said is: he was murdered. This angelic man who had to work so hard to keep his family housed and fed – he was cut down in the most barbaric way imaginable, in the middle of the afternoon, for just a few dirty coins. They attacked him together and before anyone could blink, they had stabbed him to death. If you want to ask me who dealt the killing blow, I can tell you now. It was Matkap the Drill! His real name was Macit Karakaş, and he was the nastiest, most pitiful cretin imaginable. He was one of my father's business partners. If you got up right now and tried to imitate a turkey, Ziya Bey, you would go some way to capturing the way this cretin walked, with a black raincoat that went down to his heels. But he was not the sort who could sit down in one place for long. You might think, from the way I've described him, that he cut an impressive figure, but you would be wrong, Ziya Bey. In fact he was a tiny thing, about the size of a chickpea. But what God took from him in size, he gave him in voice. Whenever he spoke, it made the ground beneath your feet creak and sway so badly you'd have thought it was an earthquake. And all the sounds around him would seem to bow to him, and the silences too. Whatever was nearby, and whatever it was, it, too, would tremble at the sound of that booming voice, until there seemed to be hundreds of Matkaps, all shouting at once. And of course this was frightening. Like it or not, you ended up wondering if something terrible was about to happen. But anyway, I've probably said enough. There's just one more thing you should know. This man was a complete and utter brute. Wherever you took him, he'd pick a fight. He'd always find some pretext, no matter what. If he couldn't, he'd just sit there, stiff as a board, searching the room for any excuse to start something. Surrounding this piece of filth were a number of men with faces like pine planks. But they were fleet of foot, Ziya Bey. They swaggered about in black cloaks that never touched their sides, using their huge hands and elbows to open the way for Matkap – as if anyone would dare to block it. They knocked people over even when they weren't in his path. And oh, how clumsy they were, how monumentally clumsy. Frowning and glowering and growling through their moustaches. If anyone would be so bold as to object to all this pushing and shoving, they would round on him at once, and by the time they were done, it wasn't a pretty sight, let me tell you! But Matkap never looked. He'd just avert his eyes. Puff up his chest and march on like a victorious general, swishing his raincoat from side to side. He had no interest in men whose faces had been smashed like cheap china. Or men who'd been sent flying against the wall with a single punch. Or the poor creatures who curled up like woodlice when his associates kicked them across the floor. For this was a man so merciless that the word alone does not come close to describing him. He was, in short, a complete and utter tyrant. A tyrant among tyrants, until he saw a child. What can I say? In the space of a moment, he ceased to be Matkap. A blink of the eye, and he became a gentle and benevolent dervish. When a child crossed his path, he never looked away. He stared at them so hard, you'd think he was trying to see inside them – into their souls. Their futures. He'd stare at them, speechless. And then he'd let out the strangest sound – a sound which seemed to belong to someone else. And that was it. He'd begin to cry. I don't know what he saw in children to make him cry. Was it their beauty? Their little quince hairs? The way they sneezed into their hands? Their tiny little bodies? The men who looked like pine planks, meanwhile – they'd have seen this coming. They'd have reached inside their pockets for the handkerchiefs he'd soon need. Sometimes, they'd even try to get there before he did, sobbing and bawling, bending and twisting, wailing and throwing themselves about. And all the while, there was Matkap in the middle, crying his heart out. There is only one word for it: surreal. The pine planks might have seen themselves as humouring their patron, though in fact they were turning him into some sort of caricature. Their false tears served only to make Matkap's tears look just as false. But there was always that moment when Matkap's tears could genuinely touch you. All of a sudden, you'd feel a slow, warm drip of goodwill. Do you know, Ziya Bey, I think I've calmed down now. Yes, when I relive that scene, I feel very sad. I'm going to have a cigarette if you don't mind. Would you like one?'

'Yes, I would,' Ziya replied.

As she reached out to take a cigarette, Binnaz Hanım allowed herself a faint smile.

'So that's how it is,' she said with a tired sigh. 'He might have killed my father, but when I remember that microbe's tears, it still makes me sad. Sometimes I wonder if you need to have some evil in you, to have any chance of being seen as good. Who am I to say, but in this world of ours, bad people do have a way of outshining the good, Ziya Bey. As I said just a moment ago, Matkap had only to see a child to turn into an extravagantly good man. Maybe, without knowing it, he was able to tap into their inner goodness somehow. Maybe when he reached out to touch a child's cheek, he was actually touching the light in that child's soul. I can't say for sure, of course. I never studied any of that God stuff, my mind just can't take it in. I can't believe there's a needle-point's worth of light in him anyway; he's all darkness, a stinking barn filled to the last square millimetre with long-tailed, fire-breathing devils. All else aside, this was already clear from the fact that he murdered my father . . . Yes, he killed my father! Without even blinking! In the space of a moment, I saw my world come crashing down – bang! – and then, before my eyes, it remade itself, from top to bottom. Just like that. And that, Ziya Bey, is when it happened: his weight joined with mine. As he vanished, I increased in volume, and then – presto! – the woman you see before you was reborn. It's not just my weight that changed that day. It was everything: my arms, my legs, my face, my eyes. I was chilled to the bone, and what's more, I couldn't stop trembling, and I had no idea what to do. And then, every time I thought that thought – "I don't know what to do" – my father's face would appear before me, and there he'd stand – my father. My father, stinking like a *meyhane*, and watching over me. He could see how distraught I was. *I'm here*, he'd say. Just the faintest hint of a smile: *I'm here*. In those days, of course, there was no price to be paid for too many tears, and nothing could stop me from retreating into a corner to cry the night away. In one sense, I was calling out for my father, whose face I could see so clearly in my dreams. I knew he wasn't coming back, but I still cried out for him. At the time, my mother was doing the same, using all her strength to beat her chest, and so were my brothers and sisters, my white-haired grandmother and the relatives who came to us from all over the city. We cried and we cried. We begged my father to come back. And oh, the day they brought the coffin to the house. That sorry coffin, draped in green. As we gathered around it, our grief knew no bounds . . . And that's God's own truth. So I shall ask you to pay no attention to what I said a moment ago, about being so sad. I am, to all intents and purposes, Matkap's most formidable foe. If I ever get my hands on him, mark my words: I'll strangle him in a heartbeat. I've only seen him a few times since, but I was too young to kill him – I didn't even have pimples then. The first time I saw him was three days after the funeral, when he came to the house, to pay his condolences. Swishing that coat of his. Did that murderer feel no shame? Standing in front of our door that day, you could still hear us wailing: three days after the funeral, our cries of grief still hung over us: black and trembling, a wailing cloud. And now here he was, stepping out of that cloud, without his men, and showing such remorse. Matkap. When my poor mother opened the door, she was so shocked and angry she didn't know what to do. Then she pulled herself together, gathered all her strength, and hissing like a yellow snake she said, "Go. Away." Just those two words. "Go. Away." We ran to her side, taking her by the arms, lest she crumble in a heap, and that leather-faced goon they called Matkap just buried his head in his shoulders, and off he went, back into the wailing cloud, and it wasn't long before we could see no more of him or his black raincoat. But still we stood there, staring into that cloud until our tears returned. It was worst for my mother. It was as if she had lost my father all over again, and the second time was far, far worse than the first. Day after day, she sat in her corner, head bowed, eyes downcast, her hands hanging limply at her side. A week later, she suddenly remembered my father's coat. Furious, she jumped to her feet. In a tearful voice, she told me to go straight to the *meyhane* to bring it back. That was how, like it or not, I had my second encounter with this Macit Karakaş, this man we knew as Matkap. And so I threw on my cardigan and off I went to the *meyhane*, and I cannot begin to tell you how scared I was. I'm not sure what scared me more – seeing Matkap, or seeing the place where my father had been killed, or touching his jacket – but I was quaking. With every step and every street, my terror grew, until there I was, at the *meyhane* door. Matkap had pinned the blame for the murder on one of his men, and given the other partner in the business a little money to get lost. He'd then had the *meyhane*'s indigo-blue walls painted pink, and changed the neon signs, and the tables, not to mention the tablecloths and pictures, and as if this wasn't enough, he'd put up a bead curtain that clicked and clattered at the slightest touch. To supervise all this he'd parked himself next to the cash register. Or at least, that where he was sitting, snug as an inkpot, when I pushed open the bat-wing doors.

Sitting there with his hands clasped, staring stupidly into the middle distance. Was he startled at the sight of me? He didn't move a muscle, but something was up. For all I know, the very force of my gaze pulled him right out of his seat, only to set him right back down again. He looked up for a moment. Bored his eyes straight into me. Then he opened a drawer. Began to rummage through it. Made a good show of being frantically busy. A businessman, with important business to attend to. And while he continued with this charade, I stared down at the concrete floor, wondering where it was my father had fallen, after being stabbed. A jowly grey-haired middle-aged waiter worked his way over to me, very slowly. Standing right in front of me, he asked me what I wanted. He knew who I was, of course. He'd seen me before. He was at pains to look pained. As if to say, "Oh, my poor, poor girl, from the bottom of my heart, I grieve for you." And oh, how old that made him seem. You know how it is with old men sometimes. How they'll try and turn their decaying bodies into featherbeds of compassion. You know the type. Old man. Heart on sleeve. A little breeze wafts by or the door slams and he dissolves into tears. With every passing day his body sinks deeper into inertia. The world revolving around him seems to do the same. Each minute rolls by slower than the last. If life were a reel of film, he'd have time to pore over each and every frame. And when life is unfurling that slowly, a single frame can really strike the heart. You know what I mean? But who does know? It might be the slow pace of life itself that drives old men like this mad. Maybe the rest of the charade is subterfuge. A sad attempt to dignify all those tears they've shed. When they cry, every last pore in their eyes opens up, and with all that light coming in, there is no hiding from the mountain peaks of memory. It may well be those mountain peaks that upset them: I just don't know. In any event, this middle-aged waiter I was telling you about. With that silly look on his face, he might as well have been one of those old men. Just say boo and he'll cry. I'm not joking. Tears welling in his eyes. Eyelashes twitching. Cheekbones clenched. I told him what I wanted, my voice trembling, and off he went, rushing to a wooden closet behind the counter and retrieving my father's jacket. With a deftness that took me by surprise, he folded it up and placed it in my arms. I was in such a state, Ziya Bey. I couldn't stop shaking. And shivering. You would have thought I had a fever. I threw Matkap a furious glance, as if to say: "What of the man who should be wearing this coat?" Which was, of course, a wasted effort. The scoundrel was still bent down, fiddling with the drawers. And so I left, without saying a word. I rushed out into the street. Dived into the crowd. Broke into a run. I began to feel better once I'd escaped from the *meyhane*, but even so, I dreaded going home. What I mean to say is, I began to imagine the scene that might await me there. I ran through the possibilities, each more frightening than the last. I had no idea what my mother would do when I walked in. Would she freeze at the sight of me, never to move again? Or would she let out a high-pitched scream, hold the jacket to her breast, bury her face in it, taking in the smell – bury her face in it, over and over, only to launch into a tirade of fury, a string of curses that had no meaning, beyond being all against Macit Karakaş? Or would she take the jacket off to her corner, and bow her head and return to her dark chasm, refusing food and drink for days to come? There was no way of knowing. It could be none of the above, but it was not knowing that unnerved me, and my heart raced faster with every step I took. Honestly, Ziya Bey. Walking home with that jacket in my arms was difficult beyond words. Even now, all these years later, that same fear comes back to haunt me. It's like someone has driven a giant nail through my heart. And nothing I can do will dislodge it. And when I go down into the city, when I walk through those same streets, sometimes I can see myself, as I was on that day. What I mean is, when I'm least expecting it, I see before me a very young girl, whose face is pale as pale. Sometimes she slips out from behind a bus, and sometimes around a corner. Sometimes the crowds drift apart like clouds and there she is. A girl whose slender legs are trembling with fear, and I share that fear. Because I'm not taking home a jacket. I'm taking home my father's absence. And that's why my burden feels so heavy, and why it pains me so. And yet I've taken it with me, wherever I've gone, wherever I rest my weary head – can you ever lose sight of a person? And for a long time I've wondered if it's his echoes I'm seeing. I'll be walking down a street, and suddenly it's like everyone I see is someone I met many years ago. Then I remember that some of these people are dead and buried, and naturally that sends a chill down my spine. Soon I'm so scared my eyes are popping out, and that is when the young girl slips back into the crowd. Tossing her hair, she slips back into the pandemonium of the streets. Time buttons itself up. I can no longer see into the past. I know, Ziya Bey, I know. You must think I've said quite enough. And if I am right about that, there wouldn't be anyone on heaven or earth who'd disagree with you. Even I couldn't tell you what's making me talk like this. Let's have another cigarette – what do you say?'

'Yes, let's,' said Ziya.

As he spoke, he looked soulfully into Binnaz Hanım's eyes.

This seemed to embarrass her, because now she averted her eyes. Then she lit the cigarette already dangling between her lips, falling back into her chair as the smoke seeped out through those lips and billowed upwards. And at that moment, Ziya could see the little girl in her. Gone were the lines that the decades had drawn on her face. It was as if they, too, had taken fright and abandoned the girl who now gazed at him in terror, wide-eyed and trembling.

'Then my mother took leave of her senses,' Binnaz Hanım continued. 'Yes, for some reason, this was the straw that broke the camel's back. She'd managed to bear the sight of my father's lifeless body, but when she saw his coat in my arms that day, she lost her mind. My mother had always been the second of the two pillars holding up our household, and now this pillar was crumbling, before our very eyes. And we children were at our wits' end, Ziya Bey. Because of course we had no idea what to do. Our despair seemed to know no bounds, but each time we looked at each other, it seemed deeper, and darker. You might have thought that all the lights in the world had been extinguished, plunging us into a nightscape so black it was almost luminous. Who knows? It might have been the darkness of our future we could see just then, shining through the sands of time. All we could do was to cry helplessly on each other's shoulders – cry into the night. What was to become of us? From time to time, we heard footsteps approaching. We'd rush to the door, sobbing and red-eyed, to see who was there, but all we could hear were footsteps receding. They ran like the wind, these footsteps, rushing in only to rush away. I like to think it was our father's spirit, back from the graveyard to see how we were. Ever so gently, pressing his ear against the door. Drinking in the music of home and then vanishing into thin air. Every time this happened, of course, it felt like losing him all over again. And once again, the vale of tears would claim us. The first to cry would be the youngest; he would stand up, saying "Who's there?" in that milky voice of his, and toddle off to the door, and as he walked he would open his arms, ready for a hug, and the wider he opened them, the more excited he became, but even so, there'd be tears welling in his eyes by the time he reached the door. I have no idea how many days we spent like that, wandering around that house of ours, bleating like lost lambs. But in due course, our grim-faced relatives surfaced. They arrived from all four corners of the city to divide us up. My aged grandmother, for instance. She took me to her draughty ruin of a house, fitting me out with a thick mattress that reeked of naphthalene. Sitting on the edge of said mattress, she stroked my hair and said, "There's never a tragedy without another in its wake, my child." She was only trying to offer me comfort, but I was in no state to understand. In actual fact, many months passed before I understood a thing anyone said to me. I stayed inside, wandering like a mute ghost from one room to the next. But my grandmother could not afford to feed me, Ziya Bey, let alone keep me in school. Once that chapter of my life had closed, I went to work in a *meyhane*. A distant relative found me the job. And after that you never saw a pen or a schoolbook in my lovely little hands. Day and night, I was washing dishes. In the early days, at least. The scullery was right underneath the big room where they served the customers − a low-ceilinged cavern that you reached via a wooden staircase so coated with grease that it stuck to your feet like gum. We could hear every chair that scraped the floor in the *meyhane* above − every laugh, every song and every curse. It wore us out, listening to that ruckus. But not because we were working like donkeys while other people were having fun. No, it wore us out because they were having fun just above our heads. Sometimes I would say as much to the other girls working there, and whenever I did, the *djinns* would get the better of me. They'd swarm around my head until I just couldn't stop myself. I'd look up at that ceiling and let loose a string of filthy curses. But the others? Not a peep out of them. Not a peep. When my rage got the better of me, they'd just exchange shifty looks. Who would be the first to tell tales? That cave we called the scullery was hard to bear − no, impossible to bear − at times like that. But never mind, because it wasn't long before I was sent upstairs to serve tables. Leaving the scullery to sink back into silence. For me, from then on, it was smiles and wayward glances and rowdy songs; it was fat-assed men who were belching one minute, and rearranging their testicles the next. It was the dark night of the soul upstairs, just as much as it had been downstairs, but the *meyhane*, at least, had lights. Each one more brilliant than the last. You know how it is − some rooms are darkened by clutter, and others by noise. Some rooms are dark because they're too empty, or too narrow or too wide. Well, in this *meyhane* the darkness was in the lights. And it was through this shimmering, *rakı*-scented gloom that I ran back and forth with my tray. Once a week I'd go and see my mother. I'd take her flowers and the finest cakes and sweets, in darling little boxes. But sadly she had no idea who I was. She called me "Auntie". My gifts would just sit there on her lap. How ashamed she looked, with those downcast eyes of hers! And so like a child! Just a glimpse of one of those white-aproned orderlies, and she'd shrink before my eyes. Shrink into me, almost. If ever one of those orderlies came towards us, she'd grab my hand, my mother would. She'd fix her pleading eyes on mine. And then, in a faint and wavering voice, she'd say, "Save me, Auntie. Please, get me out of here." Over and over, on and on. How helpless I felt when she did that. Because honestly, I had no idea what to do. A moment would arrive when I couldn't stand it any more, when I'd take my mother in my arms and hold her tight, as if I were her mother, and she my child. Then I could hold back the tears no longer. Or the hopeless sobbing. So there you have it. The story of a luck-less young girl, laid low by a calamity that never lessens, that just goes on, and on, and on. What happened next? you may well ask. But you know full well how stories like this pan out in this city of ours, which oozes evil from its every pore. You could write the script, Ziya Bey. What happened to me is exactly what you would imagine might happen, right down to the last detail. In the past we ate shit. In the future we shall do the same. You know how it is, Ziya Bey. We can rant and we can rage, but nothing short of a miracle will change it. Which is not to say I didn't try! I tried but it was all in vain, and that is why I trod the boards of that *meyhane* for so many years, just for a scrap of bread. Or to put it differently, this is where my story played itself out. And if Ercüment Şahiner had not walked into my life, who knows where I might be today? In a nursing home, I'd guess – alone with my memories, my thoughts turning to death, wheezing one minute, dozing off the next. And drooling. Drooling from both sides of my mouth. Or if not that, then maybe I'd be one of those poor souls you see going through dustbins, clutching dirty plastic bags – one of those homeless wretches that the council rounds up when the temperature goes below freezing, rescuing them from the parks and the pavements and the city's phone boxes and then calling in the TV cameras, only to throw them back on to the street a few days later . . . You're wondering what this Ercüment Şahiner did for me? No need to beat about the bush: what this man gave me was an idea. Nothing more, nothing less. It was a winter's day. I remember it well. The day before, we'd had a blizzard. From dawn to dusk, we'd watched that snow hurling down on us, thick as patches on a poor man's coat. And then, that night, the blackest frost. By morning all the rooftops of the city and all its streets were stiff with ice, and, with so few venturing outside, a silence had fallen over everything, a faint and shimmering white silence. From time to time, a sound would float in. A city bus struggling up a hill. A child screaming. I was still in bed, and each time a new sound floated in, those sleepy eyes of mine flew open. Ercüment Bey, who had spent the night in my arms, was already up claiming business to attend to. There he was in the corner, getting dressed. The glare from the snow was so strong as to cast his shadow against the wall, and as I lay there, I watched it going through its paces. Ercüment Bey was getting dressed at the same speed and with the same care as the shadow, of course: buttoning up his shirt, zipping up his trousers, fixing his tie just so, and then looking himself over, from top to toe, as if to ask, have I missed anything? Am I done? To tell you the truth, I got some sort of strange thrill from watching that shadow. It made Ercüment Bey himself seem a little less real. It turned our night together into some kind of a lie. But back to the story. When Ercüment Bey had completed his toilette, he came back to my bed, whereupon, with his usual finesse, he slipped my money under the pillow. Why I didn't wait for him to leave, I do not know. But I pulled out the money, and, before his very eyes, I put it into the chocolate box where I kept all my earnings. Ercüment Bey was back in my arms by now. Throwing a sidelong glance at the box, which was decorated with angels, he said, "Keep that money in a box like that, and you might as well just pickle it. It'll never grow, my lovely. If you have any brains, you'll put it into land." I laughed, of course. I said, "You can't buy land for three *kuruş*. I couldn't even buy a plot as long as my arm for that." Ercüment Bey got my meaning. But then said, "You might not be able to get something in the centre, but go beyond the far hills, buy some land even Allah doesn't give a fuck about, and wait for the city to come to you." Those words were like earrings, and for a few years that was all they were, dangling in my mind and from time to time catching the light. To cut a long story short, in the end I did what Ercüment Bey had suggested, Ziya Bey. A big property broker like him was sure to know what he was talking about, and so I went out to the back of beyond, to a place so remote that even caravans never passed. And bought myself a patch of land. Then after – what, thirty years – this huge wave of noise they call a city had spread so far that it engulfed my fields. One fine day a contractor knocked on my door – a young man, flashing a gold necklace. In an accent I couldn't place, he made me an offer. What do you say, sister? What if

I built two big apartment blocks and gave one to you? There are no words to describe how that threw me. It was all I could do to keep myself from crying! The truth is, I'd never imagined that the three-*kuruş* land I'd bought at the dawn of time would prove so fruitful. That's why I was so surprised. And who knows, Ziya Bey, maybe I felt a little ashamed to find myself showered with these great riches all of a sudden. I felt accusing eyes all around me. Voices saying I didn't deserve it. It didn't last long, this shyness. Once the apartments were up, it wore off, bit by bit, until one fine day it vanished like a morning mist. It happened in stages. That said – if you asked me to chart those stages, I'd have to give up before I began. Maybe it was time that gnawed away at it. Though it could be that my shame was no match for the miseries I'd suffered in earlier life, and the rancour those miseries had left me with. All I know is that I was at last able to relax. My mood lifted. I strolled through my building each morning, casting smiles right and left as I went. I was a child with a new toy, a curious child with a happy heart. How, how I loved going up and down in the lifts, just for the fun of it! How it thrilled me, to touch the banisters, to know that every single one of the doors standing in their pretty little rows belonged to me! I'd walk down every corridor, and every stairwell, until I'd seen the whole building, and then, having nothing else to do, I'd plop down on a chair on the balcony, and there I'd stay till evening. And oh! What joy I felt, as I took in the view! In actual fact, it wasn't easy. It was, to tell the truth, a fantastically tiring state of affairs. People always say that happiness makes life seem so much lighter, but for me it was so much more tiring, Ziya Bey. If there is any lightness at all, it is only the first stage. And anyway. As you already know, when happiness takes root in you, it can dazzle your mind. It can blind you. You could say that I, too, was blinded, I mean, during those long and mindlessly happy days I spent on that balcony. And all the while, Ercüment Şahiner was in my thoughts. My happy heart fairly fluttered with the gratitude I felt towards him. And so I got it into my head to thank him, to throw my arms around him, and kiss him – let him know he was my miracle's true architect. I rushed out to find him, and, what a pity, Ercüment Bey was no longer in his office. His colleagues told me that a childhood friend he'd claimed as his blood brother had left him up to his gills in debt. And so he'd fallen into the hands of a usurer. Then it went from bad to worse – Ali clothing Veli, Veli clothing Ali and both robbing Peter to pay Paul. Then the thugs came in to raid the office, and after that had happened a few times, he'd gathered up his things and fled. That was one story. Another story had it that he'd fallen in love with a slender, fair-skinned woman, who visited the office once a week. Maddened by passion, he'd buried himself in a deep, deep silence, until one day he upped and sold everything he owned to follow this woman to another city. But I can't say I found this very convincing. Ercüment Bey didn't have enough brains to lose them in such a way – so, no, I don't think he was up to it. My guess is he went into hiding after those thugs who turned his office upside down put the fear of God in him. Maybe he was inside there, shivering like a wet kitten, thinking they'd come back to kill him on the spot, never guessing it was me looking for him. One thing I know: if someone, anyone, had told me what hole he was hiding in, I would have pulled him right out – paid his debts twice over, and then, to restore him to his rightful place, I'd have gone out to the flashiest neighbourhood in the city, and bought him the biggest, brightest office going, and furnished it from floor to ceiling in the finest taste. I'd have shown him to his chair, and said, "Do sit down, my life. Do sit down." I could have done that many times over. That's how grateful I felt. No words can express the depth of my gratitude to this man. Oh, the months I wasted, traipsing from building to building, down corridors that stank of piss. I combed every street, every arcade, every land-registry office. Every office of every *muhtar* who ever ran a neighbourhood, too. Wherever a broker might show his face, there I went, to find him. Now and again, I'd come across a *muhtar* or a broker who showed me the courtesy of listening to my problem. They would take down my details, and promise to let me know if they had any news of him, but a year and a half later, not a single one had got in touch. That's when I knew I'd never find him, Ziya Bey. That was when I gave up the ghost. I returned to my chair on the balcony, empty for so long, and from dawn till dusk I took in the view. But my debt of gratitude still weighed down on me, of course. There was none of the old joy. I'd just sit there, looking emptily at nothing in particular. Gratitude is a terrible thing, Ziya Bey; the havoc it wreaks is something only the sufferer can understand. I would go so far as to say that it does a great deal more than ravage the soul: it presses down on you, turns you into a slave. A slave who is willing, even dying, to prove herself worthy. A wounded slave who is bent on opening her wounds even further . . . But anyway. So there I was, sitting on my balcony, gazing emptily at the apartments across the road, watching the cars and the crowds. Many visions came to me at that time. They fell into my mind like photographs from an album, slipping every which way. One such image showed me sewing that button back on to my uniform, my father at my side. I was turned in his direction, smiling faintly, and taking in his scent. There was another, much noisier picture, lit through wine glasses: a crowd of men. All smiling. At me. Or had they narrowed their eyes like cats to sneeze their smoke through their moustaches, all at once? Whatever the truth of this photograph, it summoned up another from the depths of my mind. In this one I was following my grandmother through a long street full of puddles. The further I walked, of course, the more darkly the slums cast shadows over my photograph. And soon they had grown into one great fake and lifeless tangle amid the rippling, quivering puddles. And now another photograph, wafting through the whole trembling mess. And in this one, I am having sex with men I don't even know. Sometimes I even see myself coming to collect my father's jacket, or washing dishes with those silent, cowering girls, or visiting my mother with those cute little boxes, or dragged to and fro by the claws of a shadow. And so it continued, Ziya Bey. It was one photograph after another, for days and weeks on end. Until somehow they drifted out of view. One by one, they vanished from my mind. The only one that remained, I must tell you, was the picture of the money I'd saved in that chocolate box. No matter how I tried, I could not shake that image from my mind. It was as if a hidden hand was holding it up to me – trying desperately to tell me something. From dawn till dusk that picture never left me. I was lost to time, lost inside time and in thrall to it. My soul was elsewhere, far away. My mind was blank. Utterly blank. I might as well have been an idiot. Maybe that's what did it – the blankness.

Because one day at long last I was hit by a new idea, a thunderclap of an idea that turned all my memories inside out. The Ercüment Şahiner for whom I had searched high and low was a broker, after all. But I had allowed this fact to slip from my mind. I had, as a consequence, felt more gratitude than was warranted, had allowed myself to become crippled by it. No doubt Ercüment Bey told everyone he met back then to invest in land. It was part of his job. That is what I told myself, and that was when I remembered that that money in the chocolate box was my own. I had paid for this building with a wasted youth spent hopping from lap to lap. Once I understood that, Ziya Bey, I was no longer willing to let tenants surrender their keys to my accountant when they vacated the premises. What I mean to say is that I came to see my tenants as having occupied my own lost years, and that is why I decided they should, at the very least, come and give me the key themselves. So that's what it's all about, Ziya Bey, this business with the key. Now let me apologise for taking up so much of your time with my chatter. And not just your time, I fear. Am I right in thinking I've also given you a headache?'

Ziya smiled faintly.

Before Binnaz Hanım could launch into another monologue, he jumped to his feet. Scooping up the key from the table that stood between them, he went a few steps closer and stretched out his hand.

A smile spread across Binnaz Hanım's face.

Catching a glimpse of the city in her eyes, he shivered.

'I'd better be off,' he said. 'Let me say my goodbyes.'

'You're leaving the city, aren't you?' Binnaz Hanım now said. 'You're going far away.'

'How do you know that?' Ziya gasped.

'I know,' said Binnaz Hanım, 'I know, yes. Actually, I know everything about my tenants. If I'm going to wander around an apartment building as big as this one, filled with scores of families and a few single men and women too – well, I need to have all the facts at my fingertips. If I didn't, God forbid, I'd lose the thread. Just because the people in this place step outside to face the world in clean, ironed clothes, swinging their fine handbags, and glittering with jewellery, just because they greet each other so nicely and smile and chatter so sweetly, don't you think for a moment they are as they seem. Behind each civilised façade you'll find lives of a different order. You'll find lives that are foul smelling and loveless, lives that decay a little bit more each day until they fall from the mortice. Some load their possessions on to trucks, you know. Vanish into the night without paying the rent; others run off with their neighbours' money, jewellery and credit cards. Some turn out to be child molesters, hunting darkly for fresh prey. Some use their apartments as drug depots, some get carted off to the police station once a week. Dragged off by their arms and legs, though who knows why, and these are only the things that happen in broad daylight. Behind closed doors, there are worse things going on. Unspeakable things. Deeds so awful that I can only hope they remain between me and the archives of the state. The long and the short of it is that – whichever way you look at it – I need to know everything my tenants are up to. As you can see, there is no other option . . . And it's no small thing – it costs me serious money and effort, of course. All the information I acquire, I store with great care in confidential dossiers, over in the corner. The only person but me who ever sees them is my little gazelle here. She helps me compile them, and – as she's so young and inexperienced – the whole thing leaves her in a constant state of shock. That most amiable and genteel of gentlemen; that loveliest of old ladies, whose eyes are brimming with tears; that creature so chaste and so morally upstanding that you cannot imagine him leaving so much as a speck of ash on a barbecue; that delicate youth; and that old man whose soft heart breaks at the sight of a wounded kitten – oh yes, they all shock her, when she sees the tricks they're up to. The word shock doesn't begin to describe it – what she sees in these dossiers shakes the very foundations of her heart and mind. Sometimes she'll put one file down on her lap and stare into the distance, as her face goes pale; sometimes, when she's listening to a recording, she has to press the button to stop the tape, and then she paces the room, wild-eyed with terror, and as she flutters this way and that she lets out that odd cry of hers. "Hiiii! Hiiii!" I cannot begin to describe how this saddens me. More than that, I'm worried that my girl will lose all faith in life itself, and all because of what she now knows. Yes, that's what I'm most afraid of, but however much I think about it, I cannot imagine any other way. If my little gazelle here didn't help me, I could never get it all filed – not by myself, anyway. Not at my age, in my condition. It simply wouldn't be possible. And nowhere on earth could I find another girl like her – a girl who knows how to keep her mouth shut. In any event, I've known for months from your dossier that you were going to leave the city. As I knew you wouldn't leave without paying, I didn't see the need to undertake a detailed investigation. As I've already said, you've had enough of the hustle and bustle of the city, and now you're going far away, to bask in the joys of nature. A place where you can hear your own heartbeat, touch the leaves, the insects, the grass and the stones. Isn't that what your heart desires?'

'It is, but it's very strange,' said Ziya, looking puzzled. 'It's not possible that you know all this.'

Binnaz Hanım said nothing. As she rose from her chair she became a ghost again, a jowly, troubled ghost whose eyes never blinked as they stared into the distance.

'You can't possibly know that,' Ziya repeated. 'I've only told one friend where I'm going, and he lives on the other side of the city. Really, how do you know all this?'

'We live in an era, Ziya Bey, where this should not surprise us,' Binnaz Hanım said, raising up her hands.

In a softer voice, she added, 'And then, if you talk to yourself about it afterwards, it's child's play. Pure child's play.'

For a moment, Ziya stood there, stunned.

Then he turned to head for the door.

Binnaz Hanım followed close behind.

One after the other, they entered the narrow, gloomy anteroom. No sooner had he set foot inside than Ziya heard paper rustling on the other side of the wall. Unable to stop himself, he turned to Binnaz Hanım. 'That's paper rustling, isn't it?'

'That hard-working girl of mine must be seeing to the new dossiers,' said Binnaz Hanım.

They continued into the corridor whose walls were lined with green tapestries. It seemed, as they walked through it (Ziya first and Binnaz Hanım close behind), as if it might never end, until they reached the door.

'You're going there to pray, if you ask me,' she said by way of farewell. 'Really, that's all I can think. To go far away and live in harmony with nature, to witness it, and to breathe that air – to my mind, that's praying. I don't know what you think, naturally.'

'You may be right. All right, then. Goodbye,' Ziya said, fearing the conversation might continue. 'Good day.'

'Goodbye,' said Binnaz Hanım. 'But don't forget – he who wishes to pray should also carry a stone to throw.'

Ziya heard her, but instead of answering, he walked quickly towards the lift. As he walked, he felt he could see all the apartment block's brown steel doors, all the plastic flowers adorning them, and the walls, the banisters, the doormats. He thought he could see Binnaz Hanım, though she had closed the door by now to pace the depths of her apartment. He thought he could see the city, and the foul smells arising from its depths. Then suddenly he saw Binnaz Hanım's maid. Or rather, the girl stepped out of the lift with a handbag on her shoulder. Lifting her head, she peered up at him coyly through those wisps of hair. And then she moved on, without saying a word, leaving only a lovely scent in her wake.

Ziya made to turn his head to watch her go, but for some reason his head wouldn't turn. And neither could he stop moving. It was, he thought, as if he'd surrendered to his own pace. It was a very strange breeze, he thought, sweeping him down the corridor. In no time he had reached the lift. He opened the door to step inside. But there was no inside. With terrifying speed, he went tumbling into nothingness. Into night without end.

2

The Dream

When he opened his eyes, it was darkness all around him, and his heart was pounding so fast as to burst from his chest. At first he struggled to understand where he was. He tried, between heartbeats, to stare out into the night. But now he noticed that his head was resting on a pillow. That calmed him down. He pulled himself up slowly, until he was sitting, drenched in sweat, feet dangling on the edge of his bed.

The air began to cool.

Feeling its caress on his skin, Ziya's first thought was to stand up, get dressed, wash his hands and face. But he couldn't get his body to obey him. There was still that strange weight pressing down on him, just like in the dream. And that was why he just sat there for about ten or fifteen minutes, head bowed, and perfectly still. Then he thought about the dream he'd just come out of. He thought about Binnaz Hanım, and what she'd said. And though he could still hear the flow of her lament, he found his way through her words, and then a little way beyond them, to think about Kader, about the bookshop where he and Kader had spent so many long days, and about the small town where he'd spent his childhood. He imagined himself on a bicycle festooned with pinwheels and brightly coloured banners, and nylon ribbons flying in the wind. But while he was pedalling through the streets of his childhood, his mind slipped away, very suddenly, to the Syrian border. And then, just as suddenly, a shaft of light slipped in, and all at once there was the scent of oranges. The crunch of pomegranates. And there, stretched out before him, was an endless expanse of sun-scorched earth. Hill after parched hill, parading before his eyes. On each was a prefabricated guardhouse. Long tangles of barbed wire. Black-mouthed trenches. And watchtowers, screaming with rust as they stretched up into the sky. Knowing what he would find there, Ziya tried to turn his thoughts to something else, but it didn't work. The Syrian border would not budge, not by a single millimetre. That field at the far edge of the Harran Plain swooped in so fast as to strike at the very heart of darkness, glowing yellow, restless and stripped bare. In its wake came the ribbons of red smoke, and the hum that turned into a roar, and the torrent of images, flowing fast and faster, but making no sense. The honking horns of the city he could now see: the hulking nightmare sitting at the edge of the minefield, sparkling with lies. And then, as if that weren't enough, the bird from the dream flew in from who knows where. And just like in the dream it flapped about furiously, as if to take in its surroundings, lighting on the tip of a watchtower and peering down, as if to inspect it more closely, whereupon the bird began to drift gently through the scent of oranges into Ziya's mind, but only for a moment. Only until the bird had settled on the roof of a guardhouse.

The bird fixed its beady eyes on the gravestones just beneath. It ruffled its wings, whirring like an aeroplane, but never taking off. Instead it settled itself in, and, pulling in its neck, began to coo. Over and over, hoarse and shrill, it called out to Syria, and Ziya could just about see the waves of sound, rippling outwards like smoke. It was almost as if this bird was saying something to these lands rendered alien by barbed wire. Or maybe it was just a sound, travelling from one side to the other. But now the bird was slowly turning towards the soldiers drawing water from the well in front of the guardhouse. None of the soldiers around the well had noticed the bird yet. They did not speak as they lowered the bucket, filled the bucket in the din of croaking frogs, and brought the bucket up again, poured the water into twenty-kilo canisters, and climbed down off the concrete platform to walk wearily into the distance in single file. They didn't just look weary, these soldiers: they looked vacant, and painfully so. They were drained of all life. As if their souls were elsewhere, as if their bodies were passing the guardhouse of their own accord. As they went on their way, they tilted ever more precariously in the direction of their cannisters, and this gave them a curious sort of shuffle. Because of this shuffle, their clapped-out combat boots left little clouds of dust like baby's breath in their wake.

Soon there were only two soldiers left at the well. One was very dark and skinny. As he pulled up the bucket, he seemed to bend over double, his legs quivering like two branches fading green. The harder he pulled, the more he puffed up his sweaty cheeks, which glistened like balloons in the hot sun.

Just then, the soldier caught sight of the pigeon.

He saw it by chance, while he was straightening out the rope. With a quick nod he pointed it out to his companion.

And that was when the bird locked eyes with Ziya. Ziya rose from his bed at once, groping his way to the window.

First, of course, he passed the yard to the left of the guardhouse. Here the soldiers were trying to boil their water. Their sooty canisters stood steaming on top of their piles of stones. Clouds billowed above them, parting now and again to offer Ziya glimpses of the soldiers as he walked on to the edge of the minefield, and into the city streets that spread out as far as the patrol paths of the rear lines. Just then he saw the bookshop they'd spent so much time in. Its window was full of newly published books, but he didn't stop; instead, willing himself desperately forward, he weaved his way through the chattering car horns, and pressed on to the skyscrapers. Cutting through this district, he kept on, past parking lots with their rows of insect cars, past the great markets lit by many thousands of lights, each one piercing the darkness with an unmatched power. Past viaducts, and past anonymous warehouses. Through a dark neighbourhood ruled by automobile repair shops and scrap-metal dealerships and into the back streets, deeper into the city and then deeper still, until he felt as lost as a distant, fleeting shadow in a shop window. It would be more accurate to say, though, that a moment arrived when he thought he truly *was* lost. And it was at this precise moment that he saw the deserted streets of his hometown looming up behind the watchtowers, and so this was where Ziya now headed.

He was no longer agitated: after walking through such chaos, it calmed him to see these white one- and two-storey houses, those woods rising above them to the left. With every step, the scent of orange groves seeping into that calm grew stronger, and so, too, did the cries of the seagulls circling in the sky above, the red, red crunch of pomegranates, and the clatter of horse carriages rolling over cobblestones. And the crunch of insects, which began to sparkle at that moment like shattered glass. By then Ziya had reached the historic fountain, the one with all those ancient words scrawled over it, and he was turning right into the town's central square. He walked on slowly, looking this way and that, stopping some distance from the shops that lined the square. When he was a child, he'd bought his sweets in these tiny little shops. And his balloons, and his chickpeas, from shops that seemed now to be no larger than ice chests. There were a few – just a few – people going in and out, carrying paper bags and straw baskets. And in the square, in the shade of the great rustling plane tree, he could still see Ali the Snowman amongst the children. He had taken the saddlebag off his horse's back, and now he was trying, with some effort, to roll one of his snow wheels on to a table covered in oilcloth. As he rolled it with his purple hands, the snow began to melt, dripping down the sides of the oilcloth. When this water reached the ground, it turned into a cooling, freshening pool that began to flow towards the children's feet. By now the snow press was spinning at the desired speed. Ali the Snowman glanced over at his handsaw. Picking it up, he began to hack at the snow wheel.

The children took one step closer to the snowflakes flying from the handsaw's blade.

And then, very suddenly, one of them asked Ali the Snowman if he knew the location of the snow well up in the mountains. He asked this as if it was something this man kept secret.

Ali the Snowman gave no answer, of course. He muttered something to himself, in a husky voice that seemed as strange, and as purple, as his swollen hands.

'I asked you for a reason,' the child now said. 'I happen to know where that well is.'

He did not bother to raise his head, but Ali the Snowman erupted. 'You don't know shit!' he snarled. 'For twenty years now, I've been the only one who knows where it is.'

'He really does know, honestly,' cried another child, rushing to the front. 'He told us all about it. Last year, when you went up there to cut out snow, he followed you.'

And suddenly, Ali the Snowman stopped moving. Fixing his eyes on the tip of the handsaw that was lodged deep in the snow, he stood very still, and breathed in deeply.

Exchanging glances, the children began to snigger.

Then the boy who had asked the question put his hands on his hips. Leaning back on his heels, he said, 'If you give me a lump of snow for free, I won't tell anyone where your well is.'

And then Ali the Snowman let go of the handsaw. Wet or not, he put his hands on his hips, and mimicking the boy's voice, he said, 'So tell me, my young lord. What if I say no? What will you do then?'

'I'd tell everyone,' the child replied. 'And then, by God, we'd head on up there, all of us, and plunder it!'

'So you're saying you'd plunder it?'

'Yes we would,' declared the boy.

A vein was bulging on Ali the Snowman's left temple. It ticked like a subcutaneous clock.

'Every time, the same old tune,' he said through clenched teeth. 'Dear God, give me patience! I've had enough of this. But you . . .'

The children fell silent.

Ali the Snowman cast them a disparaging look, and then he turned his green-flecked eyes away, and for the longest time he stared up at the cliffs overhanging the woods, and the slopes rising above the cliffs, and the shimmering purple summits, reaching up to the clouds. He stared up at them saying nothing, nothing at all. It was almost as if he was trying to make sure the snow wells were still there.

Then he turned back to the children and in an irritated voice he said, 'You don't have it in you. None of you. Go away before you drive me crazy. Be off with you! All of you! Now!'

But the boys just stood there, staring at him. They did not budge an inch.

'As God is witness,' Ali the Snowman said now. 'I'll pull you up over this snow wheel of mine, and one by one, I'll chop off your little dicks! Do you hear? No money, no snow. Get going! Now!'

But the boys, of course, did not obey him. They just stood there, greedily eyeing the snow. Then one of the boys pushed Ziya gently aside to step outside the crowd. He had freckles all over his face, this boy. His hair was blond, his skin dry, and his chest was heaving like a bellows. As he made to return to his work, Ali the Snowman peered down at him warily.

'It's such a hot day,' said the boy. 'Look – it's burning like an infidel's pussy here. Why can't you give us each a lump of snow – what's stopping you?'

Ali the Snowman did not so much as move his mouth. He just waved his arm, glaring down at the boys as if to say, 'Enough! Just go!'

And then, without warning, the boy lunged at the table.

When he saw this happening, Ali the Snowman swung around to fend him off, but it was too late. As he was turning, his arm went flying out and hit against the handle of the handsaw that he'd lodged so deeply into the snow wheel. And then, before he could ask himself what he had let himself in for, the snow wheel went flying off the oilcloth, and, leaving behind it a cool patch of nothingness, it hit the ground with a bang and disintegrated. And needless to say, Ali the Snowman did not know what to do. He just stood there, staring at the table, his eyes bulging and his mouth hanging open. The boys seized this opportunity to scatter like a flock of baby birds. In groups of three and four they flew off to take shelter in shop doors, side streets, and the nooks and crannies of distant courtyards. 'You come back here, you pimps!' he bellowed as he raced after them, stopping every now and then to stamp his feet, but he did not catch a single one. He just stood there in the middle of the square, waving and yelling, like a flag made of fury. And from time to time his voice would begin to crackle, and then a bolt of lightning would flash across the square, making a mind-splitting noise as it radiated out to catch the fleeing boys by the heels.

In time they straggled back, these breathless threesomes and foursomes, to gather around the old fountain. Their tongues were hanging out, of course, and so were their shirts. Their faces were red from fear and from running.

Even though they'd scattered far and wide, a few of them were still glancing over their shoulders, just to make sure Ali the Snowman wasn't coming after them.

Seeing the fear in their eyes, the freckled boy told the others not to worry. 'He's given up on us by now, for sure.'

Clutching his stomach, another boy bent down to the ground and, in a feverish staccato, said, 'He blew. His fuse. For good. You watch. He'll be back.'

The freckled boy said nothing. But there was contempt in his stare.

And then, with a knowing and supercilious look, he said, 'If I say he's not coming, he's not coming. Why don't you use your brain for once? Do you think he'd leave the square, with all that snow scattered everywhere?'

'He's right,' an older boy agreed. 'There's no way he'd leave the square. He's probably busy picking it all up now. But the moment he's done, we'll hear him cawing again. *Snow for burning hearts! Snow for all your aches and pains!*'

'I've never figured that one out,' said another. He was sitting on the edge of the basin with his friends, leaning into the gurgling water. 'As if snow cooled the whole body. What can snow do for a heart?'

'When a heart gets burned or broken, it's outside the body, that's what,' said the older boy. 'Maybe it's the body that's outside the heart when that happens? But how should I know? As if I could know that kind of thing.'

And then he stretched out his arms, as if to leap into the sky. He bent his legs, stared into the distance and bent his legs lower. And then all of a sudden, he cried, 'I'm so bored. Sooo bored. Let's go and stone some birds!'

The boys came back to life with this suggestion. 'Let's go. Let's stone some birds!' some cried, their faces brightening. Others jumped for joy. Some, retrieving slings from their pockets, made as if to set their sights on imaginary birds. A few crouched down to gather stones, of course. Still crouching, they waddled across the ground like ducks, pocketing stones the size of marbles. And if any boy began to flag, another boy would urge him on, saying, 'We need as many bullets as we can get, my boy!' Sometimes they began to race against each other, as if gathering the last stones on earth. Others joined, circling wildly around the fountain, screeching and swooping, sly as hawks.

Unnerved by their bloodlust, Ziya could do no more than watch until one of the boys stepped away from the pushing and the shoving to run in his direction. 'Hey! You! Why aren't you gathering stones?'

Ziya would have answered, had he been given the time. For the boy who'd asked the question now jumped up so fast he left behind a blur the colour of his shirt. A weird and deathly wind blew in – a wind as wild and loud and heartless as the boys who had given birth to it – as the boy before him doubled over, snatching the sliver of time he'd have needed to form an answer.

Then they were off, in leaps and bounds, pausing every now and then to kick a hedge, a wall, or a pile of stones. Off they went to the edge of town to line themselves up in a row as they reached the grass.

They were still lining themselves up when the older boy said, 'Whatever you do, make sure you don't stone any swallows.'

He said this sternly, with a frown and outstretched arms.

'Why not?' asked a bleary-eyed boy who was scratching his neck. 'Why shouldn't we stone them?'

'I don't know why, OK?' said the other. 'Just don't stone them.'

With these words, he took the lead. As he crept through the brambles, he kept his catapult raised and his eyes on the ground. The others licked their lips, glistening like blisters, and scattered. As they scrambled through the undergrowth, they were lost to the sun's glare. Now and again they would pop up out of nowhere, clutching their catapults, only to be drawn back into the grass-scented hush that settled more heavily with every footstep. Suddenly, they all came to an abrupt halt. With narrowed eyes and bated breath they gazed out at the bushes amid the thickets of trees, the reeds lining the stream and the distant slopes beyond them. Not a muscle moved – until the eldest sprang back into action, of course. Propelled now by the heady scent of blackberry blossoms, they followed suit. As they made their way through the orange groves, some jumped up to tug at the branches hanging over them like gathering clouds to see them spring back. The sun beat down on them, burning their nostrils with each new intake of breath, while a ghostly and shimmering mist settled over the hilltops, the riverbeds, and the outcroppings of rocks. As always, nature had found a way to breathe. Each time it inhaled, sucking away all the air, the empty spaces around the trees and rocks and hedges filled up with the chirping of cicadas and of birds. Their songs glanced off the leaves like sunlight, sparkling only to fade and tantalise these boys who wished to kill them.

Just then, the oldest boy stopped by a lone pear tree.

Of course, the others stopped with him, breathlessly shielding their eyes from the sun as they peered into the thicket of trees just ahead. First, they watched a bright yellow butterfly making its escape, tracing wide arcs in the air with its shivering wings, veering recklessly, a shivering blur of gold in the darkening green gloom until even this was lost to view. The silence in the grove grew deeper still. Deeper than a thousand butterflies, lying wing to wing. And then, somehow, the birds contrived to fill that silence. Just one or two at first, until suddenly, resoundingly, they were singing all at once. Their song seemed to drip from the leaves themselves, stretching out from branch to branch, stirring like huge nested shadows, wrapping themselves around the trees and sprouting up between the rocks like grass. For the eldest boy, there was no more time to waste; after a quick glance back at his friends, he assumed a swaggering pose. '*Bismillah!*' he cried, and let fly the first stone. He hit his target, sending it flailing to the ground. Running over to retrieve his prey, he promptly cracked its neck. For a moment he went pale. The bird's warmth must have mixed with his own somehow, found some way to his heart, touching whatever tenderness he had left in him. Or perhaps it was the bird's last song that had responded to his touch; perhaps it was this song that made the boy shudder. It seemed, almost, that he was going into shock, but then, most abruptly, the boy pulled himself up. Taking the bird by its wing, he held it up for all to see. With a nasty, pompous smirk, he tossed it high into the air.

The other boys stood there stunned and wide-eyed with envy. Then they melted into the bushes. Like tense little shadows, they advanced towards the clump of trees. The freckled boy who had lunged at Ali the Snowman's table put his hand on Ziya's shoulder, forcing him along. They stumbled on, catapults in hand, pushing their way past branches of fragrant blossoms and sun-dappled leaves, and on into the dark shadows. All around him, he could hear trampling feet. Looking back over his shoulder, he could see they were all going forward, but he could not feel his legs move or his feet touch the ground. Something was pulling the other footsteps off course. He thought it might be the ropes of couch grass, or the red earth, or the fresh shoots struggling through the undergrowth to be crushed underfoot. Soon all that remained were the stones, piercing leaves as they shot through the air, and the birds thrashing about at his feet. He leaned against a tree trunk to catch his breath. He looked away, far away. If only he could slip off into those distant hills . . .

But he could not. And now Ziya found himself looking at a small bird. Perched on a thin and almost leafless branch, it was, despite the commotion surrounding it, sitting perfectly still. It might have been a statue, a feathered statue, sculpted from silence and long forgotten: it was so still, in fact, that it paid no heed to the approaching footsteps. And that was why Ziya could not move either. Serenity had turned this bird to stone. Now he, too, was anchored to the earth. No question any more of moving. In awed and breathless silence, Ziya stared at the bird as the grass curled around his heels. What he saw that day, and all he saw that day, was the thing this bird alone possessed. The promise of serenity. This was what struck his eyes, and stopped him in his tracks for that brief interlude, what pierced his heart. It would be forty-two years before he saw another living creature in such coy and naked contemplation, and when he did, it would force him back through the tangled web that was his memory and plant him on this patch of grass that had long since turned to dust, to stare unmoving at this bird once more. Or rather, it would take him more than forty years to understand what he saw in this bird's eyes. At the time, of course, Ziya knew none of this. Truth be told, he had not the faintest idea what that day had set in motion. Only that this bird brought him peace. At the same time, he feared that one of the other boys might come creeping through the trees with his catapult mercilessly lifted. There was the need to keep watch. But each time he made to peer around the tree trunks, the earth itself seemed to ripple, and the undergrowth too. The light breeze carrying its scent was swaying as well, in actual fact. Swaying with the noise that rose and fell, heavy with its dark green silences, its uncharted distances and empty spaces. This was all very much in motion when a burly boy in a white shirt appeared from behind a tree trunk. He seemed to know about the bird already, and he made a beeline for Ziya.

Alarmed to see this boy loping towards him, Ziya glanced back at the bird. No sooner had he done so than he glanced away again, to see how much closer the boy had come. But there was no one there: just a mass of pointed branches and a rustling of leaves that served only to deepen the silence. Beneath the browns and greens of those rustling leaves, there was a canopy of daisies, a quivering of shadows, a hint of old, soiled lace. Just then – just there – another boy appeared. He raised his head, prepared for the kill. Broke into a run. Yelling as he went. He was thin as a whip, this boy, and fast on his feet. As fast, in fact, as the strange breeze he brought with him. The sun filtered through the leaves above, sending a river of sun drops flowing golden down his face and shoulders.

But then, when he was just a few paces away, this boy vanished.

Now another boy emerged, this time from behind the cool, shining creepers. Catapult raised, muscles tensed.

Throwing back his head, he began to run, fast and faster, as fast as his body would allow, until, like the others, he vanished into thin air.

That was when Ziya noticed he had raised his own catapult and taken aim at the bird. This shocked him, of course. It frightened him, too. He began to tremble like never before. It was as if those boys were now inside him, running just as fast. He could hear their footsteps echoing inside him. The louder they became, the more Ziya longed to lower his catapult, but he couldn't. In fact, quite the reverse. Without even realising, he pulled back the band. Then – who knows why, or how – he loosened his grip on the leather strap and knocked the bird off its branch. As it fell, it stayed silent and serene. Only when it hit the ground did it begin to struggle for its life.

Ziya froze.

Then something came over him. His ears began to roar. Throwing down the catapult, he ran towards the bird.

He could hardly believe it. 'May God save the poor thing,' he thought. 'Dear God,' he prayed, 'don't let it die.' But it was all too much for him – the blood, the flapping, the flying feathers – and he didn't know what to do. Tears streamed down his face as he looked away, only to lean down again to see if there was anything he could do, and each time he did so, he punched himself in the knees. To take on the bird's suffering, perhaps. Or at least, to mirror its movements and play its shocked and agonised shadow.

It was while he was flailing around like this that the bird went stiff.

Ziya didn't have the heart to look at it for long. The trees were hanging over him like a many-eyed monster. Pushing his way through the undergrowth, he raced back to town as quickly as his legs could take him, and without so much as a backward glance. His heart rebelled at the pace. He was choking, not breathing. His hair, his forehead, his trousers – they were all drenched in sweat. There was so much water running into his eyes that he couldn't see. The only time he slowed down was to wipe the sweat from his brow. But this meant he had to raise his face, and whenever he did that, the sun went straight into his eyes. He had to lower them to increase his speed again. And that is how he made it to the edge of town without seeing the red tractor with its trailer full of manure, or the horse cart, or the three women in headscarves, or the boy with the cane and the shoulder bag following close behind. Suddenly Ziya stopped. He straightened out his clothes. Blurred by anxiety, he stared at the rows of houses. For a moment, he saw people pouring out of every window and door. He heard a roar. He saw them pressing down on him, waving their arms, and shouting, 'What have you done? What have you done?' And of course, that unnerved him, made his heart beat that much faster. Best, he thought, to hide his fear. Best, he decided, to seem calm and collected. Just then, an old woman appeared before him. An old woman whose chin jutted out so far as to touch her nose. She was looming out at him from the courtyard wall on his right, lodged between the hanging vines and the tin flowerpots, and the shadows of the vine leaves swaying overhead. Beyond them were houses, and other courtyards, and trees of all sizes and telegraph poles; and you could see all these in the old woman's eyes, which were squinting, but shining with a fire as large and loud as the town itself.

She stared and stared, until finally, with a voice like a wooden rattle, she said, 'So tell me, my boy. Why were you running like a fawn from a gadfly just now?'

'No reason,' said Ziya.

Resting her elbows on the wall and leaning over as far as she could go, she said, 'Don't lie to me, boy. What's wrong?'

'Nothing's wrong,' said Ziya.

With these words, a flame shot through him and his mouth went dry.

And then there came the voice of Ali the Snowman. Floating over the rooftops: 'Snow for burnt hearts, snow for burnt hearts!' Startled, Ziya looked up with a grimace and let out a silent sigh. Then he composed himself and began walking again. But he didn't get very far. The old woman had used the vines to hoist herself over the wall as fast as a squirrel, and now she stood before him with her breasts hanging like yoghurt-pouches. It was clear from her expression that unless he gave her satisfaction she would bar his way.

She paused for a moment to adjust her scarf. In the same dry rattle, she said, 'So tell me, what made you run so fast that the soles of your feet were punching that rump of yours?'

'Nothing,' Ziya said.

The woman turned for a moment to watch the red rooftops ripple under the hot sun.

Then she fixed her eyes on Ziya's. 'Hmm.' In a warmer tone, she said, 'So nothing's wrong?'

Something in her voice was as soft as her breasts.

'Nothing,' Ziya replied.

But the old woman was not fooled. She could see Ziya was shaken, just from the way he kept shifting his weight. As her eyes slithered over his body, she wiggled her chin.

Ziya kept his eyes on the road ahead. Calmly, he walked on. But inside, he was still running, running from a fire. He couldn't catch his breath. The ache in his side was killing him. He got home that day walking slowly and calmly, though inside his body he was running. Sprinting across the courtyard, passing under the trees and through the huge shadows cast by their leaves. Hurtling through the door, racing into his room to throw himself on to his bed. He cried a few miserable tears there. He would have made a noise, too, but he gave up on that idea when something in the kitchen began to clatter. So instead he bit his lower lip and buried his head in his quilt. Above him he could hear some tapping, flaring and vanishing, and then flaring once again. Then he could hear water dripping in the kitchen. Intermittently at first, and then faster and faster and faster. Ziya kept his eyes on his patterned quilt. Rows and rows of yellow flowers with green leaves, all shivering in the wind. He followed those rows to the place where they almost converged, almost bent into each other as if to hide from an inaudible whine. At the edge of the bed they merged into a thick line that looked as if it might, at any moment, dissolve into the room. Now he could see a stain spreading across his quilt. A deep hole, that's what it looked like, until, after shifting his head, it became a small mound. For a time it stayed still, this stain, as if trying to outdo the little table in the corner. Which in the end, it did. Then suddenly it stirred. As it stirred, it grew wider. As it grew wider, it grew feathers, more and more feathers, and claws, and wings. Then it began to beat its wings just as wildly as that little bird he'd hit. Ziya watched all this in amazement through moist eyelashes while some strange force dried up the veins on his tongue and squeezed all the air from his throat. He told himself that this creature flapping so wildly before him was an apparition, nothing more, and that the bird he'd shot was far away, lying beneath the trees outside town. Still he could not shake off the thought that this was the bird's soul pursuing him.

At that moment the bird stain went stiff – stiff and still as the table behind it. But not for long: a few minutes later, the stain began to beat its wings again, and then, just as suddenly, it stopped. This repeated itself over, and over, and over again. Over and over, that sweet, silent bird he had left for dead so far away came back to life only to die once again in front of Ziya's eyes. With each death his sorrow was harder to bear. He could hear the roar of a tractor outside, and the echoes of horses whinnying in the distance. Whinnying through their discoloured teeth, throwing back their manes, sending their complaints soaring over the tops of the tractors and through the air, into every nook and cranny of the town, leaving only the scent of horsehair and sweat in their wake. Except now, blending in with them, was Ali the Snowman's shrill voice. 'Snow for burnt hearts! Snow for burnt hearts!' It did more than just blend. It was as if that voice knew how much pain Ziya was in. Forcing its way through the sweat and the horsehair, it swept right up to Ziya's window to look inside, before returning, just as fast, to the table in the village *meydan*. Ziya shivered in his bed. Then a wave of anger swept through him, and he swallowed hard. 'That stupid voice just won't leave me alone.' And then, as the stain grew yet another beak, and yet another pair of beating wings, his eyelids grew heavier, and he fell fast asleep.

Before long, Nurgül Hanım arrived. Gently, she tucked him in.

'People undress before they sleep, my boy. Does anyone sleep like this?' But after she had covered him, she lingered at the foot of his bed, smiling kindly.

Then, as if she thought Ziya was listening, she said, 'There's food on the stove. I mustn't let it burn. I'd better go back and check.'

She tiptoed into the kitchen and turned off the flame under the saucepan. Calmer now, she shuffled out into the courtyard in her nylon slippers. Passing through the shadows of the huge leaves, she went first to look over the wall. There was no sign of her husband; just a few boys some way away. The fun seemed to have gone out of whatever they'd been doing, because they were shouting at each other. One looked like he was ready to eat the others raw. Each time one boy finished shouting, and before another started, he would raise up his hands like two ferocious claws, and let out a string of filth. 'You're queers, every last one of you! So don't forget. I could make your mothers' cunts as moist as a cat in heat.' At first Nurgül Hanım did nothing – she just stood there, squinting out at them, smiling kindly. Before she was even aware of smiling, she was stroking the basil plant next to her head and breathing in its lovely scent. By now the boys' bickering had turned into rage: they were jumping on each other, rolling about in the dust.

Nurgül Hanım called out to them, 'Stop fighting, boys. Stop fighting!' Again and again she called out to them, but they paid her no heed.

Then, without willing it, she pulled off a large sprig of basil and threw it in the boys' direction. This struck her as funny, somehow, so then she took off one of her slippers and threw that as well. But even this was not enough. The slipper landed a few paces away from the boys, and they didn't even see it: by now they were tearing at each other's collars, scratching and punching and kicking without even looking where their blows were landing.

Nurgül Hanım had no idea what to do.

Then one of the boys poked his head out from under flailing arms and legs, and spotted something.

'A twister's coming!' he cried. 'Run! A twister! Run!'

With that, the boys jumped to their feet. Seeing the whirlwind that was heading down the street, they scattered.

By now the whirlwind reached as high as the rooftops. It was a muddy tube, churning noisily through the air. The things it had picked up were turning with it, of course: huge stones that looked like lead, dust, leather broken to splinters, sheets of paper, shards of glass, and leaves, rusted tin, scraps of wood, nails and rubbish, some old tasselled hats and paper bags. Mixed in with all these was a large handkerchief whose stripes and borders sparkled as it swirled. The wind whirled down the street, taking Nurgül Hanım's slipper with it before leaping up into the sky, whereupon, with an unearthly groan, it vanished.

Nurgül Hanım was still crouched below the wall, hands over her head. Her heart still pounding, she kept her eyes on the earth at her feet.

The town looked like a different town altogether now. It was still as still, dark as dark. Everyone had gone inside, slamming their doors hastily behind them, leaving only the whirlwind to roam the streets. A fearful minaret of wind – that's what it looked like, whirling down the streets of this town. Then suddenly, this whirlwind stopped, losing all sound and all shape. The things it had carried were now

dropping and falling and flying back to earth. The whirlwind had swept through town, a fog of havoc, sucking up
everything in its path – sucking down to the soul, even.
Now it had dropped it all back on to Nurgül Hanım's street,
as if to say, 'Here they are. In these symbols are your future,
your present and your past.' But Nurgül Hanım didn't look
too closely at this shower of falling debris. Instead she fought
her way through the splinters, the shards and the scraps to
retrieve her slipper, and once she had it on her foot again,
she darted back into the house lest the whirlwind return.
She had reached her doorstep when the town midwife
caught up with her, clutching three sets of prayer beads. She
no longer looked like a midwife. Her headscarf was unravel-
ling, releasing a shock of white hair. Her clothes were caked
with dust, and she was tiny enough to be mistaken for a
child born of the wind.

'I've never seen a twister like that,' she said, trying to
straighten herself up. 'Never! My days, what was that?'

Swallowing hard, Nurgül Hanım agreed. It had been horrifying. Just horrifying.

The midwife held on to the wall to catch her breath, and
then, very calmly, she surveyed the things that the whirlwind
had deposited on the street.

'So what's all this now?' she said. 'There's worse in this
mortal world, my beauty. Oh yes, far worse. When I was a
girl, a twister destroyed a whole village. On the other side
of those mountains over there, and then some. Turned it
into hell on earth. When the news spread, some people
wanted to go and have a look, so they jumped on their
horses and off they went. Those of us left behind waited at
the town gate. For two days we stood there with bated

breath, waiting for their return. And while we waited, our elders and betters got busy imagining the worst, and for two days they whispered their worst fears into each other's ears. Our hearts were with that village on the other side of the mountains. Even the ones who'd stayed home would scramble on to their earthen rooftops every half hour or so, to see if they were there yet. We didn't have tiles back then – they just got themselves ladders, went up to the roof, shaded their eyes with their hands and looked towards the mountains. Then they'd hurry inside again, like anxious little shadows. As for those who couldn't leave what they were doing, or were cripples, or too exhausted to get up on the roof – well, they would send their children to the town gate to ask if there was any news. And these children – well, they could not help noticing that this was something they could do, something that made the grown-ups sit up and listen, so they'd race over to us and ask us for the latest in the most solemn tones, and then spin on their toes to race home faster than they had come. Even on that first day, some of them had worked out ways of making the job easier, of course. Rather than huff and puff all the way out to us every hour, and all the way back to the edge of the mud huts, they began to ask for news with a system of hand signals. And we'd answer in kind. Bowing our hopeless heads. Flapping our hopeless arms. The more we did this, the stranger things became, until we were not just signalling to the children at the edge of the mud-brick houses, but to the shadowy figures in the distance. Who never asked questions. Who just stood there. What I mean to say is, we did a good deal of bowing and flapping. Come to think of it, I doubt we would have been so upset about all this if those men hadn't jumped on their horses to gallop off to that village struck by disaster. We wouldn't have felt this degree of pain, our streets wouldn't have been awash with worry and sorrow, and we wouldn't have had half the town gasping at the town gate, and the other half going up to their rooftops every other minute to look for news. If you ask me, it was pointless, galloping off to that village, because there was nothing they could do when they got there. It was at least a day's journey – a day and a half even – as the crow flies, and those jackdaws had taken no food with them. No nothing. If you ask me, they just went there to gape at the ruination. If you know anything about the mysteries of humankind, you know that there is this side to us. There's another side of us that likes to talk about the ruination we have seen and spin tall tales. But never mind. There we were, waiting at the town gate, where the grass is now, for two long days. Then, on the second day, just as the light was failing, the horses came back; heads lowered, eyes crazed, and defeated, they came down the road that winds through the gardens. It must have been their silence that made their hooves hit the earth so hard. And perhaps it touched our hearts, too. That is why, at first, we just stood there frozen. Why we all sprang to our feet at exactly the same moment and rushed towards the horses. The men were grey in the twilight. They got off those big horses and heaved great sighs. Looked all around them, as if in search of something. Bowed their heads in shame and silence. And so they remained for some time. They just stood there, saying nothing, struggling with the agonising memories they'd brought back with them, as it were. They loosened their trembling tongues after that, of course, and in voices as dry and yellow as the desert they began to tell us how the whirlwind had changed that village into hell on earth. Let me say this: what they told us was more than we listeners could bear. We were afraid even to imagine what they described. According to what they told us, the whirlwind did not hold dominion over that village for long. It was no more than fifteen or twenty minutes. But within that space of time there was not a place in that village that this blind apparition did not ravage; wailing most horribly, it careened from nook to cranny, turning dust to smoke, sucking up whatever it found in barnyards, and courtyards, and dunghills, and the streets. With shocking speed it span this silo of debris around and around, only to rise as high as the clouds and disappear. Only then did the villagers come to see how violent it had been, and how merciless. Because at that very moment, five children came tumbling down from the sky, and with these children came three lambs mired in filth and excrement, and with the lambs came chickens, pots and beehives, and pruning hooks, and glinting hatchets, and after all this, a few things that looked like sacks and pitchforks and rags, and various items of laundry. The villagers who had taken shelter here and there were dumbfounded by this terrifying scene of ruination. They ran screaming through the wreckage, to their children, their poor children, who had been ravaged beyond recognition. That same day, just after the midday prayers, they wept over these children as they gave them to the earth. But the catastrophe didn't end there, my beauty, for while they were lowering those little lambs into their little row of little graves, they heard that two other children had gone missing. So while those men were still shovelling earth into those graves, other men joined the women in their hunt for the two missing children. Running to the grain stores, they looked behind the sacks and heaps of winnowed wheat, and in the pitchers, jars and buckets that lined the entryways, the barns and the henhouses, the vegetable patches and the dung heaps, and after examining underneath the horse carts and the oxcarts, they split up into groups that combed the streets of the village, over and over, but there wasn't one trace of those two little children. To make a long story short, they at last found one of them at the very top of a giant mulberry tree, and the other stuck inside a narrow oven chimney, struggling to breathe in the thick smoke. In the end, they had to dig two more little graves next to the other five. What I mean to say is this: there are worse things in this cruel world, my beauty. Far worse.'

'Dear, dear, dear,' sighed Nurgül Hanım. 'What a terrible shame to lose all those children.'

Crouching down and leaning back against the wall, Ebecik the Midwife looked out over the rooftops. She stared at the sky, going deeper and deeper still, into the past she seemed to see there.

When she spoke again, she was almost delirious. 'Those poor children,' she said. 'It was the hour of their death. We are every one of us mere mortals. Whatever shall be, shall be, my beauty. Such is the will of God . . . But there's something I forgot to mention just now. Those horsemen of ours who went to see the village did not themselves witness any of this. They heard the story from the villagers, same as I just told you. What I mean to say is that all our men did was sit down with their hands on their knees and their heads bowed and listen to the story. And then, without suffering the slightest injury, they offered their condolences to those poor ravaged villagers and galloped on home. Having gawped at the scene of the disaster, there was nothing more these men could do, and I know whereof I speak. Maybe you won't believe me, but these men we're talking about were the very laziest men in our town. You know the type. I'm talking about the sort of men you'll see lounging against the wall, or the porch steps, or the door, like a pile of old clothes – lazy isn't a good enough word for them. Hard to believe, but they were all like this, every last one of them. So lazy they didn't even bother to greet you when you passed them, and no one had the faintest idea how they fed themselves, or who looked after them. The only thing they knew how to do, these men, was to sit there sleeping in the sun, shoot withering looks and snore. How they managed to spring to life the moment they heard about the disaster, how they found people to loan them horses at such short notice, how they shed all those lazy ways of theirs and got it into their minds to go all the way to that village – well I for one can't tell you. All I know is this. After they returned from that village, these men began to change, little by little. They had a spring to their step now. There was life in their eyes. You could almost think that the things they'd seen in that village had put an end to their laziness – popped it, like a needle popping a balloon. Soon they were walking the length and width of the town, telling the story of the whirlwind to any child who crossed their path. But now their voices didn't shake any more, like they'd done that first day. Now there were times when they spoke like a great river sparkling in the sun, or a breeze passing over a planted field. They would stop as suddenly as if they were teetering over a cliff. They would sigh tragically, but only to offer cause for hope. The story itself had changed by now. It was no longer the same whirlwind we'd heard about that first day. With each new detail, this story of theirs stretched just a bit more. The more it stretched, the more it changed in shape and appearance, until it had lost all its bearings. Soon it was riddled with logical errors and made no sense at all. You could almost say that they'd fiddled with it so much by then that it stopped being a story. By now it had as many holes in it as an old lace rag. Would you believe it – these men kept on with it regardless. They threw themselves into it, heart and soul. They gave this story of theirs everything they had. From the way they now set themselves up as the experts on whirlwinds, you'd think they had spent their whole lives with their elbows propped on a school desk. They put on such airs that soon it became their job to stand by the haystacks brandishing pitchforks, predicting when a wind might rise, and where it might come from, and how strong it might be. And there they stood, pricking their ears, and suddenly going silent, to listen even more deeply; with bated breath they'd sniff the air, to see if it told them of a whirlwind on the way. If ever the wind seemed to be going around in circles, or even if it so much as lifted up a few papers and leaves, their lips would curl and they'd hem and they'd haw and exchange knowing looks. Then they would insist that there was a whirlwind out there, somewhere far away, and that it had caused great damage, and that this little wind that was raising up a few leaves and papers had somehow broken off from it to come as far as here. Before long they had convinced themselves that however you looked at it, this little wind was the harbinger of the great whirlwind that would strike some unknown place at an unknown point in the future. So, whenever they gathered together, they'd rejoice as if they'd made a great scientific discovery and at the same time lament the great damage that whirlwind would cause. There was even a day when one of these men burst into tears while watching a cloud of dust sail towards us. Dear God, he said, it's the whirlwind. It's the whirlwind. Dear God! I saw this with my own two eyes. I swear, he went pale as pale, and the tears he shed were as big as acorns. It wasn't long before he realised he had cried for nothing. That cloud of dust on the horizon came as far as the edge of town and stopped beneath a massive plane tree. Out popped a postman on his yellow motorcycle. In the end, these men embroidered their story so much they killed it. Never mind, they've all gone to their graves now, and it wouldn't be right to dwell on them too long. It's not right to speak ill of the dead, as you well know. The silence of the dead is deeper and greater than anything we say on earth. The dead are judged, to be sure. So let us leave these men be. They're dead and buried, with their sins and their good deeds . . . As you can see, the little girl who stood in that crowd waiting for the horsemen to return is now a humpbacked, white-haired woman. And do you know, while I was waiting in that crowd for two long days all those years ago, I got so very hungry, and when I told someone in that crowd, I no longer remember who, that person gave me some meat wrapped in bread. I say meat wrapped in bread and that reminds me, what have you made for supper tonight, my beauty? Have you already made it?'

'I have,' said Nurgül Hanım. 'If you want the truth, a few hours ago I had no idea what to make. I kept changing my mind, but then I decided to make stewed haricot beans. With pilaf, pickles and semolina pudding.'

'That sounds good,' said Ebecik the Midwife, fiddling with her prayer beads, 'very good indeed, but I'm surprised, because you can't make stewed haricot beans just like that, you know, you have to decide the day before. You don't need to do much: you just bring it to a boil and let it sit in its own water. The next day you need to throw that water away, most definitely. There's nothing on this earth that does more harm. It gives you gas, it darkens the beans, and it keeps us from enjoying the sight of those beans sparkling. As God is my witness, what you need to do is to wash those beans after getting rid of that water, and then cover them with water – three fingers above the beans – and then cook them over a low flame, but at this point you must pay close attention to the rhythm of the boil. As you know, every dish has its own rhythm when it boils. So, for instance, when you're cooking bulgur, it sounds like this: lady's thigh bone, lady's thigh bone, lady's thigh bone. But when you're cooking dolmas, or pilaf wrapped in grape leaves, it should sound like this: beggar's dick, beggar's dick, beggar's dick. If you don't keep adjusting the flame, you might produce different sounds altogether, and no good can come from that. So you need to pay close attention to those haricot beans when you're boiling them. They should just bubble as softly as whispers, never more than that, and that way they won't go to pieces. They'll just lie there, playing dead. They won't stick to each other, they'll just lie there, each one sparkling like these beads of mine, each one saying, "Here I am!" After all this, of course, you need to cook your finely chopped onions with green peppers in oil, and tomato purée, and pepper purée, too. None of this putting green peppers to swim about the sauce like the sultan's caïques. You should chop them so that they are no more than twice the length of the beans. At the end of the day, this is a dish that requires a great deal of care. For example, it's a good idea to throw in two or three cloves of garlic; it brings a certain extra something to the palate. In any event, someone somewhere might be longing for this dish made just this way, so in my view, it's best to leave it there.'

Nurgül Hanım smiled softly.

'When we talk about food, we should do a good job of it,' said Ebecik the Midwife. 'People don't take food seriously, but they should. Never skimp on the food you make for your husband, my beauty. Winter or summer, he's in that classroom with those screaming children from dawn till dusk. And well, you know what they say, the road to a man's heart is through his stomach. You might think that's just a turn of phrase, but whatever you do, don't forget it. Because it really is true. It takes me back to the days of the sultans and beys and aghas. As you know, they would bestow upon their grand viziers and generals and chamberlains their own shirts and coats and jackets and boots. This was not just to make them happy, and it wasn't just to show them their worth; it was so as to become part of them. Because when their men wore these gifts, they would, without even knowing it, start thinking like their masters. And it's more or less the same with food, my beauty. Your husband is not just eating your food – he is taking in the heat that has dropped into the pot from your eyes and your hands. Even if he doesn't come to share your thoughts, he'll come closer to your way of feeling as he eats. Whatever you say, he'll warm to it. He'll look on it kindly. And that's important, how warm his looks are, and his hands. Do what you will, but mark my words. Whatever happens, it is through food that we pass on this warmth. Don't you think that it ends there, either: even if you don't kiss him goodbye at the door each morning, make sure you touch his shoulder, because no matter what, his mind will be going back to it all day. And in his mind, it will become warmer than it actually was. Then, before long, he'll long to return to it. Because wherever we happen to be, we mortals move towards warmth. But never mind. I've talked myself to a standstill. I'd best be on my way.'

'Don't go,' said Nurgül Hanım warmly. 'Look, we've talked so much about your haricot beans. Why not eat with us this evening?'

Ebecik the Midwife lifted herself up and, leaning against the courtyard wall, looked out at the smoke rising from behind the mud-brick houses at the far end of the street.

'That's very kind, my girl. Very kind indeed,' she said. 'But I'm off to my son's house tonight. We've planned a gathering, and my youngest daughter is going to join us. They'll be there already, with their eyes on the door. They're probably wondering where I am. The best of health to you!'

'And the best of luck to you,' murmured Nurgül Hanım.

Then she turned her head towards the street. After giving it a good, long look, she turned away suddenly and rushed back into the house.

Ziya was in his room, still asleep, as before.

'Time to wake up,' she said. 'Your father will be home any minute. And what's all this anyway? Sleeping in the middle of the day!'

Ziya stirred slightly.

'Don't just lie there. Time to get up!' said Nurgül Hanım in a reproachful voice. 'Your mother almost got carried off by a whirlwind and you slept through the whole thing!'

Slowly, Ziya raised his head. He was still half asleep. He couldn't understand what his mother was saying.

'Who was taking who?' he asked. 'Where?'

'The whirlwind,' said his mother. 'The whirlwind, I said. The whirlwind!'

Ziya said nothing. Sitting up, he slowly pushed his blanket to one side, and at just that moment, amongst the yellow flowers, just where he'd seen that stain that resembled a bird, he found a feather. First he just looked at it, not knowing what to do. Then he slapped his hand over it, and then he gave his mother a sidelong look, to see if she'd noticed. Nurgül Hanım had gone to the window to watch the sun falling on the leaves of the begonias; she'd seen nothing. Ziya relaxed, just a little. But at the same time, he was wondering if that stain had actually been a bird, and if that bird had left behind a feather. When his mother left the room he put the feather straight into his pocket, and went out to sit at the table in the sitting room, quiet as a shadow.

That's where his father found him when he came in.

'What's up, boy?' he said. 'What's on your mind?'

'Nothing,' said Ziya.

No sooner had he said this than he felt something warming up his pocket. It felt like the feather he'd hidden there was in flame, was on fire. This fire continued burning while they ate. At times it was a medium flame. At times it slackened, only to flare up again as high as Ziya's cheeks.

'Something's happened to you,' said his father, as they moved on to the semolina pudding. 'There's something not right about the way you're sitting.'

'Honestly, nothing happened,' Ziya replied.

And after that, to change the subject, he turned to his mother and asked, 'Were you talking to Ebecik the Midwife? While I was sleeping, I thought I heard her voice. She went on and on. Muttering and muttering.'

'We had a quick chat at the door,' his mother answered. 'But what I can't understand is how you could have heard her from so far away, especially since you were asleep.'

'It could have pierced his sleep,' said his father. 'As you know, not all sleep is the same. It has different phases. It's shallow and then it's deep, it curves and goes down tunnels and staircases and wells. Sometimes it's so thick as to carry you off this earth, sometimes it holds you underneath a veil as thin as muslin. When sleep's that thin, some things can pierce it. A sharp-edged memory, for example. Or sharp words that are still bothering us, or a thought that's settled outside our minds, in our limbs, or a feeling that's done the same, or something in our midst that we haven't even noticed – things like these can pierce our sleep. And then, you see, you can't see where it pierces on the inside, but you can on the outside. Of course it doesn't look the same from there as it does in reality: the mist of sleep makes it look a little closer, or a little further away. That's probably what happened. Ebecik's voice came in through a hole like that.'

'I don't know,' Ziya muttered in a gloomy voice, almost to himself. 'I heard everything they said, anyway. Even her words of wisdom.'

'She's fond of those,' said his father, nodding. 'And after all, a long life opens the pores of the mind.'

Ziya said nothing.

'You're making me talk too much,' said his father. 'For a moment, I felt I was still back in class, teaching.' With that he rose from the table. Stroking his stomach, he strode away to settle into the chair in front of the television.

That evening Ziya could not keep still. He wandered around huffing and puffing like a lunatic. Back in his room, he took the feather out of his pocket and tossed it into the courtyard. It sank into the night, a pale and forlorn blur until it lost itself amongst the dark and rustling leaves of his mother's begonias. When Ziya lay his head on his pillow and closed his eyes late that night, he lost himself in the same way, swaying his way down, down, down until the night came to bury him. And that is why, when he woke up in the morning, Ziya went straight to the window, to look outside with sleep-clouded eyes. He was sure the feather must be there somewhere, but all he could see was a white cat crawling out of the lilies at the foot of the wall to climb up to the roof, never once taking its burning eyes off Ziya. There was some noise just then in the neighbours' courtyard. Looking over the brick wall, he saw a few men carrying blue wooden chairs on their shoulders, a few women bending over, rising and bending over again, and a heavy-set young man going up to the roof to sit next to the chimney and watch the road while he basked in the sun.

'The wedding's about to begin,' said Nurgül Hanım, when she saw Ziya at his window. 'Since yesterday this house has been too small for you. So let's get you breakfast and then you can go outside and watch.'

'All right,' said Ziya.

After breakfast he went outside, with the bird still in his mind.

By then, the neighbours had raised a flagpole from their chimney; just underneath they had put a large pine branch, which they had decorated with red ribbons, and strings of sweets, and popcorn, and balloons of all colours. Hands on hips, head thrown back, Hacı Veli was looking up happily at the embroidered flag. Then lethargy came over him. He pulled himself together and hurried over to the cooking pots in the corner of the courtyard, stopping next to the women busy chopping meat on boards. 'Do you have enough meat?' he asked. 'Should I kill another goat?'

'It would be a waste, master,' one of the women replied. She tilted her head to one side, almost in deference for the goat that might be killed. 'Soon the girl will be coming with Reşat's gold on her forehead, bringing a ram from her household. We can't forget that.'

'All right, then,' Hacı Veli mumbled.

After giving the piles of meat a good long look, he returned to the chairs lined along the wall. Waving fretfully in their direction, he said, 'These have been waiting all morning for the musicians. What's kept them so long?'

His son had come down from the roof, and now he stood there at the bottom of the ladder, dressed in his best and looking down at his father.

'Take that ladder away,' said Hacı Veli. 'Don't let it stay there. God protect us! Just think if some children got it into their heads to climb up there and lost their footing.'

The son picked up the ladder and disappeared into the house. 'We've sent out the right favours with the right invitations, I hope?' Hacı Veli called after him, leaning in his direction as he did so. 'I hope we haven't sent handkerchiefs to the houses that were supposed to get towels, or soaps to the houses that were supposed to get handkerchiefs, or matches to the houses that were supposed to get soaps, eh?'

'Don't worry,' said the son, coming back out of the house. 'We took great care. Nothing got mixed up.'

'Fine,' mumbled Hacı Veli.

Then suddenly he remembered the tips, and thinking it would be discourteous to take out all that money and count it in front of so many people, he rushed back towards the house. His wife was just coming out with a tray of boiled vine leaves.

'What a commotion!' cried Hacı Veli when he saw her. 'I completely forgot to do the tips!'

As she passed, his wife gave him a gentle smile.

Once inside, Hacı Veli sat down on the side of the sofa, took out his wallet of dark brown leather with flowers decorating the edges, and set about arranging the tips that he would soon be handing out left, right and centre. First he set aside the money for the musicians who were late arriving. He did so with some annoyance, crushing the notes under his thumb. Then he put aside the money for the cook who would, when the time came to feed the guests, stand in front of the pots and play games with him, saying *This ladle just won't budge, sir. Oh dear, I wonder what we should do?* Then he put money aside for the men bringing the ram from the girl's house, and after that for the men bringing in the baklava on that huge engraved tray. Who else did he have to tip, who else, and for what exactly? As he racked his brain, he remembered the person who was going to pound the meat and the wheat for the *keşkek*, and the person who was going to bring in the bride, whose carriage would take the turn too fast and graze the gate on the way into the courtyard where the wedding would be celebrated. *The bride can't get down here*, he would say, *this gate is too tight. Honestly. It just won't let me in.* Then he remembered his visit to the girl's house for the dowry, and the child who would just sit there cross-legged on that trunk. As he put aside some more money, he could already hear that spoiled little voice. *I'm not budging unless I get my tip in advance, by God, not even for the president!* After doing all this he spent some time gazing in annoyance at the banknotes on the sofa, as these scenes played out in his mind.

Then suddenly he was knocked over by the blast of a clarinet. Black Davut had somehow managed to creep into the room and put his instrument right next to his ear.

'Where on earth have you been?' cried Hacı Veli, gathering up the banknotes as fast as he could. 'Did you bring the others with you?'

Black Davut answered with his clarinet.

'Shut that thing up!' cried Hacı Veli. 'Answer like a man!' His eyes sparkled with an affectionate anger. 'Are they here, or aren't they?'

Again, Black Davut answered with his clarinet.

As he did so, he looked straight into Hacı Veli's eyes, grinning childishly, as the clarinet sparkled.

'All right then,' said the other. He nodded. 'Understood.'

After that they went outside together.

Seeing the crowd in the courtyard, Hacı Veli buttoned up his jacket. Then he walked over to the musicians to shake their hands. 'Welcome,' he said. 'You have brought us great joy.' Then he took out the tips from his bulging pouch and placed them in their pockets. 'So let's get going,' he said. 'The place is yours.' He pulled the chairs back a bit further, and then he looked down at the second clarinet and the trumpet now coming out of their cases. Right then it seemed strange to him to be talking like this to people he joked with every day over a game of cards in the coffeehouse, acting as if they were strangers who had come from afar. Truth was, they no longer resembled the people he saw every day at the coffeehouse; all resemblance disappeared the moment they picked up their instruments. They were now different people altogether. They held themselves in a new way. They looked distant. Even the lines on their faces seemed to have changed. The people now pouring into the courtyard were searching the crowd as if they recognised no one, least of all Hacı Veli, and that made him feel as if he himself were drifting away from the town and all those who lived in it. As they shook his hand, and took their tips, and offered their congratulations, each one seemed to be smiling at him from a great distance. 'May the young ones enjoy endless bliss, and may they bring you many grandchildren.'

'Thank you,' said Hacı Veli to each and every one of them. 'Thank you so much.'

Then one man raised his trumpet, and another two raised their clarinets, and a fourth his drum, whose hoop was painted blue and ringed with enormous bells. Soon the courtyard was humming with their music. As the most light-footed of the townspeople came forward, they played a beautiful *Harmandalı*. Then, to give the boys a chance to dance, they played the Grand Arab *Zeybek*, the Tavas *Zeybek* and the *Kerimoğlu Zeybek*. Opening their arms like eagles, they soared higher and higher, not just in the eyes of those watching, but in the sky of their dreams. They kept coming back to earth, though. Squatting down. Dropping to their knees. Thumping the earth. Thumping the earth to its core. And when an echo returned from that dark and distant place, these boys would soar up again, to spin round and round. Without warning, they'd stop short, to gaze out into the distance, deep in thought, before they raised their arms again, taking flight on an unseen wind. And soon they were boys no longer. They were crested eagles, soaring high in the air. They took their time, these youths, and it may well be that the musicians had planned to play the *Aydın Zeybek* or the *Serenler Zeybek*, but at this point Hacı Veli came out of his corner to whisper in their ears, reminding them that the time had come for the *keşkek*-pounding ceremony.

And so they all set out for the town *meydan*, lighting up the streets with their lively chatter as they went. In front were the two strong and finely dressed youths carrying saddlebags of wheat on their shoulders; behind them a line of seven or eight people, arm in arm, dancing the *Halay*. After them came the musicians, and last came a motley crowd of guests and children. Then, just as they had passed Ziya's house, one of the dancers pulled a white handkerchief from his pocket, as fast as if he were slipping a dagger from its scabbard. At that very moment, a crowd slipped forward, skirting gracefully to the right to join the front of the dance, while the man with the handkerchief slipped to the back, to wave it with unbridled joy. The handkerchief looked almost like a bunch of pale white grapes when he waved it like that, a white glow that played for a time on the walls and the trees, swirled above the dancers' heads, and, taking flight, it whirled its way through the echoing music. The dancers seemed to be connected to it. Suddenly they sped up, overtaking the two youths who were carrying the wheat. Then the glowing handkerchief sailed to the back of the stream of sound and colour. And so it went, floating through orange-scented cobblestone streets, spinning around the corners, until it reached the mortar stone to the left of the great plane tree.

And while the music played and the dancers' hands waved and the moistened wheat on the mortar was pounded, cross-eyed Bekir joined the crowd with his many-coloured chewy sweets. He set up his stall, and lay out all the sweets he had prepared at home, and soon he was selling them to the children crowding around him. Then came Uncle Güllü, who always walked like he had swallowed a rolling pin. From his glass case of sparkling perfume bottles he brought out a small syringe, which he began to squirt on to the chests of young and old alike with the greatest solemnity. As usual, while thus engaged, he didn't waste the opportunity to exaggerate the esses in 'essence' for all to hear. Everyone knew that his syringe was empty, but they all held down their collars for him and thanked him afterwards, with false half-smiles.

Passing anxiously through this smiling crowd, Uncle Güllü went over to Hacı Veli, but instead of squirting any scent on him, he put the syringe back in its place and swiftly lifted up his glass; pointing to the little scent bottles inside it, and in a peeved voice, he said, 'Look how sweet these are, you didn't take me up on my offer, sir, but how lovely it would have been if you had.'

'It wouldn't have been lovely in the least,' said Hacı Veli. 'Did you really think you were going to introduce a new custom to this old town? Where on earth do people send scent bottles as favours for a wedding?'

'You can't be sure that this has never happened anywhere,' snapped Uncle Güllü, gazing sourly into the distance. 'To tell you the truth, I would never agree to that line of reasoning. That being the case, I can't accept your position. If you can send towels as favours, and handkerchiefs, and even soaps and matches, why can't you send bottles of scent? It used to be done, in my view. It was even quite the fashion. And anyway, you could have been the first in our town to do it, and over the years, it would have become the custom. Your name would have been uttered with awe and envy.'

'Your mind is working,' said Hacı Veli, smiling softly. 'But if you ask me, it's always working in the same direction.'

The other man fell silent, swallowing hard as he looked down at the ground.

'You're mistaken,' he said finally. 'My mind works in all directions!'

'Oh does it really?' asked Hacı Veli.

'Yes, it does,' said Uncle Güllü, nodding vigorously. 'It thinks ahead, it thinks back, it thinks to the left, and to the right. Or to put it another way, it thinks to the north and the south and the west and the east. In all four of these directions!'

Hacı Veli smiled. 'If that's the case, then it's not working at all!' Without waiting for the next question, he continued. 'Because there are not just four directions. There are at least six, my most honoured sir. The fifth direction is beneath our feet, and the sixth is above us. This thing about there being only four – that's nothing more than a tired old saying.'

Uncle Güllü sank his neck into his shoulders. 'Hah!'

And off he went into the crowd to stand next to cross-eyed Bekir, who was, he thought, the only one who understood him. And there he stayed until the wheat was pounded, calling out from time to time in a sour voice that struggled for its old sparkle. *Essence! Essence!*

And then the growing crowd began to make its way back to the wedding house, rounding the same corners to flow down the same lanes in the same high spirits, with two saddlebags full of *keşkek*.

At the back of the crowd came cross-eyed Bekir and Uncle Güllü, talking all the way. Setting up their stalls under the almond tree, they continued to sell their scents and their chewy sweets. There wasn't too much demand for the scents. Every once in a while a few panting youths would come over to point at the bottles, asking, is this scent oleaster? Is that one lilac, is that other one rose or the one behind it hyacinth? Surprised by the prices being asked, they would cast a doubtful look over their shoulders and back away. And that was why Uncle Güllü kept looking over at cross-eyed Bekir's colourful sweets. With his eyes still fixed on them, he would mumble, *Essence! Essence!* Not so much to the people in the courtyard but to the guests who lived only in his dreams.

The musicians were back in those chairs by now, playing one tune after another. But whenever they tired they took a break. And whenever they took a break, they would chain-smoke with such ferocity you'd think they'd just been rescued from a famine. Between tokes, they exchanged stories about all manner of things, each more astounding than the last. These were things they had witnessed themselves while playing at weddings in neighbouring towns and villages. Some were about normal journeys going suddenly wrong, ending with deaths so horrifying as to pierce all their hearts. Others showed how avaricious people could be, and cruel, and bloodthirsty. Some were about vicious knife fights started by drunks wandering around like lost souls, while others had former lovers coming face to face with grooms while in the act of kidnapping their veiled brides. Sometimes these stories didn't end there; sometimes, once the shock had worn off, the grooms armed themselves with guns and set off with a group of kindred spirits to save their brides. As they set off, they would salvage their pride from the wreckage to the extent that they could turn to the musicians and announce that the wedding would soon continue from where it had left off, and command them to stay where they were, no matter what.

While the musicians were telling their stories, they gathered a crowd. Some stood, some sat at their feet, mouths agape, some looked over their shoulders with bulging eyes and there were even those who lined up shoulder to shoulder, knee to knee, before the musicians' chairs. The stories lit up little flames inside them all, and from each flame came a little lick of smoke. Sometimes the stories made them laugh, and sometimes all anyone could say was, 'Oh, what a terrible shame,' and sometimes, of course, they were left half told; because whenever new guests arrived, the musicians would pick up their instruments and rush to the gate to welcome them with a tune, and accompany them inside with such delicacy and decorum that they might have been made of china, and after the musicians had escorted them inside, they would turn back to the crowd to celebrate the new arrivals with yet another tune. Or else, at the most exciting point in the story, they would catch sight of a distinguished guest leaving the wedding, and jump to their feet to accompany that guest to the gate. Each time it was the fattest of them, Black Davut, who was most tired out and sweaty from running. Yet now and again he would still pull out a handkerchief to give his clarinet a better shine.

No one was sure quite how many guests had come and gone, of course, but by now Hacı Veli's single-storey mud-brick house was buzzing like a beehive.

This continued without interruption through a second day, during which Black Davut carried on perspiring and giving his clarinet quick polishes.

Late in the morning of the third day, after the musicians had played a few tunes, they led a crowd all the way to the other side of the town, to the home of some of Hacı Veli's kinsfolk, to fetch the best man, who, like the groom, had colourful scarves pinned to his shoulders. The musicians piped both men up and down the streets of the town, slowly winding their way back to the house. Then suddenly the music stopped, for the time had come for the ritual collection. Two middle-aged men laid out an embroidered rug from Çataloba – never used, and still smelling of mothballs. The groom and his best man stepped on it timidly, and there they stood, staring at their feet. By now there were more people filing in through the gate. The women of the town made one line and the men another, going all the way up to Hacı Veli's house with their gifts under their arms. They came inside and deposited on the rug the shirts and pots and trays and kettles that they had brought as gifts. They draped the floral prints and fine fabrics over the men's shoulders. The banknotes they pinned to their collars, and they did the same with the gold pieces they had brought with them, dangling from red ribbons. No one stayed to see what everyone else had brought; it was expressly to avoid seeing any of it that they turned their eyes away so quickly. Before long they had so many prints and fabrics wrapped around their necks that they looked as if they were poking their heads through the rack at a clothes store.

After everyone had left their presents, and all those presents had been taken inside in the silk bags that a number of far-sighted women had left for them, Ebecik the Midwife appeared carrying a zinc pot, and as soon as the townspeople saw her, they opened up a long and winding corridor for her. Bent over double, she walked down this corridor with slow little steps, a shivering cloud bound for other realms. Reaching the groom and his best man, she crouched down. Dipping her finger into the pot, she dabbed a little henna on the tips of their shoes. And as she did so, she said, 'May good fortune shine on you, my handsome boy, may God give you health and harmony.' As soon as she had drawn back, the groom strode to the sherbet bowl sitting at the edge of the rug, and launched it into the air with an almighty kick that would stay in their memories. And off it flew over the heads of the crowd, glinting as the children cheered. It landed on the other side of the wall, and in no time a group of boys was kicking it down the street. And thus the collection ceremony ended. The rug was lifted up, and the instruments came back to life, filling the yard and making it tremble. The drum beat more deeply and with more lust this time. Each lithe note from the clarinets wriggled from the players' grasp, while the trumpet sent cloud after cloud of golden sound wafting across the town. And all along the way, the snare drum beat out a cheerful rhythm as it swayed this way and that.

In the late afternoon, the town imam tapped his finger three times against the microphone, as he always did before the call to prayer, and the music stopped. And in the courtyard, even the aroma of food and grass wafted through the air more slowly, the noise died down to some degree, and everyone waited for the call to prayer to finish. When the imam turned off the microphone with that strange sizzle and pop, the musicians struck up again, as a teeming crowd of men and women followed a packed and decrepit car to take the bride from her home. And suddenly there was no one in Hacı Veli's once-packed courtyard, and because there was no longer need for the cooking pots, these were taken away, too. After they had been dealt with, one of the cooks, an old woman, turned to the others and said, 'Don't just stand there, we have to clean this place up before the bride gets here' – as if the bride might take one look at the state of the courtyard and say, 'I can't live in such disorder,' and turn around to go back home. They gathered up the clothes and cups and glasses that were scattered across the courtyard. To keep the ashes from spreading when the guests returned, they got a few boys to shovel up the ashes in the corners and carry them to the back of the house, then they spread water over those corners and swept them with brooms. And then, when they were done, they washed their hands and straightened up their clothes, and there they waited, light with excitement, for the wedding party to arrive.

Before long, the wedding party arrived.

At the front was that same dilapidated car, decorated here and there with red ribbons. There were balloons of all colours tied to the door handles. Billowing behind the wing mirrors were two silk banners with writing on them. At the gate the car manoeuvred a little backwards and forwards, and when it failed to make it through, Hacı Veli gestured a little from the front seat, and they rushed to open both sides of the gate as far back as they went. And then the car swung slightly to one side, almost as if it knew what it was carrying, and now, at last, it made it through the narrow wooden opening. It drove up to the house in first gear, blowing its horn, followed by a stream of townspeople. Hacı Veli and the groom stepped out of the car, leaving the bride with her sisters and brothers. Her father stood to one side, beaming and saying nothing, while the groom and the best man went to the back of the house and, amid great excitement, clambered up on to the roof. The groom stationed himself beside the flagpole, and from there he gazed down at the people below, and the streets, the trees, the houses, and the gardens beyond them. You would have thought he was about to leave this world for another dimension, and was bidding everyone and everything in it farewell. The best man watched with him, narrowing his eyes as he joined his hands behind his head. Then he handed the groom a bulging purse. The groom took it in his palm first, as if to weigh it, and then he turned it upside down and threw it off the roof. The children who had been waiting below went tumbling after the silver coins as they clattered across the yard. In their struggle to get the most coins, some fell to their knees, others jumped across the yard like frogs, some crept as furtively as cats.

Then the groom climbed down, buttoned up his jacket, and respectfully opened the car door. As he and his veiled bride walked towards the door, arm in arm, the crowd applauded them.

A fearless boy raised his arm and in a voice everyone could hear, he called, 'Shall we fall in love?'

The bride and groom stopped walking.

The clapping stopped, and with one voice, the crowd called back to the boy, 'Let's fall in love!'

With his hand still in the air, and in a voice that was even louder, the boy cried:

> *The harvest lies before us like a carpet*
> *And here you see us, mad with joy.*
> *Uncle, we have brought the bride*
> *This mountain rose.*

The crowd began to clap again, and the bride and groom began walking again. They had gone just a few steps when another hand went up in the crowd, and a middle-aged man going white at the temples shouted out loud enough to burst the veins in his neck, 'Shall we fall in love?'

While the bride and groom stood still, the crowd again called back with one voice: 'Let's fall in love!'

Keeping his hands raised like the boy before him, the man called out:

> *Before us stands a great door,*
> *Inside all manner of grain.*
> *May he who would part these lovers*
> *Be sent crawling far away.*

The bride and groom moved again towards the door, as the crowd applauded. Then someone else in the crowd called out: 'Shall we fall in love?' Some spoke of dipping their thumbs in henna, and the first night, and heads resting on bosoms; others spoke of fresh lambs, and embroidered pillows, and prosperity; yet others spoke of water flowing like ribbons, and cypress trees, and plenty, but Ziya could no longer bear this much happiness and jubilation, and for a moment he thought he might cry. After that, he climbed over the wall, taking with him the thoughts still in his mind; the applause grew softer as he walked along the cobblestone streets towards the edge of town. In actual fact, he wasn't walking at that point. It felt more as if the town was slipping beneath his feet like a carpet, a bright embroidered carpet scattering warmth and noise in its wake, and suddenly Ziya found himself back where he had conjured up his dream. Back on the edge of that bed. He was still sitting there, leaning into the night. And now, very slowly, he stood up, and for the next few moments he walked just the same way he had walked in his dream, feeling his way across the room towards the window. Falling on to the sofa, he looked outside.

It was still pitch dark; all that could be seen was a gauzy patch of white, fluttering in the distance. And because nothing else could be seen, it was the patch of white that brought that distance into being, and once it came into being, it mixed in with the darkness and the silence that reigned over it, and once it had done so, it lost all shape, and the more it dissipated, the more strangely and heavily it loomed over the horizon. Which he could not quite see. Which he could only imagine. But it seemed to him as if it was pressing down and down on that patch of white and slowly crushing it. It grew thinner, and thinner still, until suddenly it vanished, and at that exact moment, the night began to fade. Little by little, the sky grew lighter. When he looked out at the hills in the distance, he could just about see the rocks, and the ledges, peeping through the mist. And here and there he could almost see a tree rising above the skyline. When the sky got a little brighter, he could see the plain at the foot of the hills, and the dirt road winding through it, the sheep pens to the right, the line of poplars, a few houses facing in the opposite direction, and the trees in these houses' gardens. A giant postcard, Ziya thought. A giant postcard, seen through frosted glass. To view it more closely, Ziya leaned over the sofa, and craned his neck. With reverence, he saw how gently the dirt road cast off the night. He saw how the cliffs shimmered with a serenity that seemed, as it echoed, to caress every hill and field, as the land itself became some sort of giant creature, slowly rising. He saw how the frosted undergrowth began to rustle with whispers, and how each rock, each blackberry bush, each heartless thorn came back into being, and each tree back into light. He saw how the air was thick with hisses and pops that blinked like little lanterns, jingled like little bells. And as he saw all this, he thought, what a beautiful place this is. Just imagine, a place where you can hear sound and silence, all at the same time.

With this, he stood up. Curious to see more of the place where he'd been living, he ambled slowly through the house. The walls were painted white, and there was one medium-sized room, and a narrow kitchen looking out over the side yard. Beyond it was a small, dark section with a concrete floor that could, he thought, be either a bathroom or a pantry. How different from the view he had just seen. How disappointing. For a time Ziya just stood there, staring, and asking himself if he could ever get used to such a place. But then he thought: is there anything on earth that a person can't get used to? He threw on his clothes, as quickly as he could, and stepped out of the house to do a bit of exploring, get a bit of fresh air. Once outside, he spied a wooden bench just to the left of the door. It had cushions. He settled himself down on one of them.

The sun was just rising over the hills, and there, on the dirt road, he could see Kenan walking towards him. Walking towards him, bringing with him the sparkle of every moment he had passed through to get this far, and the strange green quiver of every leaf in the vineyard.

'Good morning,' he said, still catching his breath. 'You've woken up early. *Maşallah!* I thought you would sleep until noon, at least.'

'Good morning,' said Ziya, rising to his feet. 'But why did you think I'd sleep so late?'

'Don't you remember? You were in pretty bad shape when you got here last night. You were drunk out of your mind. It was pitch dark when you got here. Your friend Ethem and I – we only just managed to get you from the car to the house. It was so hard to hold you up that the three of us went zigzagging through the vineyard.'

'I remember that, but only vaguely,' said Ziya, examining his forehead with his fingertips, as if he were trying to read the lines the night might have left there. 'I'm sorry – before leaving the city, I had too much to drink.'

They sat down together on the cushions.

'Or was it that your city friends threw you a goodbye party?'

'No,' said Ziya, smiling faintly. 'There wasn't any party. Just two friends, having a drink. The same friend who brought me here. I don't remember, but I probably introduced you to him last night.'

'Yes, you did,' said Kenan, and then he added, 'I wanted him to stay over but sadly he refused. As soon as we had brought you in, he left.'

'Don't worry. He loves driving at night. He'll have made it back to the city, no problem.'

'I hope you're right,' said Kenan.

There followed a short silence, while they both watched the hills beyond rising above the plain, the cliffs behind them sparkling in the sun and the pine forests shivering in the mist, sending up little white clouds that looked like smoke signals.

'So this is how I made my entrance?' Ziya asked drowsily. 'I arrived in Kenan Eli, drunk out of my mind?'

Kenan smiled faintly.

'Do you know what, though?' Ziya said, still sounding very drowsy. 'Even if you set out for Kenan Eli sober, you'd be drunk by the time you got here.'

'Except that Kenan Eli is not the name of this village,' said Kenan. 'This is Yazıköy. As you know.'

'Of course I know,' said Ziya.

Again they fell silent. Every time they paused, after all, the view swept in to capture their attention, and take it as far as the eye could see, and deeper, ever deeper, until, for just a moment, it became a shimmering veil of shadow, light and rainbow, only to return to itself with the speed of light. But for that same moment, Ziya's face would brighten, as if caught by a distant torch. Not just his face. It was his entire being. It was his soul.

So it was after the view had swept in and out again like this that Ziya turned slowly to look Kenan in the eyes.

'What a beautiful place this is. I can never thank you enough.'

Kenan smiled sweetly and opened his arms. 'There's no need to thank me,' he said.

There was another short silence.

Then Kenan asked, 'Why did you wake up so early? You must have been so tired, after that trip. I wish you'd managed to sleep until noon. Did you wake up because you didn't know where you were?'

'Don't even ask,' said Ziya, and he made such a grimace, you would have thought he'd just been stabbed in the stomach. 'I had the most bizarre dream. That's why I woke up so early. And this dream of mine, it wasn't just normally bizarre. It was off the scale. I still haven't managed to shake it off. Certain parts have stayed with me.'

'Dreams are like that, though.'

'This was something else, Kenan. This was beyond strange.'

'How?'

'In my dream, I was going to return my key to a woman who was supposed to be my landlady but things kept happening to me, things I could never have imagined. For one thing, this woman who was supposed to be my landlady just talked and talked and talked, there was no shutting her up. She was telling her life story, of course. And a few other people's life stories, for good measure, plus the history of the entire city . . . and in the middle of all that, she would make these bizarre pronouncements – as if someone else was speaking through her. Whereas in real dreams, as you know, there's hardly any speaking at all. Which is why, please believe me, this dream I had doesn't really seem like a dream to me.'

'Are you sure you aren't exaggerating? That's what it seems like to me. If it isn't a dream, then what is it?'

'I don't know. It was just bizarre. Beyond bizarre. For example, when I was leaving that apartment, I heard paper rustling, and because the landlady was following me out, I asked her about it, and she said it was probably her maid, going through the dossiers. But when I reached the lift, the girl who was supposed to be her maid walked out of it, carrying a handbag.'

'And?'

'What this means is that the maid was outside the apartment when I heard that paper rustling. The landlady was following me to the door, as I just said. And also. There was no one else in the apartment at that moment. So where did all that rustling come from? No, this was something other than a dream, I assure you.'

'I think you're exaggerating. And anyway, things like that happen in dreams all the time. Like once, I met myself as an old man. My older self hobbled right up to our door and rang the bell. I opened the door, and there he was, with his white hair and his long beard and his humpback, but in spite of all this, I recognised him instantly. He was wearing a dervish coat, which was white, with a silver collar that glinted like sunlight. And when he walked, he dragged his right leg slightly. I can't be sure about that, but that's how it looked to me as we walked together out of town and into the orchards. We sat down at the foot of a good-sized walnut tree and stayed there for a long time talking. And while we talked, a white bird came bursting out of his coat. It flew round and round, just above our heads. I had this dream many years ago, but I can still see my older self, with wrinkled hands, a lined forehead and that long, long beard. I have no idea if I'm going to look like that when I'm older. To tell the truth, it still worries me, even now . . . But to go back to your dream, let's just say that it's something like mine. Let's agree for a moment that the things you saw were not things you saw in a dream. If they were real, you would have to have gone back to the city in the middle of the night to return the key again. But you didn't do that. Did you?'

'Of course not. No way I could have done that. Not even if I'd wanted to.'

'And that's just it. That's what I've been trying to tell you. If you didn't go back there in the middle of the night, then it was a dream.'

Ziya raised his head to look out at the hills again, and the steep cliffs rising above them, and the pine forest, rustling green. Looking deep into the forest, he saw its noises changing colour. He felt its scent against his cheek as he breathed in its silence.

'I can't be sure,' he said. 'Maybe this is a dream, too. I just can't be sure.'

3

Peace

That first day Kenan wanted to take Ziya into the village. He spent a long time trying to convince him. 'Listen,' he said. 'My mother made all this food. They're expecting us.' But Ziya wouldn't budge. He'd not even unpacked, he said. He needed some time to catch his breath. And how much could they have prepared, anyway, when he'd only been invited the day before? And so it was that, for the first time in many years, the two friends ate breakfast together at the table they'd set up next to the wooden bench. As they ate, birdsong pecked away at the cheese plate's faded purple borders, while the flowers and the grass and the pine trees puffed out clouds of scent that hovered in the air, glistening like olives. Each time this vision came to him, Ziya would put his tea glass on the table, which seemed now to be as great and wide as nature itself, and then he'd bend over, and lift it up again. Having finished eating and poured themselves more tea, they both lit up cigarettes, and looked out over the hills and the cliffs rising above them. Or rather, Ziya looked out over the hills, leaving Kenan with no choice but to do the same.

'Did the money I sent cover all the expenses?' Ziya asked, as his eyes travelled over the cliffs.

'It did,' said Kenan. 'It was a hundred and fifty lira too much, in fact. More than I knew how to spend.'

Reaching into his pocket, he gave Ziya the money he hadn't spent.

'This barn had an earthen roof once,' he said quietly. 'It leaked in the summer rains, and in the winter snows. That's why I had it replaced when we did it up. I hired good men from town to do us a proper tiled roof. The storeroom was a good size, so I divided it into two. One part became the kitchen, and the other the bathroom . . . Then we redid the walls, inside and out. We replastered them, and then we covered the bathroom's earthen floor with pine as fresh and fragrant as the day it was cut. And then – well the doors and the windows had never been painted, and to tell the truth, there wasn't much left to them. All you had to do was touch them, and they'd crumble. So that was why we pulled them out and put in new ones. And then, as God is my witness, I spent a bit of the money you sent on furnishings. Two sofas, one table, a refrigerator, an electric stove, an oven, a gas cylinder, a bed, a few pots and pans, blankets, a quilt, and a few other odds and ends . . . You must have seen all this when you woke up.'

'I did,' said Ziya. 'And I saw all the food and drink you brought, too. Thank you. For going to all this effort for me, for taking so much time off work. Honestly. No matter how much I thanked you, it would never be enough.'

'Nonsense. I just wish I could have done more,' said Kenan, with shame in his voice. 'Of course, as time goes on, if you decide there are things you don't like, we can change them at once. Certainly there will be some things missing. So, for example, I bought an electric stove, because you said you could handle it, but if it rains more than two drops, or there's a flash of lightning in the far distance, or even if the smallest cloud decides to hang a little bit lower, the electricity begins to fizzle and pop and you can never know how long it will be before it fizzles out altogether, that's something only God knows, and that's why I need to get you a wood stove, too. And before winter sets in, we need to stack up your woodpile. Right now there's electricity, we asked the people in the nearest house and they let us run it from there, but I'm sorry to say that so far we haven't been able to sort out the water. It was never going to happen, anyway. As you know, none of these houses out here have water. And that is why you'll have to get it from the village fountain, like everyone else. My nephew Besim can help you with this, so please don't worry. Don't worry at all.'

'I won't,' said Ziya.

As he said these words, he looked out over the grapevine in the direction of the village, as if he was searching for the fountain.

'Let me clear these things away,' said Kenan, springing to his feet, and before Ziya could say, 'Stop, what's the rush?' he had filled up a tray and was rushing towards the kitchen. Ziya jumped up, too, but all that was left for him was a glass salt cellar in the corner and a few slices of bread.

'I have to go now,' said Kenan. 'I hope you don't mind me already leaving you alone for a few hours on your first day. I have to run some errands.'

'That's fine,' said Ziya.

Kenan left, rushing through the vineyard and down the dirt road that led across the plain, his dark, slight form growing thinner and thinner until it melted into the sunlight like a cloud.

After he had lost sight of Kenan, there was a moment when Ziya had no idea what to do. In spite of himself, he turned back to look at the hills and their lower reaches and the green and waving forest, and the cliffs rising above them. The silence just then was deafening; now and then the sound of a sheep bell wafted in from the plain, but even this seemed no more than a gorgeous ornament hanging from the collar of this great silence. Just then a donkey brayed in the village, and as that sound shimmered through the air, it lit up – lit up only to vanish just as suddenly. And when it vanished, Ziya went inside, opened up his cases, and took out his wrinkled clothes, which he put on to hangers and hung up in the blue fabric wardrobe in the corner.

Kenan had reached the other edge of the village by then, still in a great hurry. At last he came to a stop outside the house at the end of the street. Opening the door, he quickly slipped inside. At the sound of the door, a white sheepdog dozing by the wall on the other side of the street lifted its head to fix its glowing glassy eyes on Kenan's back, but did not bark. All it did was to open its mouth as wide as it could, to lick its chops with an enormous tongue. Then it gently lowered its head to rest on its forelegs again, and narrowed its gaze, as if preparing an ambush. For the next hour, its eyes never left the door. Even when flies landed on the sides of its mouth, it did not move. Now and again a silent torpor would contrive to close its eyes, but this never lasted long: soon enough, the dog's eyes would jerk open again and it would reassume its old pose. It did not seem to be waiting for the door so much as the sound of Kenan's feet. Though it could have been looking far, far away, towards some other point in time.

Just then a group of children aged between twelve and thirteen appeared at the top of the street. Boys and girls together, laughing and joking as they approached the dog. Some of these children were holding marbles. Others were holding bunches of grapes, and yet others were carrying sticks of various lengths, sticks that could be used to play skittles. When they saw the dog by the wall, the girls slowed right down; they retreated into a huddle still eyeing the dog, leaving the boys out in front. One of them was a dark-skinned boy who frowned and waved his stick as if to throw it. The dog made no sound. Without so much as moving its head, it fixed its blank gaze on the boy. In the face of this indifference, the boy picked up a rock the size of a pear and went one step closer. Shouting *Shoo! Shoo!* he threw the rock with all his strength. This made the dog angry. The first barks were halting but then it got up and began to chase after the children. Faced with its bared teeth and ferocious barking, the children turned on their heels and ran screaming in the direction from which they'd come. Reaching the top of the road, they vanished.

Once they were gone, the dog ambled slowly back to its station and took up its old position as calmly as if nothing had happened. Resting its head on its forelegs, it narrowed its gaze, fixing its eyes on the door. Revived by all that running, its eyes now shone more brightly than before. So brightly, in fact, that they were as good as mirrors, reflecting back the door's every detail: the whorls in the wood, the mildew on the clay, the holes in the moulding. When Kenan came outside again, he raced down the street without even noticing the dog was there.

Passing through the village *meydan*, he was noticed by one of the men sitting outside the Coffeehouse of Mirrors.

This man, whose name was Kâzım the Bellows Man, jumped to his feet. Stepping out from the shade of the trees, he cupped his hands around his mouth and with great excitement cried, 'What's the news? Has your friend arrived?'

'He's arrived,' Kenan replied.

'That's good, then. All the best!'

Sliding back into his chair, and lowering his cap, bringing its visor right over his eyebrows, he watched Kenan walk on. In a voice only he could hear, he mumbled, 'I hope my business goes just as fast.'

And though he was already nine or ten paces away, Kenan looked back over his shoulder, as he had heard these words. Then he sped up again. Huffing and puffing, he left the village, racing towards the sheep pens, turning off the dirt road to stride up the slope, and from there, wet with sweat, through the vineyards, until at last he reached the barn.

He found Ziya sitting on the wooden bench outside the house, smoking a cigarette. He looked calm and at peace, as if he had just escaped from beneath a heavy burden.

'Have you finished your business?' he asked, when he saw Kenan approaching.

'I have,' Kenan replied.

Sitting down, he, too, lit a cigarette; puckering his lips, he sent little puffs of smoke sailing into the greenery of the forest opposite.

When he had emptied his mouth of smoke, he said, 'If you like, I can take you into the village today. What would you say to that?'

'Let's do that later on,' Ziya replied. 'Why don't we take a walk in the forest now, if you have the time.'

'Shame on you,' said Kenan. 'Of course I have time!'

And so they stood up and set out through the vineyard, wending their way amid the furrows of earth, and walking down the hill, leaving behind the poplars and the sheep pens on the right to cross the dirt road, and walk on slowly, side by side, towards the forest. Just ahead, beyond the scrub, they heard the sudden echo of a clacking grouse. Ziya stopped in his tracks when he heard that, as fast as if another step might send him crashing into that clacking, and as if, the moment he crashed into it, he might die. Soundlessly, eyes shut, he stood there waiting in the grass. Kenan had stopped, too. Mystified, he turned his head, gazing in awe at his friend. Ziya opened his eyes and together they moved on. Pink and purple and yellow thorns attacked their ankles as they strode through knee-high grass, over big stones and small stones, across little fields thick with juniper bushes and fragrant with thyme, until at last they reached the oak trees. They'd been walking for forty-five or fifty minutes by then, and so, to catch their breath, they found a patch of shade to rest in; by now, they could no longer see the dirt road below. They couldn't see the sheep pens on the side of the road, either. All they could see were a few rooftops in the village and, here and there, the uppermost branches of a poplar, pulsing sunlight. And even these seemed to sink into the depths beyond the juniper bushes, as indistinct as distant memories.

'Honestly,' said Ziya, as he took out a cigarette. 'It's everything you said it was, when we were in the army. It's truly enchanted. Even the sky seems closer. Close enough to touch!'

Kenan raised his face to the sky. For a moment he stared into its depths, smiling faintly.

'Do you know what?' he said, lighting a cigarette and inhaling deeply. 'I noticed right away, when we met last night, but the truth is, I couldn't find the courage to ask you, not in the state you were in. And all morning, I've been wondering if I should ask or not.'

'Are you worried about the scars on my face?'

'Yes. How did you get them?'

Ziya swallowed hard, looking up to gaze over the gently swaying juniper bushes, and far, far into the distance.

'You're right,' he said, still looking. 'If I were you, I'd be wondering, too.'

Then he fell silent, and for a time, neither of them spoke.

'These scars,' he finally said. 'These scars come from a terrible incident that turned my life upside down sixteen years ago. There was, in one of the city's busiest avenues, a bookshop that my wife Kader and I loved very much. We visited it once a month, without fail. It was at the entrance of a bustling multi-storey shopping centre, this bookshop, and it was huge, and so well organised, and we could always find whatever book or journal we were after. It had a mezzanine that served as a cafeteria, this bookshop. It had wicker chairs with red cushions, and customers could relax there with a tea or a coffee and a little music. We loved all that, but we also loved Cemalettin Bey, the owner. You know the kind of person I mean: they don't even need to speak for you to breathe more easily, and open your mind a little – well, Cemalettin Bey was someone like that. Also, this man had this amazing sense of space, and that was why, the moment you walked in, you felt right at home. He knew if you needed him, he could tell just from the way you moved, or didn't move. And then, bam, he'd be right next to you . . . If you were not quite sure what you wanted, it was right under your nose – even if he was many kilometres away, he knew . . . So anyway, this is where my wife and I were headed sixteen years ago, on that hot summer's day, to look at a few new books, but also just to pass the time. And we had just joined the crowd pushing its way up the stairs when suddenly my watchstrap snapped. Thinking it made sense to buy a new one, seeing as I had my watch with me, I left Kader at the bookshop and made my way to the watch-maker at the other end of the same floor. You know how cramped those little shops are, with only room for one: there's always someone sitting behind a glass counter, and when you walk in, he raises his head and looks you over, almost like you were a watch. Unless, of course, he is hold-ing a watch he has just opened up, in which case he is too concerned with its innards to look up at all, and as you stand there on your side of the counter, waiting, it's almost like being caught between several different time currents, each flowing in its own direction. And all around you there are clocks ticking away, each in its own fashion, and as you stand there, that's what surrounds you, the pandemonium of clocks. And so that's how it was that day when I went into that shop. I had to wait, because the man sitting behind the counter had put on his glasses to repair a shoddy-looking watch with an instrument as fine as a horse's hair. He was totally indifferent to my presence – as if the watch he was repairing would determine the moment he'd look up at me. And just in case he had reached the most difficult moment of the job, I kept quiet, of course; but I also leaned over slightly, to see if I could find a watchstrap I liked in the display beneath the glass counter. Actually this was something of a lost cause because I didn't know anything about leather and in the end I was just going to decide on one of the expensive ones, hoping it was good. And who knows, maybe I was, without even knowing it, pretending to be busy so as not to distract the watchmaker . . . Acting like I needed to look at these watchstraps anyway, so fine with me if he carried on working . . . There is, as you know, a dark little room at the back of our minds in which we learn things by rote, and when the right conditions present themselves, we say or perform the things we learn in that room without even knowing . . . What I'm trying to say is that this is what prompted me to behave in this way. But anyway, after I'd been standing there waiting for quite some time, this sallow-faced man behind the counter slowly raised his head to look at me, and while he was doing that, a huge explosion ripped through the building. All I saw before we were plunged into darkness were flying, smashing, terrifying shards of glass. When I opened my eyes, I was in hospital, in a room painted almond green with a ceiling covered with water stains. There were bandages on my arms and legs and around my head. Voices floated in to me from the corridors and the other rooms and the far corners of the building, and every once in a while I could hear people running. All this from the bed I was lying in. It would have been better if I'd heard nothing, though, because there was no one with me, and the sound of those voices made my own empty room seem emptier. The longer I lay there, the emptier I felt inside, and I kept thinking about Kader and wondering where she was, wondering why she wasn't with me, looking into my eyes, and holding my hand. I found out the next day, of course. It seems that the centre of the explosion was in that bookshop we liked so much – that was where the terrorists had planted their plastic explosives. In due course the morgue returned what was left of my wife's body, and I failed to find the courage to look at it, not even once. In all honesty, I did want to look at it. I wanted to see her face, and touch her, one last time, but in the end I didn't. No, I didn't, I am sad to say. Even though I wanted to . . . Was I scared of seeing body parts that had been salvaged, piece by piece, from the wreckage? At the time, I just couldn't say. There were arms and legs lying all over the place, so maybe I was frightened that they'd matched them with the wrong bodies. Because something like that did occur to me that day. When you had ignorant, thick-skinned officials running roughshod over evidence and all too often destroying it with their own hands, this sort of thing could happen quite easily. But even if they exercised the greatest caution, it could still happen, simply because of the magnitude of the damage, and the chaos it had caused. It's terrifying just to imagine it. Just think: your loved one's arm in one cemetery, and her leg in another . . . In the end there were fifteen people wounded that day, and five killed. Or to be more accurate, that's what the records said – three women and two men, five people in all. When really it was six people who died. Because Kader was five months pregnant, so I did not just lose my wife that day. I also lost my child. Without ever having held it in my arms. Without ever having kissed its forehead . . .'

'I'm so sorry. So very, very sorry,' Kenan mumbled helplessly.

Ziya's eyes were brimming with tears.

'Thanks,' he said, as he reached for the pack next to his knees and pulled out another cigarette.

For a few minutes, neither spoke.

Meanwhile, the leaves of the oak tree in whose shade they were sitting began to rustle. As each new rustle flew through the air like an imaginary leaf, a tortoise came out from underneath the wild liquorice just in front of them; it took a few steps forward, crunching the grass underfoot, stuck out its head, looked around timidly, and then quickly backed away, to hide amongst the branches.

'Do you know what?' Ziya said, as he blew out his smoke. 'If I'd had a son, he'd be sixteen years old now.'

'Which means he'd be the same age as my nephew Besim.'

'So it goes,' continued Ziya, in a faint little voice. 'It's almost as if this thing we call life sent me off into that corner, with a watchstrap as a pretext. Or else, that watchmaker did it, by making me wait. Sometimes I wonder, I really do, if life put that man there, just for this purpose, if it did something to his body to slow him down and then put him in that shop to work, for fifty or sixty years, just so that it could delay me, and keep me far from the explosion. If I know anything, it's this: if that sallow-faced man behind the counter had been a little faster, there is no doubt that I would have finished my errand and returned to the bookshop at the entrance to the shopping centre, and died there, with my wife and my son. Do you know what? For many years I felt the deepest shame at not having died with them. There were even times when I was ashamed to be living the years they never could. I felt so ashamed, and was in such pain, that a time arrived when I hated life itself. I'd lose my temper, badly. There were times when the winds of fury sent me flying into a *meyhane*, times when I came to think of the others at my table as my closest friends, and went off to houses I'd never been to, with people I didn't know, to bend to the will of anyone who happened to be near me, but those days passed and I put all that behind me, soon enough. Those soap bubbles of laughter, that clanging music, those fumes and those dim lights, and all the other props people use to get close to one another – I was spending too much time with people who had given up on life, I decided. I was wasting my pain. The truth is I told none of them what had happened; they hadn't the least idea of the hell I'd been through, but still, when I sat drinking in their company, the atmosphere seeped into my private hell: the smoke they exhaled would billow across the room and settle inside me. And the endless insipid conversations, they were one long stretched-out moan. The jokes that weren't jokes, because they lacked even the slightest sparkle of wit. The kisses that meant nothing, beyond flesh touching flesh. The fights. And everywhere – lining the walls, lounging on the sofas, sitting on the floor, lurking in the bathrooms, even, and in places even worse than that – all those people, holding glasses. What can I say? I was wasting my pain, spending so much time in places like this, and that's why it didn't last long. I had my wobble, but it was soon over. One way of looking at it was that I left the life I'd known, went as far from it as I could, but then I came back again. And pulled myself together. I found refuge, with the help of that eraser of memories we call time. Or rather, I came to understand that the only way forward was to bury myself in my grief, and accept what had happened.'

'It's hard. Honestly, so hard. May God give you patience,' mumbled Kenan.

They fell silent for a spell. Leaning forward, they listened to the oak leaves, rising and falling with the breeze. Then, between each rise and fall, there came the deep rustlings of the forest. And between those, there was silence, as soft as cotton wool. And between these were the moans from which that silence came, as thick as the slopes and pastures and cliffs that surrounded them.

'So that's why I have those lines on my face,' said Ziya, and then he added, 'And what happened to you, my friend? I seem to remember you were engaged when we knew each other. Do you have any children?'

'Yes, I was engaged,' replied Kenan. 'And when I got back to the village, I quickly sold off a few pastures of marshy land and got married, with all the pipes and drums, but sadly the marriage didn't last long; we divorced after four years, because we had no children, and my wife somehow decided that this must be my fault. During those four years, there wasn't a doctor in the area we hadn't asked for help, of course, or a *hoca* whose hand we hadn't kissed, or a tree we hadn't tied a rag around, or a saint we hadn't entreated. We sold everything we owned around this time. All our money went on votive offerings, and doctors, and *hocas*. And all that time, of course, we were trying out all the treatments recommended by various famous people, just to see if they would work . . . Then one day, my wife asked for a divorce, and so we did. We parted that very day, in the ugliest way imaginable. To tell you the truth, my wife did something outrageous; having packed up her things to return to her village, she ran around town as if she were holding a doctor's report and accused me of being impotent. "You're an impotent louse! That's what you are – an impotent louse!" She was still in our courtyard when she started shouting, as loud as she could. That uncle of hers with the goitre – he was waiting outside in his car, and when she got in, I thought it would end there. But no. She kept going. She rolled down the window and stuck out her head and until they reached the edge of the village, she kept shouting, as if I had chased after her, as if I was still there. "You're impotent! An impotent louse!" But I was dumbstruck, I couldn't speak, let alone move. I just stood there, gaping. And for a time, everyone else in the village stood there, too, in their doorways, at their windows, pressed against the walls. But once the car was gone, and the clouds of dust had settled, they turned around and looked at each other. And that became my nickname. Impotent. And it wasn't long before the whispers had gone beyond our streets to the towns and villages around us. I couldn't look anyone in the eye. Even knowing that the charge was false, I bowed my head like a guilty man. A few years later, I decided I should find a good woman to take as my wife, but no one would have me. I searched and searched, but I found no one, and that was when I came to understand just what an evil thing my wife had done to me, with just a few words. All she'd had to do was shout a few words on her way out, and she'd destroyed my future. Do you know what? It's something I just haven't managed to fathom, how after four years of two people putting their heads on the same pillow, one of them could do such a thing to the other. How there is no memory left of the first day they set eyes on each other on this earth, no memory of kisses or caresses. When I think about such things, it still makes me angry. What a strange word that is, anger. For months and months, I held this huge grudge against her. Then one day it occurred to me that if I shouted out the same sorts of words as my wife had done, I would destroy her future, too. And then I thought, the poor woman, what could she have done, maybe this was why she was in such a hurry. And then, I don't know how this happened exactly, but suddenly I felt some compassion for her. My resentment went, and my anger, too. It was as if I understood her a little. Yes, I understood her, just a little. Hazy as it was, I had some understanding of what was lying underneath those words of hers. And sometimes, when I come up to this forest to chop wood, I look at the trees around me, and the cliffs, and the grass, and the tortoises rustling through the undergrowth, and the snakes sliding into view only to vanish a moment later, and all the insects, and all the birds, and almost always, I think, what a shame it is that my wife and I could not enjoy these things together. Anyway, after that various relatives and village elders got together to find me a new wife, only to return from every house they visited empty-handed. My name had gone before me, and unless I produced a certificate proving I wasn't impotent, there was nothing I could do. To make a long story short, as one year followed another, and I got older and older, the whole thing began to seem too complicated and I gave up on the idea of marrying, and accepted my fate. What else could I do? I told myself that this was the fate our Lord had written for me. So there's no family, and no children; just my mother, my sister, and my nephew and me, living together in one house, and doing the best we can.'

'Damn it,' said Ziya, shaking his head. 'You've really gone through hell.'

Kenan said nothing as he slowly lit himself a cigarette. Resting his head between his knees, he exhaled into the grass. The ants passing through paused for a moment, as if stunned by the curls of smoke, and then the line began to move again. When he noticed this, Kenan held his breath and looked anxiously into the grass, to see if any ants had died.

'Shall we get going?' asked Ziya.

'Yes, let's go,' said Kenan.

And so they stood up, leaving behind them a little mound of cigarette ends, and headed back down the same thyme-scented path they'd struggled up earlier.

'You've changed a lot,' said Kenan, as they made their way through the juniper bushes. 'You're not at all like the person you once were.'

'If you ask me, some of the differences you're seeing are differences in yourself,' said Ziya, giving him a sidelong look.

To himself he said: 'It's been thirty years since we last saw each other, for goodness sake! How could I not have changed?' But he decided it was too trite a thing to say out loud just then. And anyway, he could see the view again, through the gaps in the juniper bushes, and that took all his attention. There were poplars in this view, and sheep pens, and barns, and part of the village, and a sort of pure silence that seemed to promise peace.

And that was why, when they stood before the barn again, he said, 'I'm sure now. I'm sure that I'll spend the rest of my life here, in peace.'

'May God grant your wish,' said Kenan.

'If you ask me, it couldn't be any other way,' said Ziya, and he drew an arc in the air. 'Look at this greenery, this tranquillity, this purity. Everything is exactly as I wanted. I was so tired of dealing with life's chaos. I wanted to live a simple life, where one plus one equals two; and this is a place where such a life is possible. Yes, it really is. A place where a person can live in peace.'

Not knowing what to say, Kenan smiled faintly.

4

Yazıköy

The next day began in happy anticipation at the house Kenan shared with his family. Cevriye Hanım, already in her white headscarf, was pacing back and forth, pausing from time to time to issue brief instructions to Besim, and sometimes she crouched down next to Nefise to knead the dough and see if it was aerated enough, and whenever she stood up again, she told her to hurry up, but also to make sure she had enough dough for the *gözlemes*. Kenan was there, too: having brought in a few armfuls of oak logs to set down next to the pot-bellied stove, he was now standing by the wall like a dark and weedy ghost. In the corner of the courtyard, in front of the ash cans, the sun was shining brightly, and so, too, were the chickens strutting back and forth. And birds were twittering in the mulberry trees, and beyond the wall, the city shimmered green to the left and blue to the right, while sounds of all colours flowed between them.

'Time to light the fire, my son,' said Cevriye Hanım. 'The house needs heating up.'

Kenan knelt down, a cigarette hanging from his lips. Placing a few pine cones amongst the logs, he promptly applied his lighter, and once he was sure the fire had caught, he stood up again.

Cevriye Hanım stood next to him, watching his every move, as if she were afraid he might do something wrong.

'With the weather we're having, our guest might not wish to stay inside,' she said then. 'If it were up to me, I'd set up the table in the courtyard. I'm going off to help Nefise. You and Besim can see to the table in the meantime.'

'We'll do that,' said Kenan.

Before long he had moved the Formica table in the courtyard into the shade of the mulberry tree. After covering it with the blue floral tablecloth, they sprinkled the ground with a flask of water to keep down the dust.

Then Kenan went off to get Ziya; leaving the courtyard, a cigarette between his lips, he swiftly made his way to the barn.

After he had left, Cevriye Hanım settled herself in front of the stove, and now and then she turned to frown at Nefise. Every time she did so, she seemed about to say something, but she never did. Every time she swallowed instead, and turned her eyes back to the *gözlemes* cooking on the stove.

Only when the work was done and cleared away could she say it. They'd swept off the flour and washed their hands and now the two of them were sitting at the table.

Leaning over, she said, 'Whatever you do, don't dress up for our guest.' She spoke softly, as if sharing a secret. 'As you know, my girl, when an apple hangs high, it is asking to be stoned.'

'But I didn't dress up,' said Nefise.

Cevriye Hanım sat up and then leaned back on her chair, and gave Nefise a thorough inspection.

'What can I know?' she asked finally, her face clouding with shame. 'How can I know what you'll look like to him when he arrives?'

Nefise gazed out over the white plastic chair as if it were a cloud wafting off into the distance, and said nothing.

'Did you brew the tea?' asked Cevriye Hanım, to change the subject.

'I brewed the tea, Mother,' said Nefise. 'And I prepared a jug of *ayran*. Because he might just prefer to drink *ayran*.'

Just then the neighbour's son came tumbling into the courtyard. Taking a few more steps, he stopped to catch his breath. Leaning forward, and placing his hands on his knees, and in a trembling voice that matched his general state of panic, he said, 'My mother's had more pangs. Hurry. Hurry!'

'Dear, dear,' said Cevriye Hanım. Turning to Nefise, she said, 'You'd better go and see what's happening. It wouldn't do for me not to be here at home right now.'

Nefise jumped to her feet and ran to the courtyard gate.

'Wait a minute!' Cevriye Hanım cried, rushing after her. 'Take a few *gözlemes* with you. Make sure she eats them when they're still hot, the poor thing.'

Nefise turned around and piled a few *gözlemes* on to a little tray, which she covered with a white cloth, after which she vanished with the boy who was waiting for her at the gate,

Cevriye Hanım went back to sit down in the silent courtyard, and for a long time she did not move. Her thoughts went to her neighbour Fatma, and her pangs, and to her helpless helper Nefise, and to Numan, who had the face of a bandit, and who had been haunting their door for years now hoping to marry Nefise, and his brother Cabbar. And then, for a moment, she frowned and looked fiercely into the distance, as if Numan were standing there before her, pressing her with all manner of promises. Then she thought, no one could ever go that far, my dear. Everyone has some propriety. Then she stood up and strolled over to the chickens; bending over, she watched them for some time as they moved across the ground like little strobes of light. And as she watched, she spoke to them, very softly: 'Hey there, you blessed creatures. You have souls, too, don't you know?' Unruffled, the chickens continued on their way, brushing against her skirt from time to time as they pecked at the ground. And Cevriye Hanım walked on, very slowly, first to survey the onions lying at the foot of the courtyard wall, and then back to the table. Sitting herself down on one of the white plastic chairs, she looked over her left shoulder at the courtyard gate.

And then suddenly, as if it had been waiting for her to do just that, the gate opened up, and in came Kenan, with Ziya just behind him.

'So, Mother,' said Kenan, as she rose to her feet. 'Allow me to introduce you to my friend.'

Ziya walked over to kiss Cevriye Hanım's hand.

Though shaded by her headscarf, her unblinking eyes shone as brightly as if he were a long-lost relative.

'Welcome, my child, you have come in peace. You're here at last, so please, come in.'

They sat down at the table.

And still Cevriye Hanım kept her eyes on Ziya. She was staring at him with such affection as to put any man ill at ease. As she searched for something to say, she cleared her throat now and again.

'Where is Nefise?' asked Kenan, as he looked around him.

'She's at the neighbour's,' Cevriye Hanım replied. 'So you see to the tea, why don't you.'

Kenan stood up.

And as he did so, Cevriye Hanım turned back to Ziya. 'My child,' she said, 'we count you as one of the family. Because for years now, you have been remembered, with love, and longing, and gratitude. So please, relax, and make yourself at home.'

'Thank you,' said Ziya, looking ashamed. 'Thank you so much.'

And then, in a voice as soft as silk, Cevriye Hanım asked after his parents, and his relatives.

'I lost my parents years ago,' said Ziya. 'And quite a few of my relatives, too. They're all gone, I'm afraid. A few of my uncle's children are still with us, but we don't see much of each other. I'm not even sure where they live. It's the way things are now. Everyone's scattered.'

'I know what you mean,' said Cevriye Hanım, nodding slightly as she stared into the middle distance.

There followed a short silence.

'I know only too well,' Cevriye Hanım then said. 'This relative business, there's no way to solve it. Sometimes you crumble inside to keep the bonds alive, and sometimes you let the bonds crumble just to keep yourself together. One way or the other, it keeps most people hanging. It leaves them in the lurch. And also, we all have to suffer the same number of deaths as we have relatives. And that brings a lot of pain. And what a shame it is that there are those who only make peace with their relatives once they've lost someone. Yes, that's the way it goes. Those are the games that life plays with us. Or maybe it's the noise of life that makes us so neglectful.'

'What noise?' asked Kenan, as he placed the tea tray on the trivet.

'Oh, it's nothing,' said Cevriye Hanım. 'We're just sitting here having a friendly chat, that's all.'

Kenan smiled.

'May it continue for ever.'

Then Besim joined them. Bowing his head in embarrassment, he walked over to Ziya and held out his hand. And for a moment, Ziya thought of the son who had died in his wife's stomach. As he stood up, he felt a weakness in his knees. Grabbing the side of the table, he looked the boy over, as he thought: 'So if he had lived, he too would be a strapping young man like this by now.' As he shook the boy's hand, he felt almost as if he was touching his own son, and he shivered.

'Besim is my one and only grandchild,' said Cevriye Hanım. 'His mother and father work in Germany.'

The tulip-shaped glasses were waiting on the table now, all lined up in a row. After pouring the tea, Kenan set the tray of *gözlemes* in the centre of the table and unwrapped the cloth. Besim helped him, taking great care as he passed out the purple-patterned porcelain plates, the knives and forks and paper napkins. And then, for a time, they sat there in the shade of the mulberry tree. With a lilt to her voice, Cevriye Hanım told Ziya about her village, and her relatives; she spoke of her childhood, of days spent wandering the hyacinth-scented mountains with herds of goats, of nights in horsehair tents which rocked to the distant cries of wolves, and then she told him of the pine tree under which she had first seen her late husband. She told him how her heart had pounded, boom boom boom, and how, one spring day, she had come to be married, fully veiled atop a chestnut horse. She told him how kind and courteous and highly regarded both her late in-laws had been, how they had treated her well from the very first day, and how they had died, much too soon. How she had packed up her food each morning and slung it over her back to go and till the fields, while at the same time caring for her children in their red wooden cradles. How they had grown quickly out of their unruly childhood ways to become such lovely people. And then she talked about her eldest daughter Ayşe and her husband Fehrettin, who had left their child to go to Germany, just to earn a crust of bread, and how they had been living there for so many years now, missing their country all the while. And after she had spoken of all this, she came around to Kenan's military service.

'I'm speaking as a mother,' she said, leaning forward to look straight into Ziya's eyes. 'And I want you to know that I am eternally grateful for what you did for my son when you were in the army together.'

Ziya shot a look at Kenan.

For a moment, they came eye to eye, but Kenan lowered his head, needlessly picking up his spoon to stir his tea, as if he had only just added the sugar.

'I'm not sure I understand,' said Ziya, but when Kenan kept on stirring he looked back at Cevriye Hanım with surprise. 'What is this good thing I did for Kenan?'

Cevriye Hanım leaned back and smiled, after which she stared for a time at her napkin, misty-eyed as only the sublime can be. And all the while, that napkin's white played on her face, rippling ever so lightly across each wrinkle and crease.

'I just know,' she said. 'Refined people like you are always like this, you forget your good deeds, and even if they're not forgotten, you never speak of them. So it seems you have forgotten . . . But who knows, it could also be that you do not wish to speak of it. But in the face of such modesty, I honestly don't know what I can say now. Let's leave it there. The last thing I'd want to do would be to make you blush by embarrassing you needlessly. But I hope you'll permit me to say one last thing: I know that my son owes his life to you.'

Not knowing what to say, Ziya stared in shock at his plate.

'And today I was thinking,' Cevriye Hanım continued, 'your fate and Kenan's – they are twinned. Truly twinned. Our fates are all written by the same hand, with the same ink, to be sure, but this does not explain why your fates are twinned, I don't think. Your fates – how shall I put it – to me they look as if they were written on the same page, with the same purpose, or the same innocence, or even while dreaming the same dream. You could almost say that you came into this world to do the same thing. Look, let me do the sums: you both did your military service in the same place, and between the same dates. And then you each lost your wives. And neither of you remarried. And also, neither of you had wives who gave you children. And then, in addition to all that, and after all those years, you're both here, living in the same village. Has none of this crossed your minds?'

Kenan and Ziya exchanged glances.

'No,' said Ziya. 'I can honestly say it hasn't.'

'Me neither,' Kenan mumbled.

Cevriye Hanım looked at each in turn and smiled, nodding wisely, over and over, as if she was pulling them out of a very deep sleep.

A silence fell over them for a time.

Then, in a hoarse voice, Besim excused himself. Gently leaving his napkin at the side of his plate, he rose from the table. As he watched the boy walk towards the house, Ziya again thought he was looking at the son they had killed in his mother's belly. Reaching the door, the boy stopped in the shade of the canopy and glanced over his shoulder. And that was when Ziya noticed how much he looked like the silhouette of the young man he had seen wreathed in smoke in Binnaz Hanım's sitting room, and a shiver went through him.

'Health to your hands,' he then said, turning to Cevriye Hanım in surprise. 'Your *gözlemes* were delicious.'

'I'm glad you enjoyed them,' said Cevriye Hanım.

As she spoke, she too looked over at the door Besim had just passed through.

'Kenan may already have told you,' she said then. 'This village has just one old rickety grocery store, my boy. And nothing inside it is worth much. It doesn't even sell bread, as a matter of fact. Everyone in this village makes their own, that's why. And so, if you're going to say, "I'm not used to it, I can't eat *yufka*," then that would mean you'd have to buy your bread from town. But getting there and back, that's yet another matter. There's no regular service between town and this village, that's one thing. When the schools open, there is a clapped-out minibus that huffs and puffs its way over there arriving here at the crack of dawn, but grown-ups aren't allowed on it. There's nowhere to sit or stand in it anyway, the poor children have to huddle together like matchsticks packed inside all together. There's so little room that all their arms and legs and heads and shoulders get all mixed up. If one of those children wanted to scratch themselves, they probably wouldn't be able to find their own bodies. And with all that swaying back and forth, they'd be as bruised as ripe pears by the time they got to town. How they manage to teach them anything in that state I cannot say. And who it was who thought up this evil business of bussing children to schools, I cannot say either. A child's school should be at the other end of the street he plays in, wouldn't you say? That would allow a child to remember his school days warmly. And then, seeing as a child can always run away from school if he has a mind to do so – even if he never does, even if he always holds his pencil in the same hand, from time to time he has to see how it feels to hold it in the other, or else he'll have trouble breathing, and while he's having trouble breathing, he'll be looking at all those letters on the page. Won't he? So tell me, what's the point of it – piling those children into a metal box, and dumping them in one big lump into a concrete box. And there they stay, all day long, and when those poor children look out of that school's windows, they see strange streets that carry no memories. Not a single sly whisper, to call them back . . . But never mind. As I already said. You can't count on that minibus to get you into town and back. Once a week the Ovaköy minibus stops out there on the main road, and it picks up anyone going in for the town market, and it drops them off again around the time of the evening call to prayer. So that's the only way you can get into town, once a week. But how you'd keep your bread from going stale and mouldy in the course of that week I cannot say. What I say is that we make you *yufka* once a month. It's more supple, and all you have to do is moisten a few sheets before you eat and they're fresh as fresh.'

'Thank you,' said Ziya. 'I still haven't worked out how to manage things. If you want to know the truth, I don't really want to go into town once a week. No, I don't want that at all. But I think we'll be able to work something out, in time.'

'That's fine,' said Cevriye Hanım, 'but do keep my offer in mind. It won't be any trouble for us, just a few more sheets. My daughter and I could sit down for an hour or two and make you all the *yufka* you need for a whole month.'

There followed a short silence.

Then Ziya stood up. After thanking Cevriye Hanım and kissing her hand, he headed for the gate. 'Why don't I come with you?' said Kenan, and off the two went, walking in silence in the afternoon sun, accompanied by what might have been the faint clatter of dishes, or slippers shuffling, or childish laughter floating over the brick courtyard walls. And with these sounds came the fug of manure, rotting fruit and wet laundry. Halfway down the lane, they met a hunchbacked old man groaning under the weight of the plastic vats he was carrying from the fountain back to his donkey. As he passed them, he suddenly stopped to adjust his cap, as if ashamed to have been caught unawares; solemnly lifting his hand as high as his visor, he wished them a good day.

Ziya was still wondering what this good thing was he had done for Kenan in the army. He wanted to ask, if only Kenan would give him the chance.

'And now we have these plastic bottles,' said Kenan, waving in annoyance at the donkey behind them. 'I'm not sure if you know this, but in the old days we used wooden barrels that smelled of resin, and in each and every one of them, you could hear a whole forest rustling.'

'I know,' Ziya said.

'When I was a child,' said Kenan, leaving no time for Ziya to say any more, 'there was a bath next to this fountain we'll be coming to. Whitewashed walls on three sides, and open to the sky. They'd put these great blackened cauldrons into the oven and the water they boiled in them was laced with ash, and that's what people bathed in, that's what people used to wash their clothes. And the women beating their laundry with sticks, they'd grit their teeth, but you could still hear that strange sound they always made. Hink. Hink. Hink. And whenever they made that sound, there'd be these drops of water flying off their sticks, and as they flew through the air, each one drew its own sparkling semicircle. And with all that water flying around, the women's fronts would get wet, too, and then, of course, you'd have all those wet breasts swinging, right in front of all those boys who were fast turning into men. And every time those breasts swung, those hungry eyes swung with them. And then, when all the laundry was spread out on the hedges and the undergrowth, it would be the children's turn, and because bath time scared them, they would always kick up a fuss, or scatter like little goats or throw a tantrum, but whatever they tried, in the end it wouldn't be enough, because their mothers would take them by the arms, strip them down, and pop them into the cauldron. And then they'd go to work on them, saying, what's all this nonsense, you infidel spawn? And with each word, they would soften those children up. And then they'd beat the dirt out of them, with those sticks of theirs, and those bars of soap. They'd beat those little heads and backs till all the dirt was gone. And the sooty water would make those children's faces shine like mirrors. And the very moment their mothers let go of them, they were off, chasing after the sparrows flying up out of the dung heaps, or racing after a pedlar, if a pedlar happened to be passing through, and making an enormous ruckus. But it wasn't just pedlars with their donkeys and their big straw baskets; there were also the dyers, some days, with the yarn they'd taken from all those spinning wheels and looms and dyed white, or green, or purple, or yellow, and the tinsmiths, lugging their sacks of pots and pans from door to door, and the circumcisers that gave the children such nightmares, and the leech sellers, with their hissing bottles. The village would always somehow know when these pedlars were coming, and when they didn't, people would invent a sad story to explain it, in all innocence, of course, and then, for months, they would tell that story left, right and centre, as if it were really true. And then, at shearing time, the sheep and the goats in the pens behind some of those houses would lie down in the shadows cast by those stories, and the whirr of the shears would seep into those stories, stroke by stroke, like little scraps of yarn. And maybe something seeped out of them into those mountains over there, just behind the village. Because in those days, many of the villagers would still pack up all their belongings and take their horses and donkeys and move up to the meadows for the summer; they'd leave behind the oaks and junipers you and I saw yesterday, and on they'd go, up those thyme-scented slopes, on and on they'd go, under the swooping shadows of hawks and eagles, on and on, through the forest of the red pines, until they reached the clearing where, every summer, they set up their black tents. And the shepherds and the goatherds would take their flocks into the surrounding meadows, and how strange they looked, too, circling around and around, with those shining muskets slung from their shoulders. Floating through the rustlings of the forest you could hear bells ringing, bells the size of fists; and the milk vats, ringing with their echoes. As for the rest of us – we did the milking, we made yoghurt and we made cream, we tied cheese up into sacks, but it was almost as if all that was an excuse, almost as if what we were really doing was giving our souls some air, to spend a few months with the wind and the stars and nature's bounty. And that was why there were times when we were at one, utterly at one, with the flowers of the meadow, when even the birds seemed to chirp inside us, when the wolves and the jackals no longer called out to us from the depths of the darkness that swallowed up the pines, but from the depths of our own souls. And it would be with lighter hearts that we men and women, young and old, would walk single file down the mountain at the summer's end. And the flocks would tumble slowly down the same slopes in a cloud of bleats and dust, and soon they would be back in their old pens, and the shepherds would go back to taking them out every morning and returning them at dusk. In those days, the village didn't just have goats and sheep – we also had lots of cattle. They took up a lot of room in those pens, with their big eyes and their heavy breathing. And every morning they'd be taken out and given to a cowherd, but at the end of the day their owners wouldn't come out again to pick them up. That's because the cows could find their own way back to their owners. And the amazing thing is, not a single one ever put a foot wrong, not even once. By the time I finished primary school, people had stopped going up to the meadows, sadly. Our herds had shrunk in size by then – no one had more than a few sheep or goats, and some people converted the pens at the edge of their land into houses for the young ones, and instead of the old earthen roofs, more and more people started using tiles. In spite of all these changes, there was still a pile of manure in a corner of each courtyard, and leather patches for cracked wooden vats, and oxcarts, and candles, and threshing sledges, and prods, and spinning wheels, and chicken coops that always had foxes stalking them, and the spiced *tarhana* soup they ate for breakfast every day. And by now a lot of people had bought transistor radios, and so floating their way amongst all this we could hear Müzeyyen Senar, and Nuri Sesigüzel, and Ahmet Sezgin, and Nezahat Bayram, sending out their little clouds of heart-wrenching sorrow. I used to say they looked like decaying saddles these radios, I remember. They used to pack them so carefully in cotton-print sacks and take them with them to their fields and gardens. And then they're holding it next to their ears, saying: Oh, I hope it's not a bad winter, and then they're out there with the oxen and the donkeys, and braying just as loud. Sometimes it was because a neighbour wanted his share, and sometimes it was to make a division. Look, we've come to the end of the road.'

They were standing in front of the fountain.

Ziya looked in silence at the water rushing from the groove, and the mossy concrete trough, and the willows bordering the fountain.

'You can drink this water, can't you?' he asked.

'Of course you can,' said Kenan. 'And it doesn't taste at all bad, by the way. Look, do you see those crumbling walls back there? Those are the remains of the bath house I was telling you about.'

'But listen,' said Ziya. 'I've been wanting to ask you what that good thing was your mother mentioned just a while ago, but you haven't given me a chance to ask.'

'I know,' Kenan replied as they walked towards the shade beneath the willows. 'I could tell.'

'What could you tell?'

'That you were going to ask that question.'

They stood on the grass in the shade of the willows, face to face.

'So that explains it,' said Ziya. 'That's why you used those plastic vats as an excuse to go back to the past, to talk about whatever came into your head.'

Kenan said nothing.

'All right, then,' said Ziya. 'So tell me. What was this good deed I did for you in the army?'

'You must remember,' said Kenan, looking down in shame. 'Please don't make me tell you, please. I saw the shame in your face, when my mother brought it up; it didn't pass me by. If you ask me, it's a good time for me to introduce you to the village. Let's go to the coffeehouse and drink some tea, say hello to a few people, give them a chance to welcome you. It would look a bit strange, wouldn't it, to avoid them for too long, to stay so long out of sight.'

'You're right,' said Ziya. 'It wouldn't be right, to stay out of sight.'

Leaving the fountain and the cool shade of the willows, they walked together to the village *meydan*.

'Let's go to the Coffeehouse of Mirrors,' said Kenan. 'That's the first one we'll pass, that's why. Another time we can go to the Plane Tree Coffeehouse. They function like scales, almost. Sit down in one, and the other rises. Go to the other place, and the first one rises. That's why we all try to keep things balanced, with some of us in one, and some in the other.'

'All right, then. Let's do that,' said Ziya.

After they had walked a little further, and rounded a large turpentine tree to enter the village *meydan*, Kenan pointed out the grocery store on their left. It was a brick structure attached to a two-storey house. Its windows were painted blue, as was its door, and nailed to either side of the entrance were nets filled with brightly coloured plastic balls. Standing across the street was a group of boys exchanging sly glances.

Then one of them took a step forward. Staring through the door and into the darkness beyond, and in a husky voice, he yelled: 'Boys! Tell me what that lazy grocer does?'

Clapping their hands, they answered as a chorus. 'The lazy grocer weighs his balls!' they shouted. 'The lazy grocer weighs his balls!'

Rising to his feet, and rushing to the door, Ramazan the Grocer cried out, 'One step closer, and I'll smash your face in!' He stood there glaring at the boys. But when he saw Kenan and Ziya, he was as ashamed as if he had been the one to be shouting about lazy grocers who weighed their balls – as ashamed as if he had actually been inside, weighing them.

And then, in a dreary voice still coloured by that shame, he turned to Ziya and said, 'Welcome to our village.'

Without waiting for an answer, he turned to Kenan and, waving at the children who had escaped his grasp, he cried, 'They're crazy, those boys. Crazy! If it keeps on like this, I'll wring their necks one day, I swear!'

Kenan and Ziya both smiled at him.

They reached the Coffeehouse of Mirrors, with its trellis and its oilcloth-covered tables. Husam the waiter was standing by the door. Settling themselves at a table in the shade, they asked him to bring them two glasses of strong tea. Ziya was worried that everyone was going to pounce on him and braced himself for a rush of questions, but that was not what happened. The villagers who stood up to come over to him one by one simply smiled and said welcome and returned to their seats, and whether they'd been drinking tea beforehand, or talking, or playing cards, they just picked up where they'd left off.

Just then, Kâzım the Bellows Man rushed into the village *meydan*. Walking straight over to their table, he reached out to wrap both his hands around Ziya's, and there he remained, bowing and scraping and smiling broadly and shaking Ziya's hand as if they'd been friends for forty years. And as he did so, he said, 'I've been whiling my time away at the Plane Tree all afternoon, and God be my witness, I didn't see you until just now. I hope you will excuse me!' His eyes swept across the coffeehouse, like a child who has just been called to the front of the class to recite a poem; after greeting everyone there, he sat down at their table without waiting for an invitation. And at that moment, the atmosphere changed. Everyone perked up, as if Kâzım had come to make an important announcement. Slowly, very slowly, they put down their cards, and stopped speaking, and turned their creaking chairs in his direction. They watched him in silence, with bulging eyes. Oppressed and greatly annoyed by this attention, Ziya gave evasive answers to the intrusive questions Kâzım now asked him without preamble. And then, thinking that this man might give up asking questions if he paid him no attention, Ziya let his eyes travel over the other men in the coffeehouse. And so, for a while, he looked at their shoulders, their feet, and the hands sitting on their knees; then he looked at the chins they had cupped with their hands, and their wrinkled foreheads, and the suppressed curiosity playing in their eyes. Then, for a time, he looked at their prayer beads, and their tea glasses, and the smoke rising from their cigarettes. He looked at the raggedy old man who was sitting by himself in the sun, scratching the earth with his staff. Sensing Ziya's eyes on him, the old man turned around abruptly to stare at him from behind his beard. Then he stretched out one of his feet and erased whatever it was he had been writing, passed a quick hand over his face, lowered his head into his chest, and fell asleep. Or rather, he fell silent, while a sleep as old as the ages drew him under.

After watching him slip away like that, Ziya turned back to Kenan. 'Shall we go now?'

Excusing themselves to Kâzım and the other villagers, they got up and left.

The old man woke up as they passed. Raising his head, he grabbed Ziya by the wrist and pulled him towards him with a friendly smile. For a moment, they locked eyes, saying nothing.

'So what's this all about?' the man said, reproachfully. 'Aren't we going to have a chance to talk?'

'We will,' said Ziya.

'May you go in health and happiness,' said the old man. 'When you're bored, come and find me, and we can sit and talk.'

Ziya nodded in agreement.

And then the old man's face went sour. His eyes bored into Ziya's, as if to measure his discomfort. Then he stood up and, hanging on Ziya's arm, pulled him a few steps back

'Do you know what?' he said then. 'Don't ever say I didn't warn you on the day you came, but you're a city person. Stay here too long and your teeth will crumble.'

Ziya stood there looking at him, and said nothing.

'You know why?' the old man continued. 'Because a man's teeth come to resemble him. I know what I'm saying, and that's why I say it. That's why I just told you – come back when you're bored, and we can talk.'

'All right,' said Ziya. 'I will.'

Then Kenan took hold of his other arm and pulled him away. Leaving the old man to the sun, they walked off, side by side.

'Hulki Dede always talks like that,' said Kenan, when they were some distance away. 'He's the strangest man in the village. There's no knowing what he'll do next. Sometimes he refuses to say a word, for instance. He'll just walk through the village like a black cloud, saying nothing. Or he'll take a little sack of bread and go off to some corner, rest his staff on his knees, and stare miserably at the world around him, saying nothing. He flutters his eyes as if he's praying, he looks at the mountains, and the birds, and the children, and the clouds and the wind, as if he's chanting a prayer. And in the meantime, the bread sack at his knees fills up with ants.

But he doesn't so much as give these ants a look. Like I just said, he's in some sort of trance. He's looking into the world beyond. And after this has gone on for days and days, Hulki Dede comes back, and then suddenly he's making these big pronouncements and speaking out of turn, and it's almost as if he were trying to make up for all that silence. And you know what? The first time you hear them, the things he says sound crazy. But once those crazy words of his have been planted in your mind for a while, once they've been out in the world and met up with other words or just taken in a bit of their steam, well, it's almost like magic, they begin to change before your eyes. Once they've found their place in the world, they gain something. They gain meaning. I don't know, maybe that's just how it seems.'

'So tell me,' said Ziya. 'Who is this Kâzım who came to our table to give us such a warm welcome? Is he your relative?'

'No,' said Kenan. 'We're not related to Kâzım the Bellows Man. But he's a good man. He's always ready to help, and he's unbelievably kind and honest. No matter who it is, if there's anyone in the village needing help, he's the first to race over. Even if his own two hands were bleeding, he'd come to help. He'd never say it to my face, not now, but he also loves me dearly. He'd move heaven and earth.'

Ziya said nothing.

When they reached the edge of the village, Kenan gave his watch a quick glance. Once again, he said he had important business to attend to and would not be able to come out as far as the barn.

'You mustn't treat me like a guest,' said Ziya. 'There's no need for you to come, anyway. I am fine to go alone.'

They smiled at each other.

'There was that pigeon,' he said then. 'You know, the one that landed on the roof of the Seyrantepe guardhouse. Do you remember?'

'No, I don't,' said Kenan, shaking his head.

'How can you not remember?' said Ziya in a plaintive voice. 'Can't you remember pointing it out to me, when we were drawing water from the well to do our laundry?'

'I may well have done that, but I can't remember,' said Kenan.

Ziya fell silent. Biting his lower lip, as if to soften his disappointment, he gazed for a long time into the distance.

'Never mind,' he said in a tense voice. 'I forgot to tell you this, but in my dream the other night, I saw that same pigeon.'

Uncertain what to say, Kenan stared blankly over Ziya's shoulder, searching the sky as if he could see his whole past there, fading into nothingness.

'I remember now,' he said then. 'I do! I honestly do!'

Ziya searched his friend's face, as if to ask, 'Do you really? Or are you just saying that to please me?'

But when he spoke, it was to say, 'Right, so that was the pigeon that visited me the other night in my dream, and it didn't just visit, it smashed through my landlady's window and made a big commotion.'

'That's how dreams are,' said Kenan.

'Don't say that,' Ziya said. He was suddenly serious. 'What's happening is that this bird is following me.'

'Why?'

Slowly, very slowly, Ziya sat down on the mound next to the road. He looked tired and frightened, all of a sudden: the lines on his face seemed deeper. The light had gone out of his eyes.

Kenan went and crouched down next to him.

'Do you want to know why that bird is following me?' Ziya said, lowering his voice. 'It's because forty-two years ago, I killed a little bird, and well, you're the first person I've ever told. I was never good at aiming, and so I still can't understand how I killed it. Maybe it was just a terrible once-in-a-thousand-years coincidence. I just don't know. This bird I'm telling you about – I'd been running through the woods that day, and it suddenly appeared, right in front of me. You should have seen it. So tiny, so sweet, and so silent. And you could feel it echoing inside. Like it was your heart, your liver, your spleen, or your kidneys, like – I don't know. It just echoed, everywhere inside you. It just gathered itself inside you, this bird, calm as calm. And there, in the speck-led shade, was that little face, as radiant as a calm and distant lake. You would almost think it was watching us from another world, this bird, watching us and judging. From the moment I set eyes on it, this bird stole my heart. Was it love? I'm not sure. It was something more like reverence. Or some kind of trance. Yes, as young as I was, and for all the tumult going on around me, I saw something I had never seen before and it shone a light on me that pierced the depths of my soul. And that's why I couldn't move. I just stood there, without saying a word. And by then I was very frightened. I was frightened because of all those other boys running through the woods with their slings who would kill this little bird without a single thought. I feared for this little bird. I don't know. Maybe I killed the bird so that no one else could. Because, yes, in the end I killed it. I wasn't able to stop myself, and I killed it . . . And as soon as I did, I saw what a big mistake I had made. And after that, I couldn't stay there any longer. I turned back at once. I ran back into town, panting and sweating all the way.'

Ziya fell silent for a time, and his breathing was as heavy as if he was still running back into town.

'Do you know what?' he said then. 'Maybe what I killed that day was more than just that bird.'

'Then what was it?' Kenan asked.

'How can I be sure?' Ziya asked. 'It was like an electric current, this enormous current sending one image after another, coursing through me, and maybe that was what I killed, thinking it was a bird. I recognised it in passing, and I killed it. And then its little body fell into the grass, but its soul has followed me for ever after. Wherever I look, it's always there, hovering just beyond my lashes. Year in, year out. Sometimes it's a shadow, sometimes a silhouette. Or a leaf, or a sock, or anything else that might happen to be the length of a hand. And then, when it's chased me for a while, it begins to expand: if it's started out like a baby sparrow, it will grow to the size of a pigeon, given time. It might not stop there. I just can't know. All I know is that wherever I go, it follows me.'

'If you ask me, you're exaggerating again,' said Kenan. 'What's done is done. Like all children, you did something thoughtless once upon a time. Where's the sense in judging that child after forty-two years? And anyway, why should that bird's soul want to follow you?'

'I'm not judging that child after forty-two years. I started forty-two years ago, and I've been judging him ever since.'

After glancing quickly at the watch on his left wrist, Kenan said, 'I understand. But the pigeon on the roof of that guardhouse wasn't looking at you, as I recall. It was looking at all that activity around the well, or the graves just beyond it. Or Syria.'

'You're mistaken,' said Ziya sadly. 'Even when that pigeon was looking at Syria, it was really looking at me. And when it was looking at those graves, it was looking at me, too. I swear to you. Wherever it looked, it was also looking at me. When I was standing guard at the observation tower, it would keep flying in and out. It would land on that rusty balcony and fix its eyes on me, and stare. It would stay there all day, baking in that angry sun.'

Kenan said nothing. He just stared at Ziya, in the way someone might stare at a little child who is lost to his daydreams.

'You shouldn't fret about things like this,' he said, as he rose to his feet. 'I hope you don't mind, but I need to go now, to see to that business.'

Ziya stood up, too, and after they had said their goodbyes, he headed across the plain down the dirt road that would take him back to the barn.

That evening, he sat for many hours on the bench outside the barn. He drank tea after tea, and smoked cigarette after cigarette, and watched the mountains sink slowly into the dusk, until at last they were lost to a night as black and thick as ink. But now and then, a star pierced through it, and each little pinprick seemed smaller than the last. From the village came the dim glow of its two streetlamps, and the lights of the houses on its edge. And that was all that could be seen: the stars, the streetlamps, and a few dim lights. From one end to the other, the sky was dark and still. But floating through this black silence was a moist current that ran green.

And the silence itself went in waves, down corridors, and through doors, and there were times when Ziya could almost feel it entering inside him, to take him over. And then he thought about that first silence, the silence that was never to return, and – almost as if there were someone sitting with him – whispered, 'But really. What was that silence really, I wonder?' And then, for a time, he wondered if all the silences that had come afterwards were no more than fragments of that first silence, fallen from the sky. He thought about how big these silences could be, and how small, and then he thought how each one was different. Anxious as a child, he made a list: there were wet silences, and deep silences, light silences, and heavy silences, distant silences, pregnant silences, and warm silences. Then, all of a sudden, he thought of Besim's silence, and for a few minutes he held his breath, as he conjured him up again, there in the shade of the mulberry tree. Then he stood up and, with his tea glass in one hand, and his ashtray in the other, he looked into the black night for a moment, before heading inside. After leaving his things on the kitchen counter, he went straight to bed. The moment his head hit the pillow, he shut his eyes, turned his back on all the thoughts shimmering in his mind, and tried to go to sleep. He wanted to get up early the next morning and take a long solitary walk into the mountains. Or rather, what he wanted more than the long walk was to surround himself with nature, and its beauties. He wanted to cleanse himself in its gaze, and in its soul. He wanted to breathe the same air as the trees and the grass and the rocks, and walk with the insects, and if he could find it – if he could find a space of time great enough, resting in the shadows of those rustling leaves – he wanted to lose himself inside it.

But in the end, Ziya did not wake up as early as he had hoped; by the time he opened his eyes, the sun had already risen over the cliffs, and it had done more than that, it had already risen a spear's length above them. And that was why Ziya used a teabag instead of brewing a whole pot for his breakfast, so that he could get going without further delay. He'd not got around to slicing any tomatoes or cucumbers, and neither had he boiled an egg. All he ate with that taste-less tea was some cheese and bread. As soon as he'd finished his tea, he got up and cleared the table. He was just leaving the house with his cigarettes and lighter when he saw Besim.

The boy was holding two five-litre plastic bottles of water. He'd stopped a few paces in front of the doorway, and now he was staring shyly at the door.

Ziya felt both happy and upset at the sight of him. He ran over to him at once to take the bottles from his hands and set them on the ground. In a fatherly voice, he said, 'You shouldn't have gone to all this trouble. I could have carried my own water, once I'd run out.'

With a faint and timid smile, Besim said, 'It's no trouble at all.'

His voice was smooth, and as bright as the hair that fell over his face. And that was why Ziya just stood there staring next to the plastic bottles. Or rather, he stood there because he had no idea how to act, confronted with an innocence so natural. 'It would be fine if I don't take that walk today,' he thought. And then suddenly, he was asking Besim if he'd had any breakfast. Hearing that he had, but wishing the boy to stay on for a while, instead of going straight back to the vil-lage, Ziya told a lie. 'I'm afraid to say I've just woken up,' he said. 'I still haven't had breakfast myself.'

Besim looked at him in silence.

'So let me brew some good strong tea,' Ziya said. 'And let's take the table outside, so that you and I can sit across from each other, and have a good breakfast!'

'I've already eaten,' Besim said again.

'So what,' said Ziya, in a determined voice. 'You can sit down and have a glass of tea, at least. Look, you've just carried out those huge bottles for me. Won't you let me offer you a tea, at least?'

Besim still looked uncertain.

As Ziya said, 'Will you accept my offer?' he gave him a good, long look.

'No, thank you,' said Besim. 'My uncle has gone to see Uncle Cevval, and I need to be at home by the time he gets back.'

His hopes dashed, Ziya had no idea what to say. He made a few more attempts to keep the boy from leaving, but he was unable to persuade him. So instead he just stood there, unblinking, as Besim made his way back down the hill, and there was a moment when he had to swallow hard. And when he did so, it was because he was reliving that moment in the bookshop sixteen years ago, as violently as if it were happening for the first time; once again, the floor of the shopping centre buckled, and sheets of glass went smashing through the air, and suddenly all was darkness. And then Ziya picked up the plastic bottles, and carried them through that darkness. Not knowing where else to put them, he left them on the kitchen counter. He went outside and lit a cigarette, and thought about the walk he'd been planning, before all this happened. And then he set off.

5

The Border

Until he reached the dirt road on the plain, Ziya kept changing his mind about what direction he would take. But when he got there, he did not pause. He let the sheep pens and the poplars fall away to his right as he climbed up into the brown hills, and he kept up his speed even when he reached the high grass. He was walking as fast as if he hoped never to return. Once again, he heard the faint clacking of grouse somewhere near him; he saw the branches shudder with a nameless warmth, and he saw the trail that these shudders left behind them as they rose from those branches to flutter through the air. Then he walked for forty-five or maybe fifty minutes across that plain lined with junipers and all its yellow-headed, pink-headed, purple-headed brambles. By now he was struggling for breath, so he stopped in the shade of a large oak tree to take a short rest. And just then he heard a rustling in the leaves above, and as it rained down, he could feel something settle inside him. And once he'd sat down, he passed his hand over the grass. Then he did it again. And yet again, caressing this grass as gently as if he feared causing it harm. Then he passed his hand over the rocks. He touched the ground, too. He planted his hand on it and left it there, as if to measure the earth's pulse. After that, he lit a cigarette, and narrowing his eyes he gazed for a long time through the clouds of his own smoke at the hills and plains below. The dirt road had vanished, of course, and all he could see in the depths behind the juniper trees were the ash-coloured tips of the poplars and, here and there, a roof. Beyond these he could see the mountains, so faint and flat that they might have been sketched with a pencil.

And so that's how it was that day, and as Ziya sat there smoking, letting his eyes wander from field to hill, and roof to mountain, he thought again about what good deed he might have done for Kenan in the army. He went back through his memories, scouring each for clues, but to his consternation he found nothing. Then he stubbed out his cigarette and continued on his way, but still he couldn't stop wondering what that good deed might have been. As he left the oak forest to wander amongst the red pines that reached up, moaning, to the sky, as he padded over the path carpeted with yellowing pine needles, and climbed the hills, scaled the steep rock faces, and crossed the limpid, bubbling brooks, he kept asking himself: I wonder what good deed I did. What was that good deed I did? I wonder.

And so that's what he did that day. As he thought about his days in the army, he went deeper and deeper into the forest. And soon he was far, far from the village, and with this forest stretching endlessly in all directions, groaning and moaning, clicking and clucking, and taunting him with visions. He'd see a hill just ahead, for example, or a brook close enough for him to hear its waters burbling, or a clearing surrounded by majestic pines, awaiting him in plain view, but no matter how hard he tried, he couldn't reach them. But there were other times when he saw a cliff so far away he'd think, no, I could never get that far, but then, at just that moment, he would suddenly find himself rushing forward, at an impossible speed. And when he reached that cliff, he would stop, exalted, to catch his breath, and he'd think about how quickly he'd come this far, and as he looked around him, he'd ask himself: am I really here? And that was when he sensed a playful hand he could not see, reaching out to him from a distance he could not measure. But his faith in himself and the natural world began to falter, and the more it faltered, the more fearfully he looked around him. And then, without warning, he was walking into darkness. A silence descended. A humid silence, pierced with thorns. The great pines had merged into a single mass, and their intertwined branches had blocked out the sun, but now and again, a ray would burst through, and as he watched this dazzling shaft of light travel downwards, he wondered if it was divine. By now the darkness was seeping out from every orifice to wrap itself around the trunks of the pine trees and to tie up their branches. And Ziya was walking blind through this darkness, in which each leaf quivered. And with each new step, he asked himself what this good deed was that he'd done for Kenan.

And it was while he was walking along like this that he suddenly found himself back in the sunlight. The forest had vanished, and somehow – he had no idea how – he found himself standing at the side of the asphalt road that went from Silvan to the Malabadi Bridge. It was scorchingly hot, and standing before him, looking like the source of all that heat, was a tired blue minibus. It began to move away, and that was when he saw the battalion guardhouse on the other side of the road. There was a soldier on guard; his eyes were shaded by his helmet, but still Ziya could feel the hardness of his gaze. He didn't see danger, this soldier. It was more as if someone had suddenly presented him with a hideous picture, leaving him with no choice but to kill that hideousness with his stare.

Then he waved. 'What are doing, just standing there, you fool? Come when I call you.'

With a sinking heart, Ziya slowly crossed the road.

'Put that bag on the ground,' said the soldier coldly. 'Open the zip!'

Ziya did as he was told.

His eyes fixed on the bag, the soldier said, 'You think you're coming to a five-star hotel, do you? Well, you can stick this up your cunt! Whatever we bring here, we carry on our backs!'

Ziya did not know what to think.

First the soldier poked through his laundry with the barrel of his rifle. In spite of himself, Ziya leaned over at this point, too, to watch the barrel of that rifle poking at his pants and socks and vests and pushing them from one side of the bag to the other.

'What's this?' he asked, poking at the black plastic bag in the corner.

'It's my hair,' Ziya said.

'Your hair, is it? So tell me, boy,' said the soldier in a mocking voice. 'Where did you get your hair cut?'

'In Diyarbakır.'

'And then you didn't have the heart to throw it away, so you asked the barber to give it back, and put it into this bag. Am I right?'

Ziya said nothing.

'I've asked you a question, boy!' the soldier roared. 'Are you waiting for the sergeant major's horse to fart?'

'Yes, you're right,' said Ziya. 'I didn't have the heart to throw it away.'

'I didn't have the heart to throw it away, *sir*!'

'I didn't have the heart to throw it away, sir.'

'So now. Take that hair of yours, and take it over to that dustbin on the other side of the road there, and toss it in. Now!'

Ziya rushed over to the bin, tossed his hair away, and came back.

The soldier was waiting for him. He seemed to have grown in stature. He was holding his rifle crossways.

'Now pick up your bag and go inside,' he said, in a voice so harsh it almost slapped him across the face.

Ziya did not want to pick up his bag just then. He wanted to kick it high in the air, and send it flying far away, to a place no one knew, but of course he did no such thing. He had no choice but to bend down slowly, pick up the bag, and walk on to the grey building between the trees.

'Keep walking, oh bird of God!' the soldier shouted after him. 'Keep walking!'

Ziya shot a look over his shoulder. As far away as he was, the soldier in the guardhouse seemed even taller than before. And it seemed to Ziya as if he was no longer walking up and down the guardhouse's concrete porch. He was walking up and down his own greatness.

All the way to the building, those words echoed painfully inside him. 'Keep walking, oh bird of God!' Then he caught sight of the men waiting to the left of the building, holding bags of all colours, and he crossed the large, sandy courtyard to join them. Actually, he did not join them, he kept himself slightly apart, but even so they pulled him into their silence. And there he stood at the edge of that crowd, with those hundreds of men waiting tensely, clutching their bags, looking as helpless as a flock of lost sparrows. They started telling people where they were from, and if there were five of them from the same city, they formed their own group, and talked amongst themselves. And little by little, these conversations spread, and as the scorching sun beat down on them, their voices rose and fell. Then a fat-legged, fat-assed sergeant appeared at the door of the grey building. Strutting down to stand before them, he raised his eyes to the sky and waited, unmoving, for all those voices to die down. The young men didn't know how to read him, though, and so they continued talking, as casually as they could in such a situation. But that was when the sergeant let out a bellow that seemed to come from his eyes as well as his mouth. 'Silence, you fools! Before you turn this place into a girls' bathroom. Silence!'

The new recruits fell silent.

And then this sergeant launched into a never-ending speech. One short, cold sentence after another. What they had to do. How they were to behave. And then, after glancing at his watch, he ordered them to line up two by two, no matter what size they were. At once! No one knew what to do when they heard that, so some went running right and left, some stayed put, some backed up until they bumped into someone, and there were even some who pulled the person next to them by the arm, as if they were having a fight. Meanwhile the sergeant just stood there looking sternly at his watch. After a minute had passed, he turned back to the building, taking this crowd with him, to lead them down a gloomy corridor with grey double doors on either side, while he strutted and swayed as affably as if he were leading those behind him to inherit the earth. But by now the new recruits were wary of speaking too loudly, and that's why they looked around them carefully before exchanging whispers. And soon these whispers had melted into their footsteps, creating an odd noise that the corridor seemed to compress, making it sound more menacing than it really was. And that was when one of the doors along the corridor cracked open, and out came a huge, frowning, buttoned-up sergeant, and no sooner had he come out than he set upon the crowd, kicking and beating all who stood in his way with a ferocity that knew no bounds. And all the while he bellowed, 'Who do they think they are, these shameless louts! You think you can make noise like that in here? You think we'll put up with noise like that?' When he heard the commotion, the sergeant at the front came back, of course. Jumping up as high as he could, he set about beating up anyone in his reach. And with all this confusion, it wasn't long before everyone was getting hit, even the silent and defeated ones who were cowering in the middle. Those not yet inside had no idea what had caused this uproar, which ended as suddenly as it had begun; they just stood there craning their necks, trying to see over the other recruits' shoulders.

In the face of all this, even those who had escaped a beating felt angry, but no one wished to invite trouble on their very first day, so no one spoke. Ziya said nothing either. He just went into the depot, purple-faced, and when it was his turn, he picked up his uniform, went up to the dormitory on the third floor and, as quickly as he could, he got dressed. Putting the clothes he'd brought with him into a white plastic bag, he handed it to the orderlies who were waiting at the door and would post them back to his father. Then off he strode towards the stairs, and he was just about to head down when he caught a glimpse of himself in the mirror to the left, and what he saw shocked him. Because the man staring out at him, with his clown costume and his cap pulled down over his ears, seemed like someone else altogether. Especially those trousers, which looked like sacks, and those huge combat boots, and that expression of surprise on his face – here was a clown who could make you laugh until you cried. And that was why Ziya didn't look at him too long. To keep from looking, he fairly flew down those concrete steps.

Early the next morning, they assembled on the field that ran alongside the mess hall, and here they learned that a squad was made up of ten men, which with the leader made eleven. Four squads made a platoon, and four platoons made a company. After they were told all this, they were told to step out of line to make new lines. And in this new line, they took account of differences in size, of course. They shuffled the recruits about, keeping some in the squads where they were and moving others. The stub-nosed sergeant in charge of Ziya's platoon was more particular about this business than the other sergeants. He would stand to one side and close one eye and give each squad a long, hard look, calculating and recalculating every last millimetre of difference, and then he'd race around, saying, no, that's not the right place for you, boy, not the right place at all, and he'd change them around. And then he'd race around again, anxiously inspecting the whole platoon. And then he came up to Ziya. 'This is not the right place for you,' he said. And he pulled him by the arm and put him into the second row of the second squad, and then, for a moment, he just stood there, giving him a very odd look.

'Why did he look at you like that?' asked the dark and scrawny man in the third row.

'I don't know,' said Ziya.

'My name is Kenan,' said the man in a soft voice.

Ziya told him his name.

The ones in the first row had no interest in them; they just jutted out their chins, casting sidelong glances. It was as if they had done their military service many times over and were just back this time to watch. They would look around the yard as if they owned it, and then grimace, and then do that odd thing with their chins again, jutting them in the air.

Once the companies had been formed, and lined up neatly, the company commander emerged from the mess hall, two stars sparkling on each shoulder. With measured steps, he went to stand before them, and, propping his hands on his haunches, he delivered a long speech. In a haughty voice, he spoke to them of discipline, and responsibility, and equipment, and weapons, and honour, and how even new-born orphans had the right to a cap of water, and then, in a voice clouded by reproach, he spoke of the nation's noble lands, and he named the various conspiracies threatening national integrity, and he located their centres of operation, both at home and abroad. And then he went on to speak of their sacred duty to the nation, and of failing that duty, and of loyalty to the army. And then, leaning lightly to one side, in the manner of a great hero, he spoke most solemnly about glorious chapters of history, and of the victories that had been written in gold in those pages, and of the illustrious generals who had won those victories, whereupon he turned his head once more, to speak again about the importance of discipline. Opening his arms wide, as if to embrace the entire company, he exclaimed, 'Welcome to the prophet's hearth, my children, let us see what you have in you! Take care not to shame our forefathers in their graves, or your mothers and fathers, or me!'

And with those words, they embarked on their three months of training.

From the first day, Ziya hated the food they made there: for there was no taste to it, and every plate and dish was ringed with oil that slopped about like petrol. And that was why he and Kenan and several others stayed away from the mess hall. They just couldn't get used to it. But it wasn't easy, going to the canteen for biscuits or cakes. Because no one stood in line there. It was always mobbed – a great khaki crowd pressing against the glass, pushing and shoving, and in the end, hardly anyone could buy anything. And then the soldier in charge of the canteen had such a hard time taking orders in all that commotion that he was always getting them wrong, and in the end he would just stand there, his arms upraised, like some picture pasted to the wall. Ziya joined that crowd just once, and from then on he never went back to it during mealtimes. And after that, he and Kenan would go out to the barbed wire behind the almond trees at meal-times. Because at mealtimes, the other side was full of children from Silvan, swinging their straw baskets, selling boiled eggs, green onions, and flatbread. And sometimes they'd bring out yoghurt in muslin-covered wooden buckets and pewter or copper pots that still carried the warmth of their homes. They would lift them over the barbed wire, and in voices so dark they seemed to scrape your very insides, they would say, 'Would you like some yoghurt, sir soldier? Would you like some yoghurt?' And the more they asked, the higher their voices. That was because the sergeants came out sometimes, to tell them they weren't allowed to sell anything, and then to beat them up. But the children would run away so fast and if their plastic shoes flew off their feet, they just left them there, lying in the grass. After they'd been chased away like that, fear would keep them away for a few days, and for a few days, quite a few soldiers would go hungry. But then one warm morning, their little faces would appear again across the barbed-wire fence, and once again they'd be calling out in those husky voices of theirs, selling boiled eggs, green onions, and flatbread.

Except that they never came to the barbed-wire fence at breakfast time, these children: when the company straggled back from their morning exercise session in one great cloud of sweat, these soldiers had no choice but to file into the mess hall to drink their tea – or their soup, if that was what they were serving that day. Each morning, after callisthenics, they would set their rifles down on the field and strip to the waist, to walk back and forth with the sergeants leading them, and then, when their muscles had heated up a little, they would turn towards the Malabadi Bridge, singing folk songs as they ran, and as soon as they caught up with their instructors, they made a great arc, turning towards the Koçaş mountains, to run lap after lap in the training ground at the foot of those blue-grey cliffs, and then they would run back, by the same route, arriving in an exhausted state outside the mess hall, where they'd left their rifles. The mess squad would already have laid out their soups or teas, with a piece of bread to one side. When everyone had piled inside, their sweat would steam it up, of course; and as they sat in that narrow, low-ceilinged room, they would struggle to breathe. After breakfast, they would walk in quick time back to the training field at the foot of the Koçaş mountains, singing marching songs as they went. When they got there, they would line up and wait for the second lieutenant to inspect their company; planting his hands on his hips, he would walk back and forth, nodding now and again, as if agreeing to whatever his invisible companion was telling him, and then he would stop abruptly, and turn on his heels, and then he'd subject his men to a long, hard stare, while his expression grew steadily stranger. As if he was not just inspecting them for himself, but for the company command, and all the other commanders, in the name of the nation, and all that was inside it, as well as outside it, and probably even in the name of its enemies and friends.

Then he would look down, this lieutenant, and smile slyly, and when he raised his head again, he would bark: 'Yes, I can see that you all shaved last night, you all shaved last night, didn't you?'

'Yes, sir, we shaved last night,' the men would reply.

The lieutenant would be overjoyed to hear this answer, and his sly smile would stretch so wide as to take in all the other companies, and the training field, too.

Then the lieutenant would lean back slightly and bellow: 'Bravo! You managed to shave, like every other idiot bachelor in the world, and every man idiotic enough to get married!'

He would say this with great delight each morning, as if it was the greatest punchline in the world.

It pained Ziya to see how much pleasure this miserable lieutenant took from laughing at the helpless soldiers lined up before him, and because he was afraid this man might read his feelings, he stood at attention, averting his eyes. At the same time, it seemed to him that this man was hiding in the shadow of the metal star on each of his shoulders; that he should choose such a simple way to ridicule the men lined up before him was proof that he was wretched and afraid. So when the training began, he couldn't stop himself from looking at this lieutenant whenever the opportunity arose. The lieutenant would step away from the sergeants drilling them and watch them from a distance; planting his hands on his hips he would stroll around the edges of the field, giving every impression of entertaining deep thoughts, and every once in a while, he would allow himself a sly smile; but never for long. Or rather, it was never long before the lieutenant's spirits plunged. And that was when he fell into a strange displeasure, this lieutenant; unable to shake it off, he would stop in his tracks. Arms akimbo, he would look more closely at the men in the field, and looking more closely he would spot a number of faults. Whereupon his hands would rise from his hips to fly through the air like angry arrows, of course, as he called each wrongdoer to account. This one had his cap crooked. That one had fallen to the ground in the required way but had stood up incorrectly. And that one over there was holding his rifle like a shepherd's musket, and when he thrust his bayonet forward, he had failed to keep to the rhythm of the chant: *Strike! Lion! Mehmet! Strike!* One by one, he laid into them. Showing no mercy. He kicked them with all his strength, actually. Kicked them and punched them, until they were bleeding from the nose and the mouth, and then he would relax and say, 'Ohh,' a very deep 'Ohhhh,' and, putting his hands back on his hips, he would walk away, very slowly, with a spring to his step.

But there were times when even this routine did not bring him peace of mind. And then he would inspect the cartridge belts and cartridge pouches, the canteens and the combat boots, and everywhere he looked, he found more faults. Then he would punish the whole company with hours of press-ups, and send them all on a low crawl from one end of that dusty field to the other, and if that wasn't enough, he would cry, 'March! March!' And send them running up the Koçaş mountains. And the whole company would leave the training field holding their rifles crosswise and climb up to the middle of those grey-blue cliffs, and as they jumped like goats from rock to rock they kept looking over their shoulders, kept listening for the next instruction, but the lieutenant would just stand there, refusing to give the order to stop. And so the company would keep climbing up those burning rocks, following in the footsteps of the great mountain bandits, maybe, and when they were high enough up to be sure they were out of earshot, they sent a shower of curses raining down on that lieutenant. Donkey, son of a donkey, some said. Asshole, said others. Lowlife. Prick. And some lowed like cows, almost, letting out a string of curses, the veins in their neck bulging until they were thick as rolling pins. And sometime after all that, the lieutenant would give the order to stop, but, knowing that his voice would not carry that far up, he would have to face the cliff and flap his arms. And then the men would stop short, every one of them. As if they had actually heard him bark, 'About turn! March!' And down they would go, jumping from rock to rock as fast as their legs could carry them. As he watched them coming down, their bodies spent and steaming, their great tongues hanging, and their faces almost lost inside the clouds of their own breath, the lieutenant would permit himself a happy smile. And then he would resume his stroll around the edges of the training ground, nodding now and again in agreement with his invisible companion, stopping here and there to kick a few soldiers. But not because they'd done anything wrong. It was almost as if he kicked them so as to understand why he did so.

Once, while attacking an imaginary target with his bayonet, Ziya let his eyes slide away from it, and for this the lieutenant punched him. This happened on the seventh day of training, and they were lined up across the field, and thrusting their bayonets into the gut of the body they had been instructed to see in the emptiness before them, and when they jumped back, they made sure to twist their weapons in that gut, as they had been taught to do, to ensure that the wound was deadly. The lieutenant was far away just then, a lofty ghost, lost to his own thoughts. But then, it was like he'd been teleported. Suddenly he was there, next to Ziya, to punch him. 'Look the enemy in the face, you stupid ox!' he screamed. 'Look the enemy in the face!' When he was gone, the stub-nosed sergeant came over and in a gentle voice, he tried to comfort him. 'Let it go, Baba,' he said. 'Grit your teeth and let it go.' But his words were no comfort. For the rest of the day, Ziya hung his head, disgraced. He couldn't even look at Kenan. When they spoke, he averted his eyes. It was as if he could still hear the punch ringing in his ears. All day long, they burned. The sergeant must have been watching him from a distance, because after supper, when Ziya was sitting under the almond trees, he came to talk to him again. Crouching down, and putting a gentle, brotherly hand on his shoulder, he tried to comfort him again. 'You're not still thinking about that business, are you? Let it go, my boy. Put it out of your mind.'

He was an interesting man, this sergeant – everything he did was exactly as the regulations stipulated, but he never got mixed up in any of those stupid games. If they were on the training ground, advancing with the bayonets, on an army of imaginary enemies, and he saw the men were tired, for example, he would cry out, 'Air raid! Air raid! Down!' And at once the men would throw themselves on to the ground, face down. And as he went around doing his inspection, the sergeant would whisper to the men on the ground. 'Go on then,' he would say, in a voice full of kindness. 'Get some rest while the lieutenant's back is turned.' And then he would continue on his way, making as if to check each and every one of them, but actually telling them a few dirty jokes, and after that he would say, 'And let this be a lesson to you, when you're breaking a rule, and you want to make sure no one notices, there is no better way than this. And that's my advice to you. Wherever you go in life, make sure to lie low, because if you don't, that fat-assed, many-headed jailer we call society will burn you good.' And sometimes, when he made the whole company sit down, while one of their number read from the United Infantry Manual, known to them as the ST 7-10B, he would suddenly lift up his hand to silence him, and, looking dreamily into the distance, this sergeant would mumble, 'Did you know you had an aunt, waiting for me to return to Izmir Karşıyaka?' And then he would nod at the rifle sitting next to him, and say, 'As soon as I'm rid of this murderous thingumajig they call the G–3 infantry rifle, I'm going to marry that aunt of yours.' And then he'd take a long, deep breath.

And that breath of his was so deep that it almost seemed to pull the sea itself away from Izmir Karşıyaka, and with the sea, the seagulls' cries. And then, at the foot of the Koçaş mountains, they would see sparkling blue white-tipped waves, and passing over these waves they would see vessels of all colours, chugging happily back and forth. And then, they would see her, see her so very clearly. Waiting beneath the palm trees, stepping away from the crowd on the pier, or sitting at the back of a hooded horse carriage, looking at the flowers. What a beauty she was, this girl. She would lean forward, to look out over the Silvan training ground, but the sergeant was the only one who saw her. He would breathe in deep again, at the sight of her, and then he would begin to speak, tripping over his words as if that might make his military service end sooner. 'We're a rocket-launcher company, my friends. So let's see who can tell me what a rocket launcher launches.'

And with one voice, the company would say, 'A rocket launcher launches rockets!'

And then the sergeant would frown and say, 'So there you are! That's how serious this fucking military service of yours is!'

And everyone would look as if they knew what he was saying.

Then they'd go back to the ST 7-10B, and before they had a chance to remember how bored they were, sitting on that dusty field, and hearing the same lesson, over and over, they recited it yet again. And now the lieutenant was back, nodding as he walked around them, his hands on his hips. He raised his knees so high sometimes that he looked like a horse, pawing the earth. Pressing his head to his chest, he would stare down at the tips of his toes, and when he lifted up his head again, he'd look as if he was about to rear up on his hind legs and whinny. But then he'd go into one of his moods again, and run back over to beat up a few soldiers.

A week later, on his fourteenth day, Ziya got another beating, but this time the lieutenant had nothing to do with it. It was their turn for mess duty, and so they'd gone down to the mess hall at the crack of dawn, when everyone else was still snoring in bed. There were twenty-five or thirty soldiers peeling piles of onions and potatoes and about the same number emptying the vegetables from their buckets and washing them. Another group cleaned the hall and threw away the rubbish, and a larger group chopped up meat, while others with some small aptitude for this sort of work assisted the so-called cooks as they peered into the pots and stirred. But amongst them were a number of others who had been given no job: they had scattered through the hall. Not knowing what to do, they were just standing there gaping. Until finally, the mess sergeant noticed them. 'You!' he said, jabbing the air. 'And you! And you!' When he had gathered them all up, he took them down to a dark cellar that stank of onions and oil. At the sergeant's command, they picked up the huge vats by their handles and carted them outside, where they lined them up in the sun. Looking as tired as if he'd carted them up himself, the sergeant put his hands on his hips and said, 'These are going to be sent out to be tinned. Scrub them thoroughly with wet sand.' Then he bellowed, 'And don't forget! I'm watching. Any slackers and I'll kill them. With pleasure. I swear to God!'

And so they picked up their pads and began to scrub those huge vats with sand and water.

The sergeant stood in the shade of the wall, watching them closely. He seemed transfixed, but his hazel eyes shone like ice, signifying nothing. His thoughts seemed to have taken him far, far away. Then suddenly he came back to himself. He reached into his shirt pocket and took out a cigarette. He lit up and exhaled, and then, in a peeved voice, he said, 'No! That's not how you do it. You're not caressing a baby there. No! Get into those vats now and scrub them with your feet!'

So they got into the vats, and began to scrub them most ferociously with their feet.

There was a silence.

Ziya lifted his head, to see what was going on. He found himself eye to eye with a swarthy commander he'd never seen before. He had two stars on each shoulder, this commander. His features were as hard as steel and the fire in his eyes was real. Lunging forwards, and puffing up his cheeks, he yelled, 'What are you doing inside that vat, you animal?' And then, without waiting for an answer, he set about beating Ziya as if all the enemies he had ever imagined were lodged inside his body. And Ziya watched the grey building slam to the ground, taking the trees with it, as the sky went black. As he swayed in the blackness, now this way and now that, Ziya wondered why this commander was beating him. When he felt the man's fists on his face, he recoiled, but at the same time, and in a way he could not begin to fathom, he felt a strange sort of intimacy. As if, even if they never saw each other again, there would always be a bond between them that neither could deny. He even felt as if he and this commander now knew each other intimately, and understood each other perfectly. When this thought came to him, he wanted to shout, 'I got into that vat because the sergeant ordered me to!' but he couldn't get his tongue to work. His mouth was brimming with blood, that's why. His lips were so swollen he couldn't even feel them. Then suddenly the ground itself seemed to rise, and it crashed mightily into his face. It did not stop there: it slipped out from underneath him like a sheet, this ground, and as it slipped, Ziya tried to stand at attention, but because his knees buckled, he couldn't quite manage it. The commander was in such a rage he didn't notice, though. Teeth gritted, he kept on punching with all his might, and once he had knocked Ziya down, there was no knowing where the next kick might land. Now it was his side, now it was his groin, now his face. And then, after twenty-five minutes or maybe half an hour, he ran out of energy. As his hands fell to his sides, he looked at them, this commander, as if he were seeing them for the first time. It was as if he did not even own these fists that had just pummelled Ziya, as if he hated them for their stupidity. And then he walked away, towards headquarters, and soon he and his stars were lost amongst the trees.

Ziya was still lying on the ground, moaning helplessly and reaching out for something to hold on to, while he pulled himself up. Kenan and a few others ran out to help him at that point, but when they stretched out their arms, he pushed them away with a sudden burst of anger. Then slowly he straightened up. He turned his bloody face this way and that, as if to figure out where he was; he picked up his cap and put it back on, and hobbled off towards headquarters. When he finally reached it, he tried to go inside, but, seeing his condition, the guard wouldn't let him pass. When he heard that Ziya wished to see the battalion commander, he even lost his temper. Lowering his voice, he told Ziya that unless he wanted to ruin his military service by kicking up another fuss, he'd better leave quietly, and without anyone seeing him. His face streaked with blood and tears, Ziya continued to insist on being let in. And soon it turned into an argument, of course, and as they talked over each other, their voices reached as far as the office at the front of the corridor. Out of this room came a tall officer with a fat, round sergeant. They came together to the doorway, as if by common agreement, and there they stood, staring silently at Ziya. Then the officer gave the signal, and the sergeant took Ziya by the arm and led him quickly down the corridor, to a little room at the end that had frosted glass on two sides. He sat Ziya down on a chair, and said in a voice thick with compassion, 'What happened to you? Please tell me.' Ziya wanted to tell him the whole story, but he couldn't speak, he just looked around him, and then, when he couldn't bear it any more, he let out a little cry that sounded to him like a cat's meow. It was such a weak little cry that it sounded like it was coming from the tears streaming down his face. Seeing those tears, the sergeant did not know what to do; turning his head, he wrinkled his forehead and stared at the medicines in the cabinets. Then he made a decision; he put his hand on

Ziya's knee, and in a voice that strained to make his feigned compassion sound genuine, he said, 'All right, all right, just try to calm down.' This went on until the sergeant could no longer hold himself back. He asked what had happened. Ziya took a deep breath, and then, in a trembling voice, he told him what had happened, and when he was finished, he said that he wanted to make a complaint to the battalion commander about having been beaten for no reason.

And this was when the officer who had come to the door with the fat, round sergeant came into the room. Ignoring Ziya, he turned to the sergeant and in an icy voice, he said, 'Tell this dog that he can't just go barging into the commander's office any time of night or day.' Then he added, 'If he wants to make a complaint, then take him to the clerks so that they can take down his statement.'

The sergeant, who was standing at attention, said, 'Yes, sir.'

When the officer had left the room, the sergeant turned back to Ziya. Leaning slightly to look him in the eye, in a concerned voice he said, 'You heard that, did you?'

'I did,' Ziya said.

The sergeant said nothing. Straightening himself up, he began to pace the room, back and forth between the frosted glass and the blue curtains, leaving a cold silence in his wake. Then once again he planted himself in front of Ziya. Leaning on the steel table, he told him about other incidents he'd seen of this sort in this battalion, and what had become of the parties involved; for a time he spoke of the crude machinery of military courts, and of the endless string of hearings. Then he moved on to legal petitions, and the municipal police, and the various different types of documents, and their details. Then he spoke of their commander's character, and his habits, and his love of discipline, and the legal rights of those above and below him. As he spoke, he waved his hands about, his fingers spreading like tongues of fire, and from time to time those flames would flare out at Ziya to burn his skin. They would reach forward, these fingers, and then pull back. And every time they pulled back, his eyes would grow larger.

In the end, Ziya could make neither head nor tail of what the sergeant was saying to him; not knowing what to do, he begged him with his eyes.

'Look,' the sergeant said then. 'I can't know if what you told me is true, but the decision to make a complaint or not is yours. I am not going to make that decision for you. But at the present moment, we cannot know how the commander against whom you will be making your complaint will defend himself, or how he'll tell the story. Do you see my point? When he's asked why he beat this soldier, well, who knows what he might say? So let's see. He could say: I gave him an order and instead of obeying it, he let loose a string of curses, and why would I beat someone for no reason? Or he could say: your honour, I heard him taking the name of our glorious armed services in vain, he said each and every member of it was the son of a whore, and in the face of such insults, I couldn't restrain myself. Who knows, he could even say he caught you red-handed when you were trying to steal something. We cannot know whom the judges will choose to believe – a commander with a clean record and many years of service to the army, or a new recruit like you, with only two weeks of training under his belt. And even if we found eyewitnesses, we could not be sure how many of them would have the balls to tell the truth about what they saw. Over and above all that, we cannot know how many stages the case might have to go through, and sadly, we cannot foretell the outcome, either. Who knows, it could tie itself up in new and unexpected knots, and with every hearing, the plot could thicken, and the whole thing could drag on for four or five years. So when the happy day arrived when you got your discharge, there would be years of hearings still ahead. There are even those who are found guilty and have to leave their families and jobs behind to do a few more months of military service. So this is what you can expect, my ram. Time to get up. If you want to make a complaint, let's get you to the clerks so that they can take down your statement.'

Ziya had no idea what to do.

'So you are making a complaint, or not?' asked the sergeant.

'No,' said Ziya. He paused to swallow. 'No, I'm not.'

Then he stood up and washed his hands and face in the sink that the sergeant indicated and went outside.

That evening, while sitting under the almond trees, eating the boiled eggs and green onions that he'd bought from the children of Silvan, Ziya turned to Kenan and whispered, 'Do you see how it is, then? They beat us in broad daylight, and we can't do a thing.'

'If you ask me, that sergeant used all his wiles to talk you out of it,' said Kenan, quickly swallowing his food. 'Who knows? Maybe it wouldn't have turned out like he said.'

'I have no way of knowing,' said Ziya. 'Really I don't. All I know is this: if I'd complained, that commander would have given me no peace. And anyway, the case would have gone on for years, and as that sergeant at headquarters said, there's no way of knowing how it would have turned out. So in one way, at least, it's good that it ended like this. Let's just get through our military service as quickly as we can and then get out. I don't know if you noticed, but the lieutenant called me an ox, and the commander who beat me up today called me an animal. The officer at headquarters called me a dog. That is not just an insult to humanity, but to animals.'

Holding his flatbread to his mouth, Kenan smiled.

'With all the bad things going on around it, you're going to worry about this now? Wouldn't most people agree with you anyway?'

Rather than answer, Ziya looked over at the barbed wire beyond the almond trees, and for a moment each and every one of the Silvan children seemed to flare up and glitter with all the possibilities of life on the other side. After that, he couldn't take his eyes off them for the longest time. It was almost as if his soul had flown over the fence, to hover over those black-eyed, black-haired children and their swinging baskets.

'If you ask me, you shouldn't let anything worry you,' whispered Kenan. 'I say we just buckle down and hope for the best and finish our military service and leave. And anyway, we don't have much choice, as you know.'

Ziya nodded slowly in agreement. But then, in a harsh voice, he said, 'I hate the food. I hate that mess hall. And most of all, I hate that kitchen. I never want to see it again.'

Kenan raised his head and looked quickly up at the sky. He closed one eye, moving his lips very slightly. His face still raised up, he told Ziya that according to his calculations, they'd have one more week of mess duty while they were here, and that would be in two months' time.

The next time he was on mess duty, Ziya was very tense. He kept trying to lose himself in the crowd, and every time the mess sergeant issued an order, he watched what those around him were doing and silently did the same. Until lunchtime, they worked in that room whose walls were thick with the stink of old oil; furiously they peeled onions and potatoes, and chopped up the meat; they sifted through sack loads of lentils; they washed vegetables in the long sinks, and cleaned the hall; over and over, they mopped the blackened concrete floor. Then, with giant spoons, they ladled the food into lidded metal pots. Just before lunch was served, they threw the sacks of bread over their shoulders, and each squad went to its own company's mess hall. Fearing that something might go wrong in the commotion of passing out the food buckets, and land him with another problem, Ziya chose to pick up one of the sacks of bread. When they had filed in with all the others in the squad, those carrying the sacks went from table to table, leaving a ration of bread at each place. Ziya was making his way towards a table in the corner when the mess sergeant gestured to him from the door. 'You!' he said. 'Look here! Now!' When Ziya had turned around, he said, 'You know that you're to leave two rations of bread at each place on that table. Don't you?'

And at that moment, the Ziya who had spent the day being so very meek gave birth to a new Ziya, almost. This new Ziya stared back at the sergeant, as if he was about to bite him.

'What are you looking at, boy? Didn't you understand what I just said?'

'No, I didn't,' said the newborn Ziya. 'Why should I give the people at this table a double ration?'

'Because that's where your sergeants sit,' muttered the mess sergeant. 'Don't tell me you didn't know that, oh bird of God.'

Ziya said nothing. Returning to the tables, he started with the one in the corner, putting down a single ration of bread at each place.

'What do you think you're doing, boy?' yelled the mess sergeant.

His face was red with anger.

'I did what needed to be done,' said Ziya. 'Do these sergeants have a different God from ours? Why should they have two rations of bread, when we get only one?'

Not believing what he'd just heard, the sergeant opened his arms, as if in prayer, and stood there, wide-eyed. Then he sprang into action, fairly flying across the hall, and without so much as a by your leave, he did a right hook and then a left hook, punching Ziya in the face. He punched him so hard that the jugs and trays on the tables all rattled. And Ziya swung this way and that, grabbing at the edge of the table to keep from falling.

'Stand at attention,' yelled the sergeant. 'Stand at attention, you son of a whore!'

Ziya promptly stood at attention, but his stare was the same. It was almost as if it was his clenched teeth staring, and not his eyes. He stared with all the force of the thoughts racing through his mind, and each one was fiercer and more violent than the last.

And the sergeant stood a few paces back, glaring at Ziya as if he could read those thoughts.

Then he jabbed his forefinger at the mess hall's concrete floor, jabbed it as fast as if he was thrusting a bayonet. 'Get down, oh bird of God,' he yelled. 'Get down and take the belly-crawl position.'

Ziya got down as ordered, taking the belly-crawl position, and when the sergeant gave the order, he soundlessly wriggled his way amongst the tables. At that point, the company came marching back from the training ground, singing the Eskişehir March, and a few minutes later, they had all piled into the mess hall. When they came inside and saw Ziya crawling on the floor, they stopped short, of course. Instead of sitting down, they formed a huddled queue along the wall. And that was when the sergeant changed his tune, very suddenly. He flashed a bright smile, as if to diminish everyone and everything in sight, and then, for a few moments, he turned that smile on Ziya, and as he did so, it blackened, sending out sparks. Over and over, he yelled, 'Keep crawling, you son of a whore. Keep crawling like the dog you are, until that doggy mind of yours is back in your doggy head!' And each time he yelled out these words, he glared at the crowd that had backed against the wall, so that this would be a lesson to them.

No one made a peep, of course; with tired eyes, they watched Ziya crawl across the floor.

And so it was that Ziya crawled back and forth and back and forth across the mess-hall floor that day, under exactly 180 pairs of eyes. He felt nothing. It was as if all his senses had shut down, and there was nothing left to him but flesh and bone and a khaki uniform. So as not to further delay the company that was soon to return to the training ground, the sergeant finally told Ziya to stand up. And then he said,

'Now finish what you left half done. Go and put another ration of bread at each place on that table.'

Ziya gathered the strength that had got him back on his feet. He walked wearily over to the table where the sergeants were to sit, and he put an extra ration of bread at each place.

Then he turned around and, keeping his eyes on the ground, looking at no one, he shuffled outside. Here he passed amongst the rifles that were laid out on the ground and made his way towards the almond trees, and sat down next to the barbed wire, turning his back to the children so that they couldn't see him, and putting his head on his knees, he began to sob. Kenan came running out right behind him, but he couldn't find a thing to say. Or rather, he shied away from saying anything, for fear of saying something that might make it even worse. Instead he waited seven or eight paces away, cigarette in hand, watching Ziya's shoulders shaking as he kept his face down, and cried his heart out under the almond trees. When the sobs began to abate, just a little, he sat up straight, took out his cigarettes, and with trembling hands, he lit one. And that was when Kenan came over; without saying a word, without even asking if Ziya minded, he crouched down next to him. He had no idea what to say, anyway. There were so many things he wanted to say, so many words swirling through his mind, but he couldn't find a way to extract enough of them for a sentence. That was why they didn't speak for some time. They just sat there, smoking their cigarettes, and staring at the ground.

After a long while, Kenan said, 'Don't be upset. What's done is done. There's nothing we can do about it.'

'How can I not be upset?' said Ziya. He took a deep breath. 'As you can see, every evil comes to find me. Yes, it's true. Every evil comes to find me, and no matter how hard I try to stop it happening, I can't. Honestly. I have no idea why this keeps happening. For God's sake, Kenan. Tell me, please! Is there some sort of mark on me I can't see? A cloud maybe? Or a light? Do I look the same as everyone else, when I'm seen from a distance? Or not? Please, could you tell me? Am I dressed in khaki right now, like you, and all our friends over there?'

Kenan looked shocked.

Measuring his words carefully, he murmured, 'What a thing to say.'

'I just don't know,' Ziya continued. 'It's something I have no power over. I just think there is some sort of sign on me, to guide all kinds of evil to me. It might even be a sign too small for the human eye to see, but as I just said, it could also be some sort of light, some sort of shadow.'

'What a thing to say,' said Kenan once again. 'Are you serious, or is this a joke?'

'Do I look like I'm in the mood for jokes?' said Ziya. 'I'm serious. I meant it.'

Kenan just stared at him, shocked.

Ziya looked as if he was about to cry again. His eyes sparkled with quivering tears.

When Kenan saw this, he said, 'Just put those thoughts out of your head. Why don't we get up now? That's what I think we should do. We have to go back to the mess hall now and take the pots to the kitchen, as you know. That fool of a mess sergeant is waiting for us to come back, and the last thing we want is another bust-up. So come on now. Get up!'

Reluctantly stubbing out his cigarette, Ziya slowly rose to his feet.

By the time they reached the mess hall, the others on mess duty had long since rolled up their sleeves to clear the tables. Kenan and Ziya joined them at once, and together they carried the pots to the kitchen, down the dirt road that ran alongside the water depot.

'This will be the last time we see the kitchen,' said Kenan, hoping to console his friend. 'It's our last stint. Two more weeks and we'll be out of here.'

Ziya said nothing. Weighed down with all those pots, he could do no more than give Kenan a sidelong look. But then he turned to the left, to look at the Koçaş mountains and the clumps of undergrowth between them and, very slowly, he breathed in.

In the kitchen, Ziya remained silent. From the soulless way he washed the trays from the officers' mess, you might have thought him a machine. Just then, one of the men doing the rinsing announced in a voice as bright and cheerful as running water that they would be doing the lottery that weekend. He went on to say that his source was solid. Looking over his shoulder so that he could look the others in the eye, he said, 'There's a sergeant at headquarters who comes from my part of the country. He was the one who told me.'

Hearing the words that spelled the end of their training, they all perked up, of course. And then there was a short silence, a tense silence that flashed and glittered like those trays from the officers' mess, as each one of them wondered where in the country he might be sent next. And then someone said that anyone from a rich family was bound to get preferential treatment and there followed a heated argument in that dim-lit kitchen that stank of oil and detergent.

According to some, this piece of shit farce they called the lottery was a scam, pure and simple; they did it only so that they could say they had. 'No sir! That's not true,' said others. There was no preferential treatment. They folded up those papers and put them into sacks or metal pots and then those lots were duly drawn in full view of the entire company, and so it was total nonsense to say that there was any trickery going on, because they would each be choosing their lot with their own hands, and that was why they would, in due course, each accept their fate. It was wrong to accuse the army – the pride of the nation – of resorting to preferential treatment, or trickery, and suspicious practices of any kind, without any proof; the lottery would be just, no doubt about that, because there was no difference between rich and poor here: beneath their khaki uniforms, they were all equal.

But that is not how things turned out on the day. The ones who had, despite never once going beyond the barbed wire in all their time there, managed to have their uniforms altered for them on their second day, the ones who had spurted more money than a fountain does water, and managed to get through without a single sergeant kicking them; the ones the loudspeakers were forever calling to headquarters, if not to collect a doctor's report, then to speak to their families on the phone, and who spent weeks lolling about the dormitory, watching the training ground through the window – somehow they all made it to the lottery, and somehow they all ended up with papers that said Gökçeada, Bergama, Istanbul, Akçakoca, Denizli or Izmir. Ziya's paper said Urfa. Kenan went next. He put his hand into the black bag the sergeant was holding, pulled out a paper, and as soon as he had read it, he turned to Ziya. 'Look,' he said, in a strange but happy voice. 'I got Urfa too.'

For three months they had lived on the outskirts of Silvan, and never once had they seen the town. And the very next day, a big bus pulled up outside the guardhouse, to take thirty-five men off to Urfa, with the sergeant in tow.

As the bus pulled away, Ziya murmured, 'Did you see that? We didn't say goodbye to Şehmuz.'

'And who's Şehmuz?' asked Kenan.

'The boy from Silvan. The boy at the barbed wire,' Ziya said softly. He took a deep breath. 'You know, the boy we bought our boiled eggs and green onions from.'

Remembering him now, Kenan nodded gently.

'We didn't say goodbye,' said Ziya once again. 'After eating so much of his food. Shame on us.'

With that he turned back to the window and for a long time, as the rocky land slipped past, he thought only about Şehmuz. He thought about him for so long that he could almost see him standing there on the other side of the barbed wire, shimmering in the wind and stretching out his little arms, his little black eyes receding into love.

It was sunset by the time they reached the 123rd Mobile Gendarmerie Unit in Urfa. There was no time to get a sense of where they were. They spent a tense night in a large, grey-curtained dormitory that stank of sour sweat and strangers.

In the morning a tiny slip of a sergeant took them down to the mess hall on the ground floor, and then, walking faster than the wind, he led them over to the main building. He did not tell them to line up when they got there. Instead he stared at them, as if he had some very bad news that he could not bring himself to put into words. Then he pulled himself together, as if in response to a secret sign, passed a hand over his face, and in a thin little voice, he said, 'My friends, you are going to spend the next few days here putting up a building.' With that he led them off to the construction site next door. The site was swarming with soldiers. Some were digging inside a huge pit several *dönüms* in area. Some were carrying metal rods that were five or six metres long. Some were tying metal rods together with wire, and others were carrying stones from behind the hill in single file. But the ones carrying the stones were different from the others; most of them had hair growing down to their beards, and they seemed old enough to be addressed as big brothers or uncles. Their uniforms were in poor condition. Some were ripped at the knees and elbows, some were missing buttons, some were so short you could see their calves. And on top of all that, the soldiers looked bewildered, as if they didn't know where they were.

'Our friends over there are convicts,' the sergeant said, lowering his voice.

With that, he turned to face his men. He stared at them as if they weren't standing right next to them, but very far away.

'And now you are going to go and carry stones with them,' he said. 'Off you go. Get started!'

They lined up like the convicts and followed them behind the hill. Here there was a red pit, where a group of muscle-bound convicts was holding pickaxes, hacking up rocks, while another group of convicts crushed these rocks with a huge sledgehammer, and there was so much sweat running down their faces that you'd think that an invisible hand was looming over them, pouring water from a pitcher. During their few trips between this quarry and the pit that was to serve as the new building's foundation, they kept themselves separate from the convicts, but soon they began to mingle. Once they had begun to mingle, the convicts began to talk now and again. And that was when they heard how these men had come to be in prison, and what horrors they had seen while serving on the border. And at the end of each story, they thanked God for still being alive, and said how good it was to be in prison. And so they listened to these tales of dark nights made darker by explosions and the hiss of gunfire, and whinnying horses, and bloodcurdling cries, and herds of sheep, and bloodied tea crates lying next to people and animals who had been blown to bits, and the more they heard, the more frightened these Silvan boys became, of course. They became so frightened, in fact, that they said nothing all day long. They just looked at each other strangely, from the corners of their eyes.

The next day a big-boned, white-haired convict who called himself Dede took it upon himself to give them some advice. Gathering them together during a meal break, he sat down, put his hands on his knees and let his fingers droop. Assuming a fatherly tone, he said, 'So tell me. Did they beat you a lot during training?' They all answered at once. They'd all had enough beatings to fill a truck, they said. To which this man who called himself Dede said, 'Well from now on, it won't be the commanders who'll be giving you your worst beatings. It will be the conditions. This is one thing you should never forget.' And he smiled bitterly as he shook his head.

For a time he was silent. He looked down at the ground and swallowed.

And then he said, 'Now listen carefully to what I have to say. Most likely they'll be dispatching you to your companies tomorrow. What I mean is, some of you will be going to Akçakale, and some to Viranşehir. Wherever they send you, you are fated to end up in the middle of hell, by which I mean one of those outposts along the border. So my advice to you while all this is going on is to do whatever you can to stay in the place where they're sending you. For example, every once in a while they ask you questions. Are any of you tailors? Is anyone here a barber? And who here has worked in construction? So if you happen to have any talent whatsoever, or if you happen to be good at something, even just a little, for God's sake, don't be shy. Step right out with a confident look on your face and say, "Yes, I can do that." Or say, "Yes, that was the work I did when I was a civilian." To make a long story short, my advice to you is this: whatever you can do to stay with your company or your battalion, do it.'

'And what if we don't manage to stay with our company or battalion?' asked Kenan.

Dede looked at Kenan sharply through his dusty eyelashes and then bowed his head.

'You're already in the shit,' he said. 'Once you go out there, you've really had it.'

His words plunged them into silence. And then they got up to return, bewildered, to their work, of course. With long faces they picked up more stones, and carried them out in single file.

Two days later the waif-like sergeant rushed over. 'Put down your stones! Put down your stones!' he said to the boys from Silvan. And he took them to the front of the main building. This time he ordered them to line up two by two, and there they waited motionless in the sun for twenty-five, thirty minutes. Finally a grim and fleshy sergeant major came outside; standing on the steps, he produced a piece of paper, and in a voice that sounded as if he had swallowed a microphone, he boomed, 'Now listen to me carefully. I am going to read out the names of those who are to be sent to Suruç Company. You should step out of line if you hear your name and wait over there'. This sergeant major went on to read out the names of those to be sent to Akçakale and Viranşehir. When he had finished reading out the names, he rolled up the paper, and after giving his thigh a few nervous slaps, he said, 'If you get a move on, you can make it to your companies by evening, so get going, now.' With that, he hurried back into the building.

They piled out of the gendarmerie in confusion, and after asking anyone they met for directions to the bus station, they set off for the city centre. Once they were there, they plunged into the crowd, and here they were obliged to divide up into three groups. And each group went off in a different direction, to wander amongst the buses and minibuses on the bays. Kenan and Ziya and a few of their friends headed first for the Viranşehir minibus. After the driver dozing at the wheel had told them what time he'd be leaving, they went together to the coffeehouse at the other end of the station, where they sat themselves down on its low straw chairs and drank a glass of tea each.

'For a moment there, I was afraid they'd send us to different companies,' said Kenan. 'I'm glad we've both ended up with Viranşehir.'

Ziya gave him a little nod. He tried to accompany it with a smile, but he just couldn't manage it. He fixed his eyes on the tea glass before him and for a while he stayed very still, while he thought about the convicts' terrifying stories.

'We've landed in the same place, but our future is dark,' he said, as he pushed his tea glass aside with the back of his hand. 'God only knows what we can do.'

Kenan said nothing. He stared fearfully into the tea glass in his cupped hands.

Then they jumped up, fearing that they might have missed the bus. They rushed past the prayer-bead vendors and the rainbows they sent clicking around them. They wended their way amongst the *sucuk* vendors and *lahmacun* vendors, and through the clouds of sweat and smoke until they had reached the clapped-out minibus that would be taking them to Viranşehir. The other passengers had not yet arrived, and the driver was no longer at the wheel. There were patches of putty on the sides of the minibus. It looked like it had been sitting there, inert, for many thousands of years. Not knowing what else to do, Kenan and Ziya went to wait in the shade of a wall. Neither wanted to speak. They just stood there grimly, thinking about the stories the convicts had told them. They could still hear all the horrors that had echoes through the darkness of those stories: the bloodcurdling cries cutting through the hiss of gunfire, the whinnying horses, rearing up on their hind legs, and explosions. And each time they did so, the two men would cast their eyes to the ground in silence, and take a deep breath.

It was hot as the fire Nimrod built to burn the Prophet Abraham.

And then the shoeshine boy came up to them, his case swinging from his shoulder. Stopping two paces in front of them, he said, 'Should I give them a shine, brother soldier?'

At first neither of them heard the boy.

That's why they both looked down, as if their boots were speaking. 'Should I give them a shine, brother soldier?' the boy asked again.

'Go away, son. Go away. We're from faraway towns. If a crow squawks around here, we jump,' said Kenan. Looking as if he were about to cry, Kenan flapped his arms, as if to shoo away a chicken.

The boy turned away at once, and soon he and the case on his shoulder had vanished into the crowd.

No sooner had he done so than the passengers appeared. They rushed in from all directions, their baggy trousers flapping, and piled into the minibus.

When they reached the Viranşehir Company, it was still as hot as it had been in Urfa: the single-storey prefabricated building lined up on that great plain sizzled and swayed as if they'd been thrown into a flaming vat of oil. Sitting in the sun on the sandy field between the buildings was a two-wheeled water tanker; some soldiers had gathered around it and were taking turns drinking from the tap. First the new arrivals went up to these gasping soldiers, whose lips and tongues were parched from the heat, and asked where they should go. Pointed in the right direction, they raced across the field, and one by one they printed out and signed their names on a paper that burned to the touch. But after that, no one paid them the least attention. No one told them what to do, or what not to do. And so they waited with those who had come before them, wondering if they were being punished, wondering what they had done. For days and days they waited in the sun. Finally, on the thirteenth day, a sergeant lined them up. After pacing from one end of the line to the other, he asked, 'Does anyone here know how to type?'

'I do,' said Ziya.

They waited for the sergeant to ask if there were any tailors amongst them, or barbers, or anything else he might wish to know, but that was it. 'Come with me, then,' he said, and he took Ziya off to the building next to the mess hall. He took him into Room S-1, which was tiny, and filled with metal cabinets, sat him down in front of a typewriter and gave him a typing sample. Trying not to show his excitement at being spared the watchtower on the border, Ziya typed up the sample, pulled it out, and handed it to the sergeant who was waiting beside him. The sergeant gave it a long inspection, searching for mistakes. Then he said, 'Fine, you're the person we're looking for. Congratulations. You'll be the company's S-1 clerk.'

Ziya did not get up from the typewriter once that day. He carried on typing the documents the sergeant gave him, and that was why he did not see Kenan again until he walked into the dimly lit mess hall that evening. All day he'd been elated at the thought of being spared the watchtower on the border, but when he went over to Kenan's table and sat down across from him, he suddenly felt ashamed, as if he'd done something wrong. He felt so ashamed that he hardly knew how to hold himself, or where to look, or what to say.

'Come on now. Congratulations. You've managed to escape, at least,' Kenan said, as he made an effort to smile.

Ziya's face burned.

'It's just luck,' he said quietly.

The next morning he raced off to his typewriter as soon as he had finished breakfast. He opened the window, picked up a cloth and dusted off the desk, and gladly went to work. Twenty-five or thirty minutes later, the sergeant arrived, and he was very happy to see Ziya there typing away, of course. Then he sat down on one of the chairs lining the wall, threw one leg over the other, and, without so much as a good morning, he asked, 'How old are you?' And Ziya told him he was twenty and a half years old. He said this without pausing to think or make a calculation, and neither did he give any indication of an ulterior motive: he simply said the first words that came into his head, as if he were breathing them. And the sergeant burst out laughing. He laughed so much he almost burst his sides. So he got up. Clutching his belly, he spun around, and his belly swayed this way and that. He went out the door, still laughing. 'So he's twenty and a half, ha, ha. He's twenty and a half. Ha, ha!' Ziya sat there stunned, as he listened to the laughter bouncing down the corridor. He was still sitting there when the sergeant returned, throwing open the door. Then, as he left again, he threw back his head, as his mouth lost its shape. Ziya listened to the laughter. Ha, ha, ha. Ha, ha, ha. Then suddenly he was back with two other sergeants, and as he laughed, he kept pointing at Ziya, now with one hand, and now with the other, as if he were watching a naughty monkey at a zoo. As if he were reporting some sort of miracle. Ask him yourself, he said. He really is twenty and a half. Twenty and a half! That's how old he is! While all this was going on, Ziya tried to keep his cool, but he couldn't quite manage it. And before long he was lost in confusion.

Then suddenly the sergeant stopped laughing. With the back of his hand, and with a certain agitation, he wiped the tears from his eyes. When the other sergeants had left the room, he walked to the window, plunged his hands into his pockets, and for a time he stared out at the sandy field and the water tanker.

And then, without so much as turning to face him, he said, 'That's all for now, my ram. I'm giving you the rest of the day off. Go outside, and spend a little time with your friends.'

'All right,' said Ziya, and he left the room.

Still in confusion, he went to find Kenan. The two sat down in the shade of those ovens they called buildings. And there they sat, for three long hours, talking anxiously about what had just happened, and smoking one cigarette after another. The field on which the camp stood had no trees, so by now everyone else was sitting in the shade of the buildings; it was one long line of heads and knees and stretched-out legs, hiding from the sun while wreaths of smoke swirled over them. And with so many people crowded there together, time simply forgot how to move. And when it did, it seemed almost to become a second source of heat. It was almost as if time itself was beating down on them. Just then, an order came for them to line up outside the mess hall, and they all stood up, rushing like bent little shadows to the front of the building. A sergeant had planted himself at the mess-hall door. And while he waited for the men to arrive, he kept turning his head to catch what the corporal behind him was saying.

And now they were all standing in front of the officers. They hadn't bothered to line up.

'My friends,' said the sergeant, walking towards them. 'I have put up the lists on that window over there. Each of you should look and see what platoon you've been assigned to. You are to report to Ceylanpınar by nightfall.'

There was some rustling in the crowd.

'Quiet!' barked the sergeant. 'I haven't finished speaking. Now listen to me carefully. When you get to Ceylanpınar, you are to go straight to the mobile gendarmerie unit. The first and second platoons are stationed there. The third platoon should wait there to be picked up. In the meantime, don't think you can slip off home just because there's no officer there watching over you. The police will pick you up before you're halfway there, and then you'll have failed your military service, and all for nothing. But if there's still an idiot out there who wants to slip off home, don't hold them back! Let them go! So now find out where you're going. Hurry up!'

There followed a lot of pushing and shoving, as they cast their large eyes over the lists. But when they did find their names, they didn't move, they just stood there staring, as if by doing so they might release the miracle that would save them from the border. Finally Kenan and Ziya moved forward. Standing on tiptoes, side by side at the back of the crowd, they scanned the lists.

'Oh, no. Oh, no,' said Ziya when he found his name. 'Look what I've done. Just a few words that came out wrong, and now I'm doomed!'

'Don't take it too hard,' said Kenan, trying to console him. 'All this means is that you were never fated to stay at headquarters.'

'Maybe you're right,' Ziya murmured.

Then they put the field and the battalion behind them; boarding one of the minibuses they found waiting for them in Viranşehir *meydan*, they headed for Ceylanpınar. For an hour they passed through a dry and copper-coloured waste-land, accompanied all the way by a low moan that seemed not to come from the road so much as the depths of the bus itself; and all around them was a yellow glow pushing against a sky that seemed to grow before their eyes; now and again they caught sight of a bird in the far distance, or a bush they could barely see, or a shape that was almost certainly a tree. On entering Ceylanpınar, they were met by a procession of earthen-roofed shacks, most of which looked as if they'd been built in a day. And with them came their courtyards, of course, and the trees in those courtyards, and the laundry hanging out to dry, and the dusty clouds of children, and a garish spattering of distant and disconnected noises that, as they died away, seemed more like silence. Lurching across the potholes in the asphalt road, they arrived at a sharp bend and, hitting the brakes, the driver called out: 'So, boys, the gendarmerie is on our right, and the mobile unit on our left, so are you getting out, or what?' No one moved, except to look at the little single-storey guardhouse on their right and the grey two-storey building on their left. No one got out. And this was how they all came to alight at the village mar-ketplace instead; here they filed into a long, narrow restaurant whose walls were lined with pictures of the Kaaba Stone; after filling their stomachs to a Ferdi Tayfur song, they made their weary way back to the buildings on the sharp bend.

'What's this writing all about?' asked Kenan.

Ziya turned his head to look: painted in red letters on the wall he saw the words: *Belik is a murderer.*

'I have no idea,' he said. 'When we were passing through Diyarbakır, I saw *Freedom for the Kurds* on some walls and the name Mehdi Zana, too, and these I understood, but this one – I have no idea.'

Kenan turned back to give the wall a second look.

They saw the same slogan on a few other walls on their way to the sharp bend, and each time Kenan and Ziya could not stop themselves from looking.

On walking inside that big and menacing grey building, they were all thinking of the stories those convicts had told them, and when they looked around them, it was with the same distracted air they had seen in those convicts. A humpbacked sergeant came rushing down in some agitation when he saw them standing there; he pulled out the men who'd been assigned to the second platoon and lined them up, after which he strolled back and forth in front of them, hands on hips. Then he stopped. In a hoarse nasal voice, he asked, 'Do any of you know how to type?'

'I do,' said Ziya.

The sergeant's eyes lit up when he heard that. He asked Ziya where he was from.

'I'm from Aydın,' Ziya replied.

'It's your lucky day,' said the sergeant. 'The company commander is from Aydın, too.'

They all turned to look at Ziya, as if seeing him for the first time.

Then this sergeant said, 'Follow me,' and led them down a gloomy, high-ceilinged corridor to the company commander's office. One by one they stepped into his office, walked up to his steel table, and saluted. The commander had not yet raised his head; he was gazing icily at the yellow onion-skin documents he was still busy signing. Grimacing strangely, he held his pen in the air with one hand, while with the other he was scratching his crotch. And whenever he did that, it almost seemed as if he wanted to look down there, too, but he never did; instead he'd venture to look all the more solemn as he carried on signing. When he'd signed the last document, he'd put it face down on top of all the others, and finally raise his head to take a good look at the soldier standing before him. In a stern voice he'd say, 'Well, then. Identify yourself.' And then, without missing a beat, the soldier would identify himself. When it came to Ziya's turn, he took one step forward and said, 'Ziya Kül, son of Mehmet, born in 1958, in Aydın, at your service, sir!'

The commander shifted slightly in his chair. And then, making as if it were a coincidence that he had shifted, he gave his balls another good scratch. In a stern voice he asked Ziya which part of Aydın he was from. And what district, and what town. And then, glancing up at the ceiling, he said, 'Hmmm. So you live next door to Veli Sarı, also known as Hacı Veli. Don't you?'

'Yes, sir,' said Ziya.

'Good,' said the commander. 'So now tell me. Is Halime Çil still alive?'

Ziya just stared at him.

'Don't tell me you don't know Ebecik?' The commander raised his hand in consternation.

'Yes, sir. Of course I know her. And yes, she's still alive.'

As he said those words, he saw Hacı Veli. He strolled around Hacı Veli's house, and as he did, he suddenly saw Ebecik, and after she had looked at him for a good long while, she cleared her throat.

'Are you from our town, sir?' asked Ziya.

The commander shifted again in his seat. Glaring at his hands, he placed them on the edge of his desk. 'Son of a donkey! Know your place. I'm the one who asks the questions round here!'

Hearing his answer, Ziya turned deep purple.

'Get out!' bellowed the commander. He lowered his head as he pointed to the door. 'All of you, get out!'

And that was when Ziya caught sight of the brass nameplate standing there on its wooden base: First Lieutenant Necdet Belik. That stopped him in his tracks, but only for a moment. Then he raced out of the room with all the others. The sergeant stood waiting at the door, and when they were all out, he stepped inside, but he didn't stay in there long; two minutes later, he was out again, and from the look on his face you would have thought he'd just been punched. He turned around to give Ziya a mournful look. 'He won't agree to your staying on here as a clerk.'

Ziya gave him a blank stare.

The sergeant hurried them over to the ammunition depot. He gave them each one canteen, one G-3 infantry rifle, two cartridge belts, one cartridge clip, and eighty rounds of ammunition, recording each consignment with the blue ballpoint pen he'd pulled from his breast pocket and then signing for it. Then they all piled under the tarpaulin at the back of a rickety truck, and with the commander in the driver's seat, they put Ceylanpınar behind them, and with it, the State Battery Farm, and the dark little stream down from the Ali Yerelli and Sheikh Nasır brooks and flanked on both sides by lines of towering poplars. On they went in the direction of the asphalt road. With them in the back of the truck were several huge sacks of bread, and as they were knocked back and forth by the ruts on the dirt road, the sacks gave out clouds of powder that they could not stop staring at, if only because they were the only things visible under the tarpaulin.

And that was when Kenan slid over in Ziya's direction, just a little, and whispered: 'Let's hope we end up in the same outpost.'

'Let's hope so,' said Ziya.

He kept his eyes fixed on the clouds of powder that rose up through the darkness every time the truck swayed, contracting the tent above them only to expand it.

'Did you see the commander's nameplate?' whispered Kenan.

Ziya nodded.

Briefly, they exchanged glances.

The truck began to climb up a hill. There was barbed wire running alongside the road, and beyond it was a minefield. The truck turned around a bend and stopped. They were now standing in front of the Mezartepe Outpost, and the thick stone walls that enclosed its courtyard. The commander jumped down from the driver's seat and came around to the back. Opening the flap of the tent, he pointed to the three soldiers he saw first. 'You, and you, and you,' he said. When they had stepped down, he turned to the officer standing next to him. 'I am putting these men in your charge. Now take care of the rest.'

'Yes, sir!' said the other.

The round-faced cook standing behind the sergeant jumped up into the back of the truck. Finding the bread sack marked 'Mezartepe' and cradling it in his arms, he jumped down again with a great thud.

And then they were off again. They went back down to the asphalt road, and then it was another ten or fifteen desolate minutes, until, at a crossroads, they went hurtling up another hill, this time to stop in front of Seyrantepe Station. The commander came round to the back of the truck again, lifted the flap of the tarpaulin, and, drawing a horizontal line with his forefinger, he said, 'You two get down.'

Gathering up their things, Kenan and Ziya got down.

The truck moved on to the Ege Outpost, and as it went down the dirt road, it grew smaller and smaller, until it reached the watchtower at the end of the road, and vanished.

Once it was gone, the sergeant said, 'Welcome,' and shook both Kenan's hand and Ziya's. And then he said, 'Go straight into the dormitory without making too much noise, and go straight to sleep, my friends. Because in just a few hours, you're on guard duty.'

Ziya had turned to look at the graves just in front of the outpost.

Seeing this, the sergeant said, 'Those are two soldiers who were hit during a skirmish. They're buried here because we had no family to send them to. That's enough fooling around. Off to the dormitory! Get some sleep!'

'All right,' said Ziya.

He and Kenan went across to the prefabricated building that looked like it might collapse if you so much as blew at it. The dormitory they found to the left of the entrance was no bigger than a matchbox. They lay themselves down on the two empty bunks, but surrounded as they were by so many snores and outstretched limbs, they hardly slept. Towards evening, the cook came to wake them up. Hitting the frosted glass with the back of his hand, he said, 'Hopla! Time to get up, my fine sirs, your food is ready!' and with that he was gone. When the men had washed their hands and faces with water pulled from the well, they proceeded to the mess hall at the back. With its uneven stone walls, it looked just like a sheep pen. And there they sat down in front of their bowls of noodle soup. After this soup, which had nothing to offer them but heat, they moved on to soggy dried beans and semolina halva that was lumpy and as hard as rock. Then they went outside, taking with them a piece of bread each, to eat during the night, while on guard duty. Some went over to the well, others to the dormitory. Others went over to stand in line in front of the roofless wooden outhouse some fifteen or twenty paces to the right. And that was when a shame-faced Kenan went up to Ziya. 'I've started to itch,' he said softly. 'And scratch.'

'Don't even ask,' said Ziya. 'I have, too.'

Osman of Selçuk, who had been wandering amongst them like a cow let off his lead, noticed them whispering. He came to their side. Smiling slyly as he swung his head from side to side, he said, 'Nothing to be ashamed of, friends. You can scratch to your heart's content.'

And then he sized them up, these two, who still seemed uncertain as to how to scratch, and then, turning sad and solemn, he said, 'Don't get upset. You have lice, that's all. That's why you're itching. But while you scratch, just remember that you'll never get rid of them. Whatever you try, I can guarantee you it won't work. Sometimes we put this ointment on – spread it over every inch of skin, and as if that weren't enough, we throw all our pillows and blankets and bedding into vats, along with all our clothes, and boil them for hours and hours, but that doesn't make a shit of difference. Twelve hours later, the lice are back. Because these little critters live inside the earth, that's why. Sit down just once at the edge of the barbed wire over there, and you're infested. So that's what I'm trying to tell you. Don't be ashamed. Scratch away, and try to get used to it. You're three-day birds, anyway. Whatever way you look at it, you're here for another seventeen months. You don't mind my calling you that, do you?'

'Not at all,' said Ziya.

'Oh please,' said Osman of Selçuk. 'I implore you. Don't take offence.'

And then, hopping off towards the guardhouse, he stopped in front of the graves. And in a voice so loud you'd think his throat might burst open, he bellowed, 'Fuck off, you fucking village! Fuck off, before I fuck you more!' Sparks flew from his eyes as he stared out into the distance, teeth clenched. And it was as if he could actually see that village he wanted to fuck over.

He was still staring out there when the sergeant came out of the guardhouse, holding his blue register. In an agitated voice, he said, 'That's enough fooling around, my friends. Get over here, all of you, and sign your names.'

They went over and signed the register.

'You've signed up to the third station to the east of the D-3 outpost,' the sergeant told Ziya. 'I'm sending you out with some people who know the drill.'

'That's fine,' Ziya murmured.

Then they all got ready together; they filled their canteens with water, and lined up their rifles in a row, and attached the chargers to their rifles, took out the bolt handles and loaded the bullets and then more bullets and, leaving behind them only the cook and the night watchman and those two unclaimed soldiers in their graves, they followed in the sergeant's footsteps as he slowly led them out to the border. *So here we are*, Ziya whispered to himself, *here we are, inside that story the convicts at battalion headquarters told us.* As he whispered these words, he cast a tense gaze at the lands of Syria stretching out before them and breathed in sharply. They went down a hill that was covered with dry grass, and after they had patrolled the dirt track that went along the barbed wire from one end to the other, the sergeant put them in charge of the border and when night fell they moved with their rifles into their trenches. That was when Hayati of Acıpayam did as the sergeant must have asked, and gave them a bit of instruction.

'You see that railroad over there,' he said, turning his head in the direction of the barbed wire. 'Well that's the actual border. And between that asphalt road and this barbed wire, it's a minefield. If you see a shadow trying to cross the railroad, you must shoot without hesitation. Understood? According to the rulebook, we're supposed to tell them to stop three times and only open fire if they fire first, but don't you pay any attention to that. The book counts for nothing out here! And anyway. If we played it by the book, those smugglers would hunt us all down like grouse. And then, God forbid, we'd all be going home early, in coffins. In the meantime, don't forget that smugglers go between these countries in both directions. That means you have to keep a watch on both sides of this border. You have to do this even when there's a skirmish. Because the ones trying to cross over into Syria meet with fire from Syria while the ones trying to cross over into Turkey meet with fire from this side, and in a skirmish like that we end up getting fire from both sides. Understood?'

'Understood,' said Ziya.

And so began their ordeal at the border.

At sunset every evening, they went out to the barbed wire and until dawn, they guarded the border, together with the lice crawling over their bodies. There was more to it than just lying in their trench, training their eyes on the border. They were forever getting up and slinging their rifles over their shoulders, and going off to patrol the part of the border for which they were responsible. They did this to keep a close eye on the places that were beyond their field of vision and also, as time went on, to stay awake. They would walk down the dirt track that ran alongside the barbed wire, looking both to their left and their right, and while they walked they would whisper to each other in half sentences, careful to make as little noise as they could. And when they did so, their voices seemed to bring a little light to the dry grass, and the barbed wire, and the dirt track, and the minefield, and the night itself. But it was not enough to go out on these patrols all night. Every ten, fifteen minutes, they cupped their hands or leaned forward and hollered into the darkness: 'Whoooooop!' And then the same call would come back to them from the next station along: 'Whooooop!' And then the next station along would answer this cry, and on it would go, from station to station, echoing in the night, all along the border. It would start at the station on the shores of the Mediterranean, carrying with it the blue scent of salt, and travel the full length of the barbed-wire fence, through Hatay, and then Gaziantep, and then Suruç, and

Akçakale and Viranşehir. Moving on to Kızıltepe, it would echo for a time in Mardin, and from there it would travel the length of the Iraqi border, and the Iranian border, and the border with the USSR, station by station, until at last it reached the Black Sea.

It wasn't a military regulation, whooping like that. Quite the opposite. It was entirely irregular. But it was better known than any regulation in the book. And no irregularity was more strictly observed than this one. To draw out those o's – to whoop and listen to it pierce the night – it was a way of nudging the people in the next station, and keeping them awake; it was to say, fear not, my friends, I'm just over here next to you, and as you've just heard, I'm awake. And at the same time, should a smuggler or some such be approaching the border, whooping was a way of saying, listen, brother, don't risk your life and mine by coming any closer. It might be masquerading as a challenge, but underneath the show of force was a softness, and a silent plea. And sometimes it was a way of letting out a long and mournful sigh of frustration, or a rough, gruff curse against the conditions in which they were living, and the fate that had brought them to this place. But most important, whooping was a way for the caller to cast a veil over the fear he had buried inside him, so that no one else could see it. When it was Osman of Selçuk's turn to call out, he was never satisfied with just one whoop, of course. Shaking his fist at the night, he would cry out, 'Fuck off, you fucking village! Fuck off!'

As these calls went up along the border, there was some-times – every four or five days – a faint call from across it. According to some, these came from old soldiers who had no longer been able to bear the conditions and escaped across the border, there to marry and settle down. But others said, nonsense, those aren't old soldiers, they're those trickster smugglers, heading towards the border, and after calling out like that they would turn back, no doubt; having seen that it was impossible to cross over at this point, they would vanish into the night. While others said that it was nothing more than their own calls echoing in the depths of Syria. The terrain was so flat around here that it would, no doubt, take four or five days for a call to bounce back, and that was also why it sounded so exhausted, so much like a low moan. Whereas Veysel Hoca, who had worked as an imam in a village called Cıkınağılköy out in the sticks near Şereflikoçhisar, saw no merit in any of these theories; in his view, the souls of the soldiers who'd fallen in skirmishes over the years were still here, and when they heard the voices of those still in life, they couldn't restrain themselves, and that was why, from time to time, they whooped from the next world. But no one, not even Veysel Hoca, could know if there was any truth in any of these theories, of course, so whenever a faint little call came floating out to them from the depths of Syria, they would peer back into those dark depths with suspicion.

On his nineteenth day at the border, Ziya heard his third call floating in from Syria. It was Hayrullah of Denizli District, Adana, standing next to him that night; several hours in, they dipped into their parka pockets and took out the dry bread they'd brought with them, and after they had finished it, they went out on patrol, each in their own direction. The air had cooled somewhat, so Ziya had pulled his cap down over his ears, and he was treading softly down the dirt track that quivered before him like a piece of white gauze. All he could see on the Turkish side was a darkness so thick it almost pressed against his face; on the Syrian side, on a gentle hill some seven or eight kilometres away, there were the lights of a small village. And so it was while Ziya was gazing over at those lights that he heard what sounded like a soft moan, rising from the darkness beyond the railroad. 'Whooooop!' And with that, Ziya turned on his heels, to race back to the trench. And there, rushing in from the other side, holding his rifle crossways, was Hayrullah, and even though his face was half-obscured by darkness, you could see that he was shaking, quaking; throwing himself into the trench like some sort of sack, and struggling to catch his breath, he gasped, 'Did you hear it?'

'I heard it,' Ziya whispered.

They swung their rifles forward, and now it was their barrels looking out like two eyes over the dark minefield; with bated breath, they put their fingers on their triggers. Then suddenly they could see a tangled flock of shadows landing on the railroad, until, one by one, they moved into the minefield, rising and falling, crackling the dry grass beneath their feet. And then Hayrullah pressed the trigger, and then Ziya did, too: hearing gunfire, a few of the shadows turned around, whinnying in pain as they went. There was then a violent scuffle, as several shadows broke away from the flock; a few of them shot back at the trench: one shadow with a great load on its back lost its balance and fell on to its knees, but at the very moment as it pulled itself back up to the level of the asphalt road, it vanished. And with a speed that seemed to verge on the impossible, the shadows coming up behind it vanished, too. Hayrullah and Ziya fired a few more shots in their direction, and into the rustling grass, and then, trembling with fear and excitement, they waited. And as they did so, the night slowly expanded; as it lapped against the old border, it grew thicker, too. Seeing that the danger was over, Hayrullah muttered, 'We got off lightly this time, thank God,' but his eyes were still fixed on the border. 'Did you see them? Those were bales of tea on those horses' backs, and there were seven or eight people, at least.'

'So we've fended off a plot to bring down the national economy – is that what you're saying?' asked Ziya in a mocking voice.

Hayrullah said nothing, but he lifted up his head, just a little. His eyes were still on the rustling grass and the railroad.

And for a time Ziya fell silent. 'Dear God,' he said to himself. 'I hope none of those shadows were hit. Dear God, I hope not. I hope none of them were hit. Dear God!'

At daybreak, the sergeant came back, bringing with him the soldiers from the other stations, and they all went out to the barbed wire to look at the field. There were, as far as they could see, no dead or wounded, and neither had they left anything behind. There were tracks about the width of five ploughs coming on to the field, and just a bit of the way in, long before they reached the other side, they looped away in all directions. Later on, the commander arrived in a cloud of dust to inspect the area where the incident had taken place. Stepping down from his jeep, he put his hands on his hips and took a good long look at the field.

'So now,' he said to Hayrullah. 'Tell me what happened.'

Hayrullah gave a blow-by-blow account of what had happened, but of course he left out the whoop.

The commander left it there, asking no questions, and he didn't so much as look at Ziya. He just stood there staring at his glistening, freshly shined combat boots, and listening to what Hayrullah had to say. Then he marched sternly back to his jeep, and climbed in.

Back at the outpost, they took a statement, and instead of saying that they had used forty-seven bullets back in the trench, it said they had used a hundred and forty-seven. This was because they were all short of bullets, and that was because the soldiers sometimes fired their rifles indiscriminately as time went on, sometimes just out of exasperation, and sometimes because they were about to be discharged and wanted to make sure nothing went wrong at the last moment. Some had used most of their bullets on the mosquitoes. Especially when the State Battery Farm put on its water sprinklers, those mosquitoes came out in force, and when they did, it felt as if there were dozens of lice crawling over the men's groins and armpits and down the seams of their uniform. The mosquitoes came swarming in like clouds. All night long, they'd buzz annoyingly around their heads, and by morning their hands and faces would be covered with bites. If a driver was going to Viranşehir for provisions and ammunition, there were even those who begged him to bring them back plastic bags to put over their hands and heads while on guard duty. This, too, had its drawbacks, because if you were breathing inside a plastic bag, you misted it up, and so you had to keep reaching in to rub off the condensation, and when you did that, you dislodged the elastic band that kept the plastic bags on your hands. And that was when some soldiers lost their patience and tore those plastic bags off their heads, upon which the mosquitoes that had been sitting on their rifles rose up in clouds and zeroed in on them.

And this was why the extra hundred bullets that they included in their statement that day was not enough to meet the deficit at Seyrantepe Station. So from time to time, in an arrangement with the other stations in the area, they put flash suppressors down a few barrels to make those rifles sound like Kalashnikovs, and in the space of three weeks, they staged two fake skirmishes, claiming afterwards that it was thanks to their quick response that they had been able to drive back a group of smugglers who had been trying to sneak across the border with their horses, and when they went back to the station to make their statements, they claimed to have used far more bullets than could fit into a pouch.

Because they were new, the sergeant took Kenan and Ziya aside to issue a stern warning. 'If you say a word about this to anyone, I'll make sure you suffer,' he said.

They both promised to say nothing.

They were, in any event, living in a daze, out there on the border, and in no shape to think about such things. Kenan was having nightmares, every time he lay down to sleep. He would wake up in a sweat at noon each day, and sit up on his bunk to scratch himself, and then he would tiptoe over to the door, trying not to wake anyone as he went, and then he would flit outside, like a shadow. Ziya would find him sitting under the almond tree, next to the graves, his face all screwed up and on the verge of tears. And then he would crouch down gently on the grass next to him, of course, and the two of them would stay there for a long time, gazing out at the border and the railroad and the lands of Syria beyond it. Sometimes, when they were sitting out there, they'd see the battered carriages of the Toros Express rolling down the tracks, and it was almost as if it was afraid to break the hush reigning over that border, because it wouldn't sound its whistle even once, as it slithered across the earth like a dusty old snake towards Ceylanpınar or Gaziantep. As it faded into the skyline, the silence it left behind was hard to bear, and so, too, was the naked earth that filled it. And that was when Kenan would go pale, and let his shoulders sink a little lower. And he would get up suddenly, and leave Ziya where he was, and go behind the station to write his fiancée a letter. Or he would stay where he was, and take a deep breath, and say, 'This really is the land that God fucked over. Just look at it. We don't even have a little shop where we can go to buy matches.'

Sometimes, after looking long and hard at the dryness of the earth surrounding them, Kenan would begin to tell Ziya how beautiful his village was. For instance, one day he talked about the red-pine forest that wrapped itself around the village, while its depths throbbed and thundered. Another time, he spoke of the scent of thyme that floated down the slopes to lap against the courtyard gates. He spoke of the crystal-clear springs and brooks that wound through the forest, bubbling gently as they went. He spoke of the vineyards, and the orchards, and all the different types of fruit you could find in them, and the clacking grouse, and everywhere you looked, there were beds and beds of fragrant flowers, sparkling all the colours of the rainbow. He described all this in such detail, and with such pleasure, that Ziya could almost see Kenan's village, there before his eyes. This cheered them both. Even the light in their eyes would change, and their expressions, too: you could see in them the lively intensity that only the hopeful can enjoy. But as soon as they stopped talking about that village, the joy would drain from their faces. And that was when Kenan would feel worse than before; he would stand up, saying that he needed to go get more sleep. Scraping his boots against the earth like a dark and weary ghost, he would make his way back to the dormitory.

He tried not to show it, but Ziya was just as miserable, really. He walked around looking tired and spent with no idea what to do. Not every day, but every other day, he would return from guard duty in the morning and draw a bucket of water from the well, and then he'd gather up some scrub and make a fire with it, and when it was hot, he would set about trying to wash himself in that wooden outhouse. The outhouse was so narrow that there was hardly room to bend down to the bucket to scoop water with his tin can, let alone stand up. And also, whenever Ziya headed into that stinking place with his steaming bucket of water, some of the others would, without fail, need to go to the toilet urgently, and they would stand there, four or five paces away, shouting, 'Hurry up, man, or we'll shit our pants.' Hearing them shout like that, and seeing them through the blackened planks, he'd have to jump back into his clothes and come out, of course. Once he'd taken a little too long to pull himself together and get out of there. Hayati of Acıpayam was one of those standing outside, writhing in his white jockey shorts; now and again he would snap their elastic, and every time he did that, his eyes would bulge as he glared furiously at the door and ground his teeth. When he saw Ziya coming out, the anger went to his voice, and without meaning to, he cried, 'Why does it have to be every other day, every other day? What are you scrubbing in there, a cunt?'

Ziya apologised but Hayati was in too much of a rush to hear him, and even when he was inside, doing his business, he kept ranting. 'You can't clean things every day in conditions like this, my dear friend. There's such a thing as common sense. Here we are, living in these jerry-built huts without bathrooms, without toilets, and what am I supposed to say to these half-witted bastards who are condemned to shaving in front of that mirror we've hung from the almond tree? Which of us deserves this miserable life we're living? And anyway, I've been here now for thirteen months, and I've done time in every station in the company, and I've met each and every one of the men working in them, but I haven't seen a single rich boy, or a single man who's ever picked up a book. And if there is a single slave of God who can tell me otherwise, let him speak. Every night, we lay our lives on the line, guarding that border, and if there's fog in the morning, we wait there until it's cleared, and then, when they drag us back, well . . . just look at this food they give us, you'd need a thousand witnesses to find just one man who'd call it food! And then there's our drinking water, or rather, the stale green water we have to pull from the well every day, that we share with the snakes and the frogs and the bloodsuckers and the bugs. And then there's this place where we have to wash. Let's face it. Not even a dog would want to wash in there! Soldiers who aren't posted to the border – they do guard duty two hours a week, tops. And all of them, all of them, get to wash themselves in sparkling tiled bathrooms. And you can be sure they don't have to pour water over their heads from tin cans, like we do. And what about those letters we spend so much time writing? After pouring all our dreams into them and all our desperate longing, and signing them with our secret tears, who do we give them to? The drivers! And then what do they do? Well, they grab them away from us and toss them into the glove compartment or the pocket in the door, with all that white lead dust. When it comes time for them to post them, well only God knows what happens then! Osman! Just tell me, my fine young man! How many months has it been since you ate roasted meat? And OK, how long since you enjoyed a plate of stewed fruit? How long has it been since you had a chance to walk down a lane, or an avenue? Tell me now, so that these clouds can hear you! Go on, tell me, so that those two lost souls in those graves can hear you, too! Who would spend a day in this godforsaken place, if they had any money at all? Tell me, my fine young blade. Osman, are you still there?'

'I'm still here,' said Osman of Selçuk, as he swung from side to side, 'but you'd better hurry up, my friend! If you don't stop wagging your tongue like that and get down to business, I'm going to shit my pants!'

'I'm right, though, aren't I?' cried Hayati, like a voice from beyond. 'If I'm not right, you just go ahead and tell me, right to my face! But let me tell you, your tongue would burn if you did, and God would strike you down, turn you into a crooked old man!

'I'm that already, you idiot!' Osman of Selçuk craned his neck as far as it would go. 'Come on now. Time to get out.'

And then he couldn't stop himself. Turning towards Syria, and forgetting all the men trying to sleep in the dormitory, Osman raised his fist and bellowed, 'Fuck off, you fucking village! Fuck off!'

And when Hayati emerged from the outhouse, Osman managed to get himself in there before anyone else.

It was a calm and beaming Hayati who came to Ziya's side then, and instead of asking him if he had caused him offence, he just looked into his eyes and apologised. And Ziya apologised to him again, and then the two of them stood there together for a time, exchanging wry smiles. They smiled as if they had somehow managed to discuss everything that needed to be discussed without either saying a word, and come to an understanding. After that they went to bed, but Ziya couldn't get to sleep; he kept rearranging his pillow, and rolling over. And as he was lying there with his eyes closed, he kept thinking about those shadows he had shot at on his nineteenth day on the border, and wondering if any of them had taken his bullets. And then, even after so much time had passed, he could hear that gunfire, echoing in his ears, as loud as it had done that night, and after that, there was no going to sleep. And that was why he was so very tired when he went off on guard duty that night; he was paired up with Serdar of Velimeşe in Çorlu, at D-4, which was the furthest east of Seyrantepe's stations.

A few hours later, they began to hear those cries ringing through the black night, echoing from station to station. Whoooop! Whooooop! Then he and Serdar got up to go on patrol. Pulling down their caps and slinging the rifles over their shoulders, they went off in their opposite directions. That night it seemed darker than ever before, and heavier, and with that extra dark and extra weight came a silence that even those whoops couldn't budge. Back in the trench, Ziya was just about to take his piece of bread from his pocket when that silence slowly began to alter in texture. When the wind first swept in from the other edge of night, it brought with it a hissing, swishing sound that might have come from the empty spaces it was seeping through, or from the flatness of the grass it swept across. It travelled out in waves, and the wider it spread, the fainter it became, and soon it was lost. And then it returned, but this time there was no swish or hiss: it sounded like a whisper, an old, cracked, crumbling, half-forgotten whisper.

Just then, there was a crackle of gunfire to the west of Seyrantepe. Serdar and Ziya both jumped, turning to look in the direction of the gunfire. As they did so, they heard some angry Kalashnikovs joining in with their G-3 infantry rifles, and suddenly there were hundreds of bullets flying through the night. Amid all this gunfire, they could hear whinnying horses racing in all directions, and also shrieks, each one different than the one before, and each one more desperate.

'I can't be sure,' said Serdar. 'But that sounded like a herd of sheep. If that's what it was, this is going to turn out badly. Very badly.'

They stuck their heads out of the trench, both of them, to look anxiously in the direction of the skirmish. They were still shooting up tracers from time to time: they would go up and up, drawing a thin red line across the night sky, and then, very suddenly, they would vanish.

'Shouldn't we go over there to help them?' asked Ziya in a trembling voice.

'Haven't you learned anything in the past three months?' said Serdar, strengthening his hold on his rifle. 'It's a crime to leave your station. They'll have seen the tracers. Don't worry – they'll be out there with reinforcements soon enough. And anyway. What if the smugglers are making all that noise to the west, just so that they could box us in over there, and pass over to the east?'

'You're right,' murmured Ziya.

And there they stayed till morning, trying to protect their territory, and watching the fire-fight to the west with growing trepidation. Whenever there was gunfire, the jeeps and trucks in the field behind them would sweep the night with their searchlights, of course. Later on, a truckload of soldiers from Viranşehir joined them, together with two panzer tanks, but in the end it was not possible to stop this flock of sheep crossing like a flood of dirty wool from Turkey into Syria. As soon as there was light in the sky, they went pouring out of border control and the stations to look over to the place where the skirmish had happened. The scene that met their eyes was heart-wrenching: seventy sheep in all, lying dead on the dirt path, and in no man's land, and the minefield, and the railroad. There were wounded sheep amongst them, legs twitching as they took their last breaths. Two or three paces from the barbed wire, lying amongst the empty shells, were two horses whose bellies were riddled with bullet holes, and two men lying side by side. They were both wearing black shalwar trousers, and their scarves had been pulled off their heads. It had been Hayati of Acıpayam and Veysel Hoca in the trench just in front of them; Veysel Hoca was leaning on the wall, motionless and staring up at the sky, and letting out a light moan now and then, but it was Hayati, curled around his rifle, who'd been hit in his chest, and he had been dead for some time.

Veysel Hoca had been hit in the shoulder, and when the soldiers from the company came to collect him, they lifted him up much too roughly. They put him into an open jeep and took him to Urfa to be examined.

All the soldiers came running in from the Seyrantepe stations, wanting to see Hayati, and no one more than Osman of Selçuk, but the sergeant opened his arms to keep them from getting too close. In an anguished, ropy voice, he said, 'Stand back, my friends. I beg of you, stand back.' At these words, the men stood back, and there they waited, in tears. The only one who went in to look at Hayati close up was the commander; kneeling next to his head, he straightened Hayati's cap, and then he bent down, so that the men wouldn't see him cry.

And while he cried, Kenan was standing still next to Ziya, tears brimming in his eyes.

'Do you know what?' he said. 'None of this seems real.'

'Not to me, either,' Ziya said.

Then he turned around and looked at the two horses lying on the other side of the barbed wire, and the two men in shalwar trousers lying next to them. A soldier from the company was standing guard, with his rifle held crossways, but he had his back to them, and was looking at Hayati.

Later on that day, before Hayati departed for the village of Acıpayam in Denizli in his flag-covered coffin, the commander reassigned most of the men at Seyrantepe Station, sending some to Yıldıran and Mezartepe, and others to Boztepe, and quite a large number to Telhamut, but Ziya was not amongst them. That was why, when the rest of them loaded their belongings on to the back of the truck and climbed in after them, it was only the two of them standing there, Ziya and the sergeant. And once the truck was out of sight, they walked over to the two unclaimed soldiers lying there in their graves; as flashes of light spun out from the mirror that was hanging from the branch of the almond tree, they stood side by side in the grass and looked down at the border, and at the station where Hayati had given his life.

'After the truck drops off all your friends, it will drop other soldiers off here,' said the sergeant, in a voice so low he was almost speaking to himself. 'And also, the commander is moving me to Yıldıran Outpost, so as soon as this other sergeant comes to replace me, I'll be leaving.'

'So why did he leave me here?' Ziya asked.

'You're going back to Ceylanpınar, to work with the clerk,' the sergeant told him. 'That's what the commander said.'

And so it was that Ziya climbed up into the passenger seat of a small truck that came for him that evening, and returned to the big, grey building in Ceylanpınar; his first stop was the munitions depot, where he turned in his rifle, his canteen, his cartridge box, his charger and his bullets. The next morning, he sat down in front of a typewriter on the second floor, so that the humpbacked clerk who was to be discharged three weeks later could teach him which document was to be drawn up when, and how.

Everything had changed so fast: for him at least, the grinding hell of life on the border had suddenly given way to a story to be lived through documents on a desk. And even more important, he was the one who was shaping this story: he would wake up early to take the reports coming in from the outposts by phone; if there'd been an incident, he would take down the names of the guards who had given a rough account to their sergeants and determine how many bullets they had used, and then he would sit down at the table and roll some yellow onion skin into that creaking typewriter and begin typing at once. At such and such a time, gendarme X and gendarme Y, who were standing guard in such and such a station, under the command of such and such an outpost, itself under the command of this company, spotted intruders passing over from Syria to Turkey, and after warning them three times, and telling them to stop, the intruders answered with gunfire, whereupon a skirmish started, of which the outcome was as follows . . . this was how these stories went, making no mention of the well water, or the lice, or the wooden outhouse, or the water they had to scoop up with a tin can and pour over their heads when trying to wash themselves, or the mosquitoes, or the pieces of bread they ate in the middle of the night, in their trenches, or the letters they sent home, never knowing if they got there, or the fear, or the melancholy, or the flavourless food. Not a mention of any of this, of course. After completing a summary report that left out even the shadow of the truth, the time came to sketch out the incident itself. First he would draw a double line down the full length of the page, to indicate the route of the railroad that divided Turkey from Syria. Then he would draw another line and mark it with crosses at intervals to indicate the barbed-wire fence, and next to that he would indicate the sand track with a broken line, and in the empty space between this and the railroad he would write m i n e f i e l d, taking care to leave spaces between the letters. And if any smugglers had died in the skirmish, they were shown as stick figures lying in this minefield, or the sand track. Sometimes he had to include dead horses and dead sheep and bales of tea in these sketches. But if, say, ten bales of tea had been seized, only two or three or four would be surrendered to customs; the rest would most certainly be distributed to the guardhouses so that the soldiers could have their fill of tea. This was why Ziya almost never had to sketch in those little tea chests. And this was how he finished off those documents, which he would then put into their dossier, and take down to the commander's office, to have them signed.

Ziya already knew it from his father's letters, but the commander had yet to tell him that they came from the same town; when Ziya stepped into his office, the commander would give him a warm look, as if he could see Ebecik and Hacı Veli, standing there before him, but then he would pull himself together, so fast you might think he feared being caught in the commission of a crime, as his gaze turned to his uniform. Or perhaps, when Ziya stepped into his office, Ebecik and Hacı Veli stuck their heads in with him, and began to harangue him in whispers. Maybe that was why, if there were many documents to sign, he'd say, 'Go and wait outside,' in a very cold voice. When his work was done, he would hop into his open-topped jeep and speed off to Telhamut, eyes glued to the road, and no one would see him until noon the next day.

If there were no more documents to prepare, and no more messages from the exchange for him to transmit to the company by phone, Ziya would usually go out to the garden after the commander left. Because it was forbidden to go into the market, he would spend hours walking up and down that dry garden, with its stone walls and its arbour in the far corner. And while he was walking up and down, he could hear the horse carriages and the minibuses passing down the road on the other side, and sometimes he could hear women and children talking. And later, the aroma of that bread they cooked on their stovetops would float over with their voices, and doors opening and shutting, and curtains fluttering, and the red echoes of peppers hanging in strings from the frames of distant windows. And late in the afternoon, a little old man with his long hair growing into his beard would appear at the foot of the garden, a gaggle of children in his wake. Taking no offence as the giggling children pelted him with bottle caps, he would jump over the wall, this old man, and shuffle in his plastic slippers to the rubbish bins next to the kitchen door. Taking out the plastic bag in his pocket, he would fill it with leftovers. After seeing this ragged old man a few times, Ziya grew curious, and asked the cooks who he was.

'His name is Yabu,' one of the cooks told him. 'He's the only person in Ceylanpınar who is able to go in and out of this place without first seeking permission. Yade used to come too, but now he's dead.'

'Hmmm,' said Ziya, as he shook his head.

'If you want to know about Yabu, you should ask Seyfettin in the exchange,' said the cook, lowering his voice as if to pass on a big secret. 'He's the one who knows him best. And the things he'll tell you. They boggle the mind.'

Ziya went straight upstairs, and down to the end of the corridor next to his office, and here he found Seyfettin, lost in thought and smoking a cigarette at the front of the telephone exchange. He asked him about Yabu.

'He's one of life's sad stories,' said Seyfettin, taking a long drag from his cigarette. 'He comes here every day for leftovers, and that's all he has to eat. This is nothing new; it's been going on for a long time. Many years ago, on a hot summer's day, his wife was here, too, and she died right next to those rubbish bins. No one ever asks Yabu what he's doing there, or why he's going through the army's rubbish – we all close our eyes to it. Even the commander. Well, if he came in past the guards, waving his arms around, then maybe they'd have to ask, but he prefers to come over the wall, every time. He must have developed a taste for it.'

Seyfettin fell silent.

'Is that all?' Ziya asked.

'There's more,' said Seyfettin. 'But I'm not sure how to tell you right now . . . Yabu's not the kind of person you can describe just like that. Because he's a story. A story like you've never heard.'

'How do you mean?'

'I mean, he's a story. Yabu is a story, through and through.'

Ziya gave Seyfettin a blank look.

This seemed to make Seyfettin uneasy, and so he turned to look out the window, in the direction of Syria and the town of Ras al-Ayn; they could hear its donkeys braying and its horses neighing, and for a while they listened to those sounds floating over the border.

'It's a story I myself read many years ago, in a book,' he said.

'What story is that?' Ziya asked.

'Didn't I just tell you, that Yabu was a story? Have you already forgotten?'

Ziya stood up angrily and was about to leave the telephone exchange when he turned around suddenly at the door. 'Is this some sort of joke?' he asked reproachfully.

For a moment Seyfettin just looked at him, saying nothing.

Then he said, 'I swear to you, what I'm saying is true. And in the story I read, Yabu even had a daughter named Gazel, and she set out one night on horseback, to be married in that Syrian town we can see just out the window there – Ras al-Ayn. If you don't believe me, you can ask Yabu yourself.'

215

'What was the name of this book you read?'

'That's what I can't remember.'

'Who wrote it?'

'Sadly I don't remember the author's name either.' Opening his arms, Seyfettin added: 'His name didn't seem much like an author's name. Which goes to say that – as far as I remember – he wasn't well-known, this author.'

'All right, then,' said Ziya, and he left.

Late the next afternoon, Ziya left his typewriter and went down to the garden, hoping to see Yabu. And soon he saw him, walking between the lane's mud-brick walls, and trailed by the usual gaggle of children. And then, as those children pelted him with bottle caps that seemed not to offend him, he clutched the wall and straddled it and hurled himself into the garden like a dirty, hairy sack. And that was when Ziya walked towards him, very slowly, and gently.

'Baba,' he said, and his voice was as gentle as the look on his face. 'May I ask you something?'

Yabu looked at him in silence, his eyes caught.

'Ask me.'

'Do you have a daughter named Gazel?' Ziya asked.

Yabu slowly bowed his head, and swallowed.

In a stern voice, he said, 'This is not a question anyone should ever ask, my child.'

And then, without another look at Ziya, he went shuffling in his plastic slippers towards the rubbish bins next to the kitchen door.

Ziya felt so bad about asking the question that he died a thousand deaths, of course. He felt so bad he even stayed away from the garden for a few days; instead, when he had finished his work, he would stand next to the typewriter, gazing through the window at the town of Ras al-Ayn, smoking one cigarette after another. And they had at long last completed the new company headquarters, whereupon he left Ceylanpınar for good, anyway, in the truck carrying the contents of his office, which passed in front of Mezartepe, Seyrantepe, Ege and Boztepe stations on its way to Telhamut. And so it was that he left Yabu behind him, along with the aroma of hot bread floating from those earthen-roofed houses, ringing with the voices of women and children, and fluttering curtains, and strings of red peppers, and the creaking, clacking horse carts. And what took their place, of course, was the bare and yellow sun-baked earth, stretching mournfully as far as the eye could see.

When they reached Telhamut, with those clouds of dust pursuing them, Kenan came running up to greet him. Once the commander was out of sight they embraced each other. Then and there, they brought each other up to date. Together they unloaded the metal cabinets and tables and dossiers and carried them over to the new building, which was all on one level, with an entrance flanked by columns. Across from this building was a prefabricated guardhouse that looked just like Seyrantepe, and twenty-five paces beyond, on the other side of a barbed-wire fence, was a white flagpole and a rusty water pump. Just a bit below all this, on the other side of the train tracks, was a little station, and a hamlet made up of nine whitewashed houses, each one lower than the last. This was why there had to be a gap in the minefield behind the new building, before it continued on to Akçakale in parallel with the train tracks. Whichever direction it was coming from the Toros Express always slowed down when pulling into this station. It crept down the tracks like a tired old reptile, almost, hissing faintly, but never sounding its whistle. There was no stopping it, either, unless the commander had ordered it to do so; it would creep on quietly down the tracks, watched only by the handful of children playing in front of the mud-brick houses and the stationmaster standing guard, towards Ceylanpınar, or Akçakale. And before long, it would be lost inside the yellow earth's humming.

Living in the village's nine mud-brick houses were the railroad's employees and their families, and their lives were as dry and impossible as the soldiers'. Like the soldiers, they had to live without streets and avenues, shops and markets, parks and gardens. They didn't have a school, either, or a clinic. If they wanted to meet with friends and family on holidays or weekends, they wanted to go to Akçakale or Gaziantep or Ceylanpınar, they had to get permission from the commander. This was because the commander could at any time call out every last one of them, old and young, and line them up next to the well at the back, and do a roll-call. If anyone was missing, or if anyone had for any reason rubbed him up the wrong way, he had no qualms about giving them hell. Because the electricity ran from the State Battery Farm to the company headquarters, and from there to those mud-brick houses, he would, for example, cut off their electricity until they screwed their heads back on. And then the village itself would shudder, almost as if it was crying. A little shiver would pass across its earthen rooftops, and the grass around their walls would go yellow, sending faint reflections to swirl through the empty spaces around the well at the back, and while all this was going on, the village itself would move twenty-five or maybe even thirty paces closer to Syria. And then, amongst those faint reflections, you would just begin to see faces, some very pale faces, and as they took on substance, you would begin to see the windows these women were standing in, and the doorways. And then, clutching their children, or holding them in their arms, they would cross over to the company headquarters and stand in front of the commander's office and, for hours on end, beg for mercy.

Once, when the commander had gone on a rampage and cut off their electricity, the women brought a hollow-cheeked man with them to company headquarters. He was furious, this man; his Adam's apple kept bobbing, and he kept grinding his teeth, until there were sparks flying from his eyes, almost. Later on, when he went up to the commander's door, he could hold himself back no longer. In a trumpeting voice that shocked everyone, he said, 'The milk we keep in our refrigerators will go off, you know! Can't you take pity on the children? Why don't you just admit it – what you've done is unjust!'

That's what this man bellowed. The commander was furious, of course, to be addressed in this tone of voice, and every vein in his neck bulged. Then he turned to the women waiting outside the door and waved them away like so many mosquitoes, saying, 'Go away now. Go away.' And off they went, looking over their shoulders as they crossed over to their houses to wait next to the well at the back. And that was when the commander fell upon this man, hollering, 'I spit on your fate, you dog and son of a dog!' and punching him smack in the face. Shocked by this turn of events, the little man just stood there, red-faced and staring blankly. On the commander's orders, the cook from the guard station and one of the drivers then tied this man to the flagpole, stripping him from the waist up. Then the commander picked up his cartridge belt and went up to him, and laid into him, pelting him with a string of unspeakable curses as he beat him to a pulp. The man's eyes opened wide each time the cartridge belt landed; they swayed and they clouded, they churned and they shook, until tears were shooting out of them into two straight lines, but the commander kept on going. Every time he hit the man, the women at the well would shake, too, moaning uyyy, uyyy, tiny little moans that called to mind a *saz* playing in the wind. At last the commander hollered, 'Untie this dog,' and threw his cartridge belt on the ground. He hurried off to his jeep and off he went in a cloud of dust back to Ceylanpınar.

Having watched all this from his office window, Ziya now stood up and went down to the canteen that had opened the previous month. It had less to offer than a village grocery shop, this canteen: cologne, envelopes, paper, ballpoint pens, razors, shaving cream, a few brands of cigarettes and biscuits, and that was it. When Ziya walked in, he found the manager, Resul of Lüleburgaz, standing at the window, watching them pick up the man they had untied from the flagpole and carry him over to the mud-brick houses.

'Those poor people,' he said, when he saw Ziya coming in. 'And what a shame that there's nowhere to go, to put in a complaint about this commander!'

'Such a shame,' said Ziya, and he took a deep breath.

Lowering himself into the chair behind the table, Resul fixed his eyes on the train tracks, while he let his thoughts wander.

'I was just thinking,' he said then. 'If one of those people got on the train to go and make a complaint against this commander, they'd never be able to show their face here again. They'd have to take their whole family with them, even. If they didn't . . . I swear there'd be hell to pay from that commander, he'd kill them all and toss their bodies into the minefield. And then he'd say they'd been shot while crossing over the border, and get away with it!'

Ziya sat down across from him.

'Would he really do that?' he asked softly.

'He would, I swear,' said Resul, nodding. 'When the engineers at the State Battery Farm drink *rakı*, he hands them weapons, this man, and sends them off to be ambushed. And off they go to dig in, on their little drunken pattering feet. If they end up getting shot in a skirmish, then all this commander has to do to make them look like smugglers is pick them up and throw them into the minefield. He's not about to say he gave these civilians weapons and set them up to be ambushed. Is he?'

'I just don't know,' Ziya mumbled.

Then he turned his head to look out at the mud-brick houses. One of the women at the well was tending to the man, who still seemed to be unconscious. She was cleaning his eyes and face with water. Another woman in a white headscarf was standing next to the well, with her hand on the crank. As the sun beat down on her, she remained perfectly still.

'Can I offer you anything? Would you like something to drink?' Resul asked suddenly.

'Could I have some tea?' Ziya asked.

Resul reached under the table and took out a bottle, poured some of its cloudy white liquid into a glass and pushed it slowly across the table. 'Go on, give it a try.'

Ziya raised it to his lips without giving it much thought, but as soon as he tasted it, his face changed. Smacking his lips, he took another sip.

'It's my own creation,' said Resul, smiling faintly. 'Cologne, lemon powder, and water. What do you think?'

'I'm not sure,' said Ziya, and he took another sip.

'If you don't like it, there's a bar just over there, down that street,' said Resul. 'You can go there and find any drink you want.'

Ziya pretended not to have heard Resul's teasing words. He carried on drinking, as he looked out at the mud-brick houses.

'These commanders are all the same,' Resul said then. 'There's a commander in the next company over, for example. He loves watching soldiers' caps fly off! That's his nickname, even. Capflyer. He knows all about it, and he loves it. He hasn't been past here for some time, so you can expect him any time. He's sure to be coming by soon, no question about it, you'll see. If you hear a roaring laugh suddenly, and a gun going off, be warned. Capflyer is back. He never travels solo. He always has his clerk sitting up front with him in his jeep, and following close behind is always one of those little trucks. And in the back, he'll have his detail of bodyguards, huge grinning dimwits with lolling tongues, and they all have their fingers on the trigger. If you want to live, my advice is to hide the moment you see him coming. Because if anyone's so foolish as to walk past him, and it happens to take his fancy, he'll immediately pick up his gun, and order that man to stop fifteen metres away from him, and order him to raise the visor on his cap. And then, as you may have guessed by now, he'll pick up his gun and with a single shot, he'll send that cap flying, right up into the air . . . and then, to top it all off, he has to celebrate, he has to split his sides laughing that maddening laugh of his. If that was all he did, then fine! But no, he also has to start swinging his gun around, and shooting off in all directions, without even looking through the barrel. He's not much to look at – he's stocky, and he has a fat ass and a head like a basket, but in spite of all that, he's surprisingly quick off the mark, this Capflyer. Fast as a flea, you might say! I said this already, but just make sure you don't catch his eye. Just hide as fast as you can. That's what everyone does, anyway, along the seventy- or eighty-mile stretch between his headquarters and Ceylanpınar. Most especially the guards in the watchtower – they won't even poke up their heads. Because they're already seven or eight metres high, and that means they don't even need to raise their visors: if the fancy takes him, Capflyer pulls his gun from its holster and sends their caps flying from the top of a moving jeep! A few months ago, they took two heads at Seyrantepe. You heard about that, didn't you?'

'Heads? What heads?' said Ziya.

'You know, those two smugglers they killed. Didn't you hear this?'

Ziya gaped at him.

'Don't look at me like that,' said Resul. 'Here on the border, whenever they kill any smugglers, that's what they call it. Taking heads. And whenever they take any heads, a few commanders will get together to celebrate with a bit of *rakı.* I'm not sure if it's a tradition, but it's what they do every time. And it's the commander who can claim the head who hosts the party, of course. When they got together to cele-brate the two heads from Seyrantepe, Capflyer came, too.'

'Did they really celebrate that here?' Ziya asked.

'Why are you so surprised?' Resul asked. 'The man claimed two heads, so of course he would.'

Ziya's head began to spin. There was a roar in his ears as he looked at Resul as if seeing him for the first time.

'The drink's gone to your head, I think,' said Resul. 'I can see it on your face.'

Ziya looked down and swallowed.

'Give me some more of this poison,' he said, pushing his glass across the table. 'For God's sake, give me more!'

Resul filled the glass.

'Capflyer came that night, too,' he said, picking up where he'd left off. 'They'd set up a table right over there, under the flagpole. The soldiers had all gone out to their stations, of course. The only other ones here were Yusuf the cook, and the night watchman, and me. I knew what was going to happen, so I made myself scarce. Yusuf the cook was waiting on the table, so no such luck for him, of course. The poor man spent the night shuttling back and forth between the flagpole and the kitchen. And that was why he was doomed to capture our friend Capflyer's attention, after he'd knocked down enough drinks to relax. His head swimming with *rakı*, he took his gun out of his holster, and said, Come over here and stand in front of me, and then he ordered him to raise his visor. Yusuf had no choice but to do as he was told. He backed up until he was a good distance away, but Capflyer wasn't able to fire. What I mean is, he kept raising his gun and closing one eye as if he was going to fire, but he never followed through. Sometimes he even sucked in his breath, and when he was ready to pull the trigger, he cried out, "Bammm!" And there was Yusuf standing there, dying and coming back to life again, dying and coming back to life, and in the end he shat himself. The men at the table slapped each other on the backs and fell about laughing, just to see him like that. So that's what kind of man he is, this Capflyer. It's always the same joke, and one day, I fear, he'll take aim to send someone's cap flying, and shoot some poor bugger in the temple. You have to be on guard at all times, if you ask me. You downed that second glass pretty fast, didn't you?'

'I did,' said Ziya, in a little yellow voice that stank of cologne.

After which Ziya got up without saying goodbye and when he reached the corridor, he took the internal stairs up to the top of the building. There was no one left by the well at the back of the mud-brick houses; there was only the shadow of the well's wooden crank, and it was as smooth as a new puddle. After Ziya had stared for a long time at that shadow and the houses' darkened doors, he went to the edge of the roof and gently sat himself down on the nobbled black concrete. And then for a time he thought about Hayati of Acıpayam, killed in that skirmish at Seyrantepe Station. And he even thought of the two men in black shalwar trousers, lying near his friend's lifeless body, on the other side of the barbed-wire fence, surrounded by empty shells, and suddenly he could not hold himself back any longer. He began to cry. Then Resul came over and took him by the arm and led him to his office downstairs. He asked him why he was crying, but Ziya had no time to give an answer. Because just then, the jeep that had gone shooting off to Ceylanpınar came limping back. The commander went hurrying into the building, and as he opened his door, he called sternly out to Ziya, ordering him to come at once.

Wiping away his tears, Ziya hurried down.

When he had entered the room and saluted, he saw that the commander was seated at the front desk, looking at the pile of letters before him. He looked as if he was struggling to hold in some sort of anger or grievance, something he had clung to, long after he should have let it die away. There was a hardness in his face. Something was eating him. Then he picked up one of the letters and swung it back and forth. 'Who's this Midhat Çınar?' he asked Ziya.

'Ali Çınar's son, sir,' Ziya replied.

'Ali the Snowman's son?'

'Yes, sir.'

Screwing up his face, he threw the letter across the desk as if it were dirtying his fingers. And then he said, 'Take it.' In a mocking voice, he added, 'This Midhat Efendi has written you a letter.'

Ziya went over to the desk and picked up the letter.

'Give these other letters to the driver,' said the commander, pushing them across the desk with the back of his hand. 'Tell him to deliver them to the appropriate stations.'

Ziya picked up those letters.

The commander frowned at him sternly.

'Why do you stink of cologne?' he asked.

'I have a toothache, sir,' Ziya replied. 'I've dipped it in cologne to kill the pain.'

'That's enough!' said the commander, jumping to his feet as if to strike him. 'Get out!'

Shocked by the reprimand, Ziya got out and went back to his office and, wanting to know what had made the commander so angry, he at once opened his letter. Or rather, he reached into the envelope that had already been opened and pulled out the letter, which had been folded twice. What he saw first was the photograph in the fold. It had been cut from a newspaper, and it was a picture of Midhat from the waist up, arms crossed and smiling happily. Next to his picture was an advertisement for a film called *Hope*, and it showed Yılmaz Güney in the role of Cabbar the Carriage Driver, staring into the lens with his family; his hands were on his eldest son's naked shoulders, and he standing there, straight as a rod, frowning stonily at Ziya from underneath his bushy eyebrows, with a face so angry and mournful that it made a nonsense of Midhat's smile. Then Ziya looked at the little black-eared dog who seemed to be the eighth member of the family, sitting there on the lap of his youngest son. In the first lines of the letter, Midhat confirmed that the revolutionary struggle continued, and that he had finally secured permission to open a community centre, which he'd filled with books, and a week earlier they had brought a copy of the film *Hope* in from Aydın and shown it for free for three nights running. He went on to detail what he called his other revolutionary acts: setting up a reading group, setting up a drama club, writing 'Long Live Socialism' on the face of the fountain at the entrance to the town. He went on and on, recklessly piling on the detail, as if he did not know that all soldiers' letters were censored. In the last lines of the letter, he told Ziya how much he was looking forward to seeing him again when he got out, to which he added a string of slogans in huge letters, followed by two and sometimes three exclamation marks, each one bolder than the last.

By the time he finished the letter, Ziya was beside himself. 'Midhat, you dolt,' he thought. 'How could anyone be so naïve?' He stood up and left the office, heading to the canteen for more of Resul's brew. But it was almost as if the commander knew where he was going, for now he called him into his office.

'Go to the depot and get yourself a rifle,' he said, without looking him in the face. 'From now on, you are coming out with me on night patrol!'

'Yes, sir!' said Ziya.

And so it was that, so many months later, he was armed once again, and issued with a cartridge belt, and every night he set out in the passenger seat of that jeep, like Capflyer's clerk, to patrol the impenetrable darkness. Hours after the soldiers had gone to their stations, they would leave company headquarters, and all night long they would drive up and down the road that stretched along the barbed-wire fence, trembling like a strip of gauze. As they passed, the guards would scramble to their feet, their rifles slung over their shoulders, and salute. If there was anyone asleep inside, or smoking a cigarette, or if anyone had gone over to talk to his friends in a neighbouring trench, the commander would jump down from his jeep and beat him to a pulp. Sometimes the commander and the guard would be swallowed by the night but the air still rang with kicks and punches. When the scuffle ended, the commander would always appear in exactly the same place as he had vanished. Breathing heavily through his nose, he'd get back into the jeep, stretching out in the back seat and looking disgusted, and then he would turn to the driver, Ahmet of Polath, and bellow, 'Start driving, you animal! What are you staring at?' And Ahmet of Polath would start driving, his face darkened with anger, but saying nothing, and off they would go again, down the road. And if there was a skirmish at any point along the section of the border for which they were responsible, or an exchange of gunfire, or a tracer flying through the sky, they would head straight out to assist those guards, of course. Taking shelter behind the jeep, they would join in the shooting and stay at that post until morning.

Some nights they would sweep the darkness with their searchlights, looking for any smugglers who might have penetrated deep into Turkish territory or any others who might be approaching the border, and sometimes they would turn off all the lights and sit there in the pitch dark, as if lying in ambush. Why they had stopped in that particular place and not elsewhere, and how long they would stay – these were things that only the commander knew, of course. And he never told Ahmet of Polatlı or Ziya. Sometimes he would issue an abrupt command to move forward without putting on the lights, and the jeep would crawl blindly through the night, crackling the dry grass beneath its wheels as it moved towards the next guardhouse. When they were within shooting range, the lights would flash on, as the jeep gathered speed, until pulling up sharply at the guardhouse gate. If the guard on duty was asleep or sitting in front of the phone, chatting with some other guard, it would all end very badly; the commander would beat him until he turned to jelly. Sometimes he'd put the gun to the guard's temple, his eyes flashing in the night like some madman, and bellowing, 'I could blow out your brains, you dog and son of a dog, nothing would make me happier, I swear, I could blow your brains out!'

Because Ziya was still responsible for all the work in the office, he was only able to sleep for a few hours after returning from patrol. And like so many of the guards, he was now suffering from rheumatism, and so he did what they all had to do: to reduce the pain he had to make himself sweat, so he wrapped his knees with plastic bags and tied them tightly with string. After just a few hours, he would jump out of bed and quickly get dressed. Without stopping for breakfast, he would rush to the canteen. If Resul was alone in there, he'd say, 'Pour me a glass of that poison,' and it was only after downing a few glasses that he was able to calm down.

Sometimes Kenan would join them, slipping into a corner to drink that liquid they called poison, looked very ashamed of himself as he pretended to be drinking tea. With each sip, he'd look out the window at the mud-brick houses and a moment arrived when he could no longer keep himself from talking about the beauties of his own village. And so it was that the Telhamut canteen was cooled by that faraway red-pine forest and its fragrant flowers. And then came the bubbling of the pure waters running down its slender brooks, and the tranquil hills, with their oak trees and their juniper bushes, and the clacking grouse in the ash-coloured under-growth, and the sheep pens, and the footpaths carpeted with yellow leaves, and the steep cliffs that were red in some lights and grey in others, and the bugs that glistened in the sun amongst those yellowed-headed, pink-headed, purple-headed thorns. And after these would come the vineyards, and the fruit trees, the gorgeous fruit trees, and their per-fume, whirling through the air like soap bubbles. And in their wake, the blue skies, each one deeper than the one before, and the grassy slopes, glistening as if they'd just been washed, and those silences, always changing colour. It was Kenan's face, and the rise and fall of his voice, that lit up each one, if only for an instant. But then that light would go out, and Kenan would go limp, and before their eyes he would turn into a dark and trembling slip of a ghost. After rubbing his knees and giving himself a good scratch and gazing blankly at the empty shelves, this ghost would leave the canteen in silence. And Ziya would head for the office and the typewriter, to prepare more reports on the latest skirmishes.

The company commander would sometimes park himself at the far end of the outpost and watch him from there. He seemed to take pleasure in seeing that the night patrols and the long days at the typewriter were wearing Ziya down, and his eyes sparkled with malice in which Ziya could see the stars on his shoulder reflected. But it must not have been enough, because one day he brought a truckload of pine saplings to the company headquarters. Some were no thicker than two fingers, others no longer than sweet marjoram, and then Ziya had to plant them one pace apart from each other, all along the base of the barbed-wire fence, around the company headquarters and the guard station, and along both sides of the dirt road at the back, while the commander looked on, smiling nastily. The moment he was finished planting, the commander beckoned to him from the window, and when he reached the office, the commander said, 'You'll be responsible for watering those saplings. I don't want to see any dry soil around their bases!' And as he said this, he didn't look up once.

'Yes, sir,' Ziya said, struggling to mask his confusion.

'And don't let me see anyone else doing the watering. Understood?'

'Yes, sir,' said Ziya once again.

The commander let a soft smile form beneath his moustache as he shook his head.

And so, as if all the work he already did was not enough, Ziya was now rushing out to the water pump next to the flagpole every other minute to water the saplings. In the beginning a number of others, and most especially Kenan and Resul, took pity on him and offered to help, but Ziya stopped them every time. When they were all gathered together, he even begged them. 'Friends,' he'd say. 'The commander doesn't want anyone but me tending to the saplings, so please, please don't water them without my knowing.' And after that, they never picked up another watering can, of course; they just watched from a distance as Ziya dragged his feet, wearily carting his watering can from tree to tree. After a few days of this, Ziya's hands were full of water, too: both palms were covered with little blisters.

The blisters had not even healed yet when the commander made a new decision: one evening he strolled in with his parka draped over his shoulders and, stopping in the doorway, his face went sour under the yellow light. 'From this night on,' he told Ziya, 'you are going out on night patrol in my place.' At which he turned on his heels and headed for the mud-brick houses beyond the barbed-wire fence, and as he looked at them, it seemed to Ziya that each had receded to its own hiding place under cover of darkness. Watching him go, Ziya thought he must be off to empty out the houses and line everyone up next to the well and do a roll-call. But that is not what happened: instead the commander walked softly, very softly, until he disappeared into one of the houses. From that day on, he was forever draping his parka over his shoulders and heading over to that house. He took great care with his appearance after that first time, even; before setting out, he would give himself a close shave, and shine his boots, and put brilliantine on his hair. But the most striking thing about the man crossing through the barbed-wire fence was that he'd become a new man, as soft as the scent of a linden tree. What no one could understand, of course, was how he could go through any of those doors wearing any face at all, after venting his rage on those people, and tying them to flagpoles to beat them up, and lining them up, young and old, next to the well, and peppering them with curses while he did the roll-call. Least of all Resul, who fretted about it for many long days. His theory was that they struggled to make ends meet with the pittance the state paid them, and so opened their doors to the commander out of fear. And when they had opened the door to invite him in, and sat him down on the sofa, and put a few cushions behind his back to make him more comfortable, and offered him a coffee, even – well, they felt obliged to smile, of course, so as not to be rude to their guest, and there was no doubt about it, this was the worst of the man's tyrannies. For there could be no tyranny on this earth that was worse than making those you had tyrannised smile at you. Those poor people, after smiling like that for a few hours, the whole family would probably feel as tired as if they'd spent the whole day lifting rocks. On the other hand, since this commander could not or would not establish any sort of friendly relations with his men, it followed that he suffered from the isolation that power brings with it, and also he was probably thinking all the time about the home he'd lost, and so here he was, in this godforsaken place, pining away like a kitten in the rain, and longing for a warm hearth. And so even if those people opened their doors out of fear, and smiled at him out of fear, this powerful wretch of a man was going over there for no other reason than to enjoy the warmth of home. And this meant that he, too, was hiding behind false gestures, and if he made those false gestures as if he believed them, then in one sense, he was also tyrannising himself. In other words, it was a heart-wrenching scenario, whichever way you looked at it.

'That's what's happening, don't you think?' asked Resul after saying all this.

'How am I supposed to know?' Ziya would reply. 'What do I care about the commander? If he wants to go over and piss on them, then let him do it.'

He'd drink the last of his poison and, head spinning, climb into the jeep, which had so many bullet holes that it would soon become a sieve, and off he would go on his night patrol, with Ahmet of Polatlı behind the wheel. They would follow the same routine as if the commander had been sitting there next to him, driving up and down their section of the border, searchlights sweeping the night to the left and to the right, and never speaking. Whenever they passed, the guards would come out of their stations and stand on the side of the road, their rifles slung over their shoulders, and when they saluted they looked like shadows looming in the night. If he caught sight of Veysel Hoca, who was back from medical leave, or Hayrullah of Adana, or Serdar of Çorlu, or Osman of Selçuk, Ziya would tell Ahmet to slam on the brakes, and they would quickly exchange news. And after the jeep continued on its way, Osman of Selçuk would shake his fist at the dark, yelling, 'Fuck off, you fucking village, fuck off!'

It was not just while he was driving that Ahmet of Polatlı kept silent; even when they stepped down, he held his tongue. Even when they heard gunfire or flares rising in the sky, he said nothing. With a grimness that seemed to be part of the jeep itself, he did exactly as Ziya said. So that was why, as they were creeping slowly towards Mezartepe through a black night that was thick with the scent of grass, Ziya couldn't bear it any more, and asked him why he never spoke.

'I'm preparing myself to die at any moment,' said Ahmet. His voice was as grim as his face.

'I can understand that,' said Ziya. 'But there's not even a skirmish going on right now.'

'You don't understand at all,' said Ahmet, his voice quivering, and almost crying. 'I'm not talking about a skirmish. That's just a possibility. If that's the fate that's written on my forehead, then so be it. I'd die a martyr. But I'm not talking about something that might or might not happen. I'm talking about something that definitely will happen. I'm talking about something that is right in front of us, shouting in our face.'

Instead of asking Ahmet what he meant, Ziya looked at him.

'There isn't a soldier in this place the commander hasn't crushed, as you know full well,' Ahmet continued, keeping his eyes on the road. 'Everyone bears a grudge against him. They're all waiting for their moment. And that's why any of them could blow their top at any minute and pepper this jeep with their bullets. I'll die at the hand of a soldier, that's what I think. Wait and see. They'll fire at the commander and they'll end up shooting me with him, and for what?'

'No! Impossible!' said Ziya. The jeep was bobbing around so much that his voice sounded strangely thin. 'Nothing like that's going to happen. Don't worry.'

Ahmet swung around to fix him with a stare.

'You're very naïve,' he said then. 'The commander's sending you out in the jeep so that they kill you thinking it's him. You haven't joined up the dots yet, I see.'

'The truth is, it never even occurred to me,' Ziya murmured.

And as he did so, he shrank shivering into his seat. He was just straightening his rifle, which had slipped between his legs, when a gunshot rang through the night. First they couldn't figure out what direction it was coming from. Stopping in the middle of the road, and turning off the searchlight and the headlights, they peered out into the night. When two flares went up near Boztepe Outpost, they turned around promptly. They barrelled down the road, passing the stations one by one, but there were no more gunshots, just a few faint whoops that made the black night blacker. Ahmet's face was as rigid as if he were racing into the arms of death; he was pressing down on the accelerator as if to say, whatever shall be, shall be, but get it over with. As he drove he kept glancing with fearful eyes at the guards coming up to the side of the road. As they were racing past Ege Outpost in the direction of Boztepe, five panicky soldiers raised their arms in the air to get them to stop. With one voice they cried, Feyzullah has shot himself! Feyzullah has shot himself! And they raced towards the jeep, trailing their long shadows behind them. They followed them back to their post, of course, and there they found Feyzullah of Niğde, whose left arm had leaned on his gun fifteen minutes earlier and set off the trigger. Now he was lying dazed in a pool of blood. The hole in his arm was horribly large, and they had packed it with the lining from a parka, and to stop the bleeding they had tied his arm tightly with a strip of gauze, just above his elbow. Then they picked up Feyzullah and held him in their arms; and even though he protested, saying leave me here, I want to die, in a quivering little moan, they put him into the jeep and then they sent him on to Urfa. A week later, Mustafa of Yozgat, serving at Yıldıran Outpost, shot himself in the foot. They picked him up out of the grass and carried him weeping tears the size of chickpeas, and sent him off to Urfa, too. Reports were made of both incidents, of course, and statements taken from both men, after which Feyzullah of Niğde and Mustafa of Yozgat were both charged with acting in a manner unfit for the army.

After seeing what happened to those two soldiers, Ziya gave himself over heart and soul to his poison. It was no longer enough just to drink in the canteen: he'd have Resul prepare him another bottle, which he would hide inside his parka and take out with him on night patrol. Because he expected to die at any minute and did not wish to arrive in the next world drunk, Ahmet of Polatlı refused to touch the stuff. He spent his nights with his fearful eyes on those guards who stood like ghosts on the roadside, with their rifles slung over their shoulders, and he spent his days circling the water pump, staring at the ground and speaking to no one. And every so often he would get into the jeep that stood next to the flagpole and just sit there, for hours on end. But all the while, he would keep glancing left and right, grimacing as anxiously as if he were on night patrol already, while bullets rained down on him. Whenever Ziya looked up from his typewriter, he would see him in that jeep. So when the day came that he did not see him there, he waited at first, thinking he might have gone to the toilet, and then he got up from his desk a few times to lean out the window and look around. And then Resul came rushing into the office. Twice he lunged forward, as if he was trying to ram a door, as in a panicked voice he cried, 'Ahmet's crossed over. By God, he's crossed over!'

'What do you mean, he's crossed over?'

'Crossed over to Syria! I saw it with my own eyes!'

'We can't let the commander find out,' said Ziya, jumping up. 'Come on now. Come with me.' By the time he and Resul had gone through the barbed-wire fence, and crossed the tracks, and passed the well and come to the end of the mud-brick houses, they looked across the ploughed fields spraying gold dust in the midday sun and saw Ahmet racing into the depths of Syria. They caught up with him, breathless, at the entrance to a little treeless village. 'We beg you,' they implored. 'Don't fail your military service!' Taking him by the arm, they dragged him back. Creeping silently around the rear of the company building to keep the commander from seeing, they took him into the office, but Ahmet was still struggling to free himself from their grasp. That was why, after they'd put him into a chair, they sat down next to him, one on each side, and tried to console him, as well as calm him down. 'Would you like a little poison?' they asked. 'Shall we bring some up?' But Ahmet wouldn't answer this question; for five minutes, he remained silent, head bowed, and then he took a very deep breath and broke into sobs.

The commander had woken up by now and was standing in the door of the room next to the guardhouse, looking very drowsy. Next to the flagpole, a soldier was shaving the head of another soldier who was crouching on the ground. He didn't seem to be doing it quite right, because the soldier who was crouching on the ground kept turning around, white-eyed, to offer suggestions. Sometimes he fluttered his fingers back and forth in the air, to show him how it should be done. The other soldier would lean over and watch carefully from above, and nod. Just then, an open-topped jeep rolled in past the soldiers who had queued up in front of the toilet with their water cans, waiting for their turn to wash. In a cloud of dust, it wheeled to the right to come to a halt five paces in front of the commander. Out jumped a flushed, narrow-shouldered, humpbacked weed of a sergeant. As he loped over to the commander, it looked as if the wind was blowing him. His head bobbing, he began to tell the commander something with feverish intensity, pointing into the distance as he did so. And the commander stood there listening, still as a statue. Then he put his hands on his hips and for a time gazed down at the ground in silence. The sergeant fell silent, too. He stood with his hands at his sides, and his head bent. Then suddenly the commander raised his head, turned towards the office, and waved to Ziya to come straight over.

Ziya left Resul in the office with the sobbing Ahmet and rushed over.

'The clerk in the next company was shot in a skirmish last night,' said the commander. 'You are to go over there and show someone who can type how to prepare the report. They'll bring you back tomorrow. So now jump into that jeep!'

'Yes, sir!' said Ziya.

And then he climbed into the back of the jeep and sat down on a black leather seat that was caked with dust. The sergeant piled in after him, looking very much like one of those stick figures in the sketches he did of incidents. With that they were off, and, tracked by clouds of dust, they sped down the road for six or seven hundred metres, and into the territory of the Yıldıran Outpost, and on they went, racing towards the horizon in silence. For about an hour, they watched yellow waves ripple across the empty sun-baked hills, as the minefield on their left grew thicker and then thinner, while on their right they passed one observation tower after another, and trenches that looked like open graves. At regular intervals, they also passed the grey prefabricated guardhouses perched on their hilltops like forgotten boxes. And then there were the waves of desolation, and the silences, and the things that seeped into those silences – the rustling of grass and the deep-blue skies – until at last they had arrived at company headquarters.

When they got out of the jeep, the sergeant said, 'Follow me,' and led him straight into Capflyer's office. This was at the front of a stone building that, with its high walls and crenulations, resembled a little desert fort. Capflyer was standing at the window, hands on hips, lost in thought. Slowly, very slowly, he turned around, and Ziya could see that his eyes were red, and puffy from lack of sleep. Slowly, very slowly, he returned to his desk and then he looked Ziya up and down, up and down, as if he could hardly believe he was there. And then off he went, huffing and puffing and angrily rubbing his face, as he explained how his clerk had been killed by smugglers and gave precise instructions for the report. He didn't go into much detail, to tell the truth: all he said was that the previous night he had gone out in his jeep on night patrol as usual with his clerk, Rasim Benli, that at around three in the morning they had spotted a group of smugglers trying to cross over from Syria into Turkey, and that at the end of a skirmish lasting fifteen or twenty minutes, they had pushed them back. And also that these smugglers had left nothing behind, and that the battlefield was empty, on account of the smugglers having passed through the minefield, and he said all this through narrowed eyes, as if he was reading a book from a distance. And then, with a ball-point pen he pulled out of his shirt pocket, he jotted down a few more details – where the skirmish had taken place, the names of the guards who had taken part, and the number of bullets used – and handed this piece of paper over to Ziya, and then, in a weary voice, he said, 'Take this with you, my boy. Go over to that office and prepare the report at once.'

The stick-figure sergeant gave him a curt nod and led him out of Capflyer's office, and took him quickly down the corridor to an office at the other end. There was a row of seven windows in this office – one big one, and six little ones. The walls were milky white, radiating silence, and in the middle of that silence, a tall soldier stood waiting.

'So this is going to be our new clerk,' said the second lieutenant. 'You're to tell him what needs to be done and how. So sit down and get started.'

And though the last thing he wanted to do right then was to sit in the chair of a clerk who'd just been killed, that is what he did. Putting Capflyer's notes down on the desk, he pulled the typewriter closer to his chair and at once began to type. His student – the man the lieutenant had introduced as Cezmi – was a most nervous and absent-minded creature, and his drooping eyelids made him look as if he was already wafting through the world of dreams; knowing that his training was to last only a day, after which he would be expected to do any number of things alone, he bombarded Ziya with anxious questions at every opportunity. And every once in a while Ziya would stop typing to give him a proper answer, and every time he did so, he'd say, 'But listen, every time you're stuck or can't figure something out, you can just pick up the phone and ask me.' This would calm Cezmi down somewhat. He'd slip into the deathly silence of the corridor and return with two glasses of tea. But as soon as they'd drunk these teas and put the glasses to one side, he'd grow anxious again; standing up, he'd go over to the cupboard where they kept the dossiers, and stare at their spines. He'd pass his hands over the yellow envelopes piled up on the shelves, and rustle through the notebooks next to them, or he'd stand right next to Ziya, asking him whatever question was in his head, even if it happened to be one Ziya had already answered.

The next afternoon, after Ziya had finished the document, put it into its dossier, and taken it into Capflyer's office to be signed, Cezmi asked him a string of questions about the monthly statements he would need to prepare on the company's provisions, equipment and personnel. Leaning against the table, Ziya answered his questions one by one, in plain language. Then he handed the dossier over to Cezmi and in a tired voice he said, 'As there's nothing left for me to do, I think it's time for me to tell the lieutenant, so that they can get me back before dark.'

Glancing at the dossier in his lap, Cezmi asked, 'But does this report say, for instance, that the clerk was shot in the temple?'

'I don't understand,' said Ziya. 'Was the clerk shot in the temple?'

'Yes,' said Cezmi. 'Somehow, in the pitch dark, those smugglers managed to hit him square in the temple.'

Ziya went cold, and for a time he didn't speak. And neither could he see or hear what was going on around. He just sat there, ears ringing, falling through the darkness of his mind.

That same evening, they took him back in the same jeep, reaching Telhamut just as the sun sank into Syria. He was still very agitated: when he went into the room next to the guardhouse to give his oral report to the commander, his face was ashen and he could barely stand. And that was why, after looking him over, he said, with some reluctance, that Ziya was excused from night patrol this once. 'Go and get some rest,' he said. And then he adjusted the collar of his parka, which was hanging on the backs of his shoulders. 'But don't forget,' he said. 'From tomorrow you're going back out on night patrol as usual, and also watering those saplings.'

'Yes, sir!' said Ziya.

And when the commander had dismissed him with a wave, he went straight over to the canteen, even though he was covered with dust, and it was all he could do to put one combat boot in front of the other. He found Resul at the table, entering his daily accounts into his blue notebook. He looked up when the door creaked. Seeing Ziya, he put his pencil down on the notebook, very gently, and raised his head, ready for his friend's report.

'That won't take you too long, I hope,' said Ziya, settling into the chair opposite.

'Thanks,' said Resul. 'Welcome back.'

For a while Ziya stared blankly at the shelves.

Then he whispered, 'You don't have any poison, do you? Please, pour me a glass of that blessed liquid.'

Without a word of complaint, Resul brought out the bottle from the biscuit tin under the table and poured Ziya a glass. He did all this very slowly, and he kept stopping to stare straight into his friend's eyes, eager for his report. Until he couldn't bear it any longer, and gave voice to the question in his eyes. He sat back in his chair, as if to say that Ziya's time was up. 'I mean, really,' he said reproachfully. 'For two days now, people have been talking about this incident and nothing else, so are you or aren't you going to tell me what exactly happened in this company right next to ours?'

'I have nothing to tell you,' Ziya said, emptying his glass in one gulp. Then he wrinkled up his face. 'Fill this up for me again, why don't you.'

'Whether I fill it or not,' said Resul, 'that commander is going to catch us one of these days. And if he does, there'll be hell to pay.'

'Who cares?'

'I say we go up to the top of the stairs, that way we can keep an eye on him.'

'Fine, let's go,' said Ziya, as he emptied his second glass in one gulp.

They climbed up the internal stairs, settling down two steps from the top so that their heads and shoulders were outside. From here they could see the guardhouse, the mud-brick houses, the sand track and part of the front of their own building. The soldiers who were about to go out on guard duty were gathered around the flagpole, buckling their cartridge belts and putting on their parkas. Some were holding the bread they'd picked up on their way out of the mess hall. Then, on the sergeant's command, they lined up and mounted their chargers, pulled out their bolt handles and, throwing their rifles over their shoulders, headed out to their trenches, like a string of weary ghosts. They had been gone for some time when the night engulfed those mud-brick houses in the dip behind the railroad tracks. The night engulfed the well then, too, and the train station, and the flagpole, and the pine saplings, and the guardhouse, and the fields around them. And that was when the commander suddenly came sailing out of his room and headed for the train tracks, his parka swinging from his shoulders. Passing through the barbed wire, he turned into a shadow, until the night that had already swallowed up those houses swallowed him up, too.

'You're overdoing it with this poison,' said Resul. 'If something goes wrong, there's no going to the doctor, as you well know.'

'No one said anything about doctors,' said Ziya. 'In the hell we're in, there aren't even army doctors. And I know that.'

The two fell silent. They stared sourly into their glasses, as if their fates were written in them. And as they did so, a breeze wafted in, a very light breeze that made them shudder, even as it soothed them with the scent of grass.

'So tell me,' said Resul, taking another sip from his glass. 'Are you never going to say what happened in that company next to ours?'

'There's nothing to say,' said Ziya wretchedly. 'A giant millwheel, churning and churning. Mosquitoes buzzing in the background. Lice swarming. Guns going off everywhere. But cap or no cap, ambush or no ambush, that glorious millwheel keeps on grinding people up . . .'

'You're right,' said Resul. 'That's what it's doing. It's grinding us up.'

Again they fell silent. For half an hour, neither spoke. They just stared into the night. Every so often they could hear a whoop coming in from one of the nearer trenches to the east.

'We're turning into cologne,' said Resul. 'Inside and out.'

'That's fine with me,' Ziya said softly.

Resul put his glass down on the dark concrete step.

'No,' he said. 'I'm not drinking any more of it.'

Ziya reached out for the bottle and balanced it between his legs. Just then, another whoop sailed in from the night, a strangled sort of moan. It didn't come from the trenches to the east, though, and neither did it come from the trenches to the west. It seemed to come from the depths of Syria. Then a door swung open, very softly, in one of the mud-brick houses, releasing a fuzzy ball of bright yellow light. But now the door swung shut, taking the light with it, as the house sank back into the night.

'Do you know what?' said Ziya, turning to look at Resul. 'I can't really believe that what we're living through here is really happening.'

'When reality becomes too much to bear, it never does seem real,' said Resul. 'There's nothing surprising about that.'

Ziya bowed his head, and for a time he didn't move.

'Look,' he said, pointing into the darkness behind their building. 'That's supposed to be a minefield, right? Hundreds of horses, and hundreds of people, and thousands of sheep have passed through there since I've been here. And all in the thick of night. Feeling their way, in zigzags and circles. But in all that time, not a single mine has gone off. It's as if even the minefield doesn't really exist.'

'How can you say that?' Resul protested. 'Maybe they got lucky. Or maybe the earth has taken all it was fated to take, and that's why nothing's exploded.'

Ziya retrieved the bottle from between his legs and poured some more into his almost empty glass.

'That's enough, I think,' said Resul. 'Your liver's going to explode.'

'Never mind,' mumbled Ziya.

And he continued drinking, in the same way and at the same rate, but after a time he was no longer in control of his movements, and then, very suddenly, his head fell to his chest. 'You drank too much, my friend,' Resul whispered. Taking him by the arm, he led him down the stairs and straight into the dormitory. Here he helped him remove his clothes, and once he had him lying on his cot, he pulled his threadbare brown blanket over him.

'Even the pine saplings aren't true,' said Ziya, waving his hand. 'Every day I water them, but before the day is out, the ground is dry again. Not the next day, do you hear what I'm saying? The ground goes dry the very same day. Resul, my boy, are you listening?'

'I'm listening,' Resul replied, 'but keep your voice down, so the commander doesn't hear you.'

'Let him hear me,' Ziya said.

No sooner had he said that than he fell asleep.

The next day he watered the saplings, of course, and then went back out on patrol with Ahmet of Polatlı. Holding his rifle between his legs, he sat in the front seat and combed the darkness with his searchlight, as they drove from one end of their stretch of border to the other, and so the months passed, in a cloud of cologne. And when the commander went off to groom himself after work, never once did he take pity on Ziya, and say, 'You're tired. Take the night off and rest.' Quite the opposite. If circumstances kept them from getting to a skirmish fast enough, if that jeep that was beginning to look like a miracle on wheels happened to break down, or if they returned to headquarters in the morning just a bit too early, he lost his temper, and then there was no end to the curses Ziya and Ahmet of Polatlı had to bear. They just had to take all this shit from him and keep their mouths shut. When the commander acted like this, and when he saw those piles of bodies and animal carcasses piled up in the night, Ziya drank even more of Resul's poison. From time to time, when no one was looking, he drank it in the office and the dormitory. Ahmet of Polatlı still wouldn't touch it: instead he spent his shifts peering darkly into the night, watching those guards as they came into view at the roadsides. Once Ziya tried to force the bottle on him – and perhaps this was his way of forcing away the fear inside him. They were in the Seyrantepe area at the time, passing close to the trench where Hayati of Acıpayam had been shot. Ziya was busy with his bottle just then, so the searchlight was off; the dirt road stretched out before them, shivering in the headlights, and the night rose up from both sides of the road to press down on them, heavy and dense.

'Have a drop or two, why don't you,' Ziya said. 'It will calm you down.'

'I don't want any,' said Ahmet.

As he said this, he took his right hand off the wheel and pushed the bottle back.

'You know best, I guess,' Ziya murmured.

Just then a huge explosion ripped through the darkness ahead; and flares flew up into the night, one after the other, from several different points. And it was as if a silence from far away came crowding in on them, while the silence that had engulfed them only moments earlier went flying into the distance, and for just a few seconds, they continued this back and forth, many thousands of times over. And then they could hear a machine gun, howling and on fire, slicing through the night. Ahmet of Polatlı put his foot on the accelerator of course, and they shot off in the direction of the Mezartepe Outpost and the skirmish. Sweeping the night with their searchlight, faster and faster, their hearts in the throats. Whenever there was a lull in the gunfire, they could hear screaming. Loud, sometimes. At other times, more like moans. And now and again, in the time it would take to wag a tail, a horse would whinny. As they drew closer, a bullet from a Kalashnikov struck their rear-view mirror, and Ahmet stopped short; cutting off their searchlight and headlights, they hit the ground. The fire was not just coming from Syria: there were as many as seven or eight Kalashnikovs firing on the guards in those trenches from the Turkish side. Once they worked this out, Ziya and Ahmet decided that there was no point in hiding behind that jeep like two dumb squashes; so as bullets continued to fly across the road, they crawled into a shallow ditch; lying shoulder to shoulder, they pointed their rifles in the direction of the Kalashnikovs and began to fire.

It went on for half an hour, this skirmish, dying down only to intensify. And for that half hour, the hills to the west of Mezartepe Outpost were living hell. When the gunfire stopped altogether, Ziya and Ahmet lay gasping where they were, and there they stayed for some time, uncertain as to what might happen next. And when they were sure that the smugglers had turned back, they made themselves small and crawled down their ditch, heading towards the guards. Somewhere out there in the night – precisely where, they couldn't say – someone was singing a song, or a lullaby. They couldn't actually make out the words, which floated in and out of the silence that had come pouring back in after the gunfire. Sometimes the owner of this voice would stop. From fatigue, perhaps. Or to take a short rest. But then he would find his strength again and belt out the same song. Or lullaby, if that's what it was. And then they heard footsteps. And then the rustling of cloth, the padding of combat boots through black sand. They echoed through the night, these sounds, and then, from the same place, there came a resounding whoop. It did not rise into the air, though. It was almost as if a fatherly hand had dissolved into a sound, to reach anxiously into the darkness, to search for those it had lost. But no one called back to it. The elongated o's just hung there in the night, like giant hoops. And after that there was no more question of narrowing their sights. One after the other, Ziya and Ahmet climbed out of their ditch. Clutching their rifles, they ran down the road.

They arrived at the trench in time to see the sergeant from Mezartepe come running in from the west with his two watchmen. There was no sound coming from the trench, and, fearful that the men inside might be dead, the five of them went crunching over the empty shells to peer inside. They found Yasin of Hendek with his trembling arms wrapped around Mehmet of Elazığ. From time to time he let out a feeble moan that might have been a song, or a lullaby, elongating the i's. Hiiiii! Hiiiii!

'Are you all right?' the sergeant asked them. 'Were you hit?'

'No,' said Mehmet. 'We weren't.'

'What's up with Yasin, then?'

'We got caught between two gunfights,' Mehmet wailed. 'We ran out of bullets.'

The sergeant reached down to take Yasin's hand, and with his other hand he took hold of Mehmet. He pulled them both out of the trench. As soon as he was out, Yasin squatted down amongst the empty shells. He was still shaking, and moaning, 'Hiiiiii! Hiiiiii!' He would stop only to start again.

'He's in shock, I think,' said the sergeant.

'I don't think so,' Mehmet said. 'He got so scared when we ran out of bullets, he lost his mind, if you ask me.'

For a few minutes they hovered around Yasin, uncertain what to do. Yasin, meanwhile, took no notice of them: he was looking, wild-eyed, at some other world. And trembling, of course. And making that strange sound. 'Hiiiiiii! Hiiiiiii!' Then the sergeant crouched down next to him, took him by the shoulders, and shook him like a tree. 'Yasiiiin, come back to yourself, my boy. Yasiiiin!' he cried, over and over. Seeing that this wasn't working, one of the watchmen said, maybe he would come back to himself if we gave him two good punches. Still squatting, the sergeant raised his head as if in prayer. 'How could you think of punching him in this state?' he cried, and he bent his head. He was trying very hard not to cry. What the sergeant couldn't do, the commander did, when he arrived about an hour later. Yasin was still squatting next to the trench, lost in his own world. The commander went up to him, looked him straight in the face, and then he punched him – a right hook, followed by a left hook. 'Come back to yourself, soldier! Come baaaaack!' But this didn't work either. His strange chant just swung one way and then the other as it dissolved into the black wind. And that was when the commander rose slowly to his feet, and placed his hands on his hips. Lowering his head, as if to speak to the grass, he said, 'He's lost his mind, this one. Take him straight to Urfa.'

A week after Yasin was taken to Urfa, the commander suddenly announced that his tour of duty on the border was over. In just a few hours, he had rushed through all the formalities, and emptied the room next to the guardhouse and left, without so much as a goodbye.

The commander who came to replace him had no need for the room next to the guardhouse. He lodged with his family in a house on the State Battery Farm. He would coast in around noon, in a perfectly pressed uniform, all razor-sharp creases. He would visit the guardhouses and the headquarters, brushing the dust off his uniform as he went, and after issuing a number of instructions to the sergeants, he would climb back into his jeep and drive off. So the jeep was now stationed in front of his house at the State Battery Farm, because from time to time it would occur to him to get himself out of bed to go on night patrol. He and Ahmet of Polatlı would drive up and down along the barbed-wire fence, from one end of their territory to the other. He never even gave anyone the finger, this fair-skinned commander. He never even threatened to lose his temper or raise his voice. All he wanted was for everyone to know their responsibilities and do their job. And when he came to visit a guardhouse or company headquarters, his heart would seem to go out to these soldiers in his command. He seemed almost crestfallen. When he frowned, it was almost as if to say, 'Dear boys, you've been to hell and back.' And when he saw the narrow kitchens in which the cooks struggled to work, and the wooden outhouses, and the wells outside the guardhouses, and the cans, and the little broken mirrors dangling from the tree branches, he would turn his eyes away quickly, as if to stop himself from feeling too sorry for the soldiers, as if to keep their pain from blowing him in a wrong direction. And sometimes he would just plunge his hands into his pockets and stand there thinking – thinking about a better life he longed to live, in a better world, but without dwelling too long on the details of this life, which was nothing other than a tragicomedy, invented by children who'd outgrown childhood's games. And after staring miserably at his feet for a time, he would climb back into his jeep, settle into his seat, with its torn cover and its bullet holes, and wave goodbye as he sped off down the road to Ceylanpınar.

A number of things changed in Ziya's life, of course, after this new commander arrived. He didn't go out on night patrol with Ahmet of Polatlı any more. His rifle and his cartridge belt sat unused on his shelf. And so he would go up to the top of the steps every evening, and sit there until late at night, drinking poison. Resul would go up most nights and find him swaying like a lost ghost; he would guide him down the steps and put him into bed, whispering, 'You've really drunk too much tonight, you really have.' And then he'd cover him with his blanket. When the guards came back from their trenches in the morning, and poured into the dormitory, bringing with them the scent of grass and earth, Ziya would wake up and a wave of shame would pass through him. He would have breakfast with them and then he would sit down in front of his typewriter and work all day, all alone in that little room. And whenever Hayati of Acıpayam came into his head, or Feyzullah of Niğde, or Mustafa of Yozgat, or Rasim Benli, the clerk from the neighbouring company, he would rush outside, and seize the watering can, and – even though no one expected him to do this any more – water the pine saplings. That commander might have brought them here, just to make him suffer, but now that he was gone, watering these saplings no longer felt like torture. As certain as he was that his saplings would never grow, he still watered them, and whenever he watered them, he almost cried. And then he would leave the watering can next to the water pump, and head into the canteen, of course, and get started on the poison.

A few hours before going out on guard duty, Kenan would join them; giving himself a good scratch, he would squat near the shelves and sip his glass of poison as slowly as if it were tea. He was no longer the person he once had been. For almost a year now, he'd been going out on guard duty in fear of death every night, and sitting in that trench until morning, with only a piece of bread in his pocket, and returning to the outpost only to sink into a nightmare, while lice and mosquitoes crawled all over him. This miserable routine and all the other indignities of his life had utterly crushed him. He tried to hide it, but his legs shook when he walked and even from a distance you could see how difficult it was for him to carry that rifle on his shoulder. That's why they never gave him too much poison, even if he asked for it. And because they could not bring themselves to tell him why, they'd tried to turn it into a joke, saying, 'Now why would you need more than that? You drink the stuff like tea!' Kenan would turn away to stare at the path he'd soon be taking to the trench. He'd turn back from that hell he was already living, and try to smile. Then he would find an excuse to talk about his village, and in the little weedy voice he'd begin to describe its beauties, which by now had taken on a mythic aura. And as he spoke, his voice would grow stronger, and if a moment arrived when it was strong enough to conjure up a pasture of sun-dappled flowers, he would invite Resul and Ziya to come and see it with their own eyes.

Biting his lower lip, and shaking his head in reverence, he would say, 'Come and visit after we're discharged, at any rate. You should see how beautiful it is, just once.' And they would say, 'We'll do that. We promise.' And Ziya in particular meant it. He had listened to Kenan speak about his village so many times that he had memorised its every detail, and those details were so large in his mind that he was sure that, even if he went there alone, he would know where to find them: the fountain and the coffeehouses, the dirt road that crossed the plain, the sheep pens and the tall poplars enclosing them, the vineyards and, just beyond them, the paths leading up into the red-pine forests. And that was why his cologne-fogged voice rang with such conviction, when he stared into his glass of poison and declared that even if Resul couldn't make it, *he* would come to visit, no matter what it took. 'I'm not dying without seeing it,' he'd say each time. And Kenan would stand up, as happy as a child. Picking up his parka and his rifle, he'd say, 'So wish me luck,' and set off down the path, with his legs shaking.

But one evening he set off down that path and couldn't hold himself up. Before he had taken ten steps, he collapsed on the ground. Ziya saw this through the canteen window, and even though he was well and truly drunk by then, he rushed out to his side. He and the sergeant pulled him up, took off his cartridge belt, opened up his shirt, and threw water on his face. Kenan began to wheeze, and his whole body was shaking, and it was burning hot, too, with some sort of fever.

'He can't go out there in this condition,' said Ziya, looking the sergeant in the face. 'What do you think?'

The sergeant seemed not to know what to think. He bowed his head.

In the days that followed, Ziya did what he could to cheer Kenan up. If he saw his friend's spirits sinking, Ziya would say, 'Look at you, you're skin and bones, there's almost nothing left of you; we're not letting you drink any of this, from now on, it's forbidden.' Kenan accepted the ban Ziya imposed on him without argument. He just bowed his head. So now, when he came to the canteen to squat next to the shelves, he'd rub his aching knees and nibble on the biscuits Resul gave him.

Ziya, meanwhile, was drinking as much as ever, of course. And when he staggered back to the dormitory late each night, he fell asleep the moment his head hit the pillow. This is how he was able to escape the barbed wire and the trenches and the observation towers and the minefields and the guardhouses, and their nightly concert, and their numbing silences. And Telhamut's nine mud-brick houses, and the dormitory in which he slept, as he slipped off like a leaf down a river to another world that carried the sour stink of cologne. And that was where he was one night, with only two months of his military service left to go, when an agitated Resul shook him awake.

'Come on, man! Wake up. The commander's waiting for you outside! Get yourself armed and get out there,' he said.

Exhausted and still half asleep, Ziya looked around him. Then he jumped up and fastened his cartridge belt and ran outside with his rifle in his hands. He found the commander standing in the darkness with his hands on his hips, and looking rather pleased. To his right stood two watchmen holding their rifles crossways, and on his left stood Resul and Yusuf the cook.

'And now we have our clerk,' he said, as soon as he saw Ziya. 'Come over here. Look. We've brought in a live smuggler.'

Ziya looked in the direction the commander was pointing, and there, tied with rope to the base of one of the
columns at the front of the building, was a broad-shouldered
man the size of a wrestler. He was wearing black shalwar
trousers, this man, and a grey T-shirt that emphasised the
thickness of his neck. From time to time he'd look up to
stare straight in the commander's eyes and then he'd begin to
speak, as rapidly as a machine gun. He was speaking Arabic,
so no one could understand a thing he said, of course, beyond
the three names he kept repeating – Muhammed, Ali and
Mensur. The commander narrowed his eyes as they darted
between the soldiers and the man tied to the column, and
from time to time he shook his head, as if to say, 'Just look
at what I managed to drag in.'

Then he turned to Resul. Pointing into the darkness in
the direction of the mud-brick houses, he said, 'Go and find
someone over there who can translate for this animal.'

Resul rushed away, rifle in hand, and once he had loped
across the barbed-wire fence there was no more to him than
a pair of pounding feet.

'Look here,' the commander said to Ziya. 'You're the
clerk so you should know. Has a smuggler ever been
brought in alive on this border?'

'I've never heard of one, sir,' Ziya replied.

The commander fixed his eyes on the man tied to the
column, shaking his head as vigorously as if he'd been the
one to answer his question. Then Resul came out into
the night again, huffing and puffing and bringing with him
a middle-aged railroad worker. But he wasn't good enough
for the commander. He looked him over as if he was about
to give him a thrashing, and then he said, 'No, not this one.

Go back and find the stationmaster. Tell him to come here at once!'

And so Resul went back and woke up the stationmaster, who quickly got dressed. Ten minutes later, he was standing breathlessly in front of the commander. Seeing him, the commander said, 'Now that's more like it,' as if it were the man's uniform that would enable him to translate the prisoner's words correctly and in the right spirit. Then he pointed at the man tied to the column and in a menacing voice, he said, 'Ask this bugger where he hid the goods he was trying to take over, and how many others he had with him.'

The captive's face brightened when he saw that the stationmaster could speak Arabic, and his eyes shone like gold dust. When he was giving his answers, he almost forgot he was tied to the column and tried to stand up.

'What is he saying?' barked the commander.

'He's not a smuggler,' said the stationmaster. 'He says he's a dervish, going by the name of Mensur.'

'What the . . .?' the commander cried. 'So he says he's a dervish?'

'Yes, sir,' said the stationmaster. 'He says he's a dervish. According to what he says, he left his village this evening to attend a wedding in another village. To sate his appetite and his mind, he says. But it was so dark that he mistook the lights of Telhamut for this village, and so he crossed over the border into Turkey without even knowing it.'

'Is he trying to pull my leg?' the commander growled. 'Does he think he can pull my leg?'

The stationmaster bowed his head, as if he had somehow committed a crime.

There was a silence.

'Fine, then,' the commander said finally. 'Go back to your house!'

As Mensur watched him go, he swallowed hard.

The commander stayed there in front of the building all night long, pacing back and forth in front of Mensur like a bird of prey, stopping every so often to shake his head and touch the gun on his hip. And Mensur just sat there watching him, wide-eyed.

At sunrise the commander opened up the tarpaulin at the back of one of the trucks parked next to the flagpole, and ordered his men to put Mensur inside it. And so they untied that huge man and hurled him into the back of that truck. After winding four ropes around his wrists and ankles, they tied him to the side hooks in a way that would keep him standing. Mensur remained silent while they did all this, and he took no interest in the soldiers who were tying him up. Instead he braced his huge shoulders, and fixed his eyes on the commander. They were huge, these eyes. And luminous, and bewildered. Meanwhile, the commander just stood there, a few paces away from the truck. Every so often, he would shake his head. And each time he did so, he changed a bit more, until he had left behind the fair-skinned man who had found the border so distressing, and who had never once raised his voice, let alone a finger. Suddenly he was a different man, bursting with anger.

By now the soldiers had finished knotting the ropes. One by one they jumped off the back of the truck.

'You two,' said the commander, pointing at Resul and Ziya. 'Get back there with the smuggler! Don't take your eyes off him for a single second!'

Resul and Ziya did as they were told; climbing straight into the back of the truck, they sat down on either side of Mensur, holding their rifles crossways.

Then the commander jumped into the front of the truck, and soon they were speeding off towards Ceylanpınar, leaving clouds of dust in their wake. And there was Mensur, standing upright in the middle of the back of the truck, breathing heavily through flared nostrils as his huge body swayed from side to side. Each time he righted himself, he would, without willing it, stare straight into his guards' eyes. And each time he did this, Resul and Ziya would quickly look away, as nervously as if they'd been caught red-handed. So nervously, they didn't know where to look. Seeing the state they were in, Mensur made them more nervous still by looking down at his feet with the faintest of smiles. Then he turned to the right to look at Syria, and for a long time he gazed at its fields and its hills and the one-storey mud-brick houses in its distant villages. He was still looking at Syria as the truck left the road running alongside the barbed wire and climbed up the little hill to Mezartepe. When he saw the truck approaching, the cook adjusted his rifle. He went to the side of the building and stood at attention.

'Bring everyone out,' said the commander, as he stepped down from the truck.

The cook ran off to the dormitory to wake up the sleeping men. Bewildered, they pulled on their clothes and came out to the front of the building.

'Look,' said the commander. 'I caught this smuggler alive last night!'

Their eyes still fogged with sleep, the soldiers looked into the back of the truck. And as they did so, the commander looked at how they looked. And then, with a great deal of swaggering, he told them how they had seen something moving in the grass that night, while out on patrol, and how they had swept it with the searchlight, and bam, there was Mensur, blinking like a rabbit, and though he had made every effort to escape, they had pounced on him and, after a mighty struggle, taken him captive. The soldiers were lined up and standing at attention. They listened, wide-eyed, to the commander's every word. Mensur listened, too, even though he knew no Turkish, and every once in a while he would allow himself a gentle smile, as if he had understood what the commander was saying, and found it greatly exaggerated. On the commander's order, the soldiers stopped standing at attention and walked around the sides of the truck, to get a closer look at Mensur. The commander, meanwhile, kept his distance, going into the shade at the side of the stone wall, and lighting up a cigarette, and looking out at the view through his own billowing smoke.

After Mensur had been put on display there like a circus animal for a good half hour, they moved on to Seyrantepe, and then Ege, and then Boztepe, Telhamut, and Yıldıran. When this last show ended, Ziya assumed they would be heading back, but that didn't happen. Instead they headed west to enter the next company's territory, and to visit each of its guardhouses. And soon they had followed the road along the barbed-wire fence to the other edge of this territory, and in the early evening they arrived in front of the stone building that with its high walls and crenellations looked so much like a little desert fort. Capflyer came zipping out, faster than a flea. After shaking hands with the commander, he went to give Mensur a long, hard look. Then he gathered together all

261

the soldiers in the company headquarters, so that they could all walk around the truck whispering, and viewing Mensur from different angles. And of course the commander told his story again, in some detail. This was how they'd closed in on him. This was how he'd twisted his arm. This was how he'd grabbed him by the nape of his neck. The soldiers were still walking around the truck looking at Mensur as they listened. And the more Capflyer heard, the more he warmed to the story, and every so often he'd gaze up at the sky open-mouthed and slap his legs and let out a peal of laughter.

But Mensur had not said one thing while they paraded him around like this. He'd just stared back at them, with those large, shining and bewildered eyes. And every time the commander told how he'd taken him captive, Mensur would smile faintly, just as he had back at Mezartepe. But here at the neighbouring company's headquarters he'd stopped smiling. He'd had no food or water all day and that had sapped his strength. His head was bent forward, and he was having trouble breathing. From time to time, he made a strange little mewing sound, even. All day long, his great body had been swaying from one side of that truck to the other, and the ropes around his wrists had chafed so that now there were bloody strips of skin dangling from his arms. These strips of skin were as worn as shreds of leather rising up from an eternity in the cool depths of the River Tigris. Just as that river snakes out to fill the Harran Plain, so these shreds of skin snaked into their hearts, because somehow they knew: that plain, and with it, the world, was beyond their reach. And that was why Ziya couldn't bear to look at them. He just shivered, and looked elsewhere. Mensur wasn't looking at him or Resul any more either. Resting his forehead on his wrists, he looked down at the dust blowing across the truck floor.

When they at last left the neighbouring company's headquarters to return to Telhamut, Mensur was still watching the dust blow across that truck floor.

Ziya climbed over the ropes to speak to Resul. In a soft voice he said, 'Do you know what? The devil says . . .'

'Shut up,' said Resul. 'Don't you go telling me what the devil said. We're just following his orders, so we don't fail our military service!'

Ziya stared into Resul's eyes.

'For God's sake,' asked Resul. 'How many months do you have behind you already? Eighteen. Am I right?'

'You're right,' said Ziya. 'I have eighteen months behind me. I'm out in two months, as you know.'

'So all right. Do you want to fail your military service at this late date, and have to start all over?'

'Who'd want that? Of course I don't.'

'Then don't pay any attention to what the devil said!'

Ziya went back to his place. Leaning against the side of the truck, he turned his head to look far, far away.

When they returned exhausted to Telhamut, the commander stepped down and gave Mensur a good once-over, and then he had him tied up to the column again. He ordered Resul and Ziya to guard him. Waving his forefinger, making circles in the air, he said, 'And don't let him out of your sight. If he escapes, there'll be hell to pay!'

And that was when Ziya could bear it no longer. Standing at attention, he said, 'This man has had nothing to eat or drink since yesterday, sir. Can we give him some food?'

Stunned, the commander gave Ziya a good long look. Then he said, 'Just listen to this scoundrel. Just listen to this scoundrel.' Without another word, the commander pounced on Ziya. First a right hook, then a left. When he heard those punches ringing in the air, Mensur raised up his head. But he paid no attention to Ziya as he lost his balance, instead fixing his glittering eyes on the commander.

'The last commander told me quite a few things about you, but I didn't believe him. But now I see that he knew what he was talking about. There's no brain in that head of yours. There really isn't!'

Ziya said nothing.

The commander turned to Resul. 'You look at me, canteen man. You're free to go. Go to the dormitory and get some sleep. This prick here will be solely responsible for this man tonight!'

'Yes, sir!' said Resul.

When the commander had left in his jeep for Ceylanpınar, Ziya collapsed on to a step three paces away from Mensur, and for a time he just sat there in silence.

Resul was still standing in front of the building. 'You shouldn't hang around here,' said Ziya. 'Go fetch me a bottle of poison, why don't you, and then go to bed.'

Resul ran off to the canteen, returning with a bottle from his secret cache.

'Let's guard him together,' said Resul. 'How's the commander ever going to find out?'

'No,' said Ziya. 'We're in enough trouble as it is. And anyway, as you know, the last commander toughened me up. I can take it.'

Resul gave up and went off to the dormitory.

And then it was just the two of them. Mensur at the base of the column, and Ziya, sitting across from him. And once again, the night took hold of the mud-brick houses across the tracks and pulled them in. And now the handle of the well had vanished, too, and all he could hear was a child here and there, calling through the night. And then these sounds vanished, too, as a silence seeped in to press down on them. And that was when Ziya turned his head to give Mensur a good, long look. His head had fallen to his chest. There was nothing left to him but his hulking shadow.

'Mensur,' Ziya called.

Mensur raised his head.

'I know,' Ziya said, 'you can't understand a word I say. But never mind. I'm still saying it. I'm going to get you some food. OK?'

He bunched up his fingers and made as if to eat. Then he pointed at Mensur.

'So now,' he said, 'I'm going. OK? To get you some food.'

Mensur smiled faintly.

'But you have to keep quiet,' Ziya said. 'Sit just the way you are until I get back. Whatever you do, don't untie those ropes and run away.'

This time Mensur looked at him blankly.

So Ziya made as if to untie the imaginary ropes around his wrists. Then he waved both his hands, looked into Mensur's eyes, and in a gentle voice he said, 'No untying these ropes.' And then, enunciating each word clearly, he said, 'Stay here. Keep quiet. Wait. I'll be back.'

Then he stood up and raced off to the kitchen. He put two bowls of *bulgur pilaf* on to a tray, and a few slices of bread, and hurried back.

Squatting next to Mansur, he said, 'Hey, how are you going to eat this now?'

They stared at each other through the darkness.

'No,' said Ziya, still flummoxed. 'No, I'm not untying you. You'd try to escape, and I could never hold you back, you're too big. And I don't want to shoot at you. So this is what's going to happen. I'm going to feed you.'

He filled a spoon with *bulgur pilaf* and put it into Mensur's mouth.

'I hope you don't mind,' he said. 'It's all I could find in the kitchen.'

He gave him another big spoonful.

'I couldn't let you go hungry,' he said, as he pulled back the spoon. 'You've come here from another country. You count as a guest. Don't you think? Whether they know you or not, everyone in this country can count you as a guest.'

He gave him another spoonful.

'And it's not just the people. Every animal in this country can count you as a guest, as well. And every plant. Every fruit tree, and poplar, and every worm and every bird, and every insect . . .'

Suddenly Mensur stopped eating. He nodded, and smiled.

'Or do you actually speak Turkish?' Ziya asked.

Mensur looked at him blankly.

Ziya went back to feeding him *pilaf*.

'Try to eat faster,' Ziya said. 'I don't want the commander catching me.'

And Mansur began to eat faster, almost as if he understood. He began to chew faster, and then he started swallowing the *pilaf* without chewing. And Ziya watched him eat, offering him a bite of bread now and again. Then

Ziya took the tray back to the guardhouse kitchen and returned with a pitcher of water. As he gulped down the water, Mensur gave Ziya the warmest of smiles, and then he nodded, vigorously. And Ziya nodded, too. Just a little. Then he got up and took the pitcher to his office, so that no one could see it. After that he sat down on the step three paces away from Mensur and began drinking his poison.

'I'm sorry,' said Ziya. 'But this I cannot share.'

Mensur smiled gently.

'So let me say it now,' said Ziya. 'If that commander comes back, I'm going to toss this bottle into the night, on to those tracks over there. If I do that, don't get frightened.'

'Mensur,' said Mensur.

Ziya, who had raised the bottle to his lips, looked at him through the glass.

'Mensur,' said Mensur once again.

Putting the bottle back on the step, Ziya said, 'Oh, I see. I understand. You want to know my name, don't you?'

Mensur smiled.

'Ziya,' said Ziya. 'My name is Ziya.'

'Ziya,' Mensur repeated and he smiled.

Then the two fell silent. They sat in darkness, breathing in and breathing out. Now and again, a whoop would rise up from one of the trenches nearby. But it sounded as if it was coming from the bottom of a well. And as it soared through the night, it brought with it the scent of grass.

Later on in the night, when he went out on patrol, the commander stopped by to check on them three times. He would slip out of the night, shiny as a fox, and slip back in. In the morning, he released Mensur from the base of the column and, without tying him up again, took him to

Ceylanpınar to hand him over to the Syrian officials who had come to fetch him from Ras al-Ayn. From then on, whenever he looked at the base of that column outside their building, Ziya saw an empty space as wide as Mensur's shoulders. As he came or went, he could not stop himself from looking.

On the day he was discharged, he looked one last time into that empty space. Then he walked quickly past the flagpole and into the station. Many years earlier, two soldiers boarding a minibus in Ceylanpınar had been shot by the relatives of smugglers who died in a skirmish, and since that day, they'd sent all soldiers away by train when they were discharged. They'd stop the train that always slowed down when coming into the station, never blowing its whistle, and after they'd piled the soldiers in, the train would move on, stealthy as a snake, towards Gaziantep.

'May it soon be over, sir soldier,' said the stationmaster.

'Thank you,' said Ziya. 'And goodbye.'

He climbed into the carriage just in front of him and found himself a seat on the right-hand side. The stationmaster stared up at him enviously, as if to say, 'You've escaped now, but we'll be stuck here for God only knows how long, and without any hope of a discharge.'

And then the Toros Express began to move, and before long, they'd left the station behind with those nine mud-brick houses. Because he could still see the minefield when he looked out the window, and the barbed-wire fence, and the dirt track, and the prefabricated guardhouses perched on their little hills, Ziya could still not believe he'd been discharged. He was still expecting the train to stop at any moment, so they could recall him, and that was why he leaned back in his seat and kept his anxious eyes on his fellow passengers. As the train moved on, and people started getting up to go to the toilet or visit other carriages, he began to feel less tense, and with time he began to relax, just a little.

Later on, while he was dozing in his seat, Ziya had a curious dream. In this dream he was still on the Toros Express, and sitting in the same seat, but awake. He knew it was a dream, too, but when he looked out the window he could see the Harran Plain passing by. But then, little by little, things began to change. And before long, where there had been only barbed-wire fences and minefields and observation towers and guardhouses perched on little hills, there were now bright-green trees, spurting from the ground, almost – rising higher and higher still, to touch the sky. And before long, he could see cliffs in the distance, and hills sparkling with flowers, and rushing between those hills there were streams and brooks that looked like watery shadows, and floating above all this were white clouds that looked nothing like the clouds of the Harran Plain. And that was when the Toros Express blew its whistle for the first time, and when he heard it Ziya jumped. And then, thinking this must be the whistle ending his military service, he smiled.

In the middle of a forest, the train slowed down for some reason and, just as Ziya was asking himself why, it stopped. And there they stayed for some time, sinking into nature and a hush that rustled with the leaves. The other passengers hardly seemed to notice; they carried on as if the train was still clacking down the tracks. They looked out of the window or watched the children playing in the aisles or chain-smoked.

Then suddenly two conductors and the train engineer burst into the carriage and made a beeline for Ziya. He was wearing a cap, this engineer, and the hair beneath it was white, and his ears were as large as soup ladles. His face was covered with lines, each one deeper than the last. And just then he looked as if he had been alive for thousands of years, with only his uniform to prove his existence.

'So go ahead,' this engineer said to him. 'We stopped here in the middle of nowhere so that you could get off.'

And Ziya showed no surprise. He rose from his seat. The engineer followed him to the door and there he stayed, bending down to fix him with his green-flecked eyes.

He stayed there, watching, as Ziya moved away from the tracks to go deep into the forest. After the dry air and empty spaces of the Harran Plain, it opened his heart to be walking through such a forest. Each step he took was lighter than the last. The path flew like feathers beneath his feet. He could climb the slopes in a single breath, and soon he was deep inside a great green realm in which the air itself sang. And now he had crossed over a few more hills, and reached the red pines. As he walked the sun would peep through the branches only to vanish yet again. He walked on into a night, a garish night that rippled with so much moisture that it sometimes felt as wide as a lake. And if all its lights flashed at once, it could blind you.

And then suddenly he was in an oak forest, where the greys curled into the browns, and the browns into the yellows, while the greens bled red. Passing through the oak forest, he entered a pasture ringed by juniper bushes, and that was when he saw the dirt road below, and the sheep pens, and the poplars marking their edges, and, just beyond them, the little barn.

6

The Debt

When Numan came inside, Cabbar was sitting beneath the almond tree in the courtyard, smoking a cigarette.

'Come in,' he said, from within the billowing smoke. 'Come in, so we can see you.'

Numan came quietly across the courtyard and sat down next to his elder brother, and at once he lit up. Then he just sat there, glowering at his cigarette. Hating the world and everyone in it. The anger and resentment that defined his every movement had also seeped into his eyes, erasing the world, replacing it with a dark and silent emptiness that grew steadily harsher.

'What's come over you?' asked Cabbar. 'What's put you in such a state?'

Breathing through his nose, he said, 'I had that dream again.'

'So?'

'It's a warning. I've had it twice. There's something in it, something terrible.'

Cabbar stubbed out his cigarette and lit another.

The voice floating out of the smoke said, 'So it's the same dream, is it? Exactly the same dream as the one before?'

'Last time I saw them in Nefise's room, as you know,' said Numan. 'They weren't there this time. There were making love under the mulberry tree in the courtyard. Passionately. Savagely. Breathing so heavily that the whole courtyard was quaking.'

Cabbar looked blankly into Numan's face, as if he could not see him.

'But at the end of the day,' Cabbar said finally, 'it's just a dream. So don't get it into your head that you can go around telling everyone you meet. Some things get worse when you spread the word, as you know. If a rumour gets started about a brother and a sister having relations, it could end very badly. Once it got going, there'd be no stopping it. What's more – it's not what I would expect from either Kenan or Nefise. Do you hear me?'

Numan stared cowering into the distance.

'You just can't get over this girl, can you? How many years has this been going on now?' asked Cabbar. 'It's always Nefise, Nefise. God protect us! If you keep this up, you're going to drive yourself mad. We did everything we could. Think how many times we sent over the matchmaker. Think of all the men of consequence we sent after her, to promise jewels and dowries and property and God knows what else, but we couldn't make it happen, and we never shall. Above all, the girl doesn't want it.'

'Because she has relations with her brother,' said Numan. 'I've had two warnings.'

Again Cabbar reprimanded him. 'Don't you ever say that again. Secret relations give way to true love, as you know. If there was a fire, we'd see the smoke pouring out the door as well as the chimney.'

'But where exactly would that smoke come from?' said Numan. 'Have you forgotten that Kenan is sterile?'

Cabbar said nothing. He just turned his head to look into the distance. Then he jumped to his feet, as if he intended to race out of the courtyard then and there. Instead he began to pace up and down, with a cigarette between his lips. Now and again he muttered something in a hoarse voice that got lost in the smoke. Numan picked a piece of string off the ground and, without quite knowing what he was doing, began to unravel it from both sides. His fingers were still tingling with the warmth of his dream. And that was why they had only to graze against one of his eyelids for Nefise to strip off her clothes again, wild with desire: now she was stretching out on that mattress beneath the mulberry tree. Now she had raised those ivory-white legs of hers, and now she was drawing such lovely little circles in the air that he could almost see the bicycle pedals beneath those perfect feet. And all the while, she was sighing and moaning and beckoning and misting up the whole courtyard. Then Kenan appeared, moaning softly as he pushed himself between her parted legs, and thrust himself into Nefise's hidden depths. In and out he went, in and out, while every hair on her head fizzled and sparked. As if, at any moment, she might burst into flame. Gaping in ecstasy, Kenan's face had lost shape. Still moaning, he kept riding her hard. And as he did, he shook those hips that were pinned beneath him, of course – and those breasts, those shoulders, those sighs.

'Forget that stupid dream,' said Cabbar.

Numan looked up.

'A delusion like this can do a man in,' Cabbar continued. 'And anyway, if you really believed that what you saw in your dream were true, you'd realise that you had to give up on this girl at once. Don't you see? When as far as I can see, you still haven't given up on her. You can't stop thinking of her, and you need to come up with a reason why she won't have you, and when you can't find one, then, well, that mind of yours invents one for you. That's why you need to put this dream right out of your mind, do you understand? Nefise is a virgin with no stains on her reputation.'

'All right, then,' said Numan, and now he looked ashamed.

Then suddenly he noticed the piece of string in his hands; he cast it to the ground as if it were a worm.

'Listen,' he said then, turning back to Cabbar. 'I've just thought of something. There may be one more thing we need to try.'

'Don't you go saying we should kidnap her or anything. I won't stand for it.'

'No,' said Cabbar. 'I'm not saying we should kidnap her.'

'Then what are you proposing?'

'What I'm thinking is that if anyone can solve this problem for us, it's Ziya Bey. Nefise and the rest of them consider him a member of the family. They have a great deal of respect for him. You know this. If he can speak for us, they won't turn us down. Don't you agree?'

Cupping his hands, Cabbar fell silent. As he let his thoughts wander, he looked out over the wall, almost as if he thought he might see the edge of the village, and the vineyards, and Ziya in his barn.

'They wouldn't turn us down,' Numan said again. 'There's no way they would go against it, if we had him speaking for us. If Ziya Bey sat down with Nefise and Kenan and their mother and spoke to them for just a few minutes, we'd have an agreement. I'm sure of it. Who knows? Maybe it was fate who sent Ziya to us. I think we should go out there and tell him the whole story in detail – how it all started, and what happened next, and on from there. We can ask him to help us, and if necessary, we can beg him.'

Cabbar gave him an odd look.

'Don't get me wrong,' Numan pleaded. 'When I said we could beg him, I meant me, not you. I'd whine like a dog for Nefise if I had to. And I'd beg everyone I met, not just Ziya Bey. But one thing is clear: fate sent this man to us, to resolve this matter that's been left hanging for so many years now.'

Cabbar went and sat back down next to Numan. He looked tired, and he was breathing heavily.

'You've convinced me,' he said slowly. 'It's true – they really do consider him a member of the family. Let's hope he's a man of compassion.'

'He's a good person,' said Numan, in a voice that had more confidence than he did. 'If we tell our story in a way that does us justice, he'll understand, I think. Please, big brother. Could we go right now and speak with this man? Hey. What do you say?'

'All right,' said Cabbar. 'There's nothing else we can do, so let's go out there and talk to him.'

With that, the two brothers stood up. Lit up by hope, and puffing on their cigarettes, they set off for the barn. They had hardly passed through the courtyard gate, though, before Cabbar started in on his warnings. 'Whatever you do, don't go telling him about that dream of yours.' Numan, who kept adjusting his collar as if they were on their way to pick up Nefise herself, promised not to breathe a word of it. He had come out of his funk and turned into a big, smiling child. He kept walking too fast and then, when he noticed it, slowing down, and every time he did that, he'd give his brother another sidelong look. Every once in a while an urge came over him to skip over a branch, or a cowpat, or a bramble or a tuft of grass, but his brother's presence made him shy, and he held himself back. He skipped over them in his mind, instead, as an imagined breeze pushed him forward, lightening his step, and sending him ahead of his brother yet again.

Ziya was sitting outside the barn, staring at the mountains. His eyes were fixed on a blurry shadow that seemed to have come out of nowhere; he had, at least, never seen it there before. One side of it looked like a jutting cliff, and the other like a crooked old roof. If he looked at it too long, it became a slowly expanding clump of dark earth. He couldn't tell if it was near or very far away, because the shivering brown mass hovering above the oak forest might have been just beyond it or many kilometres further on, rising from the mists of the red-pine forests. It seemed to be moving, but too slowly for the eye to apprehend. And every time it moved, it drew closer, only to recede.

When he heard Cabbar and Numan coming through the vineyard, Ziya turned his head.

'*Selamünaleykum*,' said Cabbar, as he struggled to catch his breath. 'Would you mind if we came to visit?'

'You're very welcome,' said Ziya. 'Please, sit down.'

When the introductions were over, they all sat down on the bench that ran along the wall. Cabbar crossed his legs. Numan shrank into himself, as if to protect himself from the cold. He put his hands between his knees.

'Thanks so much for coming,' said Ziya. 'Until now only Kenan and Besim have been out here. So you're my first visitors.'

Embarrassed, Cabbar smiled faintly.

Then, for a time, they chatted about nothing and everything. When this interlude came to an end, Ziya got up to brew them some tea, but Cabbar put his hand on his arm and stopped him.

Then he said, 'Ziya Bey, we have a problem, and we've come here to talk it through with you, if you permit.'

Ziya looked at him in surprise.

'Yes,' said Cabbar. 'We came to talk it through with you, because only you can help us solve it. To tell the truth, we see no other way forward. And so we have come to take refuge in your mercy and wisdom. I'm not sure quite how to put it now . . . except to say that my brother Numan here has been head over heels in love with Kenan's sister Nefise since he was this high. Isn't that true, boy?'

'It's true,' said Numan, as he nodded.

'So there you have it. Since he was this high, my brother has been singing for Nefise, going to sleep for Nefise, and getting up in the morning for Nefise. There's no need to beat around the bush. They grew up, these two, and they blossomed, and at last they reached the marrying age. And we got up and consulted with a few wise old men, and then, with God's blessing, we went over to Kenan's house with our offer. We went, but we got nowhere. Whatever we did, whatever we said, whatever brook we drew from, we were refused. Let's throw in some gold coins, we said, and a dozen plaited bracelets, but still the answer was no. We offered to cover all the wedding costs, and buy all the furniture. No, they said. We offered to sign over five *dönüms* of marshland to Nefise. Again, they said no. And on top of all this, I swear to God, we offered to build a two-storey house at the very top of the village, for the couple to live in, once they were married, but still they refused us. Every time we came with a new offer, they found some way to turn us down. And then, after all that, they upped and said that the girl didn't want it. The girl had no feelings for my brother. And shut the door! We were dumbstruck, just dumbstruck. We were at our wit's end, Ziya Bey. We had nowhere to turn, and it was driving us to distraction. This boy here was close to losing his mind, even. He'd just sit there, arms limp, staring across at Nefise's house. Like a little bird stranded in its nest. His eyes looked like boiled eggs that had just been peeled, and when we saw that we said to ourselves, dear God, we've lost him. What I'm trying to say is that the whole family was in tatters. But in the end, we decided to keep trying, of course. We kept going back. Sometimes we sent other men in to argue our case, and each time we did so, we offered them more. But in time, the whole thing went sour. What I mean to say is that we pressed too hard, and the day came when Nefise's family cut off relations entirely. There we were, trying to join our families, and suddenly we were on the brink of becoming enemies. And so that's where our two families have been now for quite some time, Kenan especially. If he sees us coming, he hangs his head and changes direction. If he sees us inside a coffee-house, he won't come in. He just peers inside and if he sees us, he rushes right off. As I just said, we've been teetering on that bitter brink for some time now – we are this far from becoming outright enemies. And meanwhile, the children are getting older. Soon they'll be too old. And so, in conclusion, we have come here to ask you to take on the delicate task of acting as our ambassador. If you agree, if you were willing to go to the family and recommend this union, you would bring us great happiness, Ziya Bey. Be aware that without your help, it will never come to be. Things will stay as they are. And as you know, there is no task more sacred than this. But that's all I have to say. The rest lies with your conscience.'

'Don't say that,' said Ziya in a distant voice. 'This business has nothing to do with conscience.'

Cabbar turned his head and glanced at Numan.

'I don't know what to say,' said Ziya. 'I understand your position. But I really wouldn't want to get involved in this. If this is the girl's wish, and if she really has no feelings for him, what right do I have to tell her she has to love him? I don't think it would do any good for me to raise this matter with Kenan or his mother: what exactly would I say? Tell her to tell her daughter that she should start loving Numan? It's just not done . . .'

Numan suddenly leaned forward. 'You have nothing to say but no, Ziya Bey.'

Cabbar grabbed his brother's head and pushed it back. As he did so, he muttered, 'You be quiet!' through gritted teeth. 'Mind your manners, and stay in your seat!'

'I don't understand,' Ziya said. 'Why did Numan get so angry? Was I wrong in what I said?'

Cabbar dug his huge hands into his pockets, and came out with a packet of cigarettes. He lit himself one. And then, to dissipate the tension, he said, 'He's young, that's all it is. He says the first thing that comes into his head! You're older.

You can find it in yourself to excuse him. If you ask me, Ziya Bey, the best thing would be for you to think this ambassador business over. This is not the sort of thing anyone should agree to in a flash.'

'My answer won't change,' Ziya replied. 'There's nothing I need to think over. And furthermore, I don't think of marriage as a sacred business either. From the first day to the last, it's a life you lead together, in this world. So how can you say it's sacred?'

'It's divine,' said Cabbar, frowning as he puffed out a great cloud of smoke. 'But you, I see, are a man of the world!'

Ziya said nothing.

Cabbar and Numan got up then. Muttering their good-byes, they headed towards the vineyard. Just as he was about to go through the hedges, Cabbar wheeled around suddenly and in a plaintive voice he said, 'Give it some thought, Ziya Bey. I implore you. Give it a little thought and then give us your final decision.'

'There's nothing to think about,' Ziya said again. 'I've made up my mind.'

Cabbar looked down, as if to say, 'So that's it, then?' He was about to set off when he wheeled around again. Putting more warmth into his voice, he said, 'I'm curious. What were you looking at when we walked in?'

'I was looking at the mountains,' Ziya said. 'I saw something I'd never seen before.'

Seeing this as another way in, or another way to buy time, Cabbar went back to Ziya's side. Looking out at the mountains, he said, 'So where's this thing you saw?'

Ziya pointed at it, but Cabbar could see nothing there. Then Numan came over, steeped in resentment. But he wouldn't say if he'd seen something, or nothing. Then he went back through the vineyard gate, clomping angrily over the clods of earth.

And that day, Ziya watched them go. He watched until they were down the hill and back on the dirt road. Then he quickly got himself ready. Picking up an empty plastic water bottle, he walked straight into the village, past clucking chickens and sheep pens, and the donkeys braying in their shadows, and nodding at two old men as he passed them. Arriving at Kenan's house, he stood uncertainly at the courtyard gate before gently pushing it open. Nefise, who was sitting beneath the mulberry tree, looked up. Ziya was startled at the sight of her. He could no longer move. It was all he could do to cast down his eyes. This was because there was something in the way this girl was sitting that reminded him of that bird he'd shot and killed forty-two years earlier. It was as if that bird had been here all along, changing shape – first a shadow, then a leaf, and then a blur the size of a hand, and now it had turned into Nefise. And there it was, this coy and barefaced reverie. Strangely serene, as if it existed outside time. Time seemed not to touch it, even as it flowed in great waves in the shape of a village.

'Welcome,' said Nefise, pulling herself together. 'Do come in.'

At first Ziya could not speak. When he looked at Nefise, he felt the same peace of mind he'd felt forty-two years earlier, when he set eyes on that bird. But with it came fear.

'Do come in,' Nefise said again.

'So you . . .' Ziya stammered. 'So you must be Nefise. I'm Kenan's friend.'

Nefise was standing now. She seemed to be looking at him from near and from afar. And so serene. Blindingly serene.

'Yes, I guessed as much,' she said, smiling gently. 'Do come in. Make yourself at home.'

Ziya was so agitated, he didn't know what to do. His heart was pounding. It seemed to him that Nefise was pretending not to notice, so as not to add to his embarrassment. She kept shrinking into the shadows that played on her cheeks, her eyes, her brow. Just then Kenan came through the door carrying a little copper tray draped in muslin. Seeing Ziya, he smiled and rushed over to greet him.

'Welcome,' he said. 'Have you introduced yourselves? This is my sister Nefise.'

'Yes, we've just introduced ourselves,' Ziya said.

There followed a short silence.

'I was on my way to the fountain,' Ziya said, struggling to hide his agitation. 'I thought I'd drop by.'

'I'm glad you did,' said Kenan with a smile. 'Our door is always open.'

Ziya gave Nefise a sidelong look and then turned back to Kenan. 'Do you know what?' he said. 'Yesterday I took a long walk up into the mountains and while I was walking, I went through all my memories of the army, but I still couldn't remember what this good thing was I did for you.'

Blushing, Kenan stared down at the tray in his hand. And then, to change the subject, he said, 'Please don't be offended. But I have to go see my Uncle Cevval right now. If you like, we could go together, and I could introduce you.'

'Do you really think he would agree to it?' said Nefise.

Ziya did not know what to make of that.

'He won't see anyone but me,' Kenan said. 'Why don't you come with me? I'll explain along the way.'

They left the courtyard and headed for the other end of the village.

'Uncle Cevval's a bit temperamental,' Kenan began. 'It's been six years now since he's been outside. And the worst thing about it is that he has no wife or children to look after him. My aunt gave herself back to the earth some time ago. They had a flighty daughter with big ideas; she married someone from the town and moved with him to Istanbul. Six years ago he took a dislike to my mother and shut himself inside his house. Why he took a dislike to her, nobody knows but him, of course. If you ask him, he doesn't answer. He just looks at you shocked, as if it should be obvious. For a while, his friends would come to visit occasionally, in groups of three or four, and they'd try to convince him to come out again. And my uncle would sit there staring at the patterns in the rug, looking very annoyed, and saying nothing. But when they pressed too hard, he stopped listening. He accused them of being frauds. He started shouting at them, saying, "What's out there for me, anyway, aside from shit?" He even accused them of turning his house into a hotel. "You gather up all the village gossip you can find and you bring it here," he said. "Stop bugging me. Fuck you all. Now fuck off." And then he threw all his friends out. The only thing he didn't do to those poor things was beat them up. So they began to keep their distance, saying what can the man do, he's sick and tired of life. They stopped visiting, stopped coming to the neighbourhood, even. And so it was that my uncle's life shrank to forty-five or fifty square metres. As he got older, he became more frail, and if it weren't for me, it would be very hard, there's no way he could survive on his own. I take him every meal, without fail. I feed him his food, and I give him his water. And then there's his laundry, and his bath. It's all very difficult, and as for that daughter of his, not once has it crossed her mind to ask how her father's health is, or what he's up to. So anyway, that's how it is with my uncle. Maybe he'll come out to the courtyard in your honour. Do you think?'

'I hope so,' Ziya said. Then he said, 'He sounds very strange, this uncle of yours.'

They passed in front of the Plane Tree Coffeehouse. When he looked inside, Ziya could see Hulki Dede. He was as dishevelled as ever, and sitting apart from the other villagers. He had propped his left elbow on his knee, while he sketched on the ground with his staff. As he did so, his head bobbed happily. Then he straightened up. His eyes seemed fogged with sleep. He stared into the distance and then suddenly he raised his arm. He waved at Ziya. And he did so with such deep affection that it almost seemed to taper his fingers, because Ziya could feel how warm they were. And he could feel them reaching out to touch his heart. So then Ziya slowed down, just a little, to wave back. Then he speeded up again, but as they walked through the village, he saw Hulki Dede's waving hand a few more times. It seemed almost to be hanging there, just before his eyes. Or echoing through the village. He saw it for the first time on a crumbling court-yard wall. After that he saw it on the side of a horse cart loaded down with hay. And after that he saw it in the *meydan* in the ears of a donkey whose back was covered in sores.

And outside the Coffeehouse of Mirrors, they ran into Numan. Or to put it more accurately, Numan was inside, playing cards with his friends, and when he caught sight of Ziya and Kenan, he threw his cards down on the table, and stood up, and swaggered outside, like a tough guy looking for a fight, and planted himself at the side of the road. But he said nothing. He just looked at Ziya and Kenan, spinning his yellow prayer beads in furious circles. Kenan had pulled way back, and when he walked past Numan, he fixed his eyes on the grocery store just up the road. Seeing him do this, Ziya pretended not to see Numan either, to avoid a scene, but this unsettled him.

When they reached Uncle Cevval's door, the white sheepdog was still dozing at the foot of the wall opposite. When it heard their footsteps, it raised its head to gaze at Kenan with glassy eyes, but neither Kenan nor Ziya noticed as they stepped inside. The walls were white and smelled of damp. Leaning across the copper tray he held in his hands, Kenan cried, 'Uncle, I'm here. I'm here, Uncle!' Cevval called back from what seemed to be a distance, but it wasn't clear what he was saying: it was as if the walls themselves had swallowed up his weak little voice. And soon there was nothing left but a cool and half-lit carpet-covered room. Then suddenly this room was jolted from its silence. And there was Uncle Cevval, in his knitted long johns. He was as pale as his walls, almost. But his skin was riddled with blue veins that looked as if they might be empty inside. They moved whenever Uncle Cevval moved, and when they moved, they sometimes disappeared, these veins.

'Uncle,' said Kenan. 'Look. This is my friend from the army. His name is Ziya.'

Uncle Cevval turned to look at Ziya. He looked at him with empty eyes that seemed somehow full. He seemed to want something without quite knowing what it was. But his voice told Ziya that he had turned his back on the world. 'Welcome, my child,' he said softly.

Ziya thanked him, and leaned over to kiss his hand.

They set out his food that day on a worn black and white cloth that they spread over the divan, but they weren't able to get him outside. Uncle Cevval got angry at Kenan just for suggesting it. He stuck out his chin as he protested, glaring as if he was about to hit Kenan with the back of his hand. And so they had to leave him there, alone with his walls.

When they had passed again through the damp hallway and were standing outside the house, Ziya told Kenan about the shadow he'd seen on the mountaintop. He stopped to point at it. 'I hadn't noticed it earlier. What is it?' he asked. Kenan looked for a long time at the place Ziya had pointed out above his right shoulder, but he couldn't see anything.

'I don't see anything different,' he said. 'They're still the same mountains.'

'But it's there, can't you see it? That shadow up there, the one that looks like the edge of a roof or a pile of earth. Can't you see it?'

Kenan narrowed his eyes to look up at the mountains again.

The sheepdog looked up with him.

'I really don't see any sort of shadow up there,' said Kenan. 'There's no new ridge. Maybe what you're seeing is just in your imagination.'

'Never mind,' Ziya mumbled.

They headed for the fountain, picking their way down the narrow stone lane that ran beneath Uncle Cevval's house, keeping in the shadow of the almond trees as squirrels screamed in the branches above. And as they walked, Ziya's thoughts went from Nefise to the nameless shadow he had seen on the mountaintop, and then back to Uncle Cevval. After filling up his plastic bottle at the fountain, they headed back to the *meydan*, and they were just level with a nettle tree when Kâzım the Bellows Man appeared some way down the road.

'Kenan, my boy,' he cried. 'You're walking around like a dog bit your feet! Make some time so we can sit down and talk!'

'Fine. Let's talk,' said Kenan.

Ziya left them there and carried on down the road with his water bottle passing through the boys rushing towards the grocery store. As he approached the Plane Tree Coffeehouse, Hulki Dede slowly raised his head, almost as if he knew he was there. Then he jumped up and hobbled over with his staff to grab Ziya by the arm. In a gentle voice, he said, 'Weren't you and I going to have a chinwag?'

'Yes, why don't we?' said Ziya, struggling to smile. 'Shall we find a table in the coffeehouse?'

'Fuck the coffeehouse,' said Hulki Dede. 'What's the point of sitting in there with all those people. They'll just want to know what we're talking about now and try to listen in. It's not cold out and it's not hot. It's in the bald in between. If you like, we can take a stroll.'

'I don't want to have to lug this thing around, though.' Ziya pointed at his water bottle. 'Let's go back to my house. I can invite you in for a glass of tea.'

'Let's do that then,' said Hulki Dede.

They made their way out of the village, walking very slowly, chatting about this and that. When they turned left at the sheep pens to climb up the hill, Hulki Dede suddenly ran out of energy. He stopped talking, pausing every five or six steps to lean on his staff and wipe his brow with a brown-and-white-striped handkerchief, until he set off up the hill again, open-mouthed and breathing noisily. As he passed through the gap in the hedge, he apologised with some embarrassment. 'Please excuse me. This is what old age looks like,' he said softly.

They settled down on the bench outside the barn after that, and reached for their cigarettes. Hulki Dede pressed his chin into his chest and let out his smoke with such care and attention that he almost seemed to be trying to store it inside his jacket.

'Numan came up here with his brother today, to ask you to act as their ambassador,' he said. 'That's what happened, isn't it?'

'You've really surprised me,' Ziya replied. 'I wouldn't have thought it would spread that fast.'

'There's nothing to be surprised about, my son,' said Hulki Dede, raising his head to look up at the mountains. 'Yazıköy is just a dot on the map. The moment something happens, everyone hears about it. But they always pretend they've heard nothing. And also, the thing we call the world stretches only a few pastures across. Those great distances beyond us, stretching hundreds and thousands of kilometres in all directions, well, they're all here, too, on this little piece of land.'

'Do you think that even Kenan knows about Numan coming up here with his brother?'

'How could he not know?' Hulki Dede said. 'Even the village chickens have heard about it.'

For a time they fell silent. They listened to the dead leaves rustling in the vineyard. Then Ziya sprang to his feet to put the teapot on the stove. When he returned, he pointed out the shadow on the mountaintop, thinking that he must know what it was, after looking at this view for so many long years. Hulki Dede lifted one hand to his beard while he studied the mountains through fluttering eyelashes, but he could see nothing where Ziya was pointing.

'Tell me, my son,' he said. 'Why did you decide to leave the city and come here?'

'For all sorts of reasons,' Ziya replied. 'When we were in the army, Kenan seized every opportunity to talk about how beautiful this village was. He made it sound like heaven. I promised many times to come and visit, but somehow I never managed to keep my word. I kept putting it off, and making silly excuses, and before I knew it, thirty years had passed. In the meantime, I'd become sick and tired of city life. To make a long story short, I was longing for a beautiful, quiet place like this, a place where I could listen to nature, and myself.'

Hulki Dede stroked his beard and nodded. But when he spoke he did not address Ziya so much as that distant place that rustled with the echoes of those leaves. 'Do you know what?' he said. 'Nature says nothing to us. And that's why we listen to it.'

Shocked by these words, Ziya turned to stare at Hulki Dede. For a moment he doubted his very existence, but he didn't say so, of course. He just looked at him in silence, swallowing hard. And – almost as if he had seen that doubt passing through Ziya's mind – Hulki Dede now spoke to him in a voice that did seem to be of this world. 'Let's look at it like this, my son. Is there anything about this village you find strange?'

'No, there isn't,' Ziya said, struggling to hide his confusion.

'Think about it,' Hulki Dede said. 'Because there is something strange about it.'

'You really want me to say it?'

'I really do, my son. I really do!'

'The truth is, there are two strange things about this village. One is Uncle Cevval, and the other is . . .'

'The other is . . .?'

'The other is you.'

Hulki Dede smiled, and as he did so, he looked Ziya up and down, as if seeing him for the first time.

'As you know,' he said finally. 'In little places like this, when people get bored, they'll see shit on the ground and use it as an excuse for an argument. If they can't find a solid excuse then they'll say, why did you let your chicken come into my courtyard? Or: your donkey brays every time it passes my house, you must be making it do that on purpose. They gain one kind of power from quarrelling, and yet another from making peace. But they have no idea that this is why they do either. But when they're as tired as worms, they go out looking for a new excuse to argue with their neighbours. And the moment the quarrel starts, they're bursting with life again. Their spirits soar, and everything they do, or don't do, takes on new meaning. They feel themselves transformed. Not just the ones who start the quarrel, but the ones they accuse, as well. You know all this. What I mean to say is that Cevval's quarrel has gone on much longer than it should have done. Over the years, it's gone from bad to worse. What I think is, he's angry with the world, and he's blaming his sister. She's as stubborn as a goat and sadly he is, too . . . And then you say I am the other strange thing in this village? Then perhaps this village thought it could convince you more easily if it threw in a few people who weren't convincing at all. And isn't that always the case? On the edge of every belief, there are always a number of doubts, and they have to be there, to give that belief its shape. Without a shape, what worth would it have?'

Ziya said nothing.

Hulki Dede pulled down on his shirt with his little freckled hands and began to cackle. He began to rock, too, and swing his feet. Ziya had no idea what to make of this. First he stared at Hulki Dede's feet, and then at his own feet. Then suddenly Hulki Dede stopped. Taking a deep breath, he turned to look up at the darkening mountains.

'Don't you look at me,' he said. 'This is what I'm like. I come and I go. What I mean is, I can say mad things . . . So Numan came up here with his brother today, did he? Now that sounds ominous, if you ask me. Numan is a fine boy, one of the finest and bravest in our village, but he can't stop pining for Nefise, somehow. Or rather, he hasn't settled accounts with the monster inside him. But settling accounts with this monster doesn't mean killing it, of course. Don't get me wrong. I would never want him to kill it. He who kills the monster inside him turns to dust. But when he was listening to that monster living deep inside him, Numan could have said, we're just human, for God's sake! We also long for loss, my friend! So let's stay where we are. He could have said all that, but he didn't. And so now the wretched boy confuses the monster's breath for his own. Like a fool, he's walking up and down singing songs for Nefise. Who knows? Maybe, without knowing, he got a taste for loss. Maybe that's why he keeps spinning this out . . . But we've been talking so much, you forgot about the tea, didn't you, my son?'

Ziya ran inside and came back with the tea.

While they drank their tea, Hulki Dede said nothing. But from time to time he gave Ziya a sidelong glance. Then he said, 'If you don't mind, I'll be on my way now.' He rose from the bench, straightened himself out, and tugged a few times at his shirt. Propping his staff under his arm, he headed towards the gap in the hedge and into the vineyard's whispering half-light. But when he got there, he didn't go through it. It was almost as if he had emptied himself of all the things he had to say and become lighter. Because now, with an agility not to be expected in a man his age, he leapt right over the hedge. And as he did so, there was a moment when his shirt spread out like a fan. After sitting there stunned for a few moments, Ziya began to wonder why he'd not seen Hulki Dede pull himself up again on the other side of the hedge, and, fearful that he might have broken something or still be lying there, he ran over to check, but there was no one there. And neither could he hear footsteps on the darkening plain below. It was as if Hulki Dede had jumped higher than he'd needed, and vanished from the face of the earth.

He searched for a while longer that evening, and then, giving up, Ziya turned back. He cleared the table and took the tray inside. He'd had enough of people for the time being, so for a few days he went into the village only when he needed water, hurrying down to the fountain before the morning call to prayer and filling his plastic bottles in semi-darkness before hurrying away again.

One day Kenan came up and forced him to go with him to a wedding. It took place behind the Plane Tree Coffee-house, this wedding, in the brick-walled courtyard of a house whose doors and windows were painted electric blue. By the time they arrived, almost everyone in the village was there already. On the front porch was a monstrous black four-legged contraption, flanked on each side by speakers that were even bigger and blacker. Some of the hymns blast-ing out of them were sung by a chorus, and others by a man with fire in his soul. Standing in front of all this was a young man in a black suit and pointy shoes. He worked for the wedding agency in town, and there were four others min-gling with the crowd, all dressed the same. They were serving cakes and drinks to the guests, and looking as if they could not wait for the wedding to be over. As they picked up their plastic cups and flimsy paper-thin cake plates, the guests looked much the same. Nowhere in this gathering could Ziya see any sign of elation. As they listened to the songs blasting from those speakers – *prepare yourself, my friend, the Angel Azrael is nigh, dear God, take me in,* or *the earth was crying for Hamza, the sky was crying for Hamza, and the swords were searching for Hamza* – even the children stood around them, still as kittens that had spilt the milk. The grown-ups listened to these songs with a despondency even greater than their singers. They would nod sadly, as if to confirm the truth in the words, or cup their chins to stare into the dis-tance, thinking deep and mournful thoughts, and all this made it seem as if it was not a wedding going on in this house, but a funeral.

And then a fat man with a toothbrush moustache signalled to the employee standing in front of the sound system, and he changed the CD. And as soon as the music changed, the mood in the courtyard lifted. Without a word they sailed towards the front of the house, as smoothly as if the ground was slipping beneath their feet. And now the bride and groom stepped through the door. And there they stood in silence, side by side. The man with the brush moustache gave another signal, and the man on the porch stopped the CD, removed a microphone from its box, and took it over to the bride and groom, trailing the cable behind him as he ran. After he had tested it – One two three. Se se se. One two three. Se se se – he announced that the time had come for the collection ceremony and that the bride's and groom's families would go first. One by one, they came forward. A villager who knew who they all were would whisper into his ear, and the man with the moustache would broadcast their name, and then their gift. A gold piece for the bride, from the father of the groom! A wristwatch for the groom from the bride's mother! A big piece of gold from the bride's uncle!

He was watching all this when suddenly Ziya felt a pang. Then he remembered how at Hacı Veli's wedding they had all averted their eyes, so as not to see what the others had given as gifts.

He touched Kenan's arm. 'I'm heading back.'

'Why? What's got in to you all of a sudden?'

'I just want to go home and remember what village weddings were like when I was a boy,' he said.

Kenan looked at him blankly.

And that was how Ziya left him. He left the wedding behind him and went straight back to the barn. Then he collapsed on to the bench by the door, put his head in his hands, and just sat there. Then, when he had caught his breath, he lit up a cigarette and turned to look up at the mountaintops. And there it was – that nameless shadow no one else could see. Still in the same place. Still the same shape. He shivered, as if something cold had brushed against his skin. After that he began to feel cold, so he went inside.

The brambles beyond the sheep pens had gone dry by now. There was nothing left but a great expanse of scrawny branches. The leaves had fallen from the poplars, and the fruit trees, and the vines. The grass had gone brown, and the thorns, and the flowers. And in addition to all this, the air had cooled. Cooled a great deal. A mist began to fall, very slowly, over the mountains just then, spilling its white foam over the cliffs and the pine forest, until it had reached the oak trees. Here and there it tore like a piece of gauze, looking as if a tree or a hilltop had been cut adrift to float up into the sky. With these apparitions came gusts of moist air, until suddenly it began to rain. It had not been raining every day – just every other day. First it would come down gently, as if through muslin. Then suddenly it would come down much faster and more heavily. And lightning would strike the mountain's faces, bringing with it giant claps of thunder. The cliffs would blur into the trees, and the trees into the empty spaces between them. The sky would rip apart, and when it ripped, he could hear it echoing in his heart. And as he stood there watching, Ziya would feel joy in his heart, too. Sometimes he would watch through the window. Sometimes he would put on his coat and take his tea outside, to watch from the bench beside the door. When the lightning hit the face of the mountain, glittering grey and blue, it lit him up inside, too. He could even feel the rain pattering inside him, and the mist descending, and the sky spreading, while the scent of earth and stone caressed his mouth, his nose, his skin, his eyes.

He was watching just such a rainstorm that night when suddenly Besim came running up to the window. His yellow phosphorescent raincoat – a gift from his father in Germany – was streaming with water, its edges caked in mud. Seeing Ziya at the window, he opened his mouth and stared at him with fearful eyes. Then he cried, 'Ziya Bey, Ziya Bey! Hurry, Ziya Bey! They've stabbed my uncle!'

7

The Shadow

Ziya quickly overcame his shock. Throwing on his coat, he
rushed outside.

'Was it Numan who knifed him?' he asked.

'No,' said Besim. 'It was Kâzım the Bellows Man!'

A new wave of shock crashed over Ziya, and as he stared
down at the village, it was almost as if he expected to see the
attack play itself out before his eyes. And then, without waiting to ask where Kenan had been knifed, he went coursing
down to the village. Besim raced alongside him, his yellow
phosphorescent raincoat streaked with mud. When they
reached Kenan's house, the rain was still pouring down like
water from a pitcher. From time to time, the night was lit up
by flashes of lightning, and with every thunderclap, the sky
itself collapsed on them, as its echoes shuddered across the
ground. Knowing that they would arrive sopping wet, Nefise
was waiting at the door with two towels. Next to the door
there were many pairs of shoes, some turned upside down,
and some lying on their side. There were more shoes strewn
across the floor. Ziya cast aside his coat. Taking the towel
from Nefise, he stood in the white-walled hallway, and when
he had dried himself, he stepped inside.

Kenan was lying on his back in a room that smelled of dried thyme and sweat and looked out over the courtyard. He was surrounded by villagers. They had wrapped him in a brown-and-white-striped blanket, leaving his head and shoulders open. The villagers were conversing in whispers, while Kenan stared up at the wooden beams on the ceiling. When Ziya came to sit at his side, he almost smiled, and some brightness came into his face, but not for long. Soon it was lost beneath the thick blanket of whispers.

'May it pass soon,' said Ziya, putting a light hand on his friend's shoulder. 'Where is your wound?'

'In his leg,' said one of the villagers, before Kenan had a chance to reply. 'His right leg.'

Ziya fell silent. He didn't know what to say.

Turning back to Kenan, he asked, 'Where exactly?'

'Above his knee,' said another villager, shifting his weight. 'Right here, see? Close to his hip.'

Ziya felt obliged to turn around, so that the villager could point out the place on his own leg. He traced a line, to show how long the wound was. The two burly villagers sitting in front of him leaned away so as not to obstruct the view.

'I'm fine,' mumbled Kenan. 'I'll be fine.'

'We need to get you into town,' said Ziya. 'We can't leave it like this. We need to get you to a doctor.'

'What good would a doctor be?' said Kenan. 'It's not serious enough for that.'

Ziya looked deep into his eyes. A moment arrived when he couldn't bear it any more. He tried to look at the wound, but he soon gave up on the idea, after the villagers who had not seen the wound came crowding around the divan. With bated breath they craned their necks and waited, with hungry eyes.

So Ziya said, 'No, let's not open it up. It could start bleeding again, after all.'

Disappointed, the villagers drew back. Reaching out from underneath the blanket, Kenan stroked Ziya's knee a few times, as if to thank him. And Ziya could almost see him smile through the darkness. He could almost see a little light blinking on and off at the corners of his mouth. It looked very far away.

'Just look at this,' Kenan whispered. 'You spend twenty months on the Syrian border, surrounded by murderers, while thousands of bullets fly overhead, and you come out without a scratch . . . and now look at this. Do you see what I mean?'

'Don't upset yourself,' said Ziya.

'What did Kenan say just now?' asked an old, gap-toothed villager. 'What did he just whisper to you?'

'I couldn't make it out,' Ziya replied sternly. 'He's probably delirious.'

His answer rubbed the villager up the wrong way. He looked around him, as if to say, 'Tell me. Was I wrong to ask?' So Ziya sat on the divan saying nothing, waiting for the villagers to leave. As curious as he was to find out what had happened, he asked nothing. At nightfall they got up at last. 'May it pass soon,' they said, as they filed out of the room. 'May God preserve him from worse.'

When they had all gone home, Ziya turned back to Kenan and, in a reproachful voice, he said, 'And you told me Kâzım the Bellows Man was a very good person. Endlessly helpful. And merciful. And honest. You had all sorts of good things to say about him. I remember! You even said he loved you very much, that he'd move heaven and earth for you. You said all that, didn't you?'

In a shaky voice, Kenan said, 'He's all those things.'

He was staring at the wooden beam in the corner. His eyes didn't move. There was not a trace of anger in his face. Only pain.

'So then tell me,' Ziya said. 'Why did this honest and merciful man knife you?'

'We had an argument,' said Kenan. 'A pointless argument. Just this once. There's no need to dwell on it. I am not opening a case against Kâzım the Bellows Man.'

'Fine,' said Ziya. 'But what was the cause of it?'

Cevriye Hanım came into the room, smoothing her white headscarf. She sat down at Kenan's side.

'Come on now. Answer your friend. Why were you arguing with that lout?'

Propping his elbows, Kenan rolled over on his side. He placed his free hand as close to his wound as he could manage.

'Please, Mother, let's just leave it. It just happened. That's all. Don't go and say a thing about this to Kâzım the Bellows Man. Don't ask him why and don't ask him how. We're putting an end to it, here and now.'

Cevriye Hanım raised her eyes to look at her son.

'In all the commotion we forgot about Uncle Cevval's supper. The poor man is waiting there hungry.'

'I can take him something,' said Ziya. 'Don't worry.'

And so it was that Besim and Ziya took the copper tray over to Uncle Cevval that evening. They sat him down on the divan and fed this man who seemed no more than a white shadow. After taking a few slow bites, he suddenly asked why Kenan hadn't come.

'He's feeling poorly,' Besim said each time.

When they were leaving the house, Besim noticed the sheepdog lying at the foot of the wall opposite, and suddenly he went stiff. Walking towards him a few steps with his arm upraised, he shouted, 'Shoo! Shoo!' But the dog did not budge. Its eyes glowed in the darkness as it blinked. Ziya pulled him by the arm. 'Never mind, my boy,' he said in a fatherly voice. 'Best not to disturb the poor thing. Come on now, let's go.'

Besim relaxed a little. Putting the copper tray under his arm, he set off down the lane with Ziya. It had been washed clean by the rain, and as they went, Ziya cast a few sidelong glances at the boy he had addressed for the first time as his son. It felt as if it were his own son at his side, almost.

Kenan couldn't seem to get back on his feet, and so from then on it was always Ziya and Besim who took Uncle Cevval his meals. This meant that Ziya was now going to Kenan's house several times a day, and each time he approached the door, he would imagine the moment when he'd set eyes on Nefise and Besim, and his heart would skip a beat. Leaving his shoes at the entrance he would always go first into Kenan's room, of course. And at first Kenan would sit up in bed, looking paler every day – as pale as his uncle – and try to greet Ziya with a smile. But with time that smile faded. He would just lie there, lost in thought. Because he couldn't walk. He couldn't do more than hobble a few steps across his room. He would run out of energy, and go staggering across the room to fall back into bed.

And that was why, every once in a while, Ziya would take him by the arm and lead him out to the courtyard for a bit of fresh air. They'd sit there side by side in those white plastic chairs for hours on end. If it began to rain, or snow, they just threw a few blankets over their shoulders. In fair weather Kenan would sometimes get a rush of energy and try to walk. He would hobble to the mulberry tree and back again, his grimace changing shape as he went. Once, when he was hobbling along like that, he stopped and placed his hand on his bad leg, and turned his head to look up at the mountains.

'I saw it!' he cried. 'I actually saw it!'

Ziya jumped, just a little.

'For God's sake!' he said. 'You saw what?'

'That shadow you said you saw, on the mountaintop!'

When he heard his uncle shouting, Besim came running out of the house. He, too, looked up at the mountain.

'Can you see it too?' Ziya asked him.

'No,' said Besim. 'I don't see anything different. They're still the same mountains.'

'Maybe they're building an observation tower,' Kenan murmured.

Slowly he limped over to a chair next to the wall, holding his right leg as he went. He spent the rest of the day there, and each time he looked up at the mountain, it was as if he was doing so for the first time, or had forgotten where he was looking – as if his soul had flown far away and he was waiting now for its return. He would stare at it for many long minutes, unmoving, and unblinking.

A week after Kenan first noticed the shadow, it snowed in the village for an entire day. And soon every courtyard, every lane and vineyard and hill and mountain was as white as Uncle Cevval. The houses moved away from each other, as each sank into its own solitude, and sent up its own trail of grey smoke. Eager to see more, Kenan pulled himself along the walls to get outside the next day, and tried to walk in the knee-deep snow. It was late in the morning, and the court-yard was sparkling in the snow-light, almost, and as he went back and forth with a blanket hanging from his shoulders, he looked thinner and shakier than he really was. Besim was sit-ting in front of the door, a cardigan on his shoulders. He was looking at the mountains, lost in thought.

And that was the day that Kenan fell, right there in the courtyard, and died.

They washed him with their tears and the water they boiled in sooty cauldrons. They wrapped him in a shroud and over this they draped a green rug with golden tassels at each end. When they left the courtyard with that green-covered coffin, Ziya was amongst the pallbearers, but after he had gone a few steps, one of the villagers had to come to take his place. Moving with difficulty through the drifting snow, they left the village with a large and silent crowd behind them. When the pallbearers turned past the sheep pens to climb up the hill towards the barn, Ziya didn't know what to think. He looked wildly at those around him. But they continued flowing past him, their grief-stricken faces half hidden by their caps. They were purple from the cold. On they went up the hill, losing their balance from time to time as they struggled to keep up with the coffin.

Fifteen or twenty metres beyond the barn, just beyond the hedge, they entered the cemetery on the other side of the hill. In stops and starts, they carried the coffin to the grave they had already prepared. Ziya was only able to throw three shovels of earth over it; when his eyes filled up with tears, one of the villagers came and took the shovel from his hands. Ziya moved to the back of the crowd, and watched the rest through tears. After the grave had been closed, the mourners began to disperse, and he followed after them hopelessly, struggling through the snow. Sometimes, when he stumbled into a ditch or a drift as high as a gravestone, he sank into it. And then, even as he struggled to get back on his feet, he would, without willing it, look back at those snow-covered gravestones, his eyes brimming with tears. Once, when he looked back like that, he saw a gravestone behind the almond tree, and there he saw the name Hayati. That reminded him of Hayati of Acıpayam, of course. And his insides began to tingle. He could almost hear him talking to him, from inside that outhouse behind Seyrantepe. Just then, Ramazan the Grocer came up and reached out a hand to help him out of the ditch. And that is how they ended up walking side by side in silence. When they reached the bottom of the hill, Ziya slowed down to look back at the cemetery. Then he said, 'I had no idea the cemetery was that close to my house.'

'It's not the cemetery that's close to your house,' said Ramazan. 'It's your house that's close to the cemetery.'

Ziya said nothing and carried on walking.

'It's in just the right place,' said Ramazan, after they had walked a few paces. 'You know what they say. Build your house near the cemetery, and far from the mosque.'

'I do know,' Ziya said.

And that was the last thing either said until they reached the village.

Here Ziya parted company with Ramazan and went on to Kenan's house. He offered his condolences to Cevriye Hanım, Nefise and Besim. And then he walked through the crowd of wailing women and their white headscarves and went out into the courtyard. For the next few hours, he paced back and forth under the mulberry tree, a cigarette in his hand. He had no idea what to do. At nightfall he put out his cigarette and walked through the crowd of women and went up to Cevriye Hanım. He found her sitting on the edge of the divan. She had a black headband lined with yellow on her forehead. Her eyes were blood-red from crying, as she stared into space. Leaning down, he whispered, 'Shall I take over some food for Uncle Cevval?'

'Take it over, if you wish,' she said, in a voice that trembled like a leaf. 'But don't tell him about Kenan. Whatever you do, don't tell him.'

So Besim and Ziya went together to Uncle Cevval's house that night. In silence they walked past the sheepdog lying at the foot of the wall opposite; and under this dog's gaze they stepped inside. As Uncle Cevval sat quietly on the divan, eating his food, he asked after Kenan a few times, as always.

And Besim said, 'He's feeling poorly.'

When he asked the same question the next day, he got the same answer.

But on the third day, Uncle Cevval refused to believe them, for some reason. He sat there as if someone very far away was answering his question, and suddenly he stopped listening. 'That's a pile of shit. He's not poorly. You're lying to me.' As he spoke, two tears fell down his cheeks. And then Besim seemed close to tears, too. Bowing his head, he kept gulping.

And that was why, when they were outside again, Ziya patted him gently on the shoulder, and then on the head. As he did so, he felt Kenan's hand reaching out through his to Besim's father's hand, all the way from Germany, and that unnerved him.

For months and months, he and Besim went back and forth to Uncle Cevval's house, every day without fail.

When the weather grew warmer, and everything was green again, and the leaves returned to the vines and the trees, and the earth sang with morning glories, poppies, delphiniums, campion, ox-tongue, vetch and butterflies, that was when the brambles came alive with clacking grouse, while the village swooned to the scent of thyme and gum, and sunlight soared into the mountains' deepest shadows. The world had opened itself to spring, of course, but Cevriye Hanım, who had yet to remove that headband from her forehead, was still lost inside the day that had taken away her son, and she wandered through her house like a woman possessed. And there were times when she would mumble, 'Oh, Kâzım the Bellows Man, come back to the oily bullets.' Each time he went to the house to fetch Uncle Cevval's food, he would find her walking around like this, muttering curses. And each time he ached for her, though he had no idea what to say, what to do.

In the end, and without telling Cevriye Hanım, Ziya went to talk to Kâzım the Bellows Man. Besim took him over late one morning, pointing out a double door before backing away. And Ziya walked through the shade of the nettle tree, and when he reached the door he knocked a few times on its blackened boards.

'Come on in, Ziya Bey,' Kâzım called from inside.

Surprised that Kâzım had managed to see through these high walls, Ziya paused for a moment. Then, doing his best to hide his confusion and excitement, he opened the door and stepped inside. Kâzım was sitting in the left-hand corner of his courtyard on a high wooden bench. When he saw Ziya, he put out his cigarette and stood up, struggling to keep his balance, as if he were drunk or very ill. He staggered over to Ziya. His daughter, his two sons and his wife all came running into the courtyard: since Kenan's death the whole family had been under attack and so they were always on guard.

'Welcome,' said Kâzım, offering his hand.

For a moment Ziya hesitated. He was not sure if he could extend a hand to the man who had caused Kenan's death. Then he pulled himself together. With some reluctance, he extended his hand. But as they were shaking hands, Kâzım averted his eyes. He looked very pale; he had sunken cheeks. He looked taller than before and his voice was fogged, as if he was speaking from behind a curtain, or from very far away.

'I've come to talk to you,' Ziya said.

'Let's talk,' Kâzım replied. 'Come sit down with me on the bench.'

He relaxed somewhat once they were seated, but he kept looking at Ziya with anxious eyes, as if he could read his inner turmoil on Ziya's face.

'How did you know it was me knocking on your door?' asked Ziya.

'There was no need to see you,' Kâzım said. 'No one in this village ever knocks. They just push open the door and come in. When I heard that knock on the door I knew at once that it was you. And anyway, I've been waiting for you for a very long time. I guessed that you would come to see me sooner or later.'

'I see,' said Ziya.

Then they both took out their cigarettes and lit up. Ziya was not sure how to open the subject, so for a while he looked at the barn next to the courtyard, and the straw baskets hanging from its front wall, and the coil of rope, and the shovel leaning against the door.

Then he asked, 'What happened between you and Kenan?'

For a time Kâzım said nothing, as he traced a line between the little flowers on his cushion.

'Last year,' he said finally, 'Kenan took a loan from me, so that he could finish work on the barn. That's what happened between us.'

'He took a loan from you for the barn?'

'Yes, the loan was for the barn. He needed the money. The work was only half done. All the materials were just sitting there. And I took pity on Kenan, and so I lent him seven thousand lira.'

'Seven thousand lira?' Ziya gasped. 'Why did he have to take money from you, when I was sending him all the money he needed?'

'I know. You sent twenty thousand. But Kenan gave five thousand of it to a builder from town. He found this man and bargained with him and put down a deposit, but then suddenly this builder vanished. He was just another one of those conmen, I guess! And that was it – your five thousand lira gone. And Kenan had already laid out twenty-two thousand lira for this barn. In other words, two thousand more than you sent him.'

'But I don't understand,' said Ziya. He looked doubtfully at Kâzım. 'The day I arrived, Kenan told me that I'd sent him more money than he'd needed in the end. He gave me back a hundred and fifty lira.'

Kâzım smiled faintly.

'He gave you that money to be convincing,' he said finally. 'He was a good boy. An angel. May he rest in peace.'

'But I don't understand,' said Ziya, shaking his head. 'Why didn't Kenan tell me any of this? He knew I was prepared to pay whatever he needed for the barn. If he'd told me, I could have sent him more money.'

'That was my thinking, too, when I lent him the money,' Kâzım said. 'I thought that he would take the seven thousand lira from you when you arrived. But he didn't do this. He wore himself out trying to earn it back with his own efforts. This was impossible, of course. Go out to the forest every night and cut up wood and load it on to a donkey, and then ride all the way out to another village on this plain and sell it for thirty or forty lira – how are you ever going to repay a loan like that, let alone keep a family going?'

Ziya lit another cigarette. He was so upset he hardly knew what to do.

'I just don't understand why he never told me about any of this,' he said. 'If only he'd told me, I could have given him all the money he needed.'

'In the beginning, I didn't understand either,' said Kâzım. 'What I mean is that I didn't understand why he had to hide it from you. In the end, I pulled him aside and asked him outright. I can't tell you, he said. I owe my life to him, he said. How can I let a few *kuruş* get in the way, when this man saved my life? That's what he said. The long and the short of

309

it is that he was indebted to you for something you did for him when you were in the army. Something good. A very good deed. In fact, you saved his life.'

Ziya's head began to swim.

'His mother said the same thing to me,' he told Kâzım. 'But I have no idea what this good thing was.'

Kâzım gave him a long, hard look, as if to say, are you playing games with me?

'How can you not know?' he said. 'How is it possible for someone not to remember his own good deeds?'

'Do you know what it was? Did Kenan tell you?' Ziya asked.

'I know what it was,' Kâzım said. 'When I pressed him about the money, I left him with no choice but to tell me. Otherwise, he'd never have told me. Our dear departed friend wasn't the type to talk about such things, after all. According to what he told me, one day when you were in the army, Kenan fell very ill, and on his way out to guard duty, he collapsed. You ran right over, and with the sergeant's help, you pulled him up. You poured water over his face. Then you turned around and said, our friend is running a high fever, he can't go out on patrol. But the sergeant was a coward, and the commander wasn't there, and so he just hemmed and hawed and said he couldn't see what he could do. And then you picked up Kenan's rifle and put on his cartridge belt and said, in that case, I'm Kenan. And then, so that everyone would think you were Kenan, you lay him down on your own bunk, and wrapped him up well, so no one could see his face. Stay here, you said. Don't get up, on any account. And then you went out on guard duty. And that night, his station was involved in a skirmish.

And it was you who fought it out with the smugglers until dawn. At the crack of dawn you rushed back to the dormitory and took him very quietly out to the trench, so that the commander wouldn't find out. What our dear departed friend told me was that if he'd gone into that skirmish running that high fever, he'd have taken a bullet, most definitely. Because it was a serious skirmish, a few smugglers were killed and a few soldiers wounded, and sheep and horses lost their lives, too . . .'

'It's like a dream,' said Ziya. 'I remember him collapsing on his way out to guard duty, and I remember he had a fever, but the rest is a blank. I was blind drunk at the time, though.'

'How strange,' said Kâzım.

For a time neither spoke.

'So, fine,' said Ziya in a trembling, plaintive voice. 'What led to this knifing?'

'I didn't want to do it,' Kâzım said softly. 'Such a thing would never occur to me. I don't even carry a knife. Everyone in the village knows this . . . On the day of the incident, I was sitting with our dear departed friend in the Coffeehouse of Mirrors. As always I was advising him to tell you what the situation was. I was telling him that he was never going to be able to repay his debt just by taking a donkey up the mountain every night and selling wood. I was saying it would never work. And he was sitting there, clutching his knees, and nodding his head off, saying, all right, brother. You're right, brother. Hem brother. Haw brother. But then, for some reason, his mood changed. Little by little, he became more stubborn. And when he started making faces – and God is my witness, I have no idea

311

why – something strange came over me. And then, before I knew it, we were arguing, and then suddenly the flame shot up, and he was so furious when he stood up he almost knocked over his chair. He didn't know what he was doing, and that's why I'm sure he had no idea what he was going to do next. I jumped out of my chair, too, of course, and as God alone can tell you, I didn't know what I was going to do either. There was no next step. We had jumped to our feet and that was all that kept us there. I can't tell you about mine, but our friend's eyes were on fire, and he was trembling – I could almost see the waves travelling down his arms and legs. And so we stood there, ready to pounce on each other, yelling and shouting, but I have no idea what we said. And then, I have no idea how, but there, in my hand, was that infidel knife. It was almost as if someone had come and put it into my hand on purpose. Do you know what I'm saying? Or they put it near me, so that I could use it. Or my hand wandered off like an animal, without my knowledge, and came back with that knife. I still haven't found a way to understand this part of it. Honestly, I still can't understand it. It was as if someone else had control of my hand, and it was not until afterwards that I had any idea what I'd done. To tell the truth, it was only when I saw blood spurting from Kenan's leg that I realised what I'd done. And all this while, everyone else in the coffeehouse just sat there, dumbstruck. No one tried to pull us apart. They just sat there, watching the fight. Maybe it was the knife, or the way it glittered, or maybe it was because nothing had happened yet. Maybe they were under the control of some other power, too, I just don't know. If I know anything, it's this: as I stood there with that knife, the person

I was facing was not Kenan. It was afterwards he turned back into Kenan. Our beloved Kenan . . .'

Suddenly Kâzım's hands shot up to his face as he burst into tears. Ziya was already distraught beyond words, and now, as he looked at Kâzım, he had no idea what to do.

'I felt such shame,' Kâzım said as he blew his nose, 'I couldn't even go to Kenan's funeral. I spent that day pacing up and down this courtyard like a mad cow.'

'If only none of this had ever happened,' said Ziya in a mournful voice.

Then he stood up and made his excuses, saying he was feeling ill. Kâzım stood up with him. After blowing his nose again, he wiped the tears off his cheek with the back of his hand.

'Are you going to stay here in this village?' he asked.

'Yes,' Ziya said. 'In fact, I have to stay. How could I ever leave, if it meant leaving Kenan's mother in the lurch, not to mention his sister, and his nephew, and his uncle?'

Kâzım looked at him in anguish.

'I'll pay you back your money,' said Ziya. 'Tomorrow's Tuesday, isn't it? I can take the Ovaköy minibus to town and withdraw the money from the bank.'

Kâzım nodded.

The next morning Ziya woke up early and rushed down to the village *meydan*. Off he went to town in the Ovaköy minibus. But he did not see the forests they passed through, or the hills, or the curves, or the pure waters running under the stone bridges. He did not even see the town. Instead of waiting for the Ovaköy minibus, he rushed back in a taxi at midday. The moment he arrived back in the village, he walked underneath the nettle tree and went straight into

Kâzım's house to give him the money. This time he did not pause to knock on the door. He just turned the handle and opened the door and looked straight over at the *sedir* on the left-hand side of the courtyard. And there he saw Kâzım, sitting in just the same place as the day before. At the foot of the bench were two bald chickens wandering amongst their own feathers. As soon as they had greeted each other, Ziya handed him the money he'd withdrawn from the bank. Kâzım didn't count the notes. He just put them into his pocket, looking ashamed, and took in a deep breath.

'So you're determined to stay here in the village,' he said, looking straight into Ziya's eyes.

Ziya couldn't understand why he was asking this question for the second day in a row.

'Look,' said Kâzım. 'You can count me as your elder brother. And so now I am going to ask you to listen to me. There have been terrible rumours going around the village. And they're not the sorts of rumours that will just go away of their own accord . . . No one talks of anything else in our two coffeehouses. How can I put it? From the crack of dawn till midnight, they simmer away like kettles. And they're all about you, these rumours . . . Let me put it this way. There's no knowing where these rumours will go, or what they'll lead to. If I were you, I wouldn't wait until tomorrow. I'd leave this village today!'

Ziya froze in shock.

'I don't understand. What are these rumours about?'

'All sorts of things,' Kâzım said. 'Every day it's something different. I have no idea where they come from, or who got them started. How could Kenan have died from just a knife wound? He must have been poisoned. That's one thing

314

they've been saying. And if it was you who poisoned him, then Nefise must have been the reason. You'd had your eye on her since the day you arrived.'

'I can't believe this,' said Ziya, almost talking to himself. 'Where did all this come from?'

'And also,' said Kâzım, lowering his voice as he bowed his head, 'there's something else going around with all these rumours, but let's leave it there. I can't bring myself to say it.'

'What is it?' Ziya asked angrily.

'No,' said Kâzım, as his eyes slipped away. 'I can't tell you. But let me say this much. It has to do with Besim. With you and Besim both.'

Ziya's head began to swim. For a time he just stared at Kâzım. He had no idea what to say, what to do. Then, very slowly, he stood up. Passing between the two bald chickens, he headed for the door. Once outside, he walked towards the *meydan*, but he did not hear any voices coming from the houses or the courtyards, nor did he see anyone he passed. His mind was fixed on the things Kâzım had told him. The more he thought about them, the faster his feet went. It was those fast feet of his that got him back to the barn so suddenly that day. And as soon as he got there, he plopped himself down on the bench and stared in despair at that shadow on the mountaintop, until night fell.

Remembering that it was time to take Uncle Cevval his food, he stood up and went back into the village. His plan was to go into Kenan's house and pick up the copper tray and leave, so that he could spare Cevriye Hanım from hearing what Kâzım had told him.

But Cevriye Hanım was waiting for him in the courtyard. She was still wearing the headband on her forehead. She was looking very distant. He could almost see clouds crossing her face.

'I came for Uncle Cevval's food,' Ziya said.

Cevriye Hanım looked down and swallowed.

'There are rumours going around the village, my child. So I am going to ask you to stay away from Cevval. We'll look after him ourselves.'

Ziya had no idea what to say. He felt almost concussed.

He had no choice but to go back to the barn after that. Collapsing on the bench, he gazed at the mountains humming in the darkness, and for hours he cried his heart out.

When he woke up the next morning, Ziya had no desire for breakfast. Without so much as a glance at the kitchen door, he walked out of the barn. The sun had just peeped over the mountaintops, and there were great dazzling rods of greenish light flowing down from that nameless shadow, down and down, flowing as far as the sheep pens on the plain. That's why the tops of poplars lining the sheep pens were each shining like lighthouses. He stopped for a moment to look at all this, and then he went through the gap in the hedge. Turning right, he walked distracted and dishevelled towards the cemetery, which was knee deep in grass, and in the midst of all this greenery were enormous thorn bushes. And now and again, he could hear birds chirping in the branches of the almond tree, pecking at the silence, almost. Making his way slowly over the uneven ground, Ziya at last found Kenan's grave. After looking at it for some time, he sat down next to it, putting his hand on the gravestone. What he wanted to do just then was to bare his heart, tell Kenan the whole story, from start to finish, but he didn't do this. Instead he kept his lips sealed.

After giving up on the idea of talking to Kenan, he thought about the world where his friend was now. He hoped that he'd found the peace there that this world had never given him.

'Oh, Kenan,' he said then. 'Do you remember that dream you told me? There was a knock on the door one day, and there before you was yourself as an old man. But to think that the only place you've ever seen yourself as an old man was in your dreams . . .'

And suddenly he raised his head. He looked around him. Because he could hear Hayati of Acıpayam calling to him again, from that outhouse behind Seyrantepe. Osmaaaan, my fine young man, how many months has it been since you last had roast meat? He could hear that voice floating over the graves, to lose itself amongst the waving grass and the thorn bushes. So for a time Ziya sat there, pricking up his ears in case the voice came back. As he sat there, he wondered if his mind might be playing tricks on him. Then, remembering the gravestone he'd seen the day Kenan died, he stood up and headed tensely towards the cemetery gate. As he walked, he kept turning his head, studying each gravestone, looking for Hayati's name.

'And just look at where we have to wash. In all honesty. Not even a dog would want to wash in there!'

Hearing Hayati's voice again, Ziya stopped. Shivering, he looked around him.

'If you had a speck of that shit they call money, do you think you'd be wasting away here in God's desert, my fine young man? Osman, my fine young blade, are you there?'

He stopped in front of an old almond tree. It had dried up; its trunk was covered with honey-coloured sap. His eyes nearly fell out of their sockets, because there, on the

317

gravestone before him, were the words: Private Hayati Bulut. The grave that should have been in Acıpayam, in Denizli, was here in front of him. Thinking he must be dreaming, Ziya took a few apprehensive steps to touch the gravestone. He passed his hands over it, half fearing that if he touched it too hard it might go flying out of this world. When he turned around, he suddenly saw the name Macit Karakaş on another gravestone seven or eight feet ahead of him, and the name Ercüment Şahiner on another. Without knowing what he was doing, he walked first towards one, and then the other, but he couldn't reach either. Because now, before his eyes, there was a blur he recognised as Binnaz Hanım's round cheeks. Am I losing my mind? he asked himself. Frightened now, he hobbled over to the cemetery gate. And as he hurried over that uneven ground, giving no thought to the bones whitening beneath it, he saw first Veli Sarı's name on a gravestone, and then Halime Çil's name, and then, on another gravestone, he saw the name of the clerk from the neighbouring company, Sergeant Rasim Benli. And that was when Ziya cried out, Dear God, what are these people doing here, or is Hulki Dede right, is the world really only a few pastures wide? Dry-mouthed and half-crazed and gasping for breath, he rushed back to the barn.

Just as he was passing through the gap in the hedge, a huge brute blocked his way. 'Do you feel no shame?' he said. 'Doing that with a child that age?' Swinging his club, he brought it down with all his strength on Ziya's head. Ziya fell to the ground, bleeding and in shock. After the huge brute had struck him once again, he struggled to his feet and began to run down towards the plain, to the poplars. The brute pointed after him. 'He's running away, boys! He's running away!' And a few more men carrying clubs came out from behind the hedge, and together they all raced after him. Still not believing that this was really happening, Ziya kept glancing over his shoulder. When he saw they had grown in number, he gathered together what strength he had left and increased his speed. In spite of these efforts, he was captured by Numan next to the sheep pens. And when he was captured, he got another blow in the head amongst those rocks that were the size of fists. He fell to his knees for a moment. Escaping from Numan's hands, he went racing through the brambles; bent over double, running for his life, he headed for the mountains.

When he reached the oak forest, he felt half dead, and that was why he sat down behind a rock for a while, to catch his breath. As he sat there, panting, he slowly craned his neck to look down at the crowd of men below. Twenty-five or thirty men in front, all holding clubs, and scattered behind them, another fifteen or twenty people holding things he couldn't quite see, and they were all climbing up the hill. As he looked at them, he thought, 'They can't all be coming after me, surely the ones at the back have come out to stop those crazed brutes in the front.' He even looked to see if he could find anyone amongst them who looked like Hulki Dede, but he couldn't.

Then he got up and, so as not to be caught by the people still streaming up the slopes, he hurried out of the oak wood to run as fast as he could into the red-pine forest. Soon he had run all the way up to the nameless shadow at the top of the mountain and saw it was a ramshackle old hut, but by now he lacked the strength to walk a single step. So he crawled to a rock just outside it. He curled up at the foot of this rock and waited, quiet as a rabbit. His forehead, his cheeks, his shirt, his collar; they were all drenched in blood. But now he began to drift off to sleep. His eyelids grew heavy; his soul, too. And soon sleep had softened his aching head wounds, even. But he could still hear the voices of the men coming after him so his terror grew and grew. What if they caught up with him? He could hear their footsteps coming right up to the edge of the pines. Sometimes he even thought he could see the men's faces, blackened with anger, and whenever he did, he curled up closer to the rock. Then he remembered something Binnaz Hanım had said. *He who wishes to pray should also carry a stone to throw.* Remembering those words, and thinking how bad it would be if he fell asleep, he walked twenty-five or thirty metres, until he'd reached the hut. He was bent over double by the time he got there. Dirt and dust, from top to toe. He could barely stand. That's why he lifted his hand and pounded so hard on the door. And the wooden door echoed back.

I got up and pulled it open.

He burst into the room and threw his arms around me. Together we shut the door and limped slowly away from the window. Outside there were men running back and forth, shouting.

'They're looking for me,' he said in a faint, dull voice.

I whispered gently into his ear. 'I know.'

He lifted his head to look into my eyes. It was almost as if he didn't believe he was right there beside me, with his hand on my shoulder, and talking.

'Come,' I said. 'Let's watch through the window.'

'They might look in and see me,' he said in a shaky voice.

'They can't,' I said. 'You can see out through these windows, but you can't see from the outside in.'

'Like sleep that has holes in it,' he whispered.

I said nothing.

We went over to the window. The voices outside were getting a lot louder. It was just about possible to hear what the men were shouting to each other. Then suddenly they were there right in front of us, these men. One in front, and the others behind him, all bearing clubs. The man in front was Cabbar, and his face was red from anger. Red as a pomegranate. His hair flew wildly around his face. His shirt tails had come out of his trousers.

Seeing them, Ziya said, 'You're not going to hand me over, are you, if they come to the door?'

'They won't come to the door,' I said.

He glanced at me suspiciously. Then he collapsed on to the divan next to the window. Curled up into a ball. And stared outside.

One of the men running through the pine forest turned to another and said, 'I found him. I found him!'

The men in the forest turned on their heels and all came racing towards the place the voice had come from. For a while, the pine trees' lower branches swayed, the stones and the pine cones hit against each other as they rolled across the ground, the high grass rose and fell, and the blue sky pulled back, as if to escape from the grasp of the trees.

'Come on, where's that pimp?' yelled Cabbar. Angrily swinging his club through the empty air, he shouted, 'Where's he got to now?'

Numan was just behind him. Dark-faced. Grinding his teeth. Ready to kill every living soul in the world, and not just Ziya. The other villagers were standing at the ready, waiting for orders. Their anger seemed to be in their clubs, almost, and not themselves, as they swung them up and down through the air, sending tiny shivers through the forest.

'So where is he?' growled Cabbar. 'Who was it that found that pimp? Who was it?'

'I found him,' said one of the villagers. 'Look over here! Look! He's lying curled up behind that rock!'

Clubs in hands, they raced over to the rock the villager had pointed out to them. When they vanished inside the pit, Ziya turned to look at me, as if to say, they're not going to find me.

Then he turned his head again, to look outside.

There followed a short silence. The forest had frozen inside its own silence, almost. The branches went stiff, and the leaves, and the colours and the scents. Then two men came out from behind the rock. One was holding Ziya by the arms, and the other by his legs. Slowly they carried him away. The other men looked surprised. As they followed on after him, they lowered their clubs.

Ziya turned back to look at me.

In shock, he cried, 'They found me!'

Glossary

Agha (Ağa): An Ottoman era title generally associated with large land holdings. Rarely heard nowadays outside Turkey's Southeast.

Ayran: A water and yoghurt drink similar to buttermilk.

Baba: Literally 'father'. Also used as a honorific for older men or a term of friendly affection.

Bey: A title given to the leader of a tribe, including the early Ottomans, which later became a military rank and polite way of addressing men, equivalent to the feminine 'hanım'.

Bismillah!: 'In the name of God!' Short for *b-ismi-llāhi r-rahmāni r-rahimi*, 'in the name of God, the Most Gracious, the Most Merciful'. It is sometimes used as a battle cry.

Bulgur: A type of thick-grained wheat and the name of a dish made from it.

Dede: Literally 'grandfather'. Also used as a honorific for older men and as a religious title.

Dervish (derviş): A member of an esoteric (*tasavvuf* or Sufi) group within Islam who chooses to devote his or her life to following signs of God's will rather than their own. This often amounts to a vow of poverty.

Divan: A type of long couch that rests on the floor.

Djinn (Cin): Supernatural spirits in Islam sometimes rendered in English as 'genie'. There are good, bad and mischievous djinn, and they are still very much part of Turkish folk mythology.

Dönüm: An old unit of land, representing the amount that could be ploughed in a day. This varied from region to region according to custom and soil quality.

Gözleme: A type of savoury pastry pancake, often filled with cheese, meat or potato.

Hacı: One who has completed the hajj, the Islamic pilgrimage to Mecca during the Feast of the Sacrifice (Eid al Adha, Turkish: Kurban Bayramı). Used as an honorific, denoting that its bearer is both successful enough to afford the journey and pious enough to go.

Halay: A folk dance popular at weddings, in which the dancers link fingers or arms and dance in a line.

Hanım: A polite title given to women. From an ancient feminisation of the word 'khan' as in Genghis (Nişanyan 2007).

Harmandalı: A traditional dance of the Aegean region, in which dancers dance alone with their arms in the air.

Halva: A type of crumbly sweet made from either semolina, flour or sesame seeds. In some parts of Turkey, flour halva is traditionally given out to guests at a funeral wake.

Hoca: Literally 'teacher'. Used in both religious and secular senses.

Keşkek: A traditional wedding food made from beef and wheat.

Kuruş: The smallest monetary unit in contemporary Turkey. 100 kuruş is equal to 1 lira. Ultimately derived from the Old Latin 'denarius grossus', like the English 'groat' (Nişanyan 2007).

Lahmacun: A cooked flat circle of dough and minced meat, often heavily spiced.

Lira: The standard unit of currency in contemporary Turkey.

Mashallah! (Maşallah!): An exclamation of thankfulness to God, often used in place of praise due to the superstition that expressions of jealousy attract the bad luck caused by the evil eye.

Mehmet (military): The generic name used for Turkish soldiers, much as Tommy is used for British soldiers or Jerry for Germans.

Meydan: From the Arabic meaning 'wide space', this denotes an open area in a city, town or village: usually a focal point of activity.

Meyhane: From the Persian meaning 'wine house'. A type of tavern specialising in small *meze* dishes and *rakı*.

Muhtar: The elected head of a village or neighbourhood.

Rakı: An aniseed-flavoured alcoholic drink similar to ouzo or arak and typically drunk with water and ice.

Saz: A lute-shaped stringed instrument used in both traditional and modern forms of Turkish music.

Selamünaleykum or Selam: An Arabic greeting meaning 'peace be upon you' used around the Muslim world.

Shalwar (Şalvar): Loose trousers sometimes called 'Harem trousers' in English.

Sucuk: A dry, spicy beef sausage.

Sultan: The ruler of the Ottoman Empire.

Tarhana: A soup made with yoghurt, wheat or flour, vegetables and herbs.

Vizier (vezir): The Prime Minister in the late Ottoman era, often seen as the real power behind the throne.

Yufka: A thin, unleavened bread.

Zeybek: A form of music and dance native to the Aegean region.